S0-FQL-173

Secret Blood

Don Stansberry

Publisher Page
an imprint of Headline Books
Terra Alta, WV

Secret Blood

By Don Stansberry

copyright ©2012 Don Stansberry

All rights reserved. This book is a work of fiction. Names, characters, places and incidents, except where noted otherwise, are products of the author's imagination or are used fictitiously. Any other resemblance to actual people, places or events is entirely coincidental. No part of this publication may be reproduced or transmitted in any other form or for any means, electronic or mechanical, including photocopy, recording or any information storage system, without written permission from Publisher Page.

Publisher Page
P.O. Box 52, Terra Alta, WV 26764
www.PublisherPage.com
Tel/Fax: 800-570-5951
Email: mybook@headlinebooks.com

Publisher Page is an imprint of Headline Books, Inc.

www.DStansberry.com
www.HeadlineBooks.com
www.PublisherPage.com

Cover images by gary718 and VibrantImage
Author Photo by Lindsay Husk Photography

ISBN 9780938467472 hard cover
ISBN 9780938467489 paperback

Library of Congress Control Number: 2012936901

Stansberry, Don.
    Secret Blood / Don Stansberry
    p. cm.
    ISBN 9780938467472
    ISBN 9780938467489
    1. Clones—Fiction. 2. National Security—Fiction. 3. Washington (D.C.)—Fiction 4. Biblical History—Fiction.

PRINTED IN THE UNITED STATES OF AMERICA

For Patty, Shay and Sidney

Special thanks to Tod Faller, Diane Chandler, and Dr. Toni DeVore for their expertise and support throughout the project.

Prologue

The body was taken down gently, much more gently than when it was nailed and hoisted. Now centurions looked on with a mixture of fear and awe. The very men who had cast lots for his clothing now knelt and bowed their heads. Only one, a soldier, put a lance to his side to test for life. The darkness that had rolled in and blanketed the land must certainly have been a message from God. The midday twilight changed many minds about this man Jesus. His followers wept and struggled with his absence and pledged to carry on his message. Even though he had prophesied to them of his future, this was too much for many to bear.

Pontius Pilate, who couldn't find a way to circumvent the crucifixion, gathered his family and huddled in the bowels of his palace. He had heard rumors of the miracles the Nazarene had performed and feared he would be the one remembered for the Holy man's demise.

The people who had lined the streets to curse and spit on the savior now fled from Golgotha believing they had degraded the Son of God. Most left their homes, to disappear into the masses and trek back to their places of birth.

The body of Jesus was not to be left on the cross due to the ritual Preparation Day. This relieved Pilate. The fools of the Sanhedrin, he thought, the ones who handed Jesus to him, might do something even more foolish with the body, angering God even more, if that were possible. Pilate worried about the Jews also. He was relieved when Joseph of Arimathea asked to remove Jesus. A new tomb, in which no one was yet buried, would be made available.

The body was grimy and sweat streaked. Blood had crusted on the hands and feet and on the site pierced by the lance. He was wrapped in a burial cloth and carried to the tomb. Joseph led the way with Mary Magdalene walking beside the body of the Savior.

The small entrance was near the ground. A stone chiseled into the shape of a wheel rolled in a slot cut in the ground at the front of the tomb. The burial party had to crawl to enter, but once inside the cavern, there was enough room for several to stand. A shelf was hewn into the wall where they laid the body.

Mary Magdalene, with tears streaking down her face, knelt beside the body. Placing her hand on the shroud, the movement under the cloth startled her as the lifeless arm of Jesus slid inside. It had dropped from the chest and was now below the edge of the shelf, still contained within the cloth.

The wound on the hand reopened and the blood began to run. As the shroud became saturated, a crimson flower bloomed on the shroud as the holy blood pooled. Then it began to drip to the ground.

At the sight of Jesus' blood, Mary sobbed even harder. This was His blood, the blood of redemption, the blood of the covenant, dripping into the dust. An alabaster jar was handed to Mary. She held the jar beneath the dripping blood for many minutes, hoping to retain every drop. The body, in its wondrous way, began the clotting process resealing the wound and leaving the jar almost full. Only then did they leave the tomb and begin the journey of the Holy Grail.

Chapter 1

Northern Italy 1941

The driver allowed himself a small glimmer of hope. They had been driving for nearly a week over country roads that were little more than muddy gullies, through farm towns and across meadows dodging goats as they passed. The Vatican's Rolls Royce Wraith had proved itself a marvel of engineering, conquering every terrain it encountered.

Now, only an hour from their destination, a seed of optimism began to grow. The boys, also provided by the Vatican, were a perfect cover. They slept now, four in the Roll's massive rear seat, and two in the front beside the driver. They were mannerly, disciplined, and most importantly of all, they could sing.

The turn was ahead to the left, a hundred meters past a dilapidated barn. The plate sized headlights panned across the road and onto the next, which was actually a cart path. It veered to the left, then to the right, and disappeared beyond the reach of the headlights. He drove carefully, keeping away from the deepest part of the ruts and watching for partially exposed rocks that might flatten a tire.

The path wormed its way around a stone outcropping and down a hill where it flattened out. Oak trees stood ghostly white then disappeared entirely as the car passed. The darkness was so dense that only the trees closest to the path were illuminated, the ones farther back dimmer and dimmer. The driver's mind turned back to his childhood, to Bram Stoker's *Dracula* and Mary Shelley's *Frankenstein.* Their horrors inhabited a forest such as this.

His seed of hope turned into a black seed of fear. It sprouted and entwined itself in his brain. A trickle of sweat ran down his temple over his neck and into his Priest's collar. His fingers gripped the steering wheel tightly. He increased the speed slightly without knowing it.

"Are you all right, Father DeAngelo?"

It was Vito Maslo, the oldest and sharpest of the choirboys. He hadn't realized the boy was watching him.

"Yes, Vito," he said in Italian. "I am anxious to get to the church and end this business."

Before Vito could agree with Father, a single light flickered a half a kilometer ahead. They slowed to a stop. Here the path was wide enough to turn the car, but where to go? He had committed this route to memory, he knew no other course. In turning they would surely be chased which could only lead to arrest.

Better to continue and pray their cover would work.

"Boys!" he said sharply. They squirmed awake, stretching and yawning. All except for Vito Maslo, who looked calm and wide awake. "Be prepared, this is why you have practiced!"

The car started forward again, more deliberate this time. The boys were wide awake now, looking out the windows and holding the items with which they had practiced. They could hear the crunching of the loose stones under the tires. Father DeAngelo dabbed his temples with a handkerchief.

The light came from a kerosene lantern that had been placed in the center of the path. Behind the light, barely illuminated, was a black Fiat Balilla. It was parked sideways, blocking the road, looking very out of place here, in the middle of the night. A Nazi solider in a Field Gray uniform stood near the car, rifle resting comfortably in his arms.

Father DeAngelo's worst fears were confirmed. They had been waiting for them. A week of concerts, zig zagging around from church to church, had not fooled anyone. Even going east instead of traveling west to the safety of Switzerland did not confuse them. The Rolls slowed to a stop ten meters from the lantern.

The solider brought the gun up, barrel evenly pointed at the windshield of the car. Nothing happened for several seconds, and then slowly, almost as if scripted, the rear door of the Fiat opened. Father DeAngelo's heart sank even further. The man emerging from the car was Gestapo, dressed in a gray SS uniform. He was tall but thin with a narrow face and expressionless eyes. His hair was cut short and perhaps white, but that was difficult to see in the dim lantern light. He walked with a slight limp.

The Priest had been trained to read the emblems on the German uniforms which were difficult because the agencies often overlapped. This officer had something the Father had never seen, a diamond shaped black patch on his left sleeve. The letters SD were sewn inside in white. He stepped to the driver's window and motioned to roll the window down.

"Your papers, Father," he said in Italian.

Father DeAngelo handed a folder out the window and smiled at the Nazi. The officer pulled a pair of reading glasses from his tunic and studied the driver but did not open the folder. He held it out toward the solider, who stepped to the car to receive it, without lowering the gun.

"You are traveling to the Parish Church of Oswald?"

"Yes," said Father DeAngelo. "My young charges are a choir and I am their director."

The Nazi watched him as he spoke, like a lion deciding which moment to pounce.

"Yes, I watched their performance two days ago at Duomo Vecchio. Perhaps you did not notice me in the last pew. I try to keep a low profile when I attend Mass."

"I did not notice any Nazis. Are you Catholic?"

"No, Father, I am a realist. Considering the current climate of the world, a Nazi is a more practical thing to be." He looked at the boys in the back seat. "Have the young men step out of the car."

The Father motioned the boys out and stepped out himself. Vito carried a worn Rugby ball. Another boy carried a soccer ball. As soon as they exited the car the soccer ball was on the ground and being kicked from one side of the path to the other. Vito skillfully laid the Rugby ball in the shadows while two of the others got into a loud mock argument.

Another solider appeared from the darkness of a flanking position. "Search it," the officer said in German.

Father DeAngelo backed off and waited while the boys played and the two soldiers dismantled the car. To their credit the boys gave the impression the soccer game was much more important than the search.

After nearly an hour, the interior of the Rolls Royce lay in pieces in the grass and the three Germans were at a dangerous level of frustration. The seats were removed and cut open, the trunk ransacked and using flashlights they searched the engine compartment. The soldiers muttered and the officer glared at the Father who had taken a seat on an exposed root.

The officer unsnapped the strap on his holster. Both soldiers heard it and stopped searching.

Father DeAngelo heard it also. He stood as the Gestapo officer approached, pistol drawn, speaking in Italian.

"My patience grows thin. I will ask you only once, Padre. Where is it?"

The Father turned his hands palms up. "I don't know what you mean."

The Gestapo officer shot him in the stomach. The Father looked down at the barrel, then up into the Nazi's face, and then dropped to the ground. As his hands covered the wound, blood oozed from between his fingers. He lay there, breathing hard, not moving.

The boys turned at the sound of the shot and let the ball roll away into a clump of weeds. They ran to the body of the Priest, ignoring the man who had shot him.

The Gestapo Officer grabbed a small boy named Louis Dimitto. He held him by the scruff of his neck and placed the barrel of the Luger against the back of his skull.

Who is second in charge, he wondered, scanning the group of boys. Whoever it is will speak up now.

"Stop," Vito Maslo said in Italian.

The Gestapo officer smiled. "I will ask you the same question. Where is it?"

Vito unconsciously glanced at the spot where he had hidden the Rugby ball. The look did not go unnoticed by the officer. Dragging a squirming Louis with one hand, he stepped across the path to the spot. He holstered the gun and bent to pick up the ball with one hand. Smiling in a bemused way, he released Louis who sprinted back to join the boys.

The two German soldiers were interested in the ball also. They left their rifles, which were leaning against the Rolls and walked to the Gestapo officer. One of them produced a knife and they huddled around the ball, losing interest in their surroundings. Slicing the stitches, and then removing the stuffing around it, the officer pulled out an alabaster jar.

Instantly there were two sharp cracks and the soldiers crumpled to the ground leaving the officer holding the jar. A dozen men in woodsmen clothing stepped out from behind trees and into the light. Grimy, dirty and looking like they belonged in the woods, they entered with weapons raised. A slight breeze blew through the trees, the echo of the shots lingered. The men moved in unison like a pack of wolves around the Gestapo officer who had just witnessed a complete reversal of control.

"I will take that," said one of the woodsmen. He wore a maroon beret and a thick wool vest and spoke Italian with a French accent. Black hair curled from under the cap and the cuffs of his flannel shirt.

Secret Blood

The Gestapo officer's eyes darted across the scene searching for any escape from his predicament. He found none; he had no bargaining chips, no leverage. He handed the jar to the man in the beret.

"Is there any type of deal that might interest you?" the Gestapo officer asked in French. "Perhaps we might be able to barter for information, in exchange for my life?"

The man in the beret found the Rugby ball, replaced the stuffing, and was placing the jar back in it when a shot exploded behind him. The woodsmen dropped to the ground as the Gestapo officer fell backward, his gray jacket turning a deep red in the center of his chest. The shooter stood behind them, the German soldier's rifle still aimed. "He shouldn't have killed a priest," Vito Maslo said as he lowered the gun.

An hour later the torn seats were back in the Rolls Royce and the three Germans buried in shallow graves twenty meters from the path. Three of the woodsmen took the Rolls along with Father DeAngelo's body and another three took the Fiat. The area where four men had been killed appeared as pristine as it had only a few hours before. How they were to use the cars, Vito Maslo would never know.

"What happens to the Jar, now?" Vito asked the man in the beret.

The man studied Vito, the boy who had killed a Gestapo officer. Could he be trusted?

"We will travel by night, two weeks, keeping clear of the Germans and the Russians. Then we will rendezvous with the French Resistance."

"I thought you were the French Resistance," Vito said.

"We are the Order of the Dragon."

Vito considered this and decided now was not a time for too many questions.

"Then," the man continued, "you, the package, and your fellow choir members will be handed to the American military. All of you are going to America for safekeeping."

"I do not speak English," Vito said.

The man smiled. "You are young, you will learn. But I have heard they may make you change your name, or at least change some letters, so it sounds more American."

"And the Jar?" Vito asked.

"Do not worry my young friend; they already have a secure place in mind."

America, Vito pondered, the land of opportunity.

Chapter 2

Severna Park, MD
Present Day

    The church door banged open and the old lady staggered out. Her face was haggard and worn as if it were aging by the day. Her chest heaved as she leaned against the iron railing. The door swung shut behind her with a heavy wooden thud. Balancing herself against the railing, she slid down the stairs and to the sidewalk. She looked up the street then down it, not seeing the traffic or the pedestrians there. A leaf fluttered away from an oak tree that grew from a bulky cement pot on the sidewalk. She watched as it spiraled down and landed near her foot. For an instant her face went blank as she stared. Then the agony etched there, reappeared. She took an unsteady step up the sidewalk, then another. Her back stiffened and she clutched her purse with white knuckled hands. With one unsteady step after another she willed herself up the street.
    Rounding the corner she came to a group of older men, retirees probably, who gathered outside the local deli. Most were dressed in work pants and windbreakers bearing the logos of the companies from which they had retired. The conversation dwindled when they saw her demeanor. One of the gentlemen tilted his head in a hello gesture, but the rest just stepped back, giving her a wide berth.

It took only a few minutes to get home, which was a small miracle since she kept her head down the entire way, not even looking up when crossing intersections. A lady, whom she often stopped and talked with, was ignored, as if they had never met. She continued past the butcher shop and the dry cleaners where her late husband had his suits cleaned.

As she came to the gate that barred her from the rest of the world, she paused for a moment and looked at the panorama of her home. A two-story brick with brown trim, just like all the others that lined the street, a normal house in a decent neighborhood. The grass was drying up and the paint was beginning to peel a little around the front door. The chains that held the porch swing were starting to rust.

Life here had been quiet and lonely. Now for the first time she was happy she had no children. Maybe that's why Claus had been against a family all along. He knew that somehow this would happen. He probably wanted this to happen, if only to clear his conscience.

Most of the sorrow left her face as she entered the yard and closed the gate behind her. She made up her mind without realizing it. This was a path she had started down when she decided to give the journals to Father.

The key was the old kind, simple teeth, with a swirly wispy end. She took it from her purse and snapped the clasp back together. The key turned with a series of soft metallic clicks and the door opened into a dark entry. Some of the leaves that had gathered on the porch blew in with a gentle gust of fall wind. They scratched across the bare boards making the house seem even emptier than it was. An old cuckoo clock measured time over a battered table that held a chipped china tea set. The doily that protected the scratched surface fluttered in the breeze.

She closed the door and leaned back against it. She decided she would vacuum and dust, then kill herself.

Chapter 3

The sink was a little stained, so she spent an extra thirty minutes scrubbing it after running the sweeper. She went up the creaking stairs to the bedroom and put on her best and newest dress, one she had purchased for Claus's service. It was black with a pretty little lace collar, almost like the doilies on the end tables at the senior center. Except for the collar, the dress was very plain so she added a pin that had belonged to her mother, pink stones in a sterling silver mounting.

Touching up her make up in the bathroom mirror, she began to feel uneasy. Not about the suicide, that would be a relief, but about strangers in her home. She went down and unlocked the front door. If the police broke it down, there would surely be a mess, and who would clean it up?

A note would be the best way to let people know she had no part in this. It would be very dramatic to spray paint a message on her bedroom wall. Maybe that was beyond dramatic. No, they might think she was a loony, plus someone would have to repaint to have the house ready to resell. She rummaged around and found a big calendar, a gift for renewing the car insurance. On the back was a bare, pristine field large enough to write what she had to say.

When she finished writing, she drew a stick figure with long hair looking upward to the sky. Its arms were wide and its fingers splayed and upward. It looked as if it were asking the heavens for forgiveness. She taped it to the inside of the front door window.

The top of the wine bottle screwed off and she poured a glass half full. There was a full bottle of sleeping pills left in the bathroom cabinet. Claus had trouble sleeping and kept a supply available. She couldn't remember how many he took and the dosage on the bottle was so small it was impossible to read. Taking all of them would do the trick. Making sure not to drip any wine on the clean tablecloth, she carried the glass, the pills and the wine to the kitchen table.

Taking a deep breath she popped the first pill in her mouth, took a sip of the wine, tipped her head back and swallowed. After the first couple of pills her stomach began to feel queasy. What a waste, to vomit it all back up. A crusty loaf of French bread lay on the counter. She removed the wrapper and tore off a chunk, careful of the crumbs. Her stomach settled down. When the pill bottle was empty she washed and dried the glass, put it away, and wobbled into the bedroom. She began to get dizzy.

She opened a drawer in the nightstand and took out the Rosary her grandmother had given to her for her First Communion. She carefully lay down, crossed her ankles and smoothed out the material on the front of the dress. The bed began to feel very comfortable and she began to pray.

Her mind played back to her childhood, not full memories, but flashes of senses. The earthy smell of wet leaves on the day she and her best friend Katie had raked maple leaves and created a fort. She remembered the silky feel of her aunt's wedding dress and the aroma of fresh ground coffee at her grandmother's house. Most vivid was the image of seeing Jesus on the cross, and the understanding that the Savior had suffered for her.

She was about to meet the person she had worshiped her whole life. That thought brought indescribable joy. Suicide was a sin, yes, but when Jesus touched her she knew her true feelings would glow and she would be forgiven. She was going be in His presence. A smile softened her face. Those were her last thoughts as she left this world.

Chapter 4

I had just finished the evening mass and was shaking hands with the parishioners as they left. It was a dismal turn out for a Tuesday evening in the first weeks of winter. I lost my place in the homily and sputtered around as I tried to regain my composure. I also mispronounced words. Either no one noticed or they expected this type of sermon. The first six rows were empty on each side of the aisle, a great chasm between the parishioners and me. This was my second church since being removed from the first after only a year and a half.

Mrs. Garrows, a woman who had written a letter to the Bishop, complaining my homilies were boring, passed without returning my hello. A cold gust blew in as she forced open the heavy wooden door and left.

"If your sermons only had half the convictions of your heart, the pews would be brimming," teachers told me. There was a lack of confidence, not in the Word but in my ability to deliver it. "Someday you may have to find another way to serve the Lord." The same thing was happening all over again and I knew of no way to stop it. I would be sent to another church, but as an associate pastor this time.

As the sanctuary emptied I pulled off my vestment and hung it in the sacristy. The door squeaked as it closed and I instinctively looked around. It was the sound from an old movie, shrill and brittle. I stood for a moment and waited for something to happen. There was no breathing or footsteps, just an unshakeable feeling the Holy Ghost was actually here in the building. I turned and half expected to see God waiting at the altar probably to ask me to take another less important vocation.

The church had always been my refuge of solitude. I felt more comfortable in an empty church than anywhere else on Earth. But now I would have welcomed company. The air was different, like a storm was approaching. I could feel something was coming. My mouth was dry and the hair on my neck prickled. The wind outside whistled through the wooden windows. They blended into some kind of harmonic vibration that was almost melodious. I swallowed, and then looked down at my arm, there were goose bumps. Then the church door opened.

Two men came in, one after the other. Both wore navy suits with plain ties and white shirts. They had severe haircuts to match their serious faces. One carried a manila envelope. They looked around the room and their eyes fell on me. Again goose bumps tingled up my arm.

"Can I help you?" I asked. My voice sounded stronger than I actually felt.

"Are you Father Kenzee?" the shorter one asked.

I nodded and forced a smile.

"We need to ask you a few questions about one of your parishioners," the taller of the two said. "Do you have an office or someplace we could talk?"

"Certainly," I said. "Just let me get the lights." I flipped a row of switches and the sanctuary disappeared into darkness. Once I turned them off I wished I hadn't. The creepy sensation continued. "I have an office right down this hallway." I took a step and then stopped. "Are you police officers? I suppose I should ask to see some kind of identification."

Both men reached into their breast pockets and pulled out IDs in leather cases. They flipped them over in a practiced move. I looked, not really knowing what I was looking for. Agents Phillips and Farrah, FBI. I looked at their faces again.

"I'm not sure I understand."

"We can talk in your office if you don't mind." It was more of an order than a request. Agent Phillips started walking again. I was forced to start again, also. Our footsteps echoed on the stone floor.

The office door was warped and never shut properly. I used the flat of my hand to push it open. A small brass table lamp illuminated the space with a warm golden light. This was my sanctuary, my escape, a place where I didn't have to face my failures or my critics. Stacks of folders, books and bills littered the desk and the floor beside it. There were two chairs against the wall, also stacked with paperwork. I walked around the desk and sat as the two agents entered; the last paused as he tried to close the door behind him.

"That door doesn't close. The church secretary says it hasn't since the basement flooded about thirty years ago. Sorry, I usually see guests in the Parish office," I said. I was about to ask the men to have a seat but there wasn't any place to sit. "If you would like to go there I could at least offer you a place to sit."

"That won't be necessary. We would like to know about Anna Rundell. Was she a member of your congregation?" Agent Phillips asked.

"The name sounds familiar. But we have nearly five hundred members here. I'm much better at matching the face with the pew where they sit. The names I'm still working on. I can look her up in the church directory."

"See if this helps." Agent Farah pulled an eight by ten picture out of the envelope.

There was Anna lying on her bed, in her best dress, still holding the Rosary beads. She looked as if she was sleeping.

I looked at the picture and said, "Oh that is Anna. She sits on the right side about halfway back. Yes, that's right, her last name is Rundell. Is she in some sort of trouble?"

"I'm sorry to have to tell you this Father, but she's dead," Agent Phillips said.

It was an odd photo, dressed and lying on a bed, but she didn't look dead. I'd given last rites several times and seen too many corpses; this lady looked like she was resting.

"What happened? She was just here…." again I felt the goose bumps rise on my arms, "Sunday. No, wait, maybe it was last Sunday." *Why did I feel the need to lie?* I picked up the photo. "She looks peaceful, is she… dead here in this picture? Did she pass in her sleep?"

"No, looks like a suicide. Sunday was the last time you saw her?"

Again the surge of uneasiness, but why didn't I trust these men? "Yes, that was the last time." They knew I was lying.

"Do you have any records of next of kin or anyone who would be notified in case of emergency?" Agent Phillips asked. He was gazing around the room, probably wondering how I kept track of anything in here.

"No, we do not keep records of anything of that nature. Is there anything we can do here at the church? We could help with some of the arrangements. We have special funds for things like that. I should have a service for her."

"There's no need to worry about that, Father. She's already been cremated." The agents watched for a reaction.

"Cremated? Without a service? Did she request that in the note?"

"How did you know she left a note?" Agent Farrah asked, stepping a little closer to the desk.

Still stunned, looking at one then the other, I said, "I didn't. I just presumed, I suppose." They glanced at each other. They didn't believe me.

"What led you here to my church?"

"She saved church bulletins; there was a stack of them in a drawer in her bedroom. She had the Rosary Beads in her hands; this is the closest Catholic Church to her home. That's what led us to you." Agent Phillips let the last word hang.

"Am I being accused of something here?" He ignored the question.

"We will be in touch. If there is anything you think of that might be relevant to this case, you can reach me at any of these numbers." He laid a card on the desk. They turned and walked out of the office and down the hall. I followed them.

"Shouldn't this be a case for the police? Why is the FBI involved? Doesn't the district require an autopsy for mysterious death?"

"Listen, Father," Agent Farah said, "you're smart enough to realize we can't say much, but I will tell you one thing. I've seen a ton of dead bodies, some that had been left for only a couple of days in cold weather. Even then they start to decompose. That photo you saw was shot in a warm house. She had been dead nearly a week."

They turned and walked out leaving me with an odd sense of amusement. I locked the door.

Chapter 5

I knew Anna Rundell; I had listened to her confession the week before. Though at the time I was not sure I completely understood what she was confessing. And I didn't fully understand why she insisted I take her husband's journals for safekeeping. Safekeeping for what? In typical fashion, however, I walked out of the Confessional, set them down somewhere, and forgotten about them.

The journals had been under the desk all along, even though I didn't remember putting them there. After the agents left I searched for an hour before giving up in frustration. I flopped down in my chair and kicked them. Then I remembered, I had hurried back after the confession…the phone rang…it had been the hospital…I dropped the books on the floor and hurried out of the office. A homeless man wanted Last Rites. I left immediately for the hospital and the journals had been forgotten.

During the confession, Anna had seemed distraught about her husband's journals, which she had found hidden in the attic. I was not interested in reading about a dead man's infidelities. I thought they were about a secret lover or some crooked business deal. She had not gone into detail about the contents. I assured her that her husband's sins were not hers and if she could find forgiveness in her heart, she would be healed of this pain.

I gathered the three journals and packed them in my battered old briefcase. Then I turned off the office light and slipped out a side door that led to the rectory. Yellowed hostas lined both sides of the cracked sidewalk and small solar lamps lighted the way. I hurried the ten yards along the walkway peering into the darkness beyond the lights. The breeze between the buildings rolled a handful of dry brown leaves across the sidewalk. They flitted through the weak light of the solar lights and cart-wheeled into the darkness. By the time I reached the door I was sweating in the cold air. I fumbled with the keys and looked right and left before entering. The FBI? I could see it on CNN—Father Kenzee, a person of interest in a suicide.

The rectory was a venerable three-story brick house that had a massive porch across the front. Attached to the side was a landing with a side door that connected the rectory to the church. There was a detached garage at the rear of the property. A living room, kitchen, and a conference room were on the first floor and bedrooms on the second. The third floor was mostly used for storage, things like Christmas and seasonal decorations. My bedroom and study were located on the second floor and on the side closest to the church.

I carried the briefcase up the wooden staircase to the second floor and tossed it on the bed. The priest before me left a crucifix. Other than that, the walls were bare. The desk light was small and pearly green with a marble bottom. I clicked the light on and opened the briefcase. The journals themselves were comprised of three completely different books. One was small almost like a child's diary; the second was a college composition book with the flecked black and white cover. The other was an oversized ratty book that looked like something that could have been used as a ledger when records were kept by hand. The corners were threadbare and the writing on the cover had faded. They laid there, fanned out like a display. For the first time, I wondered if I should read them.

The composition book looked the least threatening so I picked it up first. The first entry was dated June of 1975. I began to read. After ten minutes of standing I pulled out the desk chair and sat without taking my eyes off the book. I finished the first one and found the next. My answering machine rang several times but I ignored every call. Now fully engrossed, I read the third. When I had finished I closed the cover and stared at the floor. Then I got on my knees and crossed myself. I wrung my hands in front of my chest then stopped as the gold of my wedding band glinted in the light. The engraved cross glowed in the lamplight like a silver lining of a cloud.

I went into the bathroom, turned on the faucet, and splashed cold water on my face. I thought of a paper I had written in Seminary. In it was a line from *Stairway to Heaven.* The line said, "In the long run there's still time to change the road you're on." I knew at that moment my road had changed. I wondered if I could put my faith in mankind ever again. I stared into the mirror, not seeing my reflection and asked why. What had we done?

I found a towel, dried my face and walked back to the desk to turn off the desk light, already wondering if I would ever sleep soundly again. As the room darkened I picked up the journal to place it back in the briefcase with the others. I sat in the darkness on the edge of my bed, lost in the implications of what I had read. I glanced out the window in the direction of the church. A thin beam flashed across the office window in the church. If the curtains had been completely closed I never would have noticed it. Because I had left them partially open, I could see the dim beams passing over the stacks of papers, crisscrossing the room and sweeping across my desk. At least two people were there with flashlights.

Chapter 6

With the journal still in my hand I crossed the room and reached for the phone on the nightstand. I hesitated, was I going to call the police? For all I knew they were in my office already. I began to panic. The room seemed smaller than it had moments ago. I closed my eyes and tried to slow my breathing.

"God, please help me to do this," I said out loud.

I stepped to my closet and automatically reached for the chain for the light. I thought better of it, got on my knees and felt around under my hanging pants. Out came a tattered backpack I hadn't used since that camping trip last summer. I pulled a pair of jeans and a hooded sweatshirt off the hangers and threw them in the backpack. I turned and went to the bed, got down on the floor again, reached under and pulled out an old pair of Nikes. Next was my sock drawer where I felt around until I found a lump in a pair of white socks. They went into the backpack also.

I started for my cell phone that was on the desk, and then I hesitated; could I be tracked through a cell phone? Where would a thought like that come from? Too much TV. I stood and looked around again. The house was quiet. A drop of sweat trickled down my temple and dropped off my jaw. The journals still lay in the opened briefcase, looking deceptively unimportant.

The strap of the backpack went over my shoulder as I reached over to snap the clasps of the case. I began to lift it off the bed then stopped. Instead I reopened the case, removed the backpack, unzipped it, took the journals and shoved them in between the sweat shirt and jeans. I crossed the room, compelled to take one more glance out the window. The beams of light were gone. The window was as dark as the others.

The wooden stairs seemed to crack and groan with every step I took. My left hand slid down the banister while the right held the backpack against my side. The side door was situated near the bottom of the stairs. Through the glass I could see two figures on the landing, silhouetted by the faint solar lamps along the walk. They were bent, and I heard a metallic clicking at the lock. I slipped past, not two feet away from them, hidden by the darkness and a linen door shade. A cold chill passed down my neck. I shivered and turned to the source. The living room window was open about an inch.

I was to the window in no time. The sash lifted without a sound. I threw one leg over the sill, leaned out, and fell with a muffled thud. I landed on my side in the soft mulch about three feet under the window. I waited for someone to rush around the house and yell "Hands Up!" but no one did. I stood slowly, then slid the sash back down and trotted through the garden and across the neighbor's yard. When I had gone a block I cut back to the street and from a safe vantage point, took a look back at the church. There was a dark van parked up the street where it would have a good view of the front door. The goose bumps came back.

For the next hour I kept to the back streets. The only sound was from my shoes as I plowed through the downed leaves. I found a dark place near some dumpsters to change clothes. As I did, I took the sock with the lump and pulled put a roll of twenties with a rubber band around them. I dropped the wad into the hood of the sweatshirt and scrunched up the material. I didn't want to get mugged and have no money, especially since I didn't have a plan or an idea of where I was going. The jeans and sweatshirt gave me an unpriestly look. I hated to throw away my vestments, but I knew I couldn't keep them. There was a second hand clothing store in this neighborhood. If I could find the donation drop off I might be able to buy them back later. They were expensive enough to begin with, now I was going to have to pay for them twice.

The air was turning colder and a frost was forming on the leaves piled by the curb. Under the streetlights they sparkled on their curled edges. The sky was clear and the stars shone brightly. I kept walking and listening for a car to pull up behind me. In another hour I saw the flashing white light that said Suncrest Homeless Shelter. A smaller sign beneath it said; Vacancy.

There was a lighted doorbell that I pressed, and then waited for movement inside. A police car slowly rolled up the street behind me. It stopped and waited until the door unlocked and allowed me in, then it rolled on. The odor hit me as I entered the building. It wasn't a foul or dirty smell, but one that covered that up. The cleaning chemicals were just barely winning the battle.

There were two men to check me in, both wearing Suncrest Shelter ID badges. They checked my backpack and had me fill out a short questionnaire. There was no body search. As soon as I was shown a bunk and was alone I reached behind my head and pulled the roll of twenties out of my hood. The bed to my left was empty but the bed to the right contained a lump under the covers that was snoring. I sat on the edge of the bed to remove my shoes. It squeaked under my weight. We had served the homeless on many occasions, but I was not concerned about being recognized. Out of context and out of costume, I thought the chance was small.

I lay there and listened to the federally funded furnace kick on, and waited for the next soft snore to come from the right. How fast had my road changed tonight? As far as I knew I had not broken any laws, but now on the run I could not see my life ever being the same again. I did not know who to turn to, so I prayed.

Chapter 7

Vatican Observatory
Castel Gandolfo, Italy

"Father, could we have a word with you?" A dark skinned girl with dreadlocks stood beside an Arabic girl with dazzling eyes. They held printouts in their hands and looked as giddy as two freshmen at their first dance.

Father Dante Minniti looked around the room at the other students. Most were gathered around monitors, and speaking in several different languages. The students here represented nineteen countries and for many, English was their second or third language of choice. All were intent on their assignment, which was to evaluate the spectrum of stars in a given area.

Father Minniti gestured toward a door and the three left unnoticed. He flipped on a light switch and led them into a conference room. The room was painted a pale green, the sparse furniture, inexpensive, and the few photos on the walls served to document the day when the Pope toured the building. They sat at a small round table.

"Now, what is it you have found?" the Father asked in English, smiling at their radiating enthusiasm.

29

Both started speaking at once, then looked at each other and laughed.

The Father cleared his throat and raised his eye brows." You, Eve, you may go first."

The girl with dreadlocks spoke in a heavy French accent. "This is the area we were given to observe, M32, near the Andromeda Galaxy." She slid the photos in front of the Father. "We were recording the Doppler shifts of the spectrum of these stars." The Priest waited patiently for her to continue.

"Then, being the inquiring students that we are," she glanced at her classmate, "we decided to look at all the earlier pictures of M32. We hacked into the observatories' files, sorry Father it was not so very difficult, and we obtained these." The other girl, Mary, slid more photos across the table to Father.

More seriously now, Mary continued. "We thought we would be able to see the gains in technology over the years and possibly write our thesis on that subject. But that is not what we discovered. Look at the area I have marked on this sheet."

The most recent pictures had a tiny dot circled. The earlier photos had the same area circled with nothing in it. The Father took the two marked photos, placed them on top of the other and held them up to the ceiling light. The other stars fit perfectly over the originals, only the circled areas were different. He placed the photos on the table beside each other and leaned forward in his chair steepling his fingers under his chin. He studied them for several minutes without saying word.

Finally he looked up at the girls and said, "I don't know."

Chapter 8

Steward Observatory
University of Arizona
Tucson, Arizona, USA

Michael Cooper sat down at the keyboard with a Tim Horton's cappuccino in one hand and a bagel in the other. He wore faded jeans, a black Ramones tee shirt and custard yellow converse tennis shoes.

The office was organized, but in a way only he could understand. Huge stacks of papers teetered on a folding table along one wall. The opposing wall contained a shelving unit constructed of cinder blocks and planks. This held dozens of texts on astronomy and astrophysics. Posters of colorful space anomalies were taped on the remaining two walls.

He leaned back in his chair as his computer blipped and beeped to life. His ex-wife used to tell him, "It's always best to check your e-mail first." Odd how e-mail has a way of dominating the rest of your day. She was right, of course, but still he would put it off until the last moment. But if he did, then he would have to stay late and THAT was a big problem which led to other big problems which led to the end of the marriage.

Now that the divorce was final he checked his e-mail first, secretly hoping for a message from her. That's what you call irony, he thought. As the messages popped up, he unwrapped the bagel. It slipped from the waxy paper, hit his leg and rolled under the desk. A fat glob of cream cheese clung to his jeans. There was no message from his ex.

Among the inner office memos, ads from Ubid, and commercials from HGTV, was a message from an old friend:

Dear Coop,
How is my old friend, the gunslinger from the Wild West?
Is the Arizona desert keeping your movie star skin tan and wrinkled?
The summer camp has begun here and I am working with a talented group of young people. Gone are the days where I can blame lint on the lens as the solution to a question I cannot answer. They have brought to my attention something very puzzling. I have attached the Doppler shifts. Feel free to discuss this with your colleagues. Figure this out my friend, and I will serve you tiramisu myself.

Peace be with you, Dante

Dr. Cooper opened the attachments and stared at the screen. He steepled his fingers under his chin exactly like his friend had done hours earlier, halfway around the world. Then he bulged out his cheeks and slowly released his breath. He hit the print button and waited for the photos to roll out. It was a very good copier; the photos were as clear as they were on the monitor. He stood, then crossed the room, went through a fire door and up two flights of cement stairs. He knocked on his supervisor's door. It was 8:15 p.m. He hated it when his ex-wife was right.

Chapter 9

The White House
Washington, D.C.

President Rienhart closed his notebook, put the pen in the leather pen holder, and rubbed a little more of the sleep out of his eyes. He was tired but happy. By far, this was the best job he ever had. His predecessor left the country in the best shape, financially, in a decade. The radicals had gone underground for now and Homeland Security had a reasonable grip on them. Oil prices were dropping almost too quickly and an American company had made an important advancement in solar technology. This strengthened the dollar in Europe. All in all, he had been left no real problems and the ones he did encounter had been dealt with successfully.

The mornings at the White House began with a meeting as to what was on the agenda for the day. These usually occurred in a sitting room just off of the President's bedroom.

"Anything else, Jimmy?" the President asked.

"No, not really Mr. President," said his Chief of Staff who also happened to be his brother.

"I hate when you say not really."

"There's a big snow storm supposed hit the northeast this morning."

The President looked at his brother. "I have the impression you're holding something back."

Secret Blood

"Well, it may not be anything at all but there has been a jump in e-mail correspondence between observatories in the last 24 hours."

The President frowned and reached for the phone sitting on the table. "Rose, do you think the kitchen has any more of that French toast I had earlier? Yep, the powdered sugar and the cinnamon. Don't worry I've got two and a half years before I run again, I'll get it off." He hung up.

He had been a quarterback in college, an Adonis at six foot three, equally blessed with good looks, muscles, and personality. He was good, but not good enough to start in the NFL, so he set his sights on politics, his true love. Genetics allowed him to age into the portrait of an American leader. He was an astute observer of human nature. He learned how to be the person people like and respect. He molded his personality from his childhood heroes. Marriage was out of the question, he courted the right women at the right time. He had landed nearly eighty percent of the female vote and fifty-five percent of the male. The Presidential campaign had been a work of art.

Genetics had not been so kind to James Rienhart, the President's brother. He was only two years older but already nearly bald. He stood four inches shorter and had been a mediocre baseball player in college. But as everyone who knew the Rineharts could attest, he was the brains of the family. Without Jimmy's guidance his brother would not have become President. To get one you had to get the set, so the President made him the Chief of Staff. James Rienhart became the second most powerful man in the country.

"Okay," the President said, "I know you are presenting this exceedingly mundane fact for a reason. What is it?"

"I don't know. This doesn't feel right. The e-mails just aren't up, they're up 3,000 percent. They aren't sending each other solar system jokes."

"How do we know about this?" the President asked.

"Homeland security keeps tabs on these kinds of things."

"If they know they are sending them, why don't they read them?"

Then Jimmy began tapping his pencil on his pad, which remained open.

"First of all there are quite a few observatories in the world, almost five hundred. Secondly, our people are security guys, not scientists. They are trained in Arabic. They look for key words and they look for patterns. Some of them can find a terrorist plot in a meatloaf recipe. These scientists speak a whole different language. Another thing, with these scientists, I mean they are friendly enough, but if someone discovers something big, like household-name big, they keep it to themselves. One big discovery can mean millions of dollars in funding. They don't like sharing unless they already have received the credit. So like I say, it doesn't add up."

There was a knock on the door and the French toast was served, with extra powdered sugar and cinnamon, and a bowl of whipped cream on the side.

Changing subjects, "Anyhow, why don't you call the kitchen and ask if there is any more of something left, you know you get them running around like crazy making more when you ask for seconds."

The President brushed that off. "So they're like the CEOs of car companies who could be friends, but still don't share their secrets," the President said after the first bite.

"Not so much as competitors, I'm sure there are friendships there, but like I say, this whole thing just doesn't feel right," he reached over and tore off a piece of the toast.

"Okay, call Frank and tell him we want to know what's going on."

"Yes, sir, Mr. President," the Chief of Staff said, finally closing his pad. "I did that at 7:05 this morning, I just wanted to get your approval."

The President smiled, "All right then, what's first?"

"A teachers group from Indiana, I think there might be a couple we had in high school. There is also a group of Baptist ministers coming for pictures in the Oval Office."

"I hope they know I'm Catholic."

"They know you went to Notre Dame, I think they'll overlook the Catholic part."

Chapter 10

I awoke much earlier than anyone else at the shelter. Apparently they were used to the chorus of snores that echoed through the room. Each snore had its own pitch and rhythm. The attendant at the front door, a different guy than last night, asked no questions but offered a breakfast if I would only wait a couple of hours. I politely declined and he handed me a flier for free aids testing. I left the building, but only after a quick look up and down the street through the glass door.

The dawn sky was steel gray with massive black clouds rolling in from the north. The wind gusts carried in sheets of stinging rain that would be turning to snow before long. The temperature had dropped since last night and my hooded sweatshirt wouldn't do for long. I pulled the hood up, hunched my shoulders and crossed the street.

I continued walking away from the church and into the commercial area of the community. After walking for several minutes I left the older buildings and the roads became wider. The mall hulked ahead on the left, the store names muted by the rain in that unnatural shade of red that mall designers seemed to love. The names were reflected backwards on the wet blacktop of the parking lot. The mall itself was dark, along with most of the other businesses that were scattered around the periphery of the parking lot. The only place that looked open was a Shoney's with a scattering of cars around it. White smoke was rising from a tube on the roof and the lights glowed in a welcoming way. The rain began to shine on the blacktop.

The restaurant was warm and smelled of breakfast. The hostess had the bleary look of someone who worked the midnight shift. She reminded me of someone named Flo on a TV show from the seventies.

Flo seated me near the island of steaming breakfast food. The eggs alone could have clogged the arteries of my congregation. They smelled wonderful. I ordered the breakfast bar and coffee from a disinterested waitress and went to the food line, still wearing the backpack.

At the table I took it off and slid it down the booth before I sat. It was still dark enough that the window reflected my image more clearly than a view of the parking lot. I looked at myself, the Priest on the run. A bread truck broke my concentration. It pulled into the red lined spot that said "Service Entrance." I chewed a piece of bacon and tried to come up with a plan. The choices were few.

The backpack lay beside me on the vinyl seat. I thought about last night. The sight of the flashlight beams was still burned in my memory. They were taking a huge risk by breaking into a church. The journals couldn't be true but still, the breaking and entering of a church? What were they thinking? What would they have done to me if I had walked in on them? For the first time I felt frightened for my own safety. I needed help. I was out of my league.

Father Craig, a good friend from my years at Notre Dame, had a bit of a wild streak, at least for a Priest. He had questioned, sometimes even challenged the doctrines. One of the professors told him he had a nimble mind; use it to help the members, not to question the elders. Another teacher mentioned that his head was too big even for the bishop's hat. He was always one step from real trouble. We always had fun together, playing pranks on fellow seminarians,

Secret Blood

little parlor games that could even amaze some of the most 'streetwise' priests. He could think on his feet.

He was the one who replaced me at the last church, which could have made things awkward between us. Father Craig had come in with his usual banter and made the transition smooth and somewhat humorous. He was still a friend, and this was right up his alley.

Deciding that putting the backpack on before getting another plate would draw attention, I skipped seconds and went to pay the bill. I asked for a roll of ten dollars in quarters and some ones for a tip. Requests were usually granted when tips were involved. The table was already being bused when I dropped two ones on the wet surface. The busboy, who happened to be a man of about forty with a snake tattoo around his forearm, looked at me. I dropped another two dollars on the table.

There was a pay phone in the 'wait to be seated' area for the few unfortunate souls who did not possess a cell phone. It was nestled between the door and the unused coat racks. Breaking the roll of quarters was harder than I imagined. I finally used my teeth in a very unpriest-like way, fed the machine four, and dialed the number of my former rectory. It rang only two times.

"Hello," said the voice on the phone. It was Father Craig. He sounded fully awake.

"Good morning, Father," I said "Have you had your cup of coffee yet today?"

"Well, if it isn't the old snapper himself," Father Craig said.

I paused for a moment. Snaps was a game we played in school. A game of coded messages.

"Oh, snap," I said, "I didn't get to wake you up?"

"Exactly, got up early today. I'm ever ready to do God's work you know. I told you this Parish work was hard."

"Yes," I said trying to keep up.

"You ought not to be out running around on a morning like this. I'll use the sisters' car to come and pick you up. I'll try to leave in the next five minutes."

I lined up the letters in my mind. They spelled GET OUT. My guess was, he was telling me that I had five minutes before they got here.

"Thanks," I lied. "I'll be here at the Parish Hall."

"Hang loose, Sampson," he said and hung up, then smiled at the FBI agents standing around him.

"What was that Sampson reference, Father?" one of the agents asked.

"I believe I'll tell you that, when you tell me what this is all about. Just maybe you would like to go have a confession also? We can go two for one."

He got hard stares from all three agents.

Chapter 11

As I hung up the phone I could hear my heart beating in my ears. A car door shut outside, then two more. I pushed open the first set of double doors to get a better view of the parking lot. A little girl and her brother were running toward the outer doors with their parents trailing behind them. Only the adults seemed to care about the slippery pavement. Small jets of steam puffed out between their scarves and their toboggans. The parents laughed, for them it was a great time to be at Shoney's. I thought about stealing their car.

I heard voices behind me and I jumped. The bread delivery guy was handing an invoice to a manager. At least he looked like a manager; he was wearing a Shoney's issue necktie. They had come through the kitchen and were laughing about something. Everybody was happy here. Little did they know that in a few moments, FBI operatives would be dropping out of black helicopters and swarming the place.

I walked out the door after the family passed and surveyed the parking lot. It was lighter now and the lot seemed even bigger than it had in the dark. I had to figure they traced the call, so my little lie about picking me up at the parish could give me another couple of minutes. The lot was big, I didn't know if I could walk across it in five minutes.

The bread truck was still idling contentedly. It was the size of a small UPS truck with a smiling loaf of bread painted on the side. I thought about stealing the truck, but how far could I get in a bread truck? It would be reported stolen too quickly. Then I noticed the back doors were ajar.

I put my hands in my pockets and casually strode down the sidewalk, looking like a shoplifter. The only person paying any attention to me was the little girl. The family had been seated in my booth and the other three were looking at menus. She had wiped a porthole in the mist on the window and was waving at me through it. I waved back and reached for the door. Inside was a steel walkway flanked by rows of shelves on each side. Not really shelves but a framework to hold the blue plastic racks of bread. I stepped up and into the walkway and got as far away from the door as I could. The empty blue containers could be stacked, so I removed two from the bottom rack, put them on the middle, and crouched in the open space. I took my backpack off and held it against my chest. It was only moments before I heard the door open. The racks banged as the driver tossed bread onto the metal shelves. Then thankfully, the door closed.

The ride was rough, but I could brace myself against the legs of the shelving and lean against the wall of the truck. For the first time in my life, I stole something. The bread smell became overwhelming, even though I had just eaten. I tore a hole in the smiling Face of a Golden Wheat Blueberry Loaf and ate the heel. If the FBI had descended on Shoney's they must have arrived without sirens. We drove for about twenty minutes. It gave me time to think.

Chapter 12

I knew there had to be some reference to the Sampson remark Father Craig had made. The only Sampson I knew was a ribs place about twenty blocks away from my old church, Craig's present one. This seemed unlikely; Sampson's was in the center of gang territory, a hot-bed of drugs and crime.

Listen to me, I thought, *I'm running from the FBI hiding in the back of a bread truck, and I'm worried about going into a black neighborhood in daylight?*

I didn't have much time to amuse myself with the irony of the situation; the truck slowed, turned a half circle and stopped. Then I heard the familiar beeping as it began backing up.

The driver's door opened, then closed as he left the truck. I waited in silence. Nothing.

I unfolded myself from my hiding place and moved toward the door. The lever moved smoothly as I opened it a sliver. I listened, then crossed myself, and stepped out. Cold air bit into my face.

I was in an alley. Big blue dumpsters were spaced along the sides of the buildings. It was wide for an alley and it ran clear through to the other side of the block. I could see cars passing on the main street. Snow was falling between the buildings and sticking to the frozen pavement. I felt the weight of the journals in my backpack. Every time I thought about them they became heavier.

I quietly pushed the door shut and slung my backpack over my shoulder then started down the alley. Anyone could have opened a back door, or looked out a window from above, but no one did. I looked back one last time and saw a sign over the door where the bread was to be delivered. It read: Deliveries for Father and Son Deli.

The snow was falling hard now. As I reached the end of the alley I realized where I was and how far I was going to have to walk to get to Sampson's. The snow was beginning to create that soft sound that only happens in snowstorms and dreams. The sound you can imagine coming from one of those old paintings of people going to Christmas parties in sleighs.

Like a lot of small cities in America, downtown had dried up here. The retail stores were at the mall and the empty storefronts were filled with junk dealers and questionable lawyers. I tried the best I could to stay under the rusty awnings and close to the buildings, but I continued to get hammered by the wind. By luck I came to a second hand clothing store. The thought of a minute's rest and some warmth was too great to pass up. A bell tinkled as I slipped in the door and stamped off my boots on the rug.

The store had a large selection of children's clothes, men's suits, and a bulging rack of winter coats. I found one that looked warm and roomy enough to hide the backpack. It had the logo of some football team on the back hidden under a folded down hood. I looked around and found some gloves. There was a very short old lady at the counter who rang me up. She was also very nice but smelled a little funny. She wrinkled her nose and pushed her glasses back as she told me to have a nice day. When she walked to the back of the store, I donated my original jacket into a pile of clothes that someone had been sorting, and put on my new one.

As I got to the door, an aged City Lines bus pulled to a stop across the street. There's the ticket, I thought. Just saved myself

Secret Blood

three hours walking through this snow. Then I heard the old lady calling out to me.

"Sir, hey, you there, you dropped one of your gloves."

I hesitated, then went back to pick up the glove. As I stood I could see the bus still there through the plate glass storefront. But before I reached the door, a black sedan pulled behind the bus and slid to a stop. Two men in overcoats got out and walked out of view to the other side. A moment later I could make out one of them moving down the center aisle looking at the passengers.

I turned back to the lady. "Thank you, you just saved me."

"Oh, yes," she said. "One can certainly get chapped hands in this kind of weather."

I pushed out the door and walked away from the bus and the black car. I pulled up the hood revealing the logo underneath, the football team name, the Saints.

Chapter 13

I walked for another hour trying to look like I enjoyed the biting wind and freezing snow. Every few blocks I would get off onto a side street until I was reasonably sure I wasn't being followed. The snow stuck to my hood and piled up there. Everything from my shoes to my knees was soaked from the unshoveled sidewalks. I was beginning to doubt that I was even going to the right place. What if Father Craig had meant something else?

From behind me came the muffled sound of a car slowing in snow. I wanted to sprint away, but again that warm feeling spread over me. The journals seemed to warm on my back. I didn't run, but I didn't stop either.

"Hey, white Dude."

I looked over. The car was long and purple, well mostly purple with some gray primer. It had a vinyl roof, which I hadn't seen for maybe thirty years. The tires had big whitewalls with chrome rims, probably worth more than the rest of the car. The driver was leaning across the bench seat looking at me out the window. He was black with a medium sized afro. He had a wide smile with perfectly spaced white teeth.

"I see you looking at me. Slow down. I'm here to give you a ride, would you slow down. Hey. Stop walking. You want to get some ribs?"

I stopped and turned to the car for the first time. "You're not with the FBI?"

"Do I look like FBI? Do the FBI groove on Atomic Dog?" He pushed a button on the CD player that had been bolted to the underside of the dashboard. Music blared; it was a mix between a gospel choir, disco, and a western.

"Uh huh, now you listenin'. Get your white ass in the car; I'm freezin' with this window down."

I grabbed the handle, pulled the door open. A speaker fell out of a hole in the upholstery and dangled inches above the snow held only by a cable. I placed it back into the hole, sat down and closed the door. Apparently the car was "pre-seatbelt" because I couldn't find one. The backpack, under the coat, caused a lump against my back. I leaned forward. The car smelled of barbecued ribs.

"Yep, I knew you was white by the way you was walkin'. Couldn't fool me by wearin' that nasty Saints coat, big old hood and all. Don't make sense, why would they make a big heavy coat for a team that plays indoors in a hot climate like New Orleans? Bet somebody got fired on that one.

"Bunch of people out lookin' for you. All of us from Sampson's, the cops, the FBI. You must be in some big trouble, white dude like you running from the cops and takin' up with gang bangers. Former gang bangers. I mean."

"Where are we going?" I asked.

"We're going to Sampson's," he said. "Why you sittin' so straight up like that? You kinda freaky with that hood all pulled up, wrapped tight. Look like Quasimoto with that big ole lump on your back. You ain't got no bomb back there do you? I don't want no damn bomb in my car." He looked as though he had just forgotten to do something.

"All right, I'm sorry. My bad. We ain't supposed to curse anymore, Mr. Stubbs says so. So you might want to forget what I just said, as a gesture of interracial cooperation." He smiled at me, showing his big white teeth again.

We pulled away from the curb and plowed through the snow. Traffic was still light and the snow was still coming down with a vengeance. The wipers kept a silent beat with Atomic Dog.

We fishtailed around several corners, something the driver seemed to enjoy immensely and came to a stop at an intersection. A dark gray sedan pulled up in the lane beside us. My heart stopped beating.

I couldn't see to the left with my hood pulled up and tight, so maybe they couldn't see my face either. With just a little luck they would see the driver and go on, if we didn't draw attention to ourselves.

"Hey, what you lookin' at?" the driver yelled. He rolled down the window with a crank. "Don't you be comin' to my neighborhood and be eyeballin' me."

Atomic Dog ended and another song started. The passenger side window slid down smoothly and one of the agents in the sedan said something I couldn't make out.

"Do I look like a Priest to you? Here we go again, two brothers minding our own business and Jack Webb eyeballs us looking for a Priest in a snowstorm. That is the worst story I ever heard. I know what you're doing. You profiling, that's what you're doing. You in my neighborhood now."

The car pulled away. The driver rolled up his window and moved on as the light turned.

"My name's Simon," he said. "And now I've saved your white behind twice."

Chapter 14

We stopped in front of a three-story red brick building in the middle of a block. The bottom floor had large picture windows covered with black tinting and the words "Sampson's Ribs" printed in gold letters. A beat up folding chair stood as a silent sentry to mark a parking space directly in front. Simon gently nosed the grill of the Caddy against the chair and pushed it until it folded up and flattened on the snow. He drove over it and parked.

This was the only shoveled sidewalk I had seen in the last few miles.

I got out awkwardly. Simon glided around the front of the car and walked with me to a set of glass doors that had the same black tinting as the windows. He pushed the door open and disappeared into the dimness.

I was hit immediately with the most wonderful aroma. The barbeque must have permeated every bit of carpeting, upholstery and wood in the place. I could almost taste it in the air. There were breakfast odors here too. Eggs, bacon, and sausage all mixed into an intoxicating bouquet.

While my eyes adjusted from the brightness of the snow, I could hear the sounds of a restaurant. People talked and laughed, and the silverware clanged against thick plates. Not like Shoney's but like a loud family. The place was packed.

"Got your boy here, Mr. Stubbs," Simon yelled. "He in disguise."

The room, which was about the size of the dining room at Shoney's, was lined around the perimeter with booths. The counter tops were Formica and the seats, a burgundy vinyl. Long tables that would seat a dozen or more filled the center of the room. The carpeting and tablecloths that covered the tables were the same color burgundy. Plastic chandeliers hung from the black ceiling.

Mr. Stubbs sat in a large booth diagonally across the room. It was away from the windows but situated in a way where everything was in view. He was a large man, not fat, but had the look of a heavyweight who had been retired for several years. He wore a white shirt open at the collar and a thick gold chain. His sleeves were rolled up and stretched tight over his biceps. There were two others sitting with him, eating. My eyes had cleared enough to see the forks rising to their mouths. The man on his right wore a dew rag pulled down low and a baseball hat backwards. The man on his left was Father Craig. He was wearing a black windbreaker and a baseball hat, the right way.

I was surprised, although I shouldn't have been. I felt like crying. His was the first friendly face I had seen in what seemed like forever. He smiled. Now I had someone to help carry this burden. I couldn't wait to unload some of it. Then it hit me, I was about to ruin his life also. Once he read the journals he would be hunted, too.

Simon and I walked through the diners. I removed my jacket, then my backpack and carried both folded over my forearm. The jacket was so bulky I had to wrestle with it to keep it bent.

Father Craig and I were the only white faces there. I moved toward Father Craig and started to sit next to him.

Mr. Stubbs said "No Father, sit down here between me and Sunshine." He patted the seat.

Father Craig nodded. Sunshine stood and allowed me to slide into the booth, then sat back down. Simon scooted in beside Father Craig. All three heads turned towards him. Mr. Stubbs cleared his throat in Simon's direction.

Secret Blood

"All right, if you don't want me here I'll go and get me some coffee." he said. He slid out and walked toward the kitchen.

"This is Mr. Stubbs and his associate Sunshine, but most people round here just call him 'Shine" because of his warm and sunny personality," Father Craig said. Shine stared straight ahead, toothpick sticking out of the corner of his mouth.

"They have offered to help us out of whatever situation we find ourselves in." I wanted to hug him for using the word "we."

Mr. Stubbs' head turned my way; Shine's eyes flickered towards me for an instant.

"Why?" I asked.

"Well, we have sort of an agreement." Father Craig said. "I can explain that to you later. Just know you are in good hands and things aren't as they seem to be. Go with the flow."

"I've decided," I said to Father Craig, "I don't think I should tell anyone quite yet. I may have lost my priesthood just by reading these journals. I don't want the same thing to happen to you."

He looked at me for a moment. The twinkle I had always known vanished from his eye.

"How can you lose your priesthood if you've done nothing wrong?"

"Shine's eyes shifted towards the door an instant before it opened. The two FBI agents walked in briskly, took their sunglasses off, and looked around. They wore expensive overcoats, no doubt to hide their shoulder holsters. Once they saw me, the taller one smiled and walked toward our booth. The smaller one followed, after pulling his revolver and holding it straight down near his thigh.

"Father, we're going to have to ask you to come with us. And please bring the backpack with you."

Mr. Stubbs rested his massive hands on the table and laced his fingers. "This gentleman is having an early lunch as my guest. He will remain here with me until he desires to leave."

"Sir," the first FBI agent said, "you would be wise to mind your own business and keep your mouth shut."

"All right then," said Mr. Stubbs, "take him. It's no skin off my nose."

I did a double take. Where was this great protection Father Craig had promised? A large nickel plated gun appeared out of nowhere directly in front of my face. I was happy to realize it was pointed at Mr. Stubbs and not me. Shine was holding the gun. For some reason I focused in on Shine's massive neck and a delicate chain that seemed to be on the verge of breaking, stretched around it. Dangling from the chain was a tiny cross.

"He's coming with me," he said without moving the toothpick. Mr. Stubbs slowly unclasped his hands and opened them in front of his chest.

The FBI agent, with the gun out, raised it and said, "Hold it right there, Slick."

Shine leisurely swiveled his head toward the agent, still keeping the gun on Mr. Stubbs. "Who you callin' Slick?"

Behind the agents there was a sound of rustling clothing and metallic clicks. They turned slowly. Every patron in the place was holding a gun. Some were pointing the guns at the person across the table. Others were aiming across the room. Many were pointed at the agents. It was impossible to tell whose side anyone was on.

"As I was sayin', the white dude and I are leaving." Shine stood, grabbed me by my collar, and pulled me out of the booth. I was just able to snag the strap of the backpack but couldn't reach the coat. He pushed me toward a swinging door that led to what I presumed was the kitchen.

We went through the kitchen and out a side door then on to the street. We hustled up to a late model Mercedes. As we did, I noticed the FBI car parked near the curb, up on blocks, with all four tires missing.

Shine smiled, displaying perfect white teeth. "I don't think we going to be followed." Shine clicked the remote and the doors of the Mercedes unlocked. He walked around to the driver's side and got in.

Chapter 15

"Where are we going?" I asked. "What about Father Craig?"

Shine pulled onto the street and said nothing. He took the first right, went a block, and then took another. We stopped in the street and he watched in the rear view mirror. Once he was satisfied, we turned right once again, down an alley that ended in a large garage door. He touched the remote on the visor and the door lifted. We were back in the same building we had just left; only we were on the other side of the block. As soon as the door lowered, I could smell the barbecue again. Shine opened his door, took the garage door opener, and slid it in his pocket.

"Come on," he said.

We walked to a stairwell and up two flights of stairs. Our footsteps echoed on the concrete, Shine said nothing. I was puffing by the time we got to a red metal door at the top. He was not even breathing hard. The same remote unlocked the red door; he opened it and went in. I followed.

The room was as large as the restaurant downstairs. Bamboo hardwood was on the floor and two of the walls were stripped red brick. One of the two remaining walls was dominated by the biggest television I had ever seen. The other was mostly composed of windows. A dark sectional with a zebra skin rug in front was aligned with the TV. On the other side of the room was a long black onyx table on which three computer screens rested. There were odd modern chairs situated around the room to bring drama to the staging. This room was not thrown together; an interior designer had worked on this one. A round table surrounded by six traditional chairs anchored the center of the room. Shine sat on the sectional, put his feet up on a black leather ottoman, and clicked on Sports Center. I dropped into a chair completely confused and held onto my backpack.

Minutes later the door was opened by remote control. Mr. Stubbs walked in followed by Father Craig. Shine didn't bother to look away from the screen. I jumped up and nearly ran to them. Mr. Stubbs gave an open hand gesture to the table. The three of us sat. I put the backpack on the table.

"What was that all about?" I asked a little too harshly. "I really thought I was being kidnapped."

"That was the idea," Mr. Stubbs said. "FBI thought so too."

"Mr. Stubbs thought, and I agreed, that we needed a little time to sort things out, without the FBI in hot pursuit. You're going to have to tell us what's going on for us to be of any help at all."

I realized there was wisdom in that, and there was also the fact I had no idea what to do next.

"No disrespect, Mr. Stubbs, but I think this should be kept between Father Craig and me for the time being. If Father Craig thinks you need to be involved more than you already are, then we'll tell you what you need to know. If that's all right."

I could tell he didn't trust me. How Father Craig got him to help this much was beyond me. He was used to controlling everything he touched; he didn't want to be out of the loop. He looked at Father Craig and raised his eyebrows. Thankfully, Father Craig nodded. Mr. Stubbs pushed his chair back and stood.

"Shine, I think we have some business downstairs."

"Uh huh," Shine said still looking at the screen. He stood and turned off the TV. They left without another word. The room was completely silent.

"Okay," he said. "What's in the backpack?"

"You are probably in as much trouble as I am, now that I've drug you into this," I said.

"What are friends for?" he said and opened his hands palms up.

"Okay, buddy, here goes." I told him about the confession and how I thought the journals had contained love letters to someone other than the wife and how the FBI came to question me. I told him about the break-in and how I slipped out the window.

"Okay," he said, "I guess the million dollar question is—what's in the journals?"

I didn't know if I could say it out loud. I didn't want to. I wanted him to read the journals and say the whole thing was a hoax and I was the butt of some joke.

"They cloned Jesus," I said.

He looked at me and smiled. He was almost to a laugh when something clicked and the smile vanished. He stood, and then sat back down just as quickly.

"Impossible," he said in a whisper. "I don't believe it."

"Well, apparently the FBI does. And Mrs. Rundell did." I pulled the journals out of the backpack. I had not seen them since I had read them. Just looking at the covers made my stomach churn.

"Go ahead, start with this one," I said. And he did.

Chapter 16

"I've got to tell you, this sounds real," he said. "But how could that be? It opens a whole Pandora's Box for the government. Did they have that kind of science in the 80s? You got that, too, right? That is when this happened?"

I watched Father Craig read through the journals. He looked as though he was going through the same emotions as I had. Disbelief, horror, then a sick feeling at what we had done. I mean "we" as a country.

"Listen, I've had a little more time to think about this than you have. There is no way for you or me to prove or disprove any of this. The FBI would want the journals back at the very worst, because they are true, and at the very least, because they don't want it to get out, and they had a looney working in their lab. But, I think it's all true, and I'll tell you why.

"The police get a call about a lady dying in her house. Why do they call the FBI? I mean how do they get involved?"

Father Craig had been pacing. Now he sat and looked at me.

"Maybe they have been watching her all along, maybe they watched her husband before he died."

"I don't think so," I said. "That means they watched everyone involved for thirty years. I think she may have left some sort of message when she killed herself. I don't know what it was but the

Secret Blood

police would have to call the FBI to check it out. Once they did, they were on it like fleas on a monkey."

Father Craig thought about that for a minute, and then nodded. "When did you have time to figure that out?"

"I had some free time in the back of a bread truck."

He looked at me without smiling again.

"Well, James Bond, what are we going to do now?"

"Since we are in need of some criminal expertise," I said, "why not ask a criminal?"

"Mr. Stubbs is a reformed criminal. But yes, you're right. I'll call him." He flipped open his phone and hit a couple of buttons. He stood and paced as he spoke into the phone.

"He's on your speed dial?" I asked.

"We've been doing some things together. He wants to change his ways, he's getting near the end of the life expectancy of a gang banger. Wants to be completely legitimate in five years. We're working out a way he can, let's say, give back some of the things he took."

"How did you start that? You and the Lord work in strange ways." I said.

"I called and asked the price to cater the Men's Organization luncheon. He said we could work out a better price if we would make it a monthly thing and he promised his employees would watch out for the church and all of the parishioners, to make sure the neighborhood was safe. I thought it was some kind of Mafia shakedown, so I said it was a deal if I could talk to all of his employees, including himself, about God's plan for them. I was shocked when he agreed. It was almost like he was waiting for a chance to do something good. He's kind of an enigma."

Father Craig sat heavily in the chair he just vacated. In the silence our thoughts drifted back to the journals.

A few minutes later the door opened and Mr. Stubbs walked in, followed by Simon. Simon carried a container of ribs which he dropped onto the table. He retrieved a new roll of paper towels, placed it beside the ribs and said. "Let's brainstorm, shall we?"

Chapter 17

I was very impressed with Mr. Stubbs. He seemed more like a CEO than a crime boss. He listened to what we had to say without interrupting and asked for no more information than what we were giving him. We left out most of the details. His advice was to go to the smartest person we knew we could trust. In his estimation we needed someone who could understand the problem but not have an interest in the outcome.

Father Craig and I thought of the same person, Dr. DeRose, a professor whom we both admired at Notre Dame. Mr. Stubbs did not offer a person to help us. Simon voted for Oprah.

"One more thing," I said. "We're not sure why the FBI was informed of Mrs. Rundell's death. How could we find out?"

Mr. Stubbs looked at me and slowly inhaled. Then he stood, walked over to a cabinet, and opened a drawer that was stocked with tracfones. He took one out, turned it on and punched in some numbers.

"You still got the source downtown? Yes, that one. I need to know why the FBI is involved in a suicide of a woman named Rundell. Last week. Yeah, well, take her out to dinner. Let me know." He turned the phone off, took out the battery, and tossed it in the garbage.

"May take a couple of days," he said.

"Now," I said. "How do we get Dr. DeRose's number?"

"We look it up on the internet," said Father Craig.

Chapter 18

Frank T. White was the senior science adviser to the President. He had known the President for a long time. They had first met when President Rienhart was Senator Rienhart. Then he could just call him John. He kept reminding himself that he had to address him as Mr. President.

The gray sky was pregnant with rain as he pulled onto the beltway. Most of the cars already had their lights on. He turned off the CD player to concentrate on the road. Book five of *Harry Potter* had been playing disc 15. Since starting this one, he had driven past his destinations three times, was lost twice, and nearly rear-ended about a dozen cars. Everyone was worrying about texting while driving; they ought to ban books on CD.

The first fat drops of rain splattered on the windshield as he pulled into the entrance parking lot. There were concrete barriers hidden by nicely trimmed shrubs at strategic points all over the lot. There were also many more light poles than usual, some did not even have lights, but odd shaped containers. He was met immediately by three armed but very polite young men in uniform.

"Dr. White, please exit the car and follow us."

He grabbed his briefcase and was ushered to a black van with darkened windows. It pulled around the building and down a tunnel, pulling up and stopping at a nondescript door. Another trio of security men advanced as the door was opened. One held the same type of machine gun as the first guards he had met, another mirrored him with what looked to be a metal detecting wand, and the third held the leash of a bomb sniffing dog.

"Hey, boy," he said to the dog, bending down to pet it.

"Please do not touch the dog, sir," said its handler.

The door swung open. A stern, portly looking woman of about fifty filled the doorway. Her salt and pepper hair was pulled back in a severe bun and she wore heavy black framed glasses. There was a reserve pair on a chain hanging from her neck. She wore a formidable ankle length dress and a coarse white blouse. Margaret Finnigan was the President's personal secretary and she was as determined as a lioness protecting her cubs. She had started out as a nun. She left the convent but not the Lord.

"Hurry up," she barked. "You're keeping the President waiting. Have you been here before?"

"No, not since he became President."

"All right, young man, here are the rules. No swearing, cussing or taking the Lord's name in vain. He will offer you something to eat and drink, do not take it no matter if you haven't had dinner in a week. Do not walk behind him for any reason. Do not offer to shake his hand unless he offers his first. Do not stare at his right eyebrow, it is higher than his left and he is sensitive about it. Most importantly, do not do anything to antagonize any of the cats that may be lurking under any of the furniture."

She pulled him by the arm into a sparse hallway and started to lead him away.

Frank, fumbling his briefcase, looked back at the security men. "I'll yell if I need you."

"No, sir," one of the men said, "You're on your own now."

Chapter 19

Frank had never been summoned to the White House before, but he was fairly certain this was not normal operating procedure. He was marched through what must have been a shortened route. They cut across floors that were being buffed, some private offices, and some still occupied. Everyone moved out of Margaret's way. Finally, they came to a set of guarded double doors complete with new chrome handles. She knocked only once, and opened the doors. She actually pushed him in.

"Your guest has arrived," she said. "Is there anything else, Mr. President?"

"No, no, Margaret, have a good evening. Frank, nice of you to come on such short notice."

Frank smiled, "Did I have a choice?"

"No, you didn't," Jimmy said.

The two brothers were sitting in burgundy leather armchairs facing each other. A beautiful oak coffee table was between them. There were several famous paintings on the walls along with rich tapestry-like curtains. It felt like a place where compromises and big deals were made. This was a place where powerful men loosened their collars and got down to brass tacks.

"Pull up a chair Frank, do you want anything to eat?" the President asked.

"No, John, I mean, Mr. President."

"Well, Okay, we won't keep you out late tonight, it's supposed to rain. My brother gets very excited over strange things, Frank. So what's all the hubbub with the astronomers?"

Frank stared at the President's eyebrows. They looked normal to him.

"Hubbub? Did you just say hubbub?" asked Jimmy. "Please do not use the word hubbub in public. If there is any way to distance yourself from young voters it's using 1950s language."

"All right then, Frank, I'll use the word commotion, if my brother feels that my choice of vocabulary will lose me any votes in an election three years from now. What is all the commotion with the astronomers?" the President asked.

"Well, Mr. President, it started at the Vatican Observatory."

"The Pope has an observatory?" the President asked. "Why?"

"I'm not sure, but I know they also have a branch in Arizona. Anyway, they have a sort of summer camp for undergrads, the very brightest young minds in astronomy from around the world. One of them, well it was actually two young ladies, one from France and one from Saudi Arabia, found something that nobody can explain satisfactorily," he paused.

"All right Frank, I'll bite, what did they find?" the President asked. The President took a sip of his coffee.

"No one knows what it is for sure. They just know it wasn't there the last time anyone looked. Everyone is going through their records to find when it appeared."

"What part of space is that?" Jimmy asked.

"The Andromeda Galaxy. It's one of our closer neighbors, about two million light years away. Anyway this kind of thing doesn't happen. Things don't just appear."

"That far away who really cares," the President interrupted. "I mean it has no real significance to us, does it?"

"Well, the thing is," Frank looked at the eyebrows again, "in the last few decades, things in space haven't been discovered by sight. It's more how gravity and light and other factors react in a specified area. If they react a certain way, we'll know something is there. So now we see something in this area we have missed and suddenly we have to rethink how we have been doing things. We've spent a lot of money on technology and it's possible this stuff might be missing things, like we are looking right past objects that are closer."

A searing pain shot through his right ankle. He looked down to see a paw attached to his sock. He gently reached down and backed the claw out of his skin.

"There is a possibility this object may be something just outside the Heliopause and our new equipment is not configured for it. It may be something rare from the Oort Cloud or the Kuiper Belt."

"Well," said the President, "if it has nothing to do with national security, the stock market, or gas prices, I'm satisfied. I'll leave it up to you science people to worry about the universe." The President stood and extended his hand. "Thank you, Frank, for coming over this evening. You're keeping an eye on the hydrogen engine tests aren't you?"

"Yes, sir, I get a report every day." He took the President's hand and shook it.

Jimmy led him to the door. "Do me a favor Frank. Keep an eye on this, too," he said in a hushed voice. "I have a funny feeling."

Chapter 20

Dr. DeRose was a very large and robust man in his sixties. His graying hair was slicked back and he sported a bushy beard. He also had a hearty laugh that was very infectious and could drink whisky with the best of them. And he was probably the smartest man I had ever met. His e-mail was listed on the Notre Dame web site. I e-mailed, told him it was an emergency and asked him for his office number. In about fifteen minutes we were talking on one of Mr. Stubbs tracfones.

"It's not a matter of national security like a terrorist attack, it's more like Watergate," I said after I told him about the confession and the package, but not the contents.

"I'm not sure what you want me to do," he said. "I need some details."

I hesitated. I had already told Father Craig and had implicated Sampson and his guys. "Okay, tell me what you would do. I have a document that may or may not be real. The FBI is chasing me and I feel like I am in danger. They have already broken into the church office. I feel the diocese wants nothing to do with this and would wash their hands of this whole mess if given the chance. The police would give me up to the FBI and that would be the end of it. And this is something that should be investigated."

"This thing you have, is it religious in nature?" he asked. I could picture him sitting at his desk in his office tapping with a pencil.

"Yes," I said.

"And I take it, that Father Craig believes this *thing* to be as important as you say it is?"

"Yes," I said again.

"And you are willing to give up your priesthood and your vows in pursuit of this?"

"Well, Dr. DeRose, I think my priesthood is already gone and I'm pursing this because of my vows."

He was silent for a moment. "You know I always liked you, but I wasn't sure you'd make a good Priest. You were like a door with a great light behind it. Sometimes I could see a sliver of that light coming through the cracks, but I wasn't so sure you had the key to get that door open. It must have been like Einstein when he was working in the patent office, he was smart enough but the fit was wrong. Just maybe this is your key. Let me have an e-mail address where I can reach you. I need to make a phone call."

It took most of the morning but Dr. DeRose finally was able to leave a message with an assistant to Jimmy's secretary. Jim Rienhart had been his buddy through most of his undergraduate years. They had even been roommates for a semester. The years had obscured many of the details of those heady days of the late sixties and seventies, but he could still remember many of the debates in class and in the organizations they both belonged to.

Jimmy would still call for help or advice on religious matters that would affect the President. They had been having dinner a couple of times a year when he still lived in Indiana, but that stopped with his brother's chance of a serious run at the White House. Campaigns begin with friends that can raise money, and Michael DeRose had the influence to do that.

But as the importance of the office had grown, so had the distance between the two men. The Rienhart duo had less time for their old friends as building new liaisons was paramount in politics at this level. Dr. DeRose no longer had a personal phone number for Jim Rienhart.

But he had another card to play. The Priest at the church where the President attended Mass was a friend. Everyone called him Father Steve because his last name had twelve letters in it. Maybe he was more of a fan than a friend. Dr. DeRose had written several books on religion and how it affects different aspects of modern life. The Priest at the church in D.C. had contacted DeRose about one of the books and an online friendship sprouted. There had even been talk of collaboration on a book. In any event, there was enough of a relationship that DeRose thought he could ask a favor. He e-mailed Father Steve. Was there a way he could get a private phone number for his old friend Jim Rienhart, the President's brother?

That afternoon he called the number and left a message.

Chapter 21

By five o'clock Father Craig had had it.

"I gotta go," he said after the third straight episode of Andy Griffith.

"I'll help any way I can, but my presence is not helping you right now, in fact, it might be hurting you. I don't think the FBI recognized me. We got out before they came back. If I can slide back into the church with a bag of ink cartridges or something like that, I can say I was out shopping all day and have not talked to you since this morning."

The door opened and Mr. Stubbs and Simon burst in.

"Time to go," Mr. Stubbs said calmly. "We've got another place set up for you that is a little less hot." Simon walked to the drawer of phones and scooped out several and dropped them into a black briefcase.

"Went from crime to ribs to God to James damn Bond in one month," he said looking at me.

"One more thing," Mr. Stubbs said. "The plant we got at the station house said the FBI was called because of a note left by the lady that killed herself. It said, The FBI is the devil, Maslow is the devil, He is risen."

I looked at Father Craig. "Maslow is mentioned in the journals," I said. "Looks like she had the story and wanted to make sure this guy Maslow is punished."

"That's my goal too," I said. "And to make sure something like this never happens again."

He paused for a moment looking very thoughtful. "There is something we haven't talked about yet, since you mentioned your goals in this thing. The end of the journals."

"You read clear to the end, didn't you?" I asked.

"The end of the journal, but that may not be the end of the story."

"I don't know what you mean," I said.

"I mean, we don't know what happened after the egg was fertilized. What if it actually worked?"

I felt the blood rush from my head. "What are you saying?"

He looked at the snow that was still falling. "What if He is alive?"

Chapter 22

Dr. DeRose was sitting alone in his living room, switching between Jeopardy and C-Span, when his phone rang. He had a plate of beef and broccoli balanced on his lap, chopsticks in his right hand, and the remote in his left. The phone rang four times before he could get to it.

"So, how's the voice of the religious right, left, and center?" Jimmy said, after DeRose said hello.

"My work is always rewarding and invigorating," he said.

"Something must be invigorating. I got messages from two different sources from you today."

"This may fall in the category of a favor. Incidents that may cause concern for the President down the road. An old student contacted me today. He is now a Priest and claims he is in possession of some inflammatory material that could be very damaging to the church and the government. He also claimed the FBI broke into his church, and were about to take him at gunpoint and would have taken this evidence if he had not escaped." He waited for a reaction but Jimmy remained silent.

Apparently there is a death already connected with this. Her name was Rundell of Severna Park, Md."

Jimmy said, "This Priest—is he a person you trust?"

"Actually yes, very much. He would not discuss much more with me for fear of involving myself. It seems his priesthood may be in jeopardy because of his reluctance to turn over this material."

"All right, let me check into this. I've got a full morning tomorrow. Tell your friend, the Priest, to sit tight and I'll try to get back to you in the afternoon. And Mike, I hope for both our sakes we are not putting the power and time of the office of the President of the United States chasing the story of a nut job."

"Nor do I," he said. "But that may be preferable to what we actually find."

Chapter 23

Father Craig left, sliding into a car with another of Mr. Stubbs' associates and returned back to the life of a humble Priest. I, on the other hand, waited with Simon at the back door of an adjacent building, connected by a hand dug tunnel to Sampson's. The snow stopped but the temperature was dropping. We both were wearing Army jackets, mine fit nicely but Simon's was immense. I had the backpack slung over one shoulder. Shine pulled up in front of the building in a gray van. A sticker on the side said, Plastic Pipe and Fitting Co.

Simon leisurely walked out, scanning both ends of the street. He opened the passenger door and tilted up the seat, then motioned to me with a nod. I walked out and climbed in. He dropped the seat back in place and sat. The door closed and we began to roll. The headlight beams swung across the brick walls, then across the dirty snow that had been plowed onto the sidewalks. I sat on a long bench seat with brown tarp-like upholstery. The inside of the van was gray also, but not by design. It looked to have years of built up grime converging in all the places not worn clean by contact.

"So," I said. "Where are we going?"

"I personally do not know. Shine here know, I doubt if he sayin'. You know where we goin' Shine?" Simon asked.

"Uh," Shine said.

"See, Shine a man of very few words, while I, on the contrary, a man of a whole lotta words. I got what you call an expansive vocabulary. I also got something right here." He reached in an inside pocket of the coat and whipped out a CD. He held it out in front of Shine's face.

"George Clinton, babe!" he started to lean toward the CD player that had been added to the underside of the dashboard as an afterthought. With Jedi-like quickness Shine snatched it from his hand and flung it right pass my ear, into the back of the van. It bounced across some plumbing tools.

"Uh," Shine muttered.

"What the hell did you do that for?" Now I gotta climb back through all that dirty….." He didn't get to finish.

Shine pointed a finger his way. "What did Mr. Stubbs say about the swearing? You got a bad mouth."

"I know. Don't say anything about it to Mr. Stubbs and I'll stop. I'm workin' on it dammit. Aw, sorry."

"So why does Mr. Stubbs want you to stop swearing?" I asked.

"It all part of the new plan," Simon said. "We ain't gonna' be street thugs no more. If we talk like thugs and look like thugs, people are gonna' treat us like thugs. Mr. Stubbs is a visionary. He said, if we do what we always done, then we're gonna' get what we always got, which was mostly dead, sooner or later."

"Is Father Craig part of this plan also?" I asked.

"Hell yeah, aw, sorry again." He looked at Shine, but Shine continued to look at the road. "When Mr. Stubbs be talking about long range plans he means real long range. Even after we dead. So we are changing our ways but not our attitudes. We are going to have legitimate business ventures but just as aggressive about them as we were in the olden days of our youth. Mr. Stubbs, he be thuggish on America. I like that. I'm gonna' mention that slogan to him."

"Uh," Shine muttered.

Simon halfway turned in his seat and looked at me. "I figured that's why we helpin' you. Father Craig is the only other white man

I ever see Mr. Stubbs talkin' to, not counting the cops. What do you think, Shine? Mr. Stubbs have us doin' this mean he goin' soft?"

Shine looked up into the rear view mirror and our eyes met. "No, it means he goin' smart. Sounds to me that you might be questioning Mr. Stubbs actions and that may be a very foolish thing to do." He was talking to Simon but looking at me.

"No, no you didn't listen right. Don't be puttin' words in my mouth. I got enough of them in there for a bunch of people. So," he said turning his attention back to me, "You like Father Craig? You a Priest or something?"

"More like something," I said.

He exhaled. "Now what we gonna' do? You all secretive, Shine act like a mute and won't talk to me, and my CD back there with the plumbing supplies."

We rode on, the frozen snow crunching under the tires.

Chapter 24

Jimmy arrived even earlier than usual the next morning. He woke out of a dead sleep an hour before the alarm buzzed. The bed beside him was empty, as it had been for the last two months. Patricia had left him. She was tired. Tired of being alone. Tired of no help with the kids. Life was not rewarding. He missed her much more than he thought he would.

The driver was not supposed to pick him up until six thirty, so he called in and asked to have the car sent early. Once he got there, he read some of the headlines on the Internet and watched his staff file in. It was still about an hour and a half before his morning meeting with the President.

The intercom buzzed. Every time it did, he wished it was his wife, but it never turned out to be. "Yes, Kim," he said.

"I have Frank White, the senior science advisor, on line four, he says it's urgent."

"Thank you, Kim, I'll take it," he waited for the click.

"Good morning, Frank, what's the good news? Find a way to run cars on water?"

"It moved."

"What?"

"The anomaly you told me to keep an eye on. The thing in Andromeda. It's gone. There is no trace of it. The astronomers are going ballistic."

Jimmy felt his arms prickle and looked down at them resting on his desk. Goose bumps. Now he knew why he had awoken early. "What, did it explode or something?"

"Nobody can figure it out. It disappeared just like it appeared. I don't want to sound like more of a geek than I am, but this is ground breaking stuff."

"All right, Frank, keep me up to date." Jimmy started to hang up, but had a thought. "Since it's so far away, does that mean whatever happened, happened a really long time ago?"

"I can't answer that. I just don't know."

"All right, fair enough, and by the way we need geeks like you in this administration." He hung up and tapped a pencil on the desk blotter.

Was it Plato who said that intelligent people see patterns? He picked the phone back up. "Kim, could you get me Director Snider at the FBI."

By the time he was to meet with the President, Jimmy had already asked Director Snider to check into the death of Mrs. Rundell and the FBI's involvement. He decided not to inform the President on any of the FBI stuff yet, but would brief him on the space thing. The President had a tendency to make light of things like this, so he made a note for him not to mention Area 51 or anything in that vein.

Chapter 25

I awoke to the aroma of bacon and coffee. It took a moment to realize I was not in my bed in the rectory. I pulled on my tee shirt I had left on the floor. Shine was at the stove cooking as I walked into the kitchen of the apartment. I didn't make a sound and he didn't turn around, but he knew I was there. "How do you like your eggs?"

He had been awake when I went to bed. I was wiped out; he looked wide awake last night, just like he did now.

"Scrambled. What time is it?" I asked.

"About seven," he said without looking at his watch. "Went to the drug store and got us a few things, laid yours on the table." I looked in the plastic bag. Toothpaste and brush, deodorant, and mouth wash.

"Thanks," I said.

He nodded without turning around. I heard a noisy yawn behind me and Simon came out through the open door of his room. He wore old stretched out navy sweats and no shirt. There was a tattoo of a stalking tiger in the center of his back.

"What's goin' on in here?" he said as he produced a pick and stuck it in the side of his afro. "Shine doin' some cookin'? Smells good, too. Shine you been up all night? I ain't heard a sound from you last night." He scooted into a chair at a small table.

"Shine has already been to a store and picked up some things for us," I said.

"Yeah, well, that don't surprise me none. Shine is Mr. Self-Discipline. I saw him stand in the shadows for about six hours straight without movin' or complainin'. It's like he ain't human sometimes. He don't talk, he don't laugh, and he don't smile."

Shine put down his spatula and picked up a plastic bag, identical to mine, that was on the counter. He tossed it to Simon. "Don't need to thank me for takin' care of your needs." Simon peeked into the bag.

"What is this?" he yelled. Reaching in, he pulled out a Barney toothbrush. Shine didn't turn around, but I knew he was smiling.

We sat around the rest of the day, waiting for some word from Mr. Stubbs, who was going to relay Dr. DeRose's message. The headline on CNN was: *Space Apparition Disappears*. I was restless, Simon paced like a wild animal in a cage and Shine sat motionless watching TV.

Lunch was a sub for each of us from Subway. For that, Shine wore a gray overcoat and dress pants. He looked like a stockbroker coming home from work. Dinner was Chinese from a little place around the corner. Shine never frequented places that might have surveillance cameras.

Chapter 26

Jimmy was just finishing his after dinner coffee with the President when Margaret gently knocked on the door. "Mr. Rienhart, Kim just called and asked you to stop by your office before you leave." She always called him Mr. Rienhart and his brother, President Rienhart.

"All right, Margaret, thank you," Mr. Rienhart said.

"Patricia still at her mother's?" the President asked. "With the kids?"

"Yep," he said and let out a slow breath. "I don't think we're going to make it this time."

"You know you can take some time off if you need to," the President said.

"I'll think about it," he said standing to go. "I have to go see who's in my office."

Director Snider was relaxing in one of the leather armchairs in the Chief of Staff's office. His tie was loosened and his feet were up on a small table between the chairs. James walked in and navigated to the chair behind his desk.

"Make yourself at home, Director," he said.

"I thought I'd better since I didn't know how long you'd be. Okay, here's what I got on your boy Maslow. That's the name Mrs. Rundell put on a poster she left on her door. He did work for us— he was on the payroll for nearly thirty years. But, he did not work

Secret Blood

for any one division. In fact, I cannot find a single division that would claim him. He had no evaluations, no supervisor, and no permanent office. This guy was a spy's spy. I can't even find a picture of him."

"How can that be?" James asked. "What kind of agency you running over there?"

"You've got to remember Jimmy, things were different back then. They could hide just about whatever they wanted. What I did find out was that he was funded through the chemical weapons division…big time. He had a bunch of science people working in his labs. And guess what? Payroll shows Mr. Rundell was one of his highest pay level guys."

James felt the goose bumps again and shivered.

"You cold?" Snider asked.

"No, so that's it? You find out anything else?"

"Maybe if I worked for the CIA that would be it. But no, lucky for you I'm FBI and I have more."

"You have to tie up anybody and beat it out of them?"

"If I did I couldn't tell anybody in this bleedin' heart administration."

"Okay, okay, go ahead."

"I called some of the retired guys, upper level people who should have known everything that was going on. Even the black ops stuff. Maslow was never at any of the meetings, and any time anyone asked who he was or what he was doing, they would get reassigned. It was like nobody could touch this guy. One senior staff member I talked to swore that Maslow was involved in a series of break-ins all over the world, including some at the Smithsonian. There were even some rumors about something he did at Fort Knox."

"So where is he now?" James asked.

"Dead. Died of cancer in '97. At least that's what the IRS thought. Who knows though, with this guy? I traced everyone that worked with him and they are all gone. Rundell was the last of the group to die."

"How did you guys get in it? You chasing a Priest?"

"All right, I knew it would come back to the FBI being the bad guy. Here's what happened. Cops find the body and the note. Since it mentions the FBI, they call us. One of the agents types in the name Maslow. And that trips a high level risk code. Something Maslow probably put in place to get a handle on any leaks that could jeopardize his work. Whatever, it's still in the system to investigate and to recover any materials. These are kind of young agents, so they think this is their big break to move up the career ladder. They do the usual canvassing and get to the priest. He starts to act kind of kinky, so they decide to find out what he is hiding. They look in the church and the chase is on. I know it's over the top. And don't worry, they are being officially reprimanded. Now, that's all I could find out. Not bad for a day's work."

James was stunned but tried not to show it. "Yeah, that's good. Do me another favor. If you catch him, do it quietly and safely and you be the one to interview him. You're on this now. If you need any help with your superior let me know."

Snider stood and put out his hand. "It's always good when the office of the President owes you a favor; don't think I won't cash in some time."

They shook and Snider left. He picked up the phone and buzzed his secretary. "Kim, are you still there?" No answer. He had never actually dialed an outside number from this phone and he wasn't sure how. He decided to call the White House operator. She had to look up Dr. DeRose's number in the phone book.

"I think I need to meet with this Priest of yours," Jimmy told Dr. DeRose.

"So you have checked out his story and found it credible?" Dr. DeRose asked.

"Let's say your trust in him was well founded. I gather he would like to put all this behind him."

"I'm not sure what he wants. He knows he is in over his head and wants some sort of closure. I take it you have called off the FBI?"

"No, they are still looking for him."

"Why?" asked Dr. DeRose, surprised.

"It's my bargaining chip, I'm sure you would do the same thing. When we meet, he gives me the material or whatever he has, or the agency will eventually track him down. I want you to tell him I will do the right thing by him and he can trust me. I would rather keep the FBI in the background as much as I can from now on. How far away is he?"

"He is close enough. Would you like us to come to you? I'm sure there are rooms available at the White House where we could come to a solution," Dr. DeRose said already knowing the answer.

"Nope. I can't let anyone know the Office of the President is meeting in the White House with a person the FBI is actively pursuing. You pick the spot and I'll be there."

"I'll get back with you in a few minutes. Let me see what we can work out."

Chapter 27

One of Shine's cell phones rang. He picked it up smoothly and quickly. "Yeah," was all he said. He listened and then put the phone down. He looked at me and said, "You the chosen one." He retrieved our coats from a closet and said, "We need to find a computer by eight o'clock. Simon, you stay here. Don't let that backpack out of your sight." Simon started to protest but Shine gave him a look that I had not seen since the last Dirty Harry movie. We walked out to the car and Shine slid the cell under one of the tires. I heard it crunch as we pulled away.

Either Shine had visited this town before or he had done some remarkable scouting when he got the toothbrushes. Most of the snow was off the street and in piles along the curb. At 7:55 p.m. he pulled into a public library and parked in a dim corner away from the parking lot lights. He took a slip of paper and a pencil from the glove box and wrote something down. He handed me a fake driver's license with my picture on it. I looked at him, puzzled.

"We got a friend at the DMV. Mr. Stubbs had it done right after the situation in Sampson's. Always handy to have an alternate ID when the Feds are lookin'."

He watched the library door as a mother and two children walked to their car.

"Listen, sometimes they ask for a driver's license to use their computers. Just say you need to use the computer. Don't make up a story; don't say anything you don't have to. Go to the chat room I have written down. If there are no vacant ones just stand behind the most nervous looking person there. In this chat room you want to find a guy called Rosey. He's going to give you information on our next move."

"Why can't we just call him on one of your clean cell phones?" I was picking up the criminal language already.

"Not what we instructed to do. I figure that whoever you contacted thinks he is being tapped now and is probably going to find a computer like we are. Make sure you write down what he says because it may not make sense right yet."

"You coming in?" I said as I opened the door. For the first time, I noticed the lights had been set not to come on when the doors opened.

"Nope, not in the instructions. Keep your head down until you get inside, in case they got security cameras. FBI has facial recognition."

I walked in and asked to use a computer. The girl at the desk was young, 18 or 19 at the most. She didn't ask for any ID. I'm not sure she even looked up at me. I followed instructions and didn't say anything else to anyone. The chat room was easy to find and before long I had my message from Dr. DeRose, AKA Rosey. I got up and left and I was sure no one would ever remember my being there. Five years in the seminary and I was being mentored by a thug. We drove back to the apartment to figure out the message.

Jimmy's phone rang. It was Dr. DeRose. "Do you need to write this down or would you rather take it off the wiretap?" DeRose asked.

"Come on now, Mike. You're acting like we are not friends. We both know I have to protect the President and not allow myself to get dragged into anything."

"Yes, you are right. But I need to know my man is protected here also."

"I'll give you my word as an old friend," Jimmy said.

"That's good enough for me. Progress is being made. Would you be able to clear your calendar for tomorrow around five o'clock?"

"Barring some major catastrophe I'll be there. I'd like to put this whole thing to bed."

They hung up. Things are getting interesting DeRose thought to himself. He was tired and getting weaker but hurriedly packed an overnight bag and called a cab.

By the time the cabby honked he had already booked a seat on the redeye to Washington. He was sure he could find a computer in the VIP lounge to send a message to his runaway friend.

Chapter 28

Shine let me out near the front of our apartment, then drove to the next block to park. He took a ratchet from the plumber's tools in back of the van and switched license plates with a nearby car. When he walked into the apartment Simon and I were working on the message. I had written down, 'Fifty cents rests on Sunday, be there at the dozen. Do-do-do looking out the opposite door'.

Simon said, "I don't know, but I think it's got something to do with Tina Turner."

Shine and I both looked at him. Shine said, "That last part, is that a song?"

"Yeah, but I think I think the song says, looking out my back door," I said.

"That's it then, the opposite of back is front, so we go in the front door and Tina will be there waiting for us. We there, babe!" Simon said. "Why he writin' all cloaked in mystery. Why we gotta figure this all out?"

"The FBI has computer programs that look for key words on internet transmissions; I think he's staying away from certain words. Okay, look at the next part, rest on Sunday. Where do you rest on Sunday?

"I rest on my couch and watch the ballgame," Simon said as he pushed back from the table and walked to the couch.

"Rest on Sunday has got to mean church, and dozen means twelve o'clock." Shine said. It made sense to me.

"So we know we go in the front door of a church at twelve, but which church? Fifty cents. That's change. Is there a change church?" I asked.

"What about a half dollar? Is there some kind of half way church?" Simon said from the couch. He was lying with his head on the center cushion and his legs draped over the arm. His feet fluttered in the air. "This guy a white guy like you? You think he know 50 Cent, the rapper?"

"I can almost guarantee he doesn't know any rappers," I said.

Shine pulled a dollar bill out of his jeans pocket and folded it in half. He studied it for a while, shook his head and handed it to me. I worked with it for a while but got no further than he did.

"Let's get some change," I said. We emptied our pockets and put all the coins we had on the table. "Let's make all the combinations of fifty cents."

That didn't work. We would have needed about fifty dollars.

"All right," I said. "Let's start with the least amount of coins and work our way up. The least would be two quarters." I slid two quarters together on the table. Next would be a quarter, two dimes, and a nickel."

I glanced at Shine. He was smiling. "What?" I said.

"That ain't the smallest amount," he said.

Immediately I knew. The Kennedy half dollar. The church Kennedy attended while he was President. The same church President Rienhart attends now.

Simon sat up, legs still dangling. "So we takin' a fugitive into D.C. to the church the President goes to, and we walk right in the front door? Only one thing I got to say 'bout that, white guy musta' thought up this plan."

The next morning Shine pulled the stickers off the side of the van and rubbed some dirty snow across the side panels. It looked odd but you would not know the stickers had ever been there. Shine bought us jeans, shirts, and new jackets from somewhere and the old clothing was thrown out with the garbage. I shouldered my backpack and closed the door behind me. Hopefully, I would be able to shed it by the end of the day.

Shine put on a ball cap and pulled it low over his eyes as we got a drive-thru breakfast at McDonalds. Simon and I got burritos and Shine got only a black coffee. We arrived at the church about a half hour before we were supposed to. Shine had navigated the beltway and the traffic like a local. We drove by the entrance and parked about a block away.

"You go scout. I'll call in about twenty minutes." Shine handed Simon a Bluetooth. Simon put it on, then a pair of sunglasses, and then pulled up his hood. I wouldn't have known him from ten feet away. He eased out of the door, closed it gently, and sauntered down the sidewalk. When he got to the church, he sat down on the steps that led to the main doors.

Shine adjusted both mirrors so he could see the sidewalk behind us. I squirmed from the back seat to the front.

"So, what if something goes wrong?" I asked.

He stared at me for a moment and stayed quiet. It wasn't that he didn't trust me. I think it was against his grain to trust anyone. "He sees anything wrong we split, he leaves and calls Mr. Stubbs, they find a safe place to pick him up."

The twenty minutes went by slowly and the backpack on my lap felt heavier than it ever had. Shine sat patiently, not moving a muscle. He reminded me of an ambush predator waiting in the jungle.

Shine took out his phone and dialed.

"He said a big man with a white beard and a Priest unlocked the door and went in. You know them?"

"Yeah, the man with the beard is the one I called. He set all this up."

"You trust him?" Shine asked.

"I guess I have to now."

To Simon he said, "Go in and sit in one of the pews and watch. Don't talk to them; don't let them make you move. If you have to, tell them you are a messenger for the chosen one. They'll leave you be."

Shine adjusted the mirror and we watched Simon enter the church. Shine reached under his seat and pulled out a bulky manila envelope. Inside was a knife that looked like it was made of plastic and an ankle harness for it. He pulled up his jean leg and strapped it on. "Carbon fiber," he said. "Church the President goes to probably has metal detectors." Above the visor was a handicapped card. He hung it from the mirror. He started the van, adjusted the mirrors, and pulled a U-turn across all four lanes of traffic. We U-turned again and parked in a handicapped spot right in front of the steps.

"Shoulda' had another guy waitin' in the van with the motor runnin'. Too late now," he said and opened the door.

Shine was wearing a black leather coat, dark jeans, black shoes, and aviator sunglasses. I had on black jeans and a burgundy leather jacket. In my haste not to forget anything, I forgot to shave, so I had a little stubble. I carried the backpack by its strap as we entered the front doors.

The entry way was large but dwarfed by the size of the interior columns. The smell was very familiar, varnished wood and candles. The vast room was humbling and comforting at the same time, just the way the architects had designed it. The vestibule was semi-dark but the altar was lit beautifully. Three people sat in the front row of pews. Two were on one side of the aisle and one on the other.

I could hear voices, one louder than the others. "I told you, the chosen one will be here when he decides the time is right."

"Dr. DeRose?" I said. A large form rose from the pew and spread his arms wide. He walked up the aisle towards me. "The chosen one has arrived," he said with amusement.

I started up the aisle to greet him. Shine appeared in front of me like a shield. Dr. DeRose froze in his tracks, and the smile froze on his face.

"You know him?" he said without taking his eyes off of DeRose.

"Yes. He's the one I called in the first place. He's all right."

"Then where's the other person you're supposed to meet?" Shine asked.

"I haven't told them where the meeting place is yet. I didn't want them setting up a trap before you got here," Dr. DeRose said in a shaky voice.

Shine was silent for a moment and then said, "Good idea." He stepped aside and Dr. DeRose enveloped me in a hug.

"Good to see you my boy, you look quite a bit different than the last time I saw you. But then again that was several years ago. Let me introduce you to my good friend, Father Steve, who has been kind enough to allow us to use his church for the meeting this afternoon."

Father Steve had savagely black hair and beautiful white teeth. He smiled wide as he shook hands. He was from India, very polite and very much in control of the goings on in his church. Like Father Craig, Father Steve was always ready to make a deal to benefit his church.

Dr. DeRose was already on the phone with whoever was going to meet us. He gave the instructions and hung up and smiled. "Everything is set. They are to be here in a few hours."

"A few hours!" Simon shouted. "We gotta' wait here another few hours?" He stood and began pacing around the altar. "Who we waitin' for that can't get here within a few hours?"

"That's a good question, who are we going to be talking to?" I asked.

"Well, I had to find someone who was in a particular position not to be hurt by whatever you have, but still have the need to do the correct thing. Someone, who had enough power not to be pressured by the FBI. That left me with an exceedingly small pool of people. In Washington most people are looking for that little bit of leverage to parlay. All in all, I was left with only one good choice, James Rienhart."

Upon hearing the name no one moved. No one except Simon. "Who's he?" he asked.

Chapter 29

At the White House James Rienhart's phone buzzed. It was Mike DeRose. He wrote the instructions down and stuck the paper in his shirt pocket. He still had two hours before he left for the church. Just about enough time to look over a compromise the Republicans were going to offer on a bill that was dying on the senate floor. He had just realized it was not a compromise at all when the intercom buzzed and the phone rang at the same time. By the time he had decided which to attend to first, Kim was knocking at his door.

He picked up the phone and cupped his hand over the receiver then yelled to Kim. "Come in." She had a slip of paper in her hand and she looked like someone who had just had their car backed into.

"Yeah," he said into the phone.

It was David Greg, the White House Press Secretary. "You know anything about this thing in space?"

"Maybe, I know there was something way out there, then nobody could find it. Is that what you're talking about?" He waved Kim over to his desk and took the note.

"It's back and a lot closer this time. We'll have to make a statement soon. Let me know when the President is ready." He hung up.

Secret Blood

The intercom was still buzzing. The note said, *Call the President*. He can't get through on any of your lines. The phone started to ring again. He hit the button on the intercom. It was the Senator from Texas, their most important ally in Congress. "You watching CNN?"

"Nope, haven't had time this morning."

"Well son, you better get your head out of the sand, reaction over here is incredible." The intercom clicked off.

The phone was still ringing. "Could you switch on CNN, Kim? And, no more calls after this one. Tell them I'm meeting with the President."

"Yeah," he said into the phone.

"It's back" Frank said.

"You're a little late," he said.

"You kidding. I had a late lunch; I got a phone call on the way back to the office. By the time I parked the car there were reporters at the doors. These guys are acting like it's *War of the Worlds*. I checked some sites on line just to confirm, and then I called you."

Jimmy looked up to the monitor where the sound had been muted. The banner across the screen said 'Breaking News'. The scrolling subtitles were saying something about the thing in space. "Okay, Frank, tell us what to do. We are going to have to make a statement soon and the President has to come off as knowledgeable."

"The statement should say something like we are in no danger. This thing is still a hundred and seventy light years away. It's something we have never seen before; acting like nothing we've ever watched before. We'll get some of the most knowledgeable people in the world together and discuss it. It will be, ah, be a great learning experience for us all."

That sounded pretty good to Jimmy. That was a great angle, the learning experience part. He was still watching the screen. "Listen," he said. "Can we do that, I mean get the brightest science people and have a discussion. What is the name of that group? You know the people that decided Pluto wasn't a planet."

"That's the IAU," Frank said, "The International Astronomical Union."

"Yeah, let's get them together and…."

"No," Frank interrupted. "You don't want to do that."

"Why not?"

"These guys have very big egos; some of them won't listen to anything except their own voice. They make fun of other peoples' ideas until the idea is proven true, then they will try to take credit for it themselves. It'd be like a steel cage death match."

"You can handle them, if someone acts up toss them out of the meeting. We'll have it here at the White House. I'll have the President step in and listen, that will usually silence any loudmouths. Can I count on you to put this together for us?"

Frank sighed in resignation. "I have your word you won't disappear on me and leave me without a whip?"

"You can count on me Frank," Jimmy said and hung up the phone.

He buzzed Kim, "Could you get me the Oval Office, please."

Over the next hour he and the President banged out a statement and watched things unfold on Fox and CNN. They called David Greg and the three of them made some minor corrections. David left to practice the statement and do some additional research.

"I've got something going on this afternoon, I may need to take a couple Secret Service agents with me" Jimmy said.

The President was sitting across a table from him. He looked at his brother until their eyes met. "Anything I should know about?" he asked finally.

"No," Jimmy said. "I'll tell you about it later. It's really nothing big, just a precaution."

"Anything to do with you wife?" the President asked.

"No, no, I'll fill you in as soon as I know what is going on. I'm going to see Mike DeRose. He seems to be involved in something interesting." The President's stare was making him a little uneasy. "I was going to tell you earlier, then this space thing came up." He pushed the chair back and stood up. "I've got to go; I'll talk to you later tonight."

The President watched him leave and sat there rubbing his chin between his thumb and index finger. Then he shivered.

Chapter 30

"I want so badly to be a good Priest," I told Dr. DeRose. "It's what I've wanted since I was a boy. But, I lack the confidence. Sometimes the homily doesn't make sense. I've found a thousand ways to mess things up. I think people like me, but they don't see me as their Priest."

He put a hand on my shoulder. "You seem very confident, and if I may say so, very competent in what you have been doing the last couple of days. I don't know of any priest who could have handled this situation as well as you have."

He cleared his throat. "Do you believe God is all powerful?"

"Yes," I said.

"What do you think he is trying to tell you through your adventure here?" he asked softly.

"I'm not sure," I said.

"I think we discussed in class, that everything you do in life is practice for your next day. Everything in the past, leads to right now, this moment. Maybe being a Priest has been preparation for something else. Do you feel God leading you somewhere with that backpack of yours?"

Simon had been talking with Father Steve a few feet away. "You sure do have a beautiful church here Father. I, myself, was raised Baptist, but I believe I may start attending church here. What time does preachin' start? Not too late, I hope. Games start early on Sunday." Father Steve just looked at him.

Dr. DeRose said, "I don't know what's in there," he gestured toward the backpack, "but it's important enough that some of the highest ranking officials in this country want it. In God's great plan I don't believe in accidents."

I was pondering this when I heard Simon say "Church this big, you're sure to have coffee and doughnuts after preachin'."

* * *

The agents looked like the stereotypical Secret Service everyone has seen in all the movies. Crisp haircut, bulky overcoats, nicely polished shoes. They had head sets in their ears and looked serious and confident at the same time. One drove the car, one in the passenger seat, and another sat beside Jimmy in the back seat.

It was a Government issue Lincoln, navy blue with dark windows. They pulled into the handicapped spot behind the van. The driver stayed with the car and the other three got out and went to the church door. The first agent opened the door for the second agent who entered and closed the door behind him. He scanned the room and found Dr. DeRose, who stood to meet him. He had been briefed on the appearance of everyone except a thin black man who looked like a vagrant.

"All set Dr. DeRose?" the agent asked.

"Yes, everything is in place."

The agent went back to the door, opened it, and Jimmy stepped in, followed by the other agent. A tiny blue light flashed as they passed a hidden metal detector. As soon as they stepped inside, the driver got out of the car, walked up the steps and guarded the church door.

Inside the two agents fanned to both sides of the sanctuary with their backs against the walls. Neither saw Shine who had blended into the shadows behind some ornate columns near the back of the room. He had been standing motionless for the last three hours.

Jimmy walked straight toward Dr. DeRose with his hand outstretched.

They exchanged pleasantries. Jimmy knew Father Steve through his brother, so only Simon and I had to be introduced.

"Maybe we should excuse ourselves to the cry room," I said. Jimmy agreed. He looked at my clothing.

"You don't look like a Priest," he said.

"Relaxed dress code," I said.

We walked to the rear of the church where the cry room was located. We went right by Shine without knowing it. The room was built so parents could attend Mass with small children who could become fussy, loud, or unruly. The front was constructed of glass so the occupants could watch and listen to Mass, but not be heard.

It was perfect for us, both sides could see we were safe, but not hear what we were saying. Two rows of chairs faced the front and behind them was a table and chairs for games.

I watched them, watching us, as we sat.

"I think we should pray before we start," I said.

"I'm not a practicing Catholic," Jimmy said.

"You haven't read what I have in the backpack."

"All right Father, whatever you think," he bowed his head but did not cross himself as I did.

I told him everything that had happened up to the part about calling Father Craig. He didn't have to know everything.

"Now, I'd like to know what you know," I said.

"I'm going to treat this like a confession, so it's all privileged information. Got that, Father?"

I smiled. "I've only known you five minutes and I've already done one of the most difficult things for a Priest to do."

"What's that Father, create trust?"

"No. Get a non-practicing Catholic to confession."

Jimmy told me about Maslow and his shadowy employment with the CIA. He went on for about ten minutes from memory. Finally he said, "Okay, what's in the bag?"

I took out the first journal and slid it across the table.

In the sanctuary Simon was standing beside one of the Secret Service agents looking at him. He only came up to the agents shoulder.

"I guess we both in the same field. You protectin' your boy and I'm protectin' mine. Course you dressed a little better than me right now, but I undercover." The agent glanced at him then continued his vigilance.

Simon stood on his toes and looked at the agent's earpiece. "You get XM on that?"

Jimmy looked up at me after only a few pages. "I can see why you felt this is important enough not to just hand over, and why you didn't want it buried by the church."

"Keep reading, it gets better." I was amazed at myself. Two days ago I was ready to vomit after reading it, now I was being flip, *it gets better.*

Simon was still with the agent mimicking the same pose, watching everything. "I know we just met, but you think you could help a brother out. Your boy in there, pretty high up in the government, got to be, to have you watchin' his back. You think he could do somethin' bout a couple of outstanding warrants?"

Jimmy closed the journal before he was halfway through. "There's too much here, I need to take it back and read it, then see if I can corroborate the dates and information." He was a little paler than when he came in.

I was afraid this was going to happen. He was going to take it and this was all for naught. I didn't see how I could stop him. But at the same time I couldn't keep running forever. In a way, I was a little relived, now the burden would be lifted.

I surprised myself by saying, "I don't think I can let you take it, not without some assurances."

"Like what?" he asked.

"Like a promise that you'll learn all you can and keep me informed," I said.

Secret Blood

He looked at me, studying my face. "A promise?" He thought for a moment. "You got it." He reached out his hand to shake. "I wish we could do everything in the government with a hand shake. Most of them I can't trust. There's something about you though, can't put my finger on it."

"Remember," I said. "This is me in disguise," I said.

"Maybe," he said. "Also, I want you to know the FBI has given up the dragnet, you're not being chased anymore. I talked to the director on the way here."

When we walked out of the cry room a few minutes later, everyone stopped talking. Both Father Steve and Dr. DeRose stood, looking very expectant.

"Have your discussions been completed satisfactorily?" DeRose asked. Jimmy held up the backpack. "I'll be in touch through Dr. DeRose," he said, then smiled, "I promise."

The two agents, one in front and one behind, walked out with Jimmy. The metal detector flashed as they passed Shine without seeing him. Like stepping over a rattlesnake in the forest.

"May I have a word with you?" Dr. DeRose asked. I joined him again in the front pew. The altar was bathed in soft light, formidable in front of us. I felt relived I was no longer the gatekeeper to this vile secret. No longer a criminal. Suddenly I realized I had nowhere to go.

"I have been talking with the Bishop. It's one of those good news, bad news, things," he said. "You are no longer the pastor at St. Marks. I believe that is the bad news. He said you were probably expecting that to happen."

I nodded. I had expected it, but it still stung.

"The good news is that you are going to be reunited with Father Craig as an assistant pastor until you are reassigned." He smiled. "So you are still a Priest, a Priest without a church, but a Priest nonetheless."

"I suppose I should be glad they even allowed me to stay Catholic," I said.

I thanked Father Steve for allowing us the use of his church and walked out to the sidewalk. The snow was starting again. It was the sharp kind that stung your face where it hit. Dr. DeRose did not have his coat and he shivered as he said goodbye. For the first time I noticed he had lost weight.

"I'll be in touch," he said. "And remember we all do not serve the Lord in the same way. I think this is a good thing."

I nodded.

Chapter 31

The next few days were very difficult for me. Father Craig and Simon helped me move by belongings from St. Marks to St. Mary's, Father Craig's church. Father Craig, a younger and much more exuberant pastor than myself, showed me around.

I would help with communion at all the Masses and do the Wednesday night Mass myself. Father Craig was very busy meeting with community groups, senior citizens, and hospital visits. I'm sure the Bishop thought I was attending all this with Father Craig, but I wasn't. I don't know if Father Craig decided I needed time to adapt to my new position, or if he just did not want me slowing him down. Either way, I appreciated being left alone. I think I had the 'Post Fugitive on the Run Blues.' My mind was in sixth gear and my life was in first.

One Sunday morning, about five minutes before Mass was to start, Father Craig and I were at the back of the church in the area where we donned our vestments. Father Craig was almost giddy. He looked up and said, "Lord, thank you for this opportunity, I think."

A few seconds later the church door opened and let in a gust of cold air. Behind it came Mr. Stubbs and a female companion, both dressed to the nines. The doorway filled with Afro-American people. As the line continued to file in, Father Craig helped with the seating. Most of the men wore what looked like nightclub clothing and the few women wore very high heels. Simon was the last person in. He looked at my vestment with the rich embroidery and golden accents. "Morning, Father Elvis," he said.

By the time everyone was seated the entire back of the church was filled. Everyone was very quiet and respectful under the watchful eye of Mr. Stubbs. As Father Craig, the two Altar boys, and I walked down the aisle I heard Simon whisper, "Why we got to sit in back?"

Before Mass was ended, Father Craig asked Mr. Stubbs to come up and speak. This astonished most of the parishioners who had been cowering in their seats the entire service. He stepped to the pulpit and his deep voice resonated through the church. "My associates and I have been a part of this community for several years. We have not always been a positive part of the community. We are trying to change our ways. In this house of God today I am promising to try to reverse the relationship we have with you. We will pledge our help to you in any situation you might face out on the street. If anyone would like to eat at my restaurant, one of my associates will see you to and from your car, or walk you all the way home if you wish. We will be in the vestibule and on the sidewalk out front to say hello after church….excuse me, I mean Mass. Thanks for your time and patience."

Many of the parishioners turned to each other and started whispering. Mr. Stubbs stared straight ahead as he walked back to his seat.

Father Craig came back up to the mike and said, "I ask you to take Mr. Stubbs up on his offer and meet some of these gentlemen, any time a hand is offered in friendship we need to receive it in the nature it is given. And besides, you will never taste a better plate of ribs." The people laughed, maybe just a little nervously.

Stubbs' men stood self-consciously receiving the people in and outside the church. With everyone socializing, Father Craig and I put away our vestments and donned our overcoats and mingled on the sidewalk outside. For the first time, I felt the congregation was beginning to take a liking to me.

I was talking to Mr. and Mrs. Minski, when someone tapped me on the back. A man in a tan overcoat with a square jaw, short hair, and a thing in his ear said, "We need a word." He motioned toward a midnight blue car idling at the corner. A plume of transparent blue smoke was rising from the exhaust. It was the only clean car in view, the rest were painted with the gray-brown film of winter. "This way please," he commanded. At the car he opened the rear door and I slid in. Jimmy Rienhart was waiting for me there. The knot in my stomach that had almost vanished in the last few weeks tightened again. The car pulled away from the corner.

"Good morning, Father Kenzee," he said. "I hope I'm not taking you away from something important." He wore a gray suit, white shirt and a burgundy tie—the standard D.C. wardrobe. There was an open folder on his lap. "I promised I would keep you updated. I'm sorry but I think this may upset you. We found him," he said. Things in the car became unfocused. I felt myself breathing quicker. I tried to stare at the back on the front seat, where the upholstery was sewn.

"Hey, you okay?" he asked. "I thought it might be a shock."

Thinking back now, I'm not so sure I didn't perceive the whole thing as a game. But now I knew there was a man walking around somewhere with His DNA.

Did he know who he was? And really who was he? Certainly not Jesus. This man was not infused with the Holy Spirit, was he? I would have to keep telling myself, it's not Him, it's not really Him.

He was still looking at me. "Bo," he said to the driver, "see if you can find a drive-through and we will get Father a coke or something to drink."

"Where did you find him?" I asked.

"Africa, of all places." He flipped a page in the folder. "You sure you want to hear this? You're still not looking so good."

I wanted to throw up. "I'm good, go ahead."

"Here's the short version. We had our best computer guys work on Maslow's files, or what was left on them. They found the DNA codes of the subject they had cloned. We have a huge database of codes from criminals, unsolved murders, political figures and aide workers around the world. Remember when Saddam's two sons were blown up? We had to wait for the DNA to check out before we were sure it was them. Same database. We keep records of countries that have diseases that could spread to the U.S. We keep an eye on anybody that has been giving aid to diseased peoples. That's how we found him." The car pulled into a McDonald's, the driver ordered three large Cokes.

"Apparently, he was given to an orphanage at birth, when Maslow was feeling pressured to inform the Agency exactly what he was working on. After that things get a little fuzzy." The driver passed two of the drinks back; I pressed mine to my forehead.

"What about the people who worked on this, can you press any kind of charges against them?" I asked.

"From everything we can find, they're all dead," he took a sip then looked back at the folder. It looked funny, the second most important man in the country drinking soda out of a straw.

"At age eighteen, He joined UNICEF, and since then He has always been involved in volunteer work in Africa; ethnic cleansing, famine, diseases. He has seen the worst of the worst."

"How do you know, the DNA Maslow had, was that of Jesus?" I asked.

"It may not be. It could be someone else's altogether, but it corroborates what we have found in the Rundell journals and Maslow's computer files. We have convicted people on much less information."

"How in the world did we get DNA? Did we have the knowledge to clone people in the eighties?" Now my mind was swirling with questions.

"I don't know if anyone else had the knowledge, but again, no one knew we did either. The DNA is still a bit of a mystery. We do have some information about some break-ins at the Smithsonian and Fort Knox around that time, so we're still looking into that part."

His phone rang. "Yeah," he said. "Just now? How far? I'll be right there."

He looked me. "I've got to go. Anyway, do you want to meet Him?"

I didn't know how to answer.

"We picked Him up and we're bringing Him in, it'll take a couple of days though." He closed the folder. The driver was already heading back.

"I'll have to think about it," I said.

Chapter 32

By the time Jimmy had gotten to the White House things were in full emergency mode. The thing in the sky was back. Fox news was now calling it 'The Ghost' because of its ability to disappear. It was now about halfway from where it was first spotted, by far eclipsing the speed of anything in the known universe. During its last appearance a group of scientists had speculated that it was not actually in the position reported the first time it was spotted. They said it was not moving, but that our line of sight was curving around a black hole. Others thought it was passing through a series of black holes and popping up every so often like a prairie dog watching for a hawk. What worried everyone, even though no one would admit it, was the fact that it had closed the gap between us in a radically short amount of time.

Of course, any event that frightens the public has an effect upon the world economy. These effects cannot be predicted unless similar events have happened before. There are cultural differences that factor in also. It's a systemic problem all national leaders try to evade. If you can't predict the affect, then control the cause. Limit panic, stop the fear, and tell everyone it's going to be all right.

As soon as Jimmy got to the Situation Room he spoke with the President, the Press Secretary, and Frank White in that order. He talked to White on the speakerphone.

"What about the meeting you were supposed to set up Frank?" he asked a little too sharply. He had forgotten about the meeting himself, sidetracked by the Maslow business. Once the thing disappeared from the sky, people outside the world of science lost interest. He had also.

"I tried," Frank said, "I couldn't get the top three people here at the same time. They all had big interviews lined up. Two of them were on Larry King, and almost got into a fistfight. That kind of press can bring huge funding."

"You're going to have to twist some arms and get some of them here," the President said. "We can't act like we are doing nothing, like we are."

"Here's what we do," Jimmy said. "We make a list of ten really bright people. Of the top three astronomers, who is the most soft spoken?"

"McPhearson, by far." Jimmy said.

"We'll release the list of names tonight; that will be part of the President's statement. Leave off the names of the other two astronomers. I'll bet by tomorrow morning they'll be calling wanting to know why they're not on the list. Then, they'll get their rear ends here."

The rest of the afternoon was spent mapping out a strategy to go with the press release. Speech writers and analysts co-authored the ten page brief with Frank, who knew the correct nomenclature. By six o'clock the release was on its way and everyone was ready to go home.

Before Jimmy left, the President pulled him aside. "Thanks for your help today. About half the time I'm convinced you should be President and not me."

"Don't ever think that way." He was nearly out the door and turned back around. "But we do make a pretty good team."

"Off the record," the President said, "This thing out there, doesn't scare you does it?"

"No, why?"

""I heard you tell Frank, the first time he was here, that you had a funny feeling. Now it's come back twice. You've always said it's no good to believe in coincidence. Now it feels funny to me."

He looked at his brother and lied, "Nothing to worry about," he said.

Later that night at home, he sat in his chair at the dining room table. He was eating a frozen meatball sub he found in the freezer. An antique clock ticked in the den, keeping the same endless pace. The wind whistled through the old wooden windows. From where he sat he could see the kitchen phone nestled in its receptacle. He could reach it in about three steps and hear her voice. But instead he took five steps and dropped his plate into the sink. Then he took eleven steps upstairs to a very empty and cold bed.

Father Craig had left for hospital visits by the time I returned to the church. I had not been accompanying him on these because many of the patients did not like strangers seeing them in hospital garb. I was still a stranger and Father Craig was not. Though I was getting closer, I sometimes thought that I would never be the person anyone would reach out to for help. I was getting better at what I did, but what I was doing had nothing related to leadership or becoming the person that was sought after in times of need. I was still "Barney Fife."

I walked in the church and down the aisle to the front row. The crucifix hung over the altar in its glory, spotlighted in rich detail. For some people an empty quiet church was a little frightening. Many don't even understand why there is an eerie feeling. I've never felt that way. In fact I've always felt more at peace alone in church, than surrounded by people.

As a child I would look at the crucifix and wonder why we chose to idolize Jesus at his most horrid moments. Why worship his death? Over the centuries the greatest artists painted Him hanging on the cross, as a way I guess of showing his sacrifice. Whatever the reason, it has always made me thankful He was on my side.

I couldn't not go to meet this person. But I knew I couldn't expect too much. He wasn't Jesus. He was just the first of probably a long line of people being cloned. Maybe he wasn't even the first. If there is one thing we have learned from science, if it's possible to do something, we will, regardless of the ramifications.

What if he was a jerk? What if suddenly you found you were the only known living relative of the Son of God? The questions about this man multiplied until I could no longer think straight.

I knew, deep down, there was only one real question. Why me? I looked back up the crucifix, still worshiped after two thousand years, and thought, I'm not worthy.

I felt something cover me like a warm blanket. I wasn't surprised when I looked at my arm and it was covered with goose bumps.

Chapter 33

"It was great," Frank said the next morning on the phone. "Just like you said, as soon as we released McPhearson's name the other two were on the phone within minutes."

"I'm glad it worked out, I'll have my office coordinate and disseminate the information to your office so they can contact each one. I'm also going to need the names for background checks; you can send that to my secretary. Anything else I can get you?"

"You mean besides a bullhorn or a gun?" Frank said.

"They can't be that bad."

"I'd like to use Grandma and let them see what we see. If this is going to be more than just a photo op, we have to get them all the data. We have it—we might as well use it. I'll reposition WISE also."

Jimmy was quiet. Grandma was a secret spy satellite that was creatively funded. Through some unsavory deals, a long-range optics package was added to make it a little more legitimate. The long-range capabilities had never been tested. WISE (Wide-Field Infrared Survey Explorer) was an infrared science mapping telescope in space.

"How long will it take to get it in position and aim it?"

"With the maneuvering system it has, just a few key strokes. But please don't use the term 'aim' around the scientists."

Secret Blood

"Here's what we will do. You go ahead and get the people you need and start. I'll talk to the President about it. That way if he gives the okay, and I will encourage him to do so, we will already be up and running. We shouldn't take any heat for the screwball funding since it wasn't our administration who built it. If Homeland Security has a problem, tell them to call the President."

"Sounds great, I'll get back to you with the names."

"One other thing. The satellite people have signed non-disclosure agreements. We have to have the people in your group sign one also. Don't let them in the room unless I have a signature."

"Why?" Frank asked. "You don't want them to know about Grandma?"

"It's not that. I If we do get a good picture I don't want mass hysteria if the thing is a giant eyeball looking back at us."

Kim held a finger up as Jimmy walked back into his office. "Wait a second," she said into the phone, "he just walked in. Director Snider on hold for you, Mr. Chief of Staff," she said cheerfully.

"Don't call me that," he said closing his door.

"Yeah," he said when he picked up the phone.

"Yeah? That's how you greet me; after all I've done for your administration? I got your guy flying in a few hours, what do you want me to do with him?"

"Don't you have some place to keep him?"

"Me? No. I'm about finished with this mess. I figure the guy has something to do with Maslow, but you won't tell me anything. You say go pick him up and we do. You say bring him back to the States and we do. All of this is on the FBI's dollar. I can't process him and put him in a room with a guard and not have some explaining to do."

"Okay, I understand your position. Got any ideas?" Jimmy started tapping his pencil on his desk.

"Of course I have ideas, I'm the FBI. I got a good look at his medical records. This guy is frickin' amazing. I don't think he has ever been sick, and he has been in the most God-awful places in the world. The places they name diseases after. Let's put him in a disease center and tell him we need to study his blood. Looks like he's immune to everything. Then you can interrogate him all you want."

"We are not going to interrogate anyone. We just need to talk to him about a few things," Jimmy said.

"I heard that before."

"No, I mean it, as soon as we are through, he is free to go wherever he wants."

"Heard that before, too. You just have someone there to pick him up when the plane lands, then I'm done, not that it hasn't been fun," Snider hung up.

Jimmy sat quietly with his eyes closed for an indefinite time. The next thing he knew his phone was ringing. How long had he been out? He looked at his watch. He had been asleep for nearly an hour.

It was David Greg, the Press Secretary, on the phone. "There is a story on the internet," he said, "stating that The Ghost is really an alien spaceship coming to attack us. For some reason this story has legs. It's going viral. Some of the networks are responding to it."

"This kind of thing goes around all the time," Jimmy said. "In twenty-four hours no one will even remember it."

"I know, and we will squash it, but the reason I'm telling you is, you have that bunch of intellects coming in and it seems the paparazzi have left the movie stars and are watching us. Government cover-up is the biggest story around. So, we better be on the level because there are going to be pictures and questions. Every cell phone is worth a thousand words."

"All right, David, thanks for the heads up," he said. This was going to be trickier than he thought.

The Director of the CDC was an acquaintance that he could ask a favor of; he had a lot of acquaintances now that his brother was President. He explained about needing a room and blood tests since he was coming from Africa. The Director was eager to help. Next he asked Kim to connect him with his old buddy Mike DeRose.

Chapter 34

"What?" I said into the receiver. Father Craig, who handed me the phone, watched the color drain from my face.

"Who better?" Jimmy said. "Get the two guys you had with you when you were a fugitive. They seemed pretty efficient. All you have to do is meet him at the airport and drive him to the CDC."

"Why not the government? Why are you involving private citizens?" I asked.

He explained all the ramifications of allowing the press to get hold of this. This poor guy would be hounded the rest of his life, the administration would take some kind of hit for not informing the public earlier, and religious tensions may erupt all over the world. Sounded legitimate to me, but I was still hesitant.

Father Craig was still looking at me, mouthing the words, who is it? What do they want? He was exaggerating his movements so much I had to smile.

"All right," I said. "Tell me what to do." I wrote down the information. "You haven't told me his name."

"Emmanuel Shepherd."

I drew a breath. "I guess Maslow had a sense of humor."

"Yeah," he said. "Funny thing, Maslow never gave him a name, just dropped him off at the orphanage. He was named by the nuns."

The goose bumps came back.

"I still don't know why you won't come with me?" I said to Father Craig.

"Because I haven't been chosen, you have. You still don't realize this is about you. Mrs. Rundell didn't walk into my church, she found you. Her confession was to you, not me."

"It was because my church was closest," I said.

"Because you were sent there, don't you see the divine intervention here? It keeps coming back to you. This is where our paths begin to separate. You've always had a different calling. Let's face it," he smiled, "you have been a much better fugitive than a pastor this last year."

By nine o'clock that evening everything was ready. Shine pulled up in the same van, no doubt with different plates on it again. This time the logo read, Trans-Atlantic Book Store. The snow was drifting down slowly, just enough to keep the wipers on the slowest speed. It had warmed up to the high thirties and the streets were shiny with melted snow. We headed toward the airport.

"Do you do anything like a normal Priest?" Simon said. "Hangin' with you is like bein' with Tom Cruise in a *Mission Impossible* movie." He looked at Shine. "And you know who always gets killed first; the brother is always the first to go. Ain't that right Shine?"

"Shut up," Shine said. "Turn on the radio."

"I'm just sayin', that's the way it always is."

"All we're doing tonight is picking up someone at the airport and dropping them off," I said.

"Right," Simon said. "I know, with you involved it ain't gonna' be that easy."

I watched the long line of headlights as we drove, wondering who the people were in the cars. A businessman driving home to the warmth of a family. A service man returning from the war. A girl bringing home her boyfriend to meet her parents. The world felt good for a few moments. Simon was scanning through the channels and stopped on one playing *I Wanna Take You Higher* by Sly and the Family Stone. We turned onto the ramp for the airport and I started giving Shine the directions.

We headed to the military side of the airport. Ours was the only vehicle on this road. The intermittent streetlights shone an eerie pink as they curved into the distance.

"I don't want none of this," Simon said. We drove under a sign that said Military Personnel Only - Checkpoint Ahead. Shine turned down the radio and kept driving.

Floodlights illuminated the guardhouse. There was a gate, like the ones at railroad crossings, painted yellow and black, lowered across the road. Two guards with white helmets waited anxiously for our arrival. They were both black.

One of the soldiers held up a hand. We stopped beside him and Shine rolled down his window.

"I need to see some ID sir," the soldier said. Shine looked at him but didn't move.

"I have a password," I yelled from the dark backseat. The soldier raised a flashlight and shone it towards me. The other soldier was about ten yards away moving around to the passenger side with his hand resting on his firearm.

"What is the password sir?" he asked.

"Faith," I said. It must have been Jimmy Rienhart's attempt at humor.

The soldier shined the light into the back of the van, and then turned it off.

"About a mile up the road there are signs leading to three airstrips. You will need to continue traveling on this road until you see the road marked C. Take that exit and proceed onto the tarmac until you see the gate. Stop there. The aircraft will taxi up to you. ETA is twenty minutes. Have a good evening sir."

The gate went up and Shine accelerated out of the lighted area and into the darkness.

"The plane will taxi up to us?" Simon said. "I knew it. We into something nasty, Shine. We in a government plot now. 'Oh, don't worry—we're just picking someone up at the airport.' Yeah, who we pickin' up, Fidel Castro?"

Chapter 35

We followed the road marked C until we came to a brilliantly lighted area. As the soldier said, there was a chain link with a substantial gate near the edge of the runway. I had imagined a military air base to be a beehive of activity, with jeeps, army trucks, and people around. This place was deserted. Light towers similar to the one at high school football stadiums bathed everything for hundreds of yards. The landing strip had been plowed but everything else was still under several inches of snow. There were no footprints or tire tracks anywhere. The scene was eerie, as all busy places are, when no one is around. The bright lights reflected off the white snow and accentuated the complete absence of life.

We waited. Shine sat motionless as if he could sit for hours. Simon fiddled with the radio until he found a song by the Jackson Five, *I Want You Back*. Shine's fingers tapped on the steering wheel.

"This is sure out of the way. I hope they know we're here," I said.

"They know," Shine said. "Got cameras at the top of two fence posts." He nodded at two areas, one to the right and one to the left.

"Looks like your boy comin' in now," Simon said.

A light, looking as small and bright as a star appeared in the distance. It circled back and began its descent. A row of landing lights glinted to life in the middle of the landing strip. By the time we could actually make out the shape of the plane, the landing gear was out and the tail was dropping. The snow along the edges of the strip swirled as the plane's wing tips passed.

It roared past us as it touched down and reversed its engines. Even with the snow softening the sound, it was loud. It rolled out of sight as it continued decelerating. Shine gripped the steering wheel while Simon readjusted the radio.

I fidgeted as I waited for the plane to return. Simon couldn't wait to see who was going to get off and Shine just stared forward. Finally, it taxied up and stopped at the gate. Too close, I thought, for that size of plane. The engines whined down.

Almost before the plane stopped moving, a door opened and a man stepped out onto the tarmac. He walked toward us, holding an envelope against his side. He was wearing a green flight suit and a helmet, the straps hanging loose at the bottom. I slid my door back and hopped out into the chilly air. As I did the gate magically rolled open and the soldier stepped through.

"Good evening Father," he said, while extending his hand. "Is everything in order?"

"I suppose so. I'm not so sure what you mean."

"I'm not so sure either, I guess I want to be sure he is in good hands. This is a little irregular."

"I can assure you he is with friends," I said still a little puzzled.

"Yes sir," he handed me the envelope under his arm. "He's just, um, is such a good guy. I've spent the last few hours with him and, I don't know…. He's really easy to talk to."

He began walking to the plane, then stopped and looked back at me. There was something else he wanted to say, but I could tell, in that instant, he wasn't going to say it. I didn't want him to say anything; I wanted him to act as though this was just a package being delivered. I wanted the next person to get off the plane to look chubby and blonde and goofy. I felt scared and blasphemous and unworthy. I started my mantra. It's not really Him. It's not really Him. But it wasn't working.

The soldier was walking Him to me. He was wrapped up in a red micro fiber parka, jeans and army boots. Looped over one shoulder was a rolled pack made of what looked like canvas. He looked like George Harrison on the White Album. As they came closer I could see he was very tan and his hair was dark and shoulder length.

"Father, this is Emmanuel," the soldier said.

I stared into his eyes, I couldn't help it. They were so deep and dark and wise that I could barely lift my hand to shake his.

He took it in his. I'll never forget, there on that cold night, in the empty airfield, the warmth of his hand shake, the sincerity in his eyes.

I struggled to say something. "Welcome," was all I could manage. He released my hand and broke the spell. "I'm sure you would like to get in out of the cold weather after coming from Africa," I said.

"It's much different than what I'm used to" he said in a deep voice. I suppose it wasn't as deep, as it was commanding.

He turned to the soldier and shook his hand. "Thank you for your kindness, Tom, And I will pray for your sister," he said. Tom nodded and walked back to the plane.

"Our car is over here," I motioned to the van.

"In Africa we call that a van," He said with a smile. It wasn't a smart comment; he was trying to put me at ease. It worked.

"I guess that's what we call them here, too," I said.

Shine and Simon watched us as we approached. I slid the door open and we got in. "These are my friends, Shine and Simon," I said. Simon turned around to get a better look.

"Damn man, you look like Jesus."

I was horrified. I glanced at Emmanuel. He was smiling. Did he know who he was? Or wasn't.

"I've been told that a few times," he said.

Shine turned the van around, swinging the headlight beams across the pristine white snow, leaving the plane behind us. Suddenly the radio volume increased and *Spirit in The Sky* came on.

"Where we headed?" Shine asked. I gave him the address.
"It's the CDC," I said.
"The CDC?" Simon asked. We got a secret man from Africa and we headed to a disease center? Oh Lord, what have we got ourselves into now?"

You have no idea, I thought to myself.

Chapter 36

The ride was quiet. The radio played and Emmanuel slept. I watched him the best I could, without being obvious. As we neared the CDC section of the hospital, Shine said, "We may have picked up a tail."

"What," I said.

"Not sure, but he might have picked us up after we left the airport." He sneaked a look in the rear view mirror. "He's not what I would call stealthy,"

"Can you lose him?" I said, realizing how cheesy I sounded as soon as I said it.

"That kind of thing is in the movies. I could try but it's going to end up as a wreck or a police stop, and I would rather have neither," Shine said.

"What can we do then?"

"I can have a talk with the gentleman, but I want to make sure he's following us clear to the CDC."

He did. As we entered the parking lot we slowed and the car pulled into a dark space at the edge. We reversed quickly and backed directly in front of him. He was trapped.

Shine produced a ski mask from somewhere in his leather jacket and pulled it on. He put the van in park and said, "I'll be right back." He opened his door, got out, and closed it behind himself.

I watched through the mirror on the van door. In two steps he was beside the car. He smashed out the driver's window with his elbow and reached inside. I looked around, sure another car would pull up, but we were lucky. When I looked into the mirror again he was walking back to the car swinging something from his hand.

He got back in, put the car in drive, and then pulled off the ski mask. The whole thing took about thirty seconds. He dropped a camera between the two front seats and grasped a set of keys in his left hand.

"The gentleman did not want to remove the film, so I had to remove the camera."

He put the van in gear and pulled out of the parking lot. About two blocks away he stopped the van again and rolled down his window. The man, more courageous at this distance, stepped out of his car and watched us. Tapping the horn twice, Shine held the keys out the window and dropped them. We accelerated. A half a mile away we pulled into a Pizza Hut parking lot near a dumpster. Shine got out and replaced the Trans-Atlantic Books sticker with one that read Woody's Hotdogs. Simon replaced the license plate and they threw everything that was used into the dumpster.

"You think maybe we ought not to go to the CDC tonight?" I asked.

We ended up going back to the apartment above Sampson's. I nudged Emmanuel as Shine pulled the van to the curb. He had slept through the whole thing. This was a different entrance and a way I had not been taken prior. I could hear the laughter and music and smell the meat.

"This is the medical building?" he asked.

"No. We had a little trouble there. We have decided to come here for the night, and then see about the hospital tomorrow," I explained.

He was a little put out by this; I could tell by the way he stiffened.

"I need to return as soon as possible, there are people, who are in dire straits in Africa."

Simon, who had been uncharacteristically quiet during the ride, slid from the passenger door and looked around. Emmanuel and I got out and followed Simon up the stairs. Shine disappeared in the van.

The apartment was warm and welcoming. We had called ahead after the incident with the photographer. The fireplace had been lit and the fridge stocked. A door, that I had not even noticed the first time I was there, stood partially open. I could just see the end of a bed through the opening.

Emmanuel smiled shyly and said, "I have not slept in a bed in years. I will sleep on the floor, you may have the bed."

"I'm not staying here tonight," I said.

"Maybe you should," said a voice behind me. It was Mr. Stubbs. "Father Craig called. A message has been sent down the line; you are to remain here tonight. It appears the problem that Shine handled is not an isolated event, it's too hot for you two to be moving around tonight. Simon you stay here with them," he said.

"Aw man, why can't Shine stay here tonight." Simon said. He stepped closer to Mr. Stubbs. "This new dude is spooky," he whispered. "He creeps me out, it's like he knows stuff about me."

They both looked at Emmanuel and he looked back at them, smiling with brilliantly white teeth.

"See what I mean," Simon said.

"Shine will be in the building, you stay here in the apartment," Mr. Stubbs said. He turned and walked out.

"Well then, I guess I will be staying. Are you sure you don't want the bed?" I asked.

"No, I'm afraid I may like it and not be able to sleep when I return home," Emmanuel said.

"I'll take the bed, if you two can't decide," Simon said. "In the meantime I'm going to send down for some food. You all want some ribs?"

I decided we would.

"Would you like to take a shower or change clothes?" I asked.

Secret Blood

"Yes, I think I would like that," he said. He looked around, then smiled and gathered his things. He went into the room and closed the door.

"Who is this guy?" Simon asked me. Government flies him in on a jet and he stands there all quiet, like some kind of a monk. He hasn't slept in a bed."

Before I could answer the bedroom door opened and Emmanuel said, "I'm not sure how to turn on the water."

Emmanuel stepped out of the bedroom showered and fresh. His hair was pulled back in a ponytail and still wet. He wore a crumpled, white linen shirt that was wrinkled and about two sizes too large. The jeans he wore were faded, threadbare, and also too big. He was barefoot, but even his feet were tanned.

The ribs had arrived and filled the room with an overwhelming aroma. Buckets of potato salad and corn on the cob were also delivered and sat open on the table. Simon sat, ready to eat, watching the big screen with his empty plate on the coffee table. He stood and went to the table as Emanuel walked in.

"Who else is eating with us?" Emmanuel asked.

"Nobody, dig in," Simon said.

"Do you mean all this food is for the three of us?" Emmanuel asked. He walked to the table and stared at the food.

"It's gonna' be for just two of us if you don't get a plate and fill it up. I'm hungry and I've seen the Priest here eat. If we have to order more they'll make us pay for it next time." He sat at the table, but turned away from us to watch the TV. The Lakers had just gotten the tip.

Emmanuel sat quietly. I passed down a paper plate and a napkin for him. He scooped a small amount of potato salad onto his plate along with an ear of corn. I gave each of us a half rack of ribs. As I reached for my corn I caught sight of Emmanuel still sitting motionless and watching me. He made no movement toward his food.

"Do we not give thanks before we eat?" he asked me.

I nodded and felt foolish. I was ashamed it had not crossed my mind.

"Simon," I said, "hit the mute button. We're going to a say a prayer."

"What?" he said turning around. He saw we were ready to give thanks and looked as ashamed as I had felt. I gave a brief blessing and the three of us said, "Amen."

Emmanuel took his time and ate slowly, savoring each bite. His skin was deeply tanned and lined like a migrant worker who is outside year round. It was taut across the muscles in his thin arms. He was so dark that the stubble on his face blended in. Only his eyes looked unworn.

Simon jerked on the couch. He tossed his plate, which had been balanced on his lap, onto the coffee table. The corn rolled to the edge and stopped. "Kobe gets every call and still complains!"

"So what is it you do as a volunteer, Emmanuel?" I asked.

"I drive to villages," he said between bites, "and decide which places to send the doctors first. Many times doctors need not come."

"Because everyone is well?" I asked.

"No, because everyone is dead."

I didn't know what to say, I could only look at my corn.

"Our jobs are not so different," he said. "I try to save lives, you try to save souls. I only wish I had your power over evil."

"My church has a Soup Kitchen," I said weakly.

He looked confused. "It's a place to give away food," I said.

At that moment I felt like such an imposter. I worked in rich clean vestments in a place where sunlight streamed through beautiful stained glass windows. My favorite was one in which Jesus was kneeling on a rock with his hands clasped before him gazing up to Heaven. The light is flooding over him as if God is saying "I'm right here and everything will be all right."

I looked at Emmanuel. He had no inspirational windows, no embroidered clothing, and no food. He has only the strength of his character. I could not imagine the hardships he endured daily, the horrors he had seen.

"On the best days we inoculate and distribute rations. On the worst we dig graves." He cut off a small bite of meat and chewed it for a while. "We do not like to dig small graves because small graves are for the children."

Simon had turned the volume back up, but was staring at a spot on the floor, listening to us. His expression was one I had not seen before.

"You see," Emmanuel went on, "the government owns the oil fields and China needs the oil. The government troops protect the oil lines. In many cases China will hire mercenaries to protect the oil. In the past, the people have protested the lack of government responsibility by destroying the oil lines. The soldiers will come in and destroy entire villages, even if they have done nothing wrong. Much of the aid sent by other countries does not reach the people. The soldiers take it. The people are helpless."

"Except for people like you," I said.

"It is a large place\,." he said. "And there are so few of us."

Simon was still staring. On the TV, Mike Brown, was screaming at a referee.

"How do you do it, keep going every day in such horror? How do you wake up in the morning knowing the terror you could face?" I asked, wondering if my faith would be strong enough.

"I have been to villages where children have been chained to stakes then set afire and the parents made to watch. I could not live any other life knowing these things are happening and I am doing nothing."

Outside I could see snow filtering down between the window and a distant streetlight. The apartment was warm and the smell of the food was present and although I was still hungry, I couldn't eat another bite.

Chapter 37

The next morning I awoke to the sound of a helicopter. It flew over the building a few times then off into the distance. The throbbing of the rotors diminished with each mile.

I rolled over and looked at the floor. The blanket and pillow, Emmanuel had used, were folded and stacked in a neat pile. At the time I was not concerned about Emmanuel's absence. I guess I should have been more appreciative of the safety factor. I never dreamed he would venture out of the apartment.

I could hear Simon snoring from his place on the couch. I decided to shower and shave, since again the toiletries had been provided.

The shower gave me time to think. The next move, I guessed, would be to contact Dr. DeRose to see what Mr. Rienhart wanted. I felt we were being very unfair to Emmanuel. We seemed to have lied to him at every turn. We had taken him out of a place he felt he needed to be, forced him to stay with us; for what reason? Just so we could see that he actually existed? Or did Rienhart have an ulterior motive? Was he as curious as we were?

As I turned the shower off, I heard the cell phone ring. Someone answered it. I toweled off and dressed, then made the bed. I entered the living area just as Shine came in the front door with a bag of groceries. Simon rose from the couch, sleepy-eyed, and rubbed his face. Another helicopter flew overhead.

"Something's going on," Shine said, as he sat the bag on the counter. "A lot of traffic, police cars zooming around. Turn on the TV."

Simon hit the button and the giant screen blinked into life. The first image was a close up of a whale spotlighted in darkness. The caption under the picture said Chesapeake Bay.

"Man, that's only a few blocks from here, no wonder the copters been flying around," Simon said as he turned up the volume. It caught the reporter in mid-sentence.

"…was first spotted last night. Since then hundreds maybe thousands of all species of whale have converged in the bay. Of all the experts we have contacted to date, they say, that a gathering of this magnitude has never been recorded anywhere before. All private and commercial ships have been asked to drop anchor and stay where they are until further notice. We will…"

"Where's Emmanuel?" I asked.

Simon looked around at me, then around the room. "I thought he was in there with you, sleepin' on the floor."

"His stuff is all folded up. I thought he was out here with you."

"Well, he ain't, the dude's bolted."

Shine went in the bedroom. "Backpack is still here, shoes are gone." He went to the closet. "Coat's gone too."

"While I'm thinking about it," Simon said, "You got a call on the cell. Wanted to know why the package wasn't delivered last night and when it was going to be delivered? Dude said he would call back." As if on cue the cell phone rang.

"What's going on?" Jimmy Rienhart asked. "I know you picked him up, I watched the tape."

"Someone followed us to the CDC in Hyattsville. He was taking pictures." I said.

"So that was you. I have a report that a man was accosted and robbed in the parking lot."

I stared to pace with the phone. "How did you know that?"

"I didn't get confirmation that he checked in, so I had the police check the route between the airport and the CDC . So where are you?"

"Can't really say, but we're safe," I lied.

"Okay, I'll trust you on this one. Can I speak with him?"

"Still sleeping," I lied again, "and I hate to wake him after the trip he has had."

"Have him at the CDC at three, I'll have some undercover in the parking lot to be sure you are not bothered. And don't take that bookstore van you had last night. The Hyattsville police are still looking for it." He hung up.

I looked at Shine and Simon. "What are we going to do?"

"First thing we do is call Mr. Stubbs. He can put a dragnet on our area," Shine said. "Then we split up and look ourselves."

Chapter 38

Emmanuel trudged down the avenue, a bulging grocery bag in one hand and a bucket of leftover ribs in the other. The morning was cold but bright and the brittle layer of ice on the sidewalk crunched beneath his feet. He also heard the helicopters overhead. In Darfur, the sound was a prelude to death. The pilots would spot the migrant village and send in the troops. They would come in Toyota pickups with their machine guns and knives. A siren from a distant police car brought the street back into focus.

Earlier, he had asked a man the way to the closest soup kitchen. The directions were confusing but he had pointed in this direction, and Emmanuel started off, hoping it was not too far. But the biting cold and the unsure footing began to tire him out. On a summer day the streets would normally be full of people to guide him. But today everyone was bundled in the warmth of their apartments. Sweating and freezing at the same time, he began to tire. The desert with its high temperatures and moving sands were less draining than this.

At the White House Jimmy had just hung up the phone. He didn't believe the Priest. He trusted him but something was fishy. He couldn't do much about it now without drawing a lot attention. He was beginning to wonder why he brought Emmanuel here in the first place. He didn't even remember a conscious decision to do it, which was odd because he always measured risk against benefit.

He had already had his morning briefing with the President. They had agreed the top story would be the science summit concerning The Ghost. The morning talk shows had it as the lead and the newspapers had printed the headlines. Mysterious objects in space struck at the core of many of our beliefs, nearly as much as death and the afterlife.

The alarming aspect to Jimmy was that some left field religious groups were starting to spin The Ghost toward their doctrines. "We don't need another Heaven's Gate," he had told the President.

He began to tap his pencil when Kim buzzed in. "Mr. Reinhart, Frank White, on line one."

"Yeah, Frank."

"It's gone again."

"The Ghost?"

"Yep. Vanished. Just as we had Grandma ready. It will hit the news outlets in about ten minutes."

"Okay, listen. Here's what we're going to do. Go ahead with the meeting; put them into groups or something so we can get something to give the press. Even if they don't agree, we can say Dr. X believes it to be this, but Dr. Y thinks it's something else. Let the press know ideas are being kicked around.

Don't say anything about Grandma, if we've got no pictures for them there is no reason to admit she even exists. Get with David Gregg afterward and let me see the release before it goes out."

"Got it," he said. "I'm really not looking forward to this meeting."

"Hey, these people should be thanking you for choosing them. Let them know that. Take charge."

"Right," he said dismally.

"One more thing, "Jimmy said. "What's up with these whales?"

The dragnet was on. Mr. Stubbs had a calling system in place that activated a squadron of watchers throughout the neighborhood. The people he called associates, like Shine and Simon, were in cars.

Secret Blood

Once he was found, we were the ones to pick him up. Simon and I were riding together in his Caddy.

'He don't seem so spooky now," he said. "I kinda' respect what he doin' too. Just dumb though. Those people never gonna' have any kind of life." I stayed silent and watched out the window. There was a guy sitting on the edge of a storefront window, just staring at the traffic light.

"Hey," Simon yelled after rolling down his window. "You seen a white dude, long hair and scraggly beard, kinda look like Charles Manson?"

"Man, I ain't seen a white dude in this neighborhood that didn't look like Charles Manson."

"Crack head," Simon said and rolled up the window. "Strange name though, Emmanuel. Sound like some kind of Christmas name. That's too long a name. Needs to be shorter. Like Manny. Manny Sanguine, man it's been a long time since I said that name."

"Who's Manny Sanguine?" I asked.

He smiled for a beat then said, "Catcher, played for the Pirates in the seventies, my Mama's favorite player. She was from Pittsburgh, see, and we had these tapes. Glory years of the Pirates, we'd sit around and watch the tapes like they were happening right then, like they were live. Manny would get up to bat and he would be smiling. You could see his smile through his catcher's mask too. He'd even being smiling when he struck out. Mama'd say 'There's a man who loves his job.' He'd swing at anything; high, low, outside, inside. He'd take a cut at it. I think that's what Mama liked about him; you knew he was always going to swing away."

"Where is your Mother now?" I asked.

"His mouth tightened, "She's here, up around 49th street."

"So, you get to visit her?"

"Nope, I tried, but Mama don't like my life style. Said she don't want no son gang banger. Said that…."

His phone rang.

"Aw no," he said as he accelerated wildly around a corner. "Somebody saw him on Dixie and Mound Ave. heading west."

"That's good isn't it, we've found him."

"That's not our turf. He can get jammed up over there. Those dudes find out he's with us, he's as good as dead." The Cadillac roared around more corners, tires squealing. Simon stayed low in the seat and spun the big steering wheel with both hands.

We turned a corner and coasted up to an intersection. The one street sign said Dixie and the other said Mound. With the exception of several overflowing trash cans and a mangy dog sniffing through them, the place appeared deserted.

"I'd hide in the back and let you drive, but it wouldn't do no good. They know my car. Hard to hide a baby like this."

He picked up the cell phone and hit a speed dial. "Hey, we rollin' slow down Dixie. You better rally the troops. No, don't see anything yet, that's what got me spooked."

The streets were lined with cars, most in poor condition. In places, the snow had been plowed up and over cars, leaving them only partly exposed. Most of the buildings were two-story brick with crud caked in the windows, both first and second story. I felt like a cowboy riding his horse into a canyon and the bad guys were hiding behind rocks at the top.

Simon drove slowly, never stopping at the lights even when they were red. We could see several blocks ahead. Nothing moved except for a plastic bag that tumbled across the street.

Then, about six blocks ahead, I could see some movement in the road. People were moving toward the center of an intersection. Simon kept the car at the same speed, rolling right into the canyon. We stopped about 50 feet from the intersection.

Emmanuel was there with his back to us. In front of him were five men in a line facing him. They all wore sunglasses and oversized jackets. They looked as menacing as anyone I have ever seen. Emmanuel was still holding his food. From behind, he didn't look like he felt threatened at all. He looked a little annoyed.

"Stay in the car," Simon said. "Leave the motor running. And give me your best prayer." He opened the door and got out.

"Willie Hicks," he shouted. He opened his arms wide and smiled brightly. "What's 'sup babe?" Before getting halfway there, all five men pulled guns out of their coat pockets.

"What you doin' here Simon, your GPS not workin' in your swank mobile?"

This got a hearty laugh out of the other men. One of them was already on a cell whispering and staring at Simon. Another man came out of a building to our left. He was monstrous. He was a good 450 pounds and about 6 foot 9 inches. Big enough to have his own climate and weather patterns.

"No, Willie, my man here, Emmanuel, he got a little lost and he been roamin' around, he's from outta' town and he got no idea who you are. So, what I'll do is just walk him back to the car, and we can pretend like none of this ever happened." Simon grabbed hold of Emmanuel's coat sleeve and tried to pull him back to the car.

"Simon you always been a fool, but you not foolish enough to think that gonna' happen," Willie said.

For the first time since we arrived Emmanuel spoke. "I'm only taking food to the hungry. If I thought you were hungry I'd give it to you, but you do not look hungry, if anything that gentleman there looks over nourished." The plump man did not smile.

"If you wish to rob me, I have nothing, except this coat. That you can have." Emmanuel put down the food, unzipped his coat and laid it on the pavement. "There, you can have it, now I would like to get this to the needy." He took a step and the men brought up their guns. I got out of the car and stood behind the open door. A single snowflake wafted down between Simon and the men holding the guns.

* * *

Frank White raised both hands, no one noticed. The meeting room had a long rectangular table, which anchored five chairs on each side. Frank was at the end of the table with a smart screen behind him, which was dark. To the left of the screen was a door to the hallway. White House protocol should have been for him to sit in the middle of one side as the President does with his cabinet, but Frank felt neither comfortable nor safe there.

The meeting had been confrontational from the start. Dr. Neighbors did not want to sit beside Dr. Merrifield. Dr. Lewis wanted sit near Frank to try to control the meeting. Papers were passed with written analysis, much to the dismay of others with conflicting views.

One man was more obstinate than the others. His hair hung over the collar of his crumpled shirt. Both eyebrows were long and unruly. He flung aside the papers that were passed to him and growled at any one who looked in his direction. Finally, he scooted his chair away from the table and shouted.

"These are the so called great minds you have brought together? You wish to know what it is that appears and disappears in the sky?" His eyebrows bounced and the room went silent. "Now I will tell you, since for once you are listening to me. It is a globular cluster such as we have never seen before!" The room exploded into angry shouts, more frenzied this time.

Frank turned and walked out the door behind him. He stood with his hands on his hips and inhaled. He wouldn't go back in until the egos had burned down a little, or a lot. It might take a while.

"How's it going?" Frank looked in the direction of the voice. A small group of people was walking toward him on the rich blue carpeted hallway.

"How's it going in there, Frank?" Jimmy repeated. He walked with a couple of the White House security men.

"It's terrible, they only want to give their opinion and listen to no one else. Someone was shouting in the room. They could hear it even with the door closed. There was a thud and a picture of FDR fell from the wall and broke with a tinkle on the carpet.

"Let me try," Jimmy said, He looked at the security men. "You two watch from the crack in the door, I'll motion if I need you."

They walked in, leaving the door ajar. At seeing two people, the group lowered the volume to a mummer. The table was awash in papers.

In a voice, only slightly louder than his speaking voice, Jimmy said, "The President would like to thank you for your input this morning. If time becomes available in his schedule he would like to join you. I will brief him in a few minutes as to your findings."

"He needs to hear no findings," the man with the eyebrows shouted, "The Ghost is a globular cluster!" The room burst into shouting again.

Jimmy motioned to the door and pointed at the man. He had no idea what was happening and was still shouting as they lifted him out of his seat. "Would you come with us, sir?" one of the guards said as they dragged him around the table. The English had left him and he began yelling in Russian as he was pulled through the door, heels leaving little trenches in the carpet.

The only sound in the room now was the hum of the vast air conditioning system. The group sat open mouthed.

Jimmy smiled, "Mark down one vote for globular clusters."

Chapter 39

"There is no need for weapons," Emmanuel said. His voice showed no trace of fear. He stood still, in his thin white shirt and faded jeans. The wind whipped between the buildings, ruffling his un-tucked shirt and blowing his hair. Then, everything happened at once.

From behind me I heard a squeal of tires. Cars were pulling in from all directions. A navy blue Monte Carlo roared up beside me and slid in perpendicular, blocking the street. As the cars skidded to a stop the doors flung open and people piled out, all running for cover, guns drawn. Shine was in the lead, nickel plated guns in both hands and his black leather coat flying out behind him. What I hadn't noticed was the windows in the building that flanked us. The panes had been lifted and gun barrels protruded out at a dozen places. More were visible behind cars and first stories of the buildings. All told, there were about seventy people facing off.

The first shot sounded like a pop. I'm not sure which side fired first, but after that everything moved in slow motion. I could feel the concussion of the guns all round me. A spray of bullets punched a looping line of holes in the door of the car beside me. On the other side of the street, windshields exploded showering the pavement with bouncing crystals. The blue smoke of gunpowder hung near the windows that were being used as sniper nests. Those windows were blasted, sending shards of glass raining down onto the street. I could hear the sound of tires deflating and see brick chips flying away from bullets impacting the upper stories.

The noise was like the finale of a fireworks display, a symphony of different weapons striking a variety of surfaces. At the onset, Simon had instinctively taken cover behind the nearest car. I think he had expected Emmanuel to do the same. But he hadn't.

He stood in the same spot, eyes closed, head tilted. His arms were outstretched, palms up like he were asking something of God. People were shooting at him, I could see them, but nothing came close. He stood stone-like through the whole thing.

A shot penetrated the radiator of the Caddy. The steam sizzled out. The onslaught continued for what felt like hours. So many rounds had been fired that the air around the intersection was hazy. I could taste the cordite that I had been breathing.

I felt someone grab my ankle and pull. The next thing I knew I was laying on the pavement staring into the face of a black man I had never seen before.

"Get down, you fool!" he shouted over the barrage. Without realizing it, I had been standing beside the car watching the whole time. He moved away, ducking through the cars.

The windshield blew out of the car. The rear one shattered also. I crouched behind the trunk and looked out through both openings. I could barely see Emmanuel though the haze. Debris was scattered across the pavement. Auto parts and shell casings littered the ground. Puddles of oil, and radiator fluid, spread across the street. On the other side, most of the rubble consisted of broken masonry and glass.

In the distance I heard the sound of sirens, and only then did the sound of gunshots diminish. People started yelling and pulling back. There were still a few pops, but after what we had just gone through, it sounded feeble. On the other side of the intersection I could see gunmen leaving their cover and running into buildings.

All around me, men were getting into cars and peeling out. I remembered a time, before we fumigated the church, I had lifted a cardboard box in the basement and roaches scattered in all directions. This reminded me of that. I saw Simon run around a car and sprint to Emmanuel. He was holding a pistol in his right hand. Once he reached the spot where Emmanuel stood, he grabbed him around the waist and began to pull him back toward me. Only then did Emmanuel lower his arms. He was smiling.

The sirens were getting louder. Simon looked at his car. Only one window remained intact. The front tires were both blown out and there were three holes in the front grille. Everyone else had left.

"Gotta' go this way," Simon said. "Away from the police."

Before we had taken five steps, a van accelerated from the right side of the intersection and slid to a stop in front of us. Simon raised the gun and aimed at the driver's darkened window. The window rolled down. It was Shine.

"Get in," he yelled. We were in and moving before the sliding door was shut. We sped through the intersection leaving only a coat, a bag, and a bucket of ribs in the street. Unfortunately, the bucket of ribs proudly displayed the name Sampson's.

Chapter 40

Jimmy was feeling good about himself; even though he knew there would be some repercussions later. He walked through the beehive of activity that was the White House and suddenly had a powerful urge to call his wife Patricia. These were the kind of stories she loved to hear. When they were first married and in the dreaming stage, small victories like throwing a loud mouth out of a meeting put the fun in politics. They would plot and plan in restaurants and laugh in bed. Many of the Presidents most noteworthy speeches came from their playfulness. He realized he was smiling.

The urge to call her popped again, it had been a few weeks since they had spoken. No, he decided sadly, it's been a couple of months. I need to call; I'm going to go to the office right now and call. No excuses, no promises, no expectations, I'll just tell her how much I miss her. I'll have Kim call the number right now so I can't back out, again.

He walked into the office as Kim looked up. They both started talking at the same time. He smiled and said, "You first."

"The President wants to see you as soon as possible. Frank White wants you to call him as soon as possible. Both sounded very excited."

"I just left Frank, when did he call?"

"I just hung up with him." She clasped her hands on her desk and smiled. "Okay, now what were you saying?"

"Nothing," he sighed. "If anyone needs me I'll be with the President."

Chapter 41

They were watching TV in one of the outer offices. The President's jacket was thrown across the top of a chair and his shoes were under the coffee table. He was slouched down on the couch, his stocking feet on the table. A pale ring of calf showed between the bottom of his pants leg and the top of his sock.

Jimmy sat beside him, intrigued in the spastic movement on the screen. The sound was turned off, the closed caption on; the way the President liked it. He watched the news this way, scrutinizing the body language of the people being interviewed.

"Can you believe this guy?" the President said. "His name is Reverend Grace. This is the Hour of Grace Show."

A portly man waved his arms and perspired through his shirt and sports coat. A bright yellow tie, sweat stained at the knot, had escaped the jacket and fluttered every time he changed direction, which was often. It was like watching an old Meatloaf video without the long hair. He was on a large stage lined with enormous baskets of flowers and a cross hung in the background.

"He keeps quoting Revelations," the President said. "He's talking, or screaming I should say, about The Ghost. He's up to almost a half million tweets already. There is a movement going on with some of the far right religious groups."

"You mean the Doomsday groups," Jimmy said.

"Yeah, but there is growing interest all around. A guy like this can get a lot of people thinking; can take advantage of a lot of people too. You know, end of the world with an angle. Send your money to us; you're not going to need it. This is the kind of thing that can go mainstream and get out of hand."

"All right, let's find out who this guy is and what his deal is. Then we can decide if he will burn himself out or if we will need to leak something," Jimmy advised.

A banner flashed across the bottom of the screen, spelling out Breaking News.

"Maybe you better turn this up," Jimmy said.

The president fumbled with the remote until he found the volume. The serious face of a news man filled the screen.

"... News Chopper Four has exclusive video caught only moments ago. This was filmed as our helicopter was returning from covering the whale invasion of Chesapeake Bay. The footage shows what appears to be a shoot-out between rival gangs somewhere near Dixie Avenue." The camera angle was wide initially. From blocks away the shot showed cars speeding to a spot in one direction and men on foot sprinting to the same spot from the other. The crew obviously knew something was happening on the street but they were not sure what, or on which person, to focus. The cameraman soon found a person. As the camera zoomed in, Emmanuel was taking off his coat and dropping it on the street.

Jimmy had only seen Emmanuel on the video at the airport, but he had seen Simon in person. The helicopter paned to the right and both of their faces came into view. He thought, *oh no, they are going to show him getting killed right here on television. He's only been in the US a few hours and already he's involved in a gunfight.*

From the camera angle which was now straight down, the viewer could see every shot. At first a soft pop and a tiny puff of smoke, then a barrage of shots, that went on and on. The cameraman pulled back the shot to get both sides firing, but after that he focused in on the man in the flowing white shirt and jeans, standing in a strange stance, ignoring the gunfire and never once being struck.

"Look at that guy. He's standing like that statue on the rock over Rio de Janeiro," the President said. Jimmy could only watch in disbelief. Cold chills ran up his back. The bullets kept flying.

No one on the ground seemed to notice the helicopter above. They were shooting and scooting, changing positions as much as possible, which made it even more improbable that the man standing in the middle was not being hit. Thankfully, the camera pulled back again revealing a line of police cars snaking their way through distant streets, blue lights flashing.

The reporter's voice returned. "Amazingly, police report there were no deaths resulting from this firefight and at this time no injuries have been reported."

A female voice joined the reporter. "Steve, I have just received a report that none of the hospitals in the area have reported treating any gunshot victims this morning." The screen showed the van pulling away. The camera swung back to the cops arriving at the scene, guns drawn. By the time the camera had come back to the van, it was gone.

""My God, he saved them all," Jimmy said.

"What?" the President asked.

"Didn't you see, he stood there and just ....just willed it. He didn't get hit, nobody else did either. The bullets flew right past and hit something else. That was him, the one I told you about."

The President sat up straight. "That's HIM? What's he doing here in the states? You said no one could find him."

"We couldn't at first, then we did and I had him brought in. He got here last night."

"Why? The whole business was buried! What could we possibly get out of this? Nothing, I can see, but controversy that we don't need."

Jimmy sat quietly. His brother had never spoken to him this sharply. "I can't honestly say. I don't really remember making the decision, or what led up to it. I just did it." He sat looking down at the couch and feeling very hollow. And as he did, he thought about Patricia again.

"All right, I'm sorry I jumped. It just doesn't seem like you to do something so off the cuff." He slid his shoes on and stood up. "Maybe you're just working too hard, I got to tell you, you look tired. When is the last time you took even an afternoon off? When's the last time you talked to Patricia?"

"Things keep coming up. I'm going to call. Maybe, once this Ghost thing is over, I'll call and we can go to some kind of counseling."

"Maybe, by then, it will be too late," the President said.

* * *

Jimmy pulled a cell phone out of his breast pocket and dialed his office.

"Kim, can you get me the Priest's number right now? I want to talk to him on my phone. His number is on the blotter on my desk."

"Yes sir, let me go get it."

"Wait, I also need the number of my cell phone, the one I have to carry around all the time." She told him his number and went to look for the other one. He picked up a pen and wrote his number on his palm. He turned up the sound on the TV and watched some more of the Reverend's antics. Whatever he was, he sure knew how to whip up a crowd. The audience was on the edge of their seats shouting Hallelujah on cue. She came back and gave him the number. He dialed.

"What is going on?" Jimmy could feel his voice rising. "Have you seen the news? This can't happen! No one can know who he is or why he's here."

"I'm sorry, he slipped away. He was trying to take food to a shelter. I don't know what else to say, I'm sorry and it won't happen again," I said.

"You're right it's not going to happen again. I want him here where I can keep an eye on him," Jimmy had the words out of his mouth before he knew what he was saying. It was like driving, knowing you were lost, but instead of stopping and asking directions, you just keep on going down that road.

"Get him here as soon as it gets dark. He'll be recognized now. He can't be running all over town. I'll have credentials waiting for him."

He gave me the directions to get there. I felt I'd been given another challenge and failed it again.

Chapter 42

"You what?" the President said. He looked over a pair of reading glasses perched on his nose.

"You can't honestly tell me you don't want to meet him. The Ghost is gone, we've gotten the scientists evaluations, at least we will as soon as Frank summarizes them," Jimmy said.

"Jimmy you're slipping. Six months ago you would not have done this, at least without consulting me."

"Six months ago I was a happily married person."

* * *

"I know I ain't seen nothin' like it," Simon said. He had talked nonstop; from the shootout, to back to the apartment. Then once the adrenaline dropped, he fell asleep. Now, after seeing the five o'clock news he was jabbering again. The networks had picked up the tape along with another view shot by someone's cell phone. It showed Emmanuel from street level and was a more impressive documentary of a man facing certain death, and living through it. Stations around the world were now calling the footage 'The Miracle Shootout.'

"Ain't seen nothin' like it. Like he had a force field around himself." Simon repeated, "'Cept maybe on *Star Trek* when they used one to protect the Enterprise." He was thoughtful for a second, and then he whispered to me, "He ain't no kind of damn wizard or something is he?"

I laughed, I couldn't help it, he asked so seriously. I even saw Shine smile.

The thought had crossed my mind several times since this afternoon also, it was a miracle. I could feel it. I was involved in a miracle. I wanted to giggle. Each time I replayed it in my head and saw Him standing there, I was filled with such joy I was overwhelmed. I had to leave the room once, because I felt tears trickling down my cheeks. Simon felt it also, only he expressed it by continually talking.

Emmanuel had become engrossed by the large TV. He roamed the channels more enthusiastically than anyone I had ever seen. It became apparent he was not watching for entertainment but for people in need. He had grown up with the very poor, whose main occupation each day was to find enough food to eat. So when he clicked over the ads for chicken or burgers I was surprised.

He stopped on a channel showing an Alice Cooper video. "I would like to meet this man," he said.

Of all the people, I thought, *He wants to meet him?*

"Why?" I asked

"He seems very disturbed; I think I could help him." He watched for another moment then went on through the channels.

The next time he stopped long enough to actually listen to something, he landed on the Rev. Grace show. It was on several different channels at different times for maximum exposure, or for the devoted to watch repeatedly. Emmanuel stared at the huge figure on the screen, which was agitated, loud, and violent as he spouted scripture. Emmanuel sat calmly, a melancholy look of pity on his face.

"That's what we call an 'ugh' preacher," Simon said. "Cause he says 'ugh' between every fourth or fifth word."

We listened, Simon was right. It turned into a chant. Emmanuel did not turn the channel.

The apartment phone rang. Shine listened. "Got to get out of here," he said. "The police are downstairs snooping around the restaurant."

In three minutes we were in the stairs that led to the hidden garage. New license plates and a sign that read "Louie's Lighting." This time the roof of the van had been painted blue. The garage door rolled up, we coasted slowly through the alley that ran parallel to the main street. We took a left then stopped at an intersection. It was still cold, but a few people were moving about. Everything looked normal to me; we were just leaving a little earlier than we had planned.

About a block down, three guys stood on the corner with their hands in their jacket pockets, shoulders hunched. All three wore toboggans of different colors. The one with the red toboggan took his off and put it under his right arm and looked at us. Shine hit the accelerator.

The van had only gone a few yards when a SWAT truck turned in and blocked the street. Shine hit the brakes and the van squealed to a stop. Another SWAT truck blocked the street behind us.

"Hold on," he said and thrust the van into reverse. My first thought was that he was going to ram the SWAT truck. We were heading straight at it when he swerved to the left and up onto the sidewalk. The van sideswiped the storefronts and knocked down street signs. We passed the SWAT truck that had been behind us, as a SWAT team, dressed in black riot gear, piled out. They raised their rifles but did not shoot. Just as we reached the corner where the lookout had been standing, a radio car, unknowingly, came to a stop at the intersection.

With an almighty bang we crashed. The two vehicles twisted sideways in the street, parts still tumbling down the pavement as Shine jumped out. Emmanuel and I were in a heap on the floor. Simon had flown completely over me and was in the back with the pipes and plumbing equipment.

Shine was yanking on the sliding door to try to extract us. It had bent in the collision, the metal was grinding as he pulled. He wrenched it open enough to get us out when a policeman tackled him in a flying leap. They rolled on the pavement for an instant before Shine disappeared under a mound of black uniforms.

Emmanuel and I were hauled through the opening and thrown up against the crumpled side of the van. My face was mashed against the metal and held there while I was frisked. The same was happened to Emmanuel. Two cops were with each of us, one holding and one patting down. Neither of us struggled, but behind us things were not as civilized. Shine had managed to fling away the pile of police on top of him and was back on his feet. Our 'friskers' left us to join in the war with Shine, leaving only one policeman each, to keep us still. The policeman that had Emmanuel was rougher than need be, maybe because he was the one seen most clearly on camera, maybe because he had a chance to get a cheap shot.

Simon, who had disappeared under the plumbing supplies, shot out of the door and launched himself at the cop manhandling Emmanuel. He grabbed the cop's head from behind with one forearm under his chin and the other across his nose. His left hand caught hold of the cop's right ear. As the cop turned, Simon was lifted from his feet and swung around as if he were attached to a maypole. He lost his grip on everything except the ear. It ripped from the head and left a bloody slash that sent a gush of blood down the man's face. Simon was as stunned as everyone else, except maybe the one-eared policeman.

"Now see what you made me…" He didn't get to finish the sentence. His body went as taunt as a guitar string, then he fell to the street still twitching. Behind him stood a black clad figure with a Taser.

Emmanuel dropped to one knee beside Simon and held hands up to the police.

"Enough!" he shouted.

Chapter 43

"Mr. Rienhart," Kim said over the phone, "you really need to contact Frank White. He has been calling every few minutes."

"Slipped my mind," Jimmy said. "What's his number, I'll call right now." I have to get someone to program the numbers in, he thought.

Jimmy dialed, Frank answered.

"I need to show you something, you and the President both."

The tone of his voice frightened Jimmy. He had never heard Frank sound scared. He thought for a moment, working out a time when they could meet.

"How about tonight, the President is full up until about nine."

"You sure we can't do it sooner? I'd like not to carry this one alone."

"Tonight will be fine, see you then, Margaret will be waiting."

He folded the phone and slid it back into his pocket. For the moment everything was quiet. Both of the major situations were in remission. Later he would get to meet Emmanuel. At the thought, he felt a tingle of nerves. The awe had worn off a little, but in his mind's eye he saw the figure standing in the hail of bullets. He had saved them all.

His phone buzzed again. It was the Priest.

"We've run into a little trouble," I said. "Do you think you could send someone down to the third precinct and bail us out?"

It took about three hours and a lot of screaming, most of which was done by the city police. I was the easiest to bail out. Shine was arrested for resisting arrest and several other felonies. He had a fake ID. His violations were serious but routine for the officers. They were willing to let us go. With the other two it was a different story.

Emmanuel had no ID at all, and he was the one they had been looking for since the shootout footage emerged. Simon had ripped off the ear of one of their own and there was no way he was going to get out easily.

The situation grew more and more tense until the director of the Secret Service called the Chief of Police, who in turn called the precinct commander. All told, I think we were very lucky not to have spent at least one night in jail.

We were not put in the regular lock up, but placed in separate rooms. Luckily for me, I had my Catholic ID and was allowed to make my phone call quickly. We were treated a little differently thereafter, but just the same, the police did not want us to just waltz out of there.

I watched Emmanuel interact with the policemen. Each time a person came near he would stand and shake their hand, then say something that got a reaction of some kind. Some of the cops would just stare, some would smile. A couple of them laughed. He made an impression on each.

I'm sure Emmanuel would be the only one the White House would have extracted, had we not been privy to all the 'goings on' the past couple of days. Shine, Simon, and I could give the story to any news outlet and the administration could be in some hot water. The station was swarming with men in suits with pods in their ears. So we were escorted to a line of blacked out Yukon's idling on the street. This may have been the greatest turnaround since the release of Nelson Mandela. We were whisked out of jail and taken directly to the White House.

Secret Blood

Until now, Simon and Shine did not know where we were going. I had not told them where we were dropping Emmanuel. As we got closer and it became apparent, Shine looked as though he was looking for an escape route. Simon's eyes got bigger and bigger.

"I wasn't so sure 'bout Mr. Stubbs anti-thug policy at first, but dang, it sure workin' now. We social climbers."

We were rushed in through the visitor's entrance and were met by a very serious lady named Margaret. Shine kept it together, but he looked like a lion waiting for a chance to leap. Armed guards were everywhere and just as serious as Margaret, although less threatening. We soon found out she was very much in charge. She read us a list of rules. Do not swear, do not shake the President's hand unless he offers first, and do not stare at the President's left eyebrow. The list went on.

She herded us through series of hallways with carpet so thick I couldn't hear my own footsteps. Portraits were spaced every few feet, each with its own small spotlight and brass plaque. There were also paintings of famous battles from the Revolutionary War and the Civil War. Between the paintings were beautiful crystal sconces. Simon stopped to examine one.

"Chris Tucker got some just like that in his house," Simon said, "I seen it on Cribs."

"Those were a gift from Charles De Gaul and the people of France," Margaret said.

"That's where Chris got them too," Simon said, "He big over there."

Margaret led us through a maze of hallways, but did not stop until we reached a group of four doors. There were two on one side of the hallway and two on the other. She stopped and waited for our attention.

"These will be your rooms. Since you were not able to prepare for this evening because of your unfortunate incarceration, everything you need to make yourself presentable will be provided. Each of you will be given clothing appropriate for a casual dinner at the White House. The clothing you have on now will be cleaned and deloused if necessary. The styles chosen will be reflective of your age and personal style if a style can be identified," she smiled at Simon. When she turned to open the door for us, Simon made a face at her.

"I saw that," she said without turning around. "A valet will bring your attire for dinner in an hour."

"Now," she said producing a clipboard, "I need your sizes, and have to ask the dubious question, boxers or briefs?"

About an hour later I had showered and looked around the room for the tenth time. We were given nice white robes to wear until our clothing arrived. The terrycloth was soft and had a likeness of the White House where a breast pocket would have been. I felt stupid wearing it. I was relieved when someone finally knocked on my door.

A man in a butler's suit handed me a hanger wrapped like dry cleaning. I felt like I should tip him, but I didn't have any money on me.

They had chosen for me a black mock turtleneck and acid washed jeans. I don't know if I had ever looked so stylish in street clothes. They also sent a pair of black Italian loafers. I looked so good in the mirror that I said a silent prayer to help me with my vanity.

Another knock jolted me from my self-indulgence. I opened the door and Simon was strutting back and forth in the hallway. He wore a lime green sweater and black jeans with long pointy black shoes.

"Hey, babe," he said, "Do I look like an associate of a vast rib business conglomerate? I didn't think that Maude-lookin' white woman had it in her." He looked at his reflection in a painting. "Man, all I need now is one of those sweet watches, a Rolodex."

Shine stepped out of his room looking a little embarrassed but clearly putting Simon and me to shame. Next to him we looked like a couple of hayseeds.

Secret Blood

He wore a white silk shirt open at the collar and gray pants. The dark gray belt matched his shoes. It wasn't the clothing as it was the way they fit. His waist looked like about a thirty and his chest a fifty. Even without flexing you could see every muscle. He looked like a racehorse. A thin gold chain and cross hung around his neck.

Simon looked at him. "I think old Shine here could even give Denzel a run for his money." Shine didn't get a chance to respond. Emmanuel stepped out from his room.

He wore the same clothes he had worn for the last two days. White baggy shirt and the faded jeans. He smiled at us when he saw our outfits.

"Uh oh," Simon said, "That battle ax ain't gonna' be happy with you."

We were standing looking at Emmanuel when someone behind us said," Good evening, how's everyone doing?" It was Jimmy.

I shook hands and reintroduced Simon and Shine. Then I introduced Emmanuel. When their hands touched something happened. I'm not sure what it was, but I felt it as much as they did. I was overcome with an unexplainable mixture of joy and serenity. I can't say the air brightened or I could hear angels singing, but that's how I felt. For the first time in a long time I felt good about the world and maybe for the first time ever, I felt good about myself. Shine and Simon noticed it too.

Jimmy and Emmanuel were smiling at each other, neither wanted to release their grip.

Finally Emmanuel released the grip and said to Jimmy. "Will your wife be joining us for dinner?"

Instinctively Jimmy touched his wedding band. "No," he said only a little louder than a whisper.

"Perhaps I could meet her some other time then." He looked at Jimmy as if they were sharing a secret. "You've been blessed, I can tell. God has a plan for you."

Jimmy Rienhart, the man who runs the White House, did not know what to say.

"I believe I also have a plan, although I do not know what it is yet. I was told I was brought here for my blood, but I have yet to see a doctor. There is something else happening here. Either you are the only one who knows what it is, or no one wishes to tell me."

"Maybe that is something we can discuss with the President," Jimmy said.

We started down the hall with Jimmy and Emmanuel in front and Simon and Shine with me.

Simon was having trouble walking. He was taking huge steps and wiggling each foot before he brought it down.

"I think that nasty Margaret ordered my drawers too small, on purpose."

We were dining in the residence, which was pretty much off limits for the press. We passed Marine guards who were stationed at points on the grounds. Jimmy acknowledged each group. I fought the urge to look back at Simon, who was behind me, to see if he was fooling around with the guards.

We stepped into a lobby-like area where the guards doubled and a secret service agent sat behind an ornate desk.

"Good evening, Mr. Rienhart. The President has already been seated."

"He's probably already eating too," Jimmy joked. Then he turned to us and said, "He's my brother but I still call him Mr. President. Respect the office, but be yourselves." He looked at Simon, "except for you."

The room was large but not huge. The molding in the room was a carved hickory. The chandelier hung above the table, which was positioned beside a window, I presumed, because the heavy golden curtains were drawn. There was a couch and chairs in the other part of the room, in front of a fireplace. A small fire danced across the logs, which made the room feel cozy.

As Jimmy expected, the President had already buttered a piece of bread and was about to take a bite. He put the bread down and stood to greet everyone. He wore a blue cable V-neck sweater and khaki pants. The sweater had a green stripe around the neck, relaxed but Ivy League. Introductions were made and everyone shook hands. I waited for the electricity to pass again when Emmanuel shook hands with the President. It didn't happen.

"So, this is the fugitive Priest I've heard so much about? I bet you can give some exciting homilies," the President said as we shook hands. I smiled but said nothing. I liked this guy, voted for him. A year ago the chance of meeting a President would have excited me, but now it seemed second rate, compared to being near Emmanuel.

The table was rectangular, two chairs on each side and two chairs at the ends. The President sat at one end with Emmanuel at his right and I sat to Emmanuel's right. Jimmy sat at the other end and Shine and Simon across from me. A waiter, I guess you'd call him, came for the drink orders. The only choices were water, soda, or coffee. Everyone ordered water.

"In parts of Africa the people could not imagine being able to get clean water so easily. It would be unimaginable to drink as much as you want," Emmanuel said. The President adjusted in his seat.

"In many ways we do not know how lucky we are," he said. The silence began to seep in.

"I know how to fix that," Simon said.

"Fix what?" Jimmy asked.

"Countries not havin' water."

"How?" the President asked. Shine rolled his eyes.

"All right. I sometimes have a little extra time to think about things, with the job choices I have made, you know sitting in cars waiting for something to happen. So I came up with this. Space is a vacuum, right?" He took a sip of his water then continued. "So if you're in a space ship and it gets a hole in it, you get sucked out. Space got this tremendous sucking power. I know it do. I watch the Science channel. So we develop this very strong but light material and make a real long tube out of it. Then we get some kind of platform in a geosynchronous orbit. You know what that is?"

The President and Jimmy nodded. Emmanuel, Shine, and I shook our heads.

"It's a satellite or somethin' in space that stays over the exact same spot in the ground. So you put somethin' like that over the ocean, hook up the tube and let space start sucking up the water. In space, in the shadows it's real cold, right? So the water freezes and you got these huge big icebergs floatin' around. Them finally you attach giant parachutes with remote controls. The ice flies down real slow to where you want it." Simon stopped and looked around the table at the rest of us. We stared back at him.

Finally, Jimmy said, "wouldn't it melt on the way back down?"

"Dude," Simon said out of the corner of his mouth, "That's where we get the rain."

Luckily the door swung open and the salads were brought in. After that, an amazingly tender roast beef with red skinned potatoes and green beans. The conversations swirled around Africa and the world's hunger problem. As everyone ate and talked I kept stealing glances at Emmanuel. He was polite but quiet, even more so than usual. I had the feeling something was building.

"Mr. President," Emmanuel said finally. "Why am I here?"

The air went out of the room. Three of us knew and three didn't. I'm sure the three that didn't were wondering the same thing. Each of us looked at the President. He placed his fork on the table and gently wiped his mouth.

"Son, this country has done a terrible thing. No one in this room or in this administration is responsible, as far as we can tell none of the people who are responsible are still alive. The fact remains that the U.S. government is responsible for your being here. You are, as far as we know, the first person to ever be cloned."

Emmanuel looked down at his plate. I could feel him reaching down inside himself, to find his feelings.

"Son, are you all right?" the President asked.

Emmanuel lifted his head and smiled slightly. "I was raised in an orphanage. I thought my parents didn't want me."

"Because you're in an orphanage, it doesn't mean your parents don't love you," Shine said. I looked at Shine, then Simon. Simon

Secret Blood

raised his eyebrows in an 'I don't know where that came from' expression.

"There's more," the President said. "Would you like to have some time to digest this, or would you like to hear the whole thing now?"

"I think I would like to hear anything else you can tell me. I am healthy and help others less fortunate than I am. My past is cloudy but I am not scared by it."

"Okay, then." The President took a deep breath. "Jimmy you know the facts better than I do."

Jimmy took up where the President left off. "The work was done by a splinter group of the CIA. The widow of one of the members gave the information to Father in a confession. Of all the work they had done over the years, your case was the only one that was successful. The DNA was taken from a vase that was about two thousand years old."

"Two thousand?" Simon said. "That would be about year zero."

"Exactly," said the President. "You were cloned from the blood of Jesus Christ."

For the first time I heard the fire crackling in the fireplace. The President said nothing else. We waited for some response from Emmanuel. There was none at first, and then he took a sip of water and said, "In that case I've really underachieved." He smiled. That broke the tension.

Desert was fresh baked apple pie with brown sugar and cinnamon ice cream. Emmanuel was hard to read. I kept glancing at him. He looked over to me and said, "You knew about this all along?"

"Yes," I said. I did not know what else to say.

He nodded.

In the awkward moment, I caught the end of a conversation between Jimmy and Simon.

"… got that figured out, too. I call that my umbrella solution."

"We'd be very interested in stopping global warming," the President said.

Simon started, "The oceans control the climate right? So we got to cool off the oceans. And how do you do that, you put part of it in the shade. How do you do that? Space screens. Rocket up screens that keep unfolding, real thin, light stuff. Could be like silver foil only stronger. Put it in another geosynchronous orbit. Don't ever let the sun hit that part of the ocean. Currents keep the cool water movin'."

"Yes, but the ocean's so big that it would take a pretty big screen. That's pretty pricey, I think the going rate to put something in space is about $10,000 a pound," Jimmy said.

"Yep, pretty pricey," Simon said. "How much Katrina cost you? How much if the polar caps melt and New York goes underwater? That price don't seem so high all of a sudden, do it?"

"Well..." said the President.

"That a deep subject," Simon said. "And what else is, if you can reflect that light, somebody might be able to aim it back down to solar plants on the ground, get rid of all the carbon fuels. And," he went on, "we might scare somebody over in North Korea, start rattling some sabers, we shoot a light beam near enough to let them know we could toast them if we so minded."

The President said, "That's getting close to Reagan's Star Wars Plan."

"*Star Wars, Star Trek*, Star Jones, I don't care what you call it, we gotta' cool down the oceans. We can make the screen the size of Texas if we want, just keep sending up the rockets."

"When do I go home?" Emmanuel asked.

"Well, whenever you like," the President said "Jimmy is the person who thought we should bring you here and tell you in person."

"I'd like you to stay," Jimmy blurted out, then looked self-conscious.

"I would, too," I said without having planned it.

"For how long?" Emmanuel asked.

"I don't know," Jimmy said, "I just have this feeling that you are supposed to be here."

"I shall have to think about it," he said. "I feel guilty being here, eating this wonderful food, while I could be of help elsewhere. Lives may be depending on my return. There is so much suffering."

"I understand," Jimmy said.

There was a knock at the door and a secret service agent came in. He walked to the President, bent low and whispered something.

"Okay, let's see." The agent stepped to the window and pulled the cord. The curtains split and slid to the sides, revealing the White House grounds that were illumined by halogen floodlights. The ground was a seething mass of brown.

"What are those?" Jimmy asked as everyone crowded around the window.

"Doves," the President said. "Millions of them."

We all looked at Emmanuel.

As Jimmy walked us back to our rooms for the night he said to Emmanuel," I hope you will consider staying for a couple of days longer."

"I have a great deal to think about. I do not want to go back still having questions unanswered, but right now, I'm not sure what the questions are."

We walked back to our rooms in silence, each of us lost in our own thoughts. I was really kind of interested in what Simon and Shine thought of the evening. I knew that neither was very religious but each had a sort of spirituality. They had rules they lived by, and the more I was learning about them, the more I understood the rules. I knew they would never let each other down, no matter how they complained about, or made fun of one another. I was glad I was on their side.

We dispersed into our own rooms knowing our White House visit would not be long.

Chapter 44

Frank White was already seated at the table when Jimmy returned. The President had a coffee cup in his hand and there was another sitting on the table, steam rising.

"Come on Jimmy, Frank's about to bust an artery."

A battered laptop was open on the table beside the coffee. Frank did not look up as Jimmy sat down. He kept typing passwords into the computer. "He's forgotten his password," the President said, smiling.

"Not my password, a special password I used, specifically for this," Frank said decidedly frustrated.

"I remember Mom losing things that way. She put something in a special place so she wouldn't lose it, then she'd forget where she put it," Jimmy said. "Then she'd pray to somebody, who is the patron saint of lost things."

"Listen, you guys I've been sitting on this all day and I need to show somebody. After I called you today to tell you The Ghost had disappeared, it reappeared and Grandma got some pictures."

"Where did it reappear?" the President asked.

"That's scary point number one. It's a lot closer. It's traveling at speeds we did not think possible," Frank said, still typing.

"Okay," Jimmy said. "Can you tell where it's heading?"

"Scary point number two. It has veered off at an angle."

"So that's good, it's not still headed toward us," The President said.

"Maybe. I can't work up any numbers by myself; I need to talk to somebody who is qualified. The scary thing is that for the first time it has changed direction. On its own." He typed in another password. "Oh, that was it, Bosco." The pictures Frank was looking for started to materialize line by line.

"Scary point number three," he said and spun the screen around so the President and his brother could see.

The pictures were really video and much better quality than Jimmy had expected…or had wished for.

The image on the screen boiled and twisted in the blackness of space. It was mostly spherical except in the areas where it slowly bulged. A transparent membrane kept whatever forces within from ripping the sphere to pieces and escaping. The inside swirled with violence and malevolence. Whatever was there was throwing itself against the walls, flashing purple and scarlet, like all the evil in the universe compressed into one form. It snarled silently and went in and out of focus, wrenching and churning like a reptilian monster without shape. The whole mass looked to be rolling through space, the interior not attached to the outer skin.

"My God," the President said softly. "Who else has seen this?"

"The three of us and some of the tech crew at NASA. This was e-mailed to me but it was a semi-secure link. Why do you ask?"

"People would be scared to death," Jimmy said. "Looking up into space at night and knowing that something like that is speeding toward us. It's like being in a little boat and knowing there are sharks all around but not being able to see them."

"Jimmy's right, we have to keep this quiet until it passes. There will be worldwide panic if these become public," the President said. "But we need to have a plan just in case this leaks. There's got to be a plan for a scenario similar to this, doesn't there?"

They looked back at the screen and watched the writhing mass.

"I know we have projections for the earth being struck, but I don't know if we have studies on the reaction of the country if an impact is imminent," Jimmy said. "I'll work on a panel of people tonight and get with you in the morning Frank, just to make sure we have the right science people. We'll have the names by nine and meet just after lunch."

The President hadn't taken his eyes off the screen. "Is it me, or does it look like it knows we're watching it?"

"I had the same feeling," Frank said. "Once we got Grandma set it reappeared just so we could see it."

"You guys are just projecting your fears. I want to have plan ready just in case the rest of the country gets hold of this," Jimmy said again.

"Well you had better hurry," Frank said, "because in about a week, any eighth grader with a telescope is going to be able to see it."

Chapter 45

My suite was comprised of a sitting room, a bedroom and a bathroom that was as large as my living quarters at the seminary. It probably wasn't as nice as a high rollers room in Las Vegas or at The Greenbrier, but it was certainly the best I had ever seen. The draperies and bedding looked lush and expensive, the woodwork was understated but meticulous, and the art was abundant and authentic.

I sat for several minutes drinking it all in, contemplating the extremes of modern life. What in the world was I doing here? I consider myself a devoted man. The church has been my life for as long as I can remember. My convictions have never wavered; I've always wanted to live my life for the Lord.

So how did I get here, so far away from my parish and my priesthood? The President called me Father, but in no other way am I behaving like a priest. I sat there in my new stylish clothes. I was confused, but I hadn't lost my faith. If anything I think my faith was stronger than ever. After a while, I decided that my future was not in my hands. Maybe it was time to visit Emmanuel.

I left my door ajar and knocked on his. He said, "Come in."

The door was unlocked and I stepped in and closed it behind me. He was on the floor, legs crossed, like he had been meditating. His hands were on his knees, palms up, and his back was very straight. He opened his eyes and smiled brightly. I was taken aback—it was the brightest smile I had seen from him.

"You look very… rejuvenated," I said.

"And you look very confused," he said. "It seems we are at opposite ends of the same spectrum. Until a few hours ago my past was murky, unknown to me. Now I have a very strong feeling of my future, I know what my life's work will be." He stood and twisted, stretching his back.

"You, on the other hand, are solid on your past. You know where you've been and are happy with the decisions you have made. But, because of my presence your future is unclear; your path has been lost."

"You got all that from meditating?" I asked.

"No, I got that from looking at you. I was not meditating, unless you can call prayer meditation. I was praying for the people of the villages that I serve."

His room was very much like mine in design, although the colors and fabrics differed. He sat on the couch and motioned for me to sit in the chair across from him. Same clothes, but the shoes and socks were gone.

"I know you came to check on me and I thank you for that, but I can assure you I am and will always be fine. The shadows of my past have lightened and what was once confusing is now becoming clear. These are things I can deal with. I'm sorry it was a burden on you."

I leaned back and relaxed, "It's much less of a burden now that I have seen what you have become and how you are living your life. Although I'm not sure how the Vatican is going to take the news."

"That would be an interesting phone call, but it is not one that I myself am going to make," he said. "But what of you, what have you decided to do for your faith?"

"I don't know, I've pretty much settled on letting the Lord guide the way," I said.

"I have a prediction," he said, smiling again. "I'm very good at these you know. I have a feeling you are going to have a calling within a calling, as Sister Teresa described it."

"Do you mean Mother Teresa?" I asked, "You knew her?"

"I spent much of my youth in India, with her. This was after her first heart attack. I would run many of her errands. In the evenings she would teach me different languages. There were others there that would teach me those she could not. She taught me charity, humility, and about the Grace of God." He stood to get some water in the bathroom and offered to bring me a glass, I declined.

"This is so good, I'm afraid I am indulging myself," he said between sips. "She often spoke of her decision to leave the convent to help the poor and dying. She said it was a calling within a calling. Her first calling was to God and within that calling another surfaced later. And that was the calling to help the sick."

"My prediction is that you will hear a second calling, and then your life's work will begin."

I felt the tingle in my arms, the feeling you get right before the goose bumps rise. He's just a man I kept telling myself.

* * *

"What do you think about this cloning business?" Shine asked Simon. Simon looked up in surprise, not often asked his opinion by Shine on anything.

"All I know is, I'm the one who called him spooky and thought he looked like Charles Manson, and now I need to be reborn or somethin' or I'm goin' to Hell. Now that I know who he is, he doesn't even look white any more. He looks more like an Arabian."

Simon had come to Shine's room looking for a TV, which his room didn't have. None of them did, which was ludicrous to Simon. It was around eleven o'clock and neither were used to going to bed so early.

"What we supposed to do now?" Simon asked.

"Maybe they are hoping you can come up with another world saving plan, like Project Parasol."

"That's the Umbrella Solution, and I could tell you didn't believe in it then, but the President did. I saw the look in his eyes, he gonna' try to steal my idea and say he thought it up. But he can't do that cause I got all you as witnesses."

They sat and let that sink in for a moment. Then Simon said, "I wish my Mama could see where we are now. Maybe tomorrow I can get the President to speak to her on the phone. Naw, she wouldn't believe it was real. I might let him take credit for one of my plans if he let me stand behind him when he talkin' on TV. Maybe I could even call her and tell her to turn the channel and be talking to her while I'm on. She wouldn't think I was a no-good then."

Shine listened and nodded, "What you gonna' do, stand behind him and wave your arms like those goof balls do at ballgames? Your Mama sure gonna' be proud then."

"Don't really seem fair though, we startin' to go legit then we got Jesus comin' back like it's the Second Coming," Simon said. "You think it's the end of the world?"

Shine leaned back on the couch with a toothpick stuck in the corner of his mouth. "Don't know," he said. "Too deep for me."

Chapter 46

The President was Jimmy's last phone call of the night. Between himself and Frank, they had rounded up everyone he thought they needed and it was only eleven o'clock. He wanted the President's input on a couple of them.

"Here's who we have; Frank—science, Gen. Parker—Department of Defense, Ken Jenkins—Homeland Security, Ronald King—Department of Energy, Brenda James—Secretary of State, Jude Johnson—CIA, and I guess we will have to include the Judge."

"Oh no, can't we send him somewhere?" the President asked his brother.

Judge Aston was the Vice President and wanted badly to be President. He wasn't actually a Judge. It was a nickname he thought worked well. He'd had it since campaigning for class president in Jr. High. It rolled off the tongue nicely. He was only on the Rienhart ticket because he could carry New York. They had to appease him through the next election, and then they wouldn't have to worry about him anymore.

So far they had managed to keep him out of the spotlight and away from most of the affairs of the President. Many of the comments that were made during the primary still stung and there were accounts of some dirty tricks that could not be traced directly back to his camp, although he was the main beneficiary. Neither the President nor his brother trusted him.

"If he's not on the panel he'll sniff it out and leak it, and he'll make sure it's to his advantage and not ours. If he's on the panel he can't discredit it," Jimmy said. "Might be a way to keep an eye on him."

"I still don't like him around," the President said. "Is that everybody?"

"That covers it, except that maybe we should have someone to advise us on the religious aspect. I don't know. If we are preparing for the country's reactions, the religious component is a large part of that."

"Makes sense to me," the President said. "How about Father Steve?"

"No, I think he's too Catholic, we need someone with a wider vision of religion in this country. Plus the fact that we're Catholic might make it look like we aren't interested in any other point of view. I was thinking of Mike DeRose. He's well known and has a spoon in a lot of different pots." Jimmy waited for the President's reaction.

"That sounds good. I still don't like the Judge snooping around though."

"Keep your friends close," Jimmy said.

"And keep your enemies closer, I know," said the President. "I hate to bring this up, but to be prudent, we need to keep the Continuity of Government ready. Make sure all the new Senators are up to speed."

"We are going to meet in the Situation Room, so when this leaks, and you know it will, we will know who the leak is.

"Everybody's either in town or they are flying in tonight, so we will be able to start first thing in the morning. I told them it would be a working breakfast and not to plan anything for the rest of the day." Instead of tapping his pencil Jimmy used his thumb to spin his wedding band around on his ring finger.

"You know," he said, "this is going to be big. I can't get the vision of that thing out of my head."

"Get some sleep," said the President, "I'll see you in the morning."

Jimmy slumped in the chair and hung up the phone. The house was way too quiet. It felt eerie without her, like being the only person to attend a visitation at a funeral home. Jimmy walked upstairs, took off his tie and threw it into a drawer. He sat on the bed, kicked off his shoes and unbuttoned his shirt. The phone sat on the nightstand, mocking him. I can pick up the phone and call any leader in the free world, but I'm afraid to call my wife. His subconscious mind knew why, but he would not admit it to himself. If he called her he was afraid she wouldn't talk to him. As long as they didn't talk, he would still be married.

He threw his shirt in the overflowing hamper and went into the bathroom and started the shower.

The bed was so comfortable that I felt like I was floating. I had the most extraordinary feeling that Jesus had taken me by the hand and led me into a lifetime of service amongst the clouds. I knew it wasn't so, but I allowed myself to believe. Maybe that's what faith is, opening up without reservation, the abandonment of reason for the sake of belief. There wasn't too much theology in it, but in the beginning I felt happy and rejuvenated.

I was deep asleep when the dream started; I knew I was deep because it was so hard to come out of it. Emmanuel and I were walking in a park in some city. I remember seeing children playing on a playground. There was an old man walking a dog that had a knitted sweater around its stomach. I remember that dog because I thought it must be really uncomfortable, its summertime and it's hot. There was an ice cream truck somewhere playing that twinkling music like from a music box. It came around a corner and the kids all ran to it. Mr. SOFTEE was painted on the side and the man stopped the truck and opened that little window where you could order.

Someone was mowing grass with a Lawn Boy mower. I couldn't see it but you can tell from the sound of the motor and the smell of the exhaust. It must be the mixture of gasoline and oil because there is no better smell than grass cut with a Lawn Boy. I could smell the mower and see the kids in a line beside Mr. SOFTEE and everything was just about perfect.

The sliding window of the Mr. SOFTEE truck opened and brilliant white clouds began flowing out and slurping across the ground. It muffled everything. I couldn't hear the Lawn Boy or the children playing. I couldn't see the grass or the street or even my shoes.

Then an orange cloud rolled across the sky. Lightning bolts silently veined through it. As it came lower it turned purple and blue and angry puffs of smoke engulfed the trees in the park. Leaf by leaf the trees burst into flames and the clouds rolled toward the playground. The paint boiled on the pipes that supported the swings and the parts made of plastic melted.

I yelled to the children to get out of the way but there was no place to hide, the clouds were everywhere. A telephone pole beside me went up like a Roman candle. Emmanuel was still with me. He spoke to me in French, a language I can't speak, but I could understand him. He said to me, "You're not the chain, but you're a link." The fire rolled over the ice cream truck and was headed for us.

I opened my eyes. I could see but I was so terrified that I couldn't move; if I could have I probably would have screamed. I reentered reality slowly, subconsciously taking deep breaths. Little by little, I got control of myself and flung off the blankets. My tee shirt was damp and clingy. I popped out of bed without turning on the light and pulled open the drapes. I had to prove to myself that everything was still normal.

Sufficiently persuaded by the drizzle of rain that was falling on the parking lot pines, I allowed myself to sit and try to relax. It would be awhile before I would try to sleep again.

Chapter 47

The Situation Room is a series of thirteen rooms located directly under the Oval office. It is equipped with the latest and most powerful communication devices and video screens. A President can view a terrorist camp photographed from a drone or watch an anti-American demonstration in Korea on the screens in the Situation Room. Ninety five percent of the information a President acts on is viewed in the Situation Room.

The Situation Room was chosen for this particular meeting to stem the tide of panic. If the pictures of The Ghost got out, it would be by the hands of someone on this panel. They were apprised of this as each entered.

The only seat vacant was that of the Vice President. He was third generation, old political machine, and he showed his clout by making the others wait for him, or so he thought.

"Go ahead Jimmy; we aren't going to wait on the Judge any longer."

As soon as the door closed, the Judge opened it and walked in like the faithful were assembled just for him. He entered like a parody of Tony Soprano.

"I'm sorry. I was detained," he said as he took his chair. Each person had an attractive, nameplate signifying their seat.

Jimmy started, "As of this moment this is a hypothetical situation. That may change." He stood and turned on the projector. The fan hummed in the quiet of the room.

"This is the latest image of The Ghost; it was taken by an asset that is not normally used in this capacity." The only sound was that of the committee members leaning in their chairs.

"You mean it's a spy satellite," the Judge said.

"Yes Judge, I think everyone here can read between those lines," the President snapped.

"Okay, I'm just saying."

"It's scary looking," Jimmy said. "I had nightmares about it last night. What we would like from each of you is a projection. What would the nation's reaction be if an impact were imminent? And those of you who have the expertise, the reaction around the world."

"We need to create a model of the reaction and then have a plan ready if the situation materializes," the President added.

Jimmy turned the screen off. "Look at this from your prospective, think outside of the box."

Gen. Parker who was the Dept. of Defense said, "What kind of time frame are we looking at? Six months, six weeks, or six days. That may make an impact on the reaction."

"Good question General," Jimmy said, "Let's try to get a reaction for each length of time." He was about to start another sentence but Frank was making a face at him.

"Frank, you got something to add?"

"Yeah," he said. "I didn't want to be premature on this, but as long as the question was raised…"

"Go ahead Frank, spit it out," the President said.

"We've gone over this several times, so I think we are spot-on with the timing. The Ghost will intercept with the orbit of the Earth in 22 days."

The room went deathly quiet. Gen. Parker put his face in his hands.

"You okay, General?" Jimmy asked.

"My daughter's pregnant. She's due in about two months. Are you saying my grandson won't be born?"

Frank broke the silence. "Remember when I told you it wasn't heading toward us anymore and that might be a bad thing. Well, it was. If it headed at us, it would have missed us, because we are still moving in our orbit of the Sun. It changed its course to cut us off."

"We do have other agencies looking into a defensive alternative. I will keep you updated on that as necessary," the President said.

"Again," Jimmy said, "I have to ask you to please keep this quiet. No one, family, friends, or clergy can know about any of this. Use only the people you can trust to help with the projections and let them know we will prosecute any leaks. It looks like we may be in for the biggest panic the planet has ever known."

He felt it, saw it in the faces of those looking back at him. The dread and fear. "The emotions you are feeling now, those are what the people of the world are going to feel. Some may receive the news gently and some will not. We want to be able to handle what we can and let God do the rest."

"Back here, same time tomorrow," the President said.

Chapter 48

"I gotta get out of here," Simon said. "The accommodations are nice but this is like being in lock-up."

We had gathered in Emmanuel's room, and filled in our request for breakfast. The choices were limited but it was breakfast and this wasn't a restaurant. We were all up early, except for Simon who was woken by Shine.

"How long we gonna' have to stay?"

I hated to admit it but I was itching to get out, too. My talk with Emmanuel had fired me up and I was ready to get on with whatever I was going to do. I wasn't sure what exactly it was, but I didn't think I could get things started by staying here. For the first time in years I didn't feel I was doing poorly in my job. The fact that I didn't really have a job was probably a contributing factor.

A knock on the door and the food was served. Three of us ate heartily. Emmanuel had toast and juice. He smiled and ribbed us a little about how much we ate.

"I do not think we will be leaving very soon," he said. "For some reason Mr. Rienhart wants us here, with him. He has convinced his brother of this also."

"I think he wants you here, we're just extra baggage," Simon said.

The phone rang. Simon picked it and said, "Hello, Presidential dungeon." He listened and then gave the phone to Emmanuel. "Yes, that would be wonderful, good bye."

"Mr. Rienhart is going to come down and see what we would like to do today. He has canceled his meetings for the rest of the day."

Jimmy thought he was going to be greeted by happy, excited faces but he was not. He had suggested a tour of Washington for the group, chaperoned of course, but they did not seem interested in that or any other idea he came up with.

"Well, what would you like to do?" He finally asked.

"Go home," Simon said.

"Do you know Alice Cooper? That is a person I would like to visit," Emmanuel said.

"Don't think so," said Jimmy.

"How about a hospital?" I said.

"Yes!" Emmanuel said enthusiastically.

"Are you crazy?" Simon said.

"Promise you won't take off again?" Jimmy said to Emmanuel.

At least one happy face smiled back.

Jimmy made the arrangements. He looked a bit disappointed when we showed up in our own clothes. Emmanuel insisted on wearing what he always had and the rest of us felt overdressed for a hospital visit.

The St. Margaret Mary Children's Hospital was a showcase for family friendly health care. The reception area completely contrasted the stark, drab hospitals of my youth, which could have doubled as reformatories or mental institutions. Everything here was designed to mask or deflect the sorrow of children in pain. But no one could do anything about the smell. Hospitals always have that smell.

The staff was extremely professional, but still friendly and received us enthusiastically which may have been difficult, considering what a diverse group we seemed to be.

And there was always Shine. No matter where we were, he was always treated as though he was some kind of dangerous animal. No one ever spoke to him directly; no one would even look him in the eye. They kept their distance and glanced, then turned away. He had an air of menace, a violence that lay just below the skin, like a shark. The security guards, as did the Secret Service, spoke into their walkie-talkies when he entered. It always seemed to me that none of them wanted to face him alone.

The entourage included seven people, Jimmy, Emmanuel, Simon Shine, two Secret Service agents, and me. One of the agents stayed in the lobby and the other stayed with Jimmy.

We split into groups without realizing it. Jimmy and I were in a group with the agent trailing behind. Shine and Emmanuel formed an unlikely pair but they worked well together. Emmanuel, a smiling, gentle man who could bring out the best in everything, and Shine, who scared the bejeebers out of everyone. Simon kind of hung out in the hallways, not knowing what to say. He had never been around kids, never been in the hospital; not even to visit. These things were alien to him and all he wanted was to get out of the place.

We started on the second floor and worked our way down the hall talking to the kids and their parents. This floor was easy; a lot of broken bones and minor surgeries, and most stays were only a couple of days. It would get harder.

Simon was lurking in the hall when the bell for the elevator chimed and a kid rolled out in a wheel chair. His left leg was elevated and in a neon green cast. He wore a pair of khaki shorts and a white tee shirt under a Lakers jersey. He glanced to the left, then the right, and rolled up to Simon.

"Who are you?" he asked.

"My name's Simon," Simon said trying to get into the spirit of the visit. "What's your name?"

"I'm not telling you. You think I'm stupid, telling a stranger my name?

What you doing out here in the hall?"

"We're visitin' people in the hospital," Simon said not quite as friendly as before.

"Out here in the hallway? Who you visiting out here?" The kid gave him a good looking over. "You don't look right, I think I better get security." He started to roll away.

"Go ahead, see what it gets you." Simon said. "They will probably throw you out instead."

The boy spun his wheelchair around. "Why would they throw me out?"

"Cause you are messin' with me and I am here with the President's brother and Jesus," Simon said. He crossed his arms and raised his eyebrows.

"You are not. What are you some kind of sicko coming to hospitals to lie to kids?"

"His bodyguard is a hard case, look like some kind of genie. I could have him toss you if I wanted."

They stood staring at each other until Jimmy and I came out of the last room and walked past them to the elevator. A few moments later Emmanuel and Shine came out of another room and strode past Simon and the kid. The kid's eyes got wide when he saw Emmanuel, but when he looked at Shine he frowned.

The elevator doors opened and we got in, while Simon strolled toward us. He got in the car and turned and gave the kid a smirk.

The wheelchair raced to the car and banged into the doors as they were closing. Jimmy pressed the open button and the kid rolled in.

"That guy's black," he said.

Shine looked down at him.

"So?" Simon said.

"A genie can't be black. Genies are blue."

"What you sayin'? A black man can't be a genie 'cause of his color? What, you some kind of a racist?"

"Oh, God," Jimmy said. "We're supposed to be helping the patients here, not calling them racists."

"Yeah," the kid said.

The elevator chimed and the door opened to the next floor. Everyone got out including the kid. They stood in the hall while the doors closed softly behind them.

"Where you goin'?" Simon said.

"With you," the kid said. "You're not doing anything but standing in the hallways anyhow."

The rest of us laughed, Simon stared at the kid.

"You and him got a lot to discuss," Shine said, "given that he got a Kobe shirt and you think he's so over rated."

"Over rated?" the kid said. "You have got to be kidding."

"Not only over rated but gets all the calls, too," Simon said.

After that, it was on, not aware of anything except each other's arguments. The next two hours were spent trying to outdo each other.

On the fourth floor Shine and Emmanuel came across a girl who was recovering from a fractured skull. Her brain had swollen and the pressure was causing a great deal of pain. The doctors were discussing whether or not to drill a hole in the skull to alleviate pressure. She had two black eyes and a very swollen lip.

During the visits Emmanuel did the talking and Shine would show encouragement only with his presence. He was kind but unattached. He acted like he was afraid he would scare the kids. This girl was different. He told her she was going to get well. He actually touched her arm when he spoke to her. He promised he would be back to see her.

A nurse came in to administer medication and told us she would be getting sleepy shortly. She nodded when he told her he would be checking up on her. Her eyes closed before we left. Shine followed the nurse out of the room.

"What happened to her?" he asked. The nurse stepped away from him but her eyes never left his.

"The report says she fell down the stairs," she said.

"What do you say?" Shine asked.

"I've never seen injuries from a fall on both sides of the head," she said.

Shine was still, like a snake waiting in a bush.

"Before I leave I'd like the girl's address."

"I'm sorry sir, but there is no way I can do that," she said.

"I want it on a piece of paper, in my hand, before I leave."

The nurse recoiled, "But, sir,"

"In my hand," he said.

She turned and walked away quickly. Emmanuel came out of the room and stood beside Shine as he watched the nurse walk away.

"Of all the children, why the interest in her?"

"She reminds me of someone," he said.

The long term and critically ill kids were housed on the top floor. Conditions with impossibly long names, chemo and radiation were the order of the day here. To these kids, shaved heads and permanent shunts were as routine as skateboards and video games.

But Emmanuel was at ease here as he had been at the White House and the shootout. He spoke quietly and listened to the parents and kids alike. He made each child smile.

When we finished we hopped the elevator and rode to the lobby. Simon and the kid, who now had been named Kobe, laughed and made fun of one another.

As the doors slid open a sturdy nurse was waiting there, with arms crossed across her ample chest.

"You, young man have been rolling around too long. You are busted," she said. "I've been all over this hospital. Just stay right there in that elevator. When we get to your room I am going to handcuff you to your bed."

"You coming back?" he said after we got out.

"Maybe we can watch a Lakers game and I can point out some of Kobe's weaknesses. Take two games to point out all of them."

The doors closed with the nurse holding onto the wheelchair and the kid looking at us. The Secret Service agent had the SUV up, idling at the entrance. As we were climbing into the vehicle, a nurse walked out and handed a folded piece of paper to Shine. She walked back into the hospital without saying a word.

* * *

That night Shine met with Jimmy. A bond had formed between them since the hospital visit. Jimmy realized Shine was something special and under different circumstances he would have risen to a different level of society.

All Shine had to say is, that he had to do something for the little girl they had talked to in the hospital. Jimmy arranged for him to take a Secret Service van and leave the White House grounds after midnight. He had memorized the address and knew the route he would take.

Forty minutes later he pulled the van to the side of the street. He got out and walked two blocks through a broken down neighborhood, across a yard littered with car parts, and up on a porch of a house with cracked steps. He unscrewed the light bulb in the dirty porch light and threw it into the front yard. He pulled open the dull aluminum screen door and pounded, then stepped back, still holding the door.

The man who stepped out was larger than Shine, both in height and weight; but it was a soft bulk. He had the kind of body that would intimidate most people because of the sheer size, not because of any kind of strength or skill. He was a bully and had been all of his life.

"Who the …." was all he could manage before Shine grabbed a hand full of greasy hair and pulled him into the darkness of the porch. He hit the man with a short right hook to the temple that would have dropped most people. His eyes began to roll back as Shine forced him against the wall, put a forearm under his chin and leaned hard against his throat. Shine's face was an inch away. The man's eyes refocused as he struggled to breathe.

"Your breath stinks," he whispered.

Shine brought an uppercut to the man's solar plexus.

"That your little girl in the hospital?"

The man could just get enough air to reply, "Step-daughter."

Shine forced the forearm tighter and the man gave a small grunt. He reached under his leather jacket and pulled out a flat black Smith and Wesson .357. He shoved it against the man's upper lip with enough pressure to make it bleed.

"Now, if I ever hear any harm comin' to that little girl or anyone else in this family I will kill you. Do you understand?"

The man nodded.

"I think you do understand, but the real question is, do you believe me?"

The man shook his head again.

Shine pulled the tip of the barrel down over his mouth and cleft and held it under his chin. It left a red line in his skin. Shine reached in his pocket, brought out a bullet and shoved it into the man's mouth.

"I want you to do something for me. Feel the size of that bullet; go ahead roll it around with your tongue." Shine waited.

"I'm gonna' let you keep that bullet, just so you can remember how large it is and the size of hole it will make in your skull." The man kept moving it around his mouth.

"Got it?" Shine asked.

"Yeah," the man grunted.

Shine hit him in the side of the head with the gun. "Manners, yes what?"

"Yes, sir," the man said.

"I am employed by a large organization, and we all will be watching, so don't plan on moving and carrying on the same way, because I'll know. Got that?"

"Yes, sir," the man said.

"Now, I'm going to allow you to turn and face the wall. If you turn around while I am departing, I will shoot you dead right now. If you would like to live to see the daylight again, you will quietly enter you home, if you can call this a home, when you cannot hear me whistling. Do you understand that?"

The man nodded vigorously, he wanted nothing more than for this to be over.

Shine turned him around and shoved him into the wall holding the gun against his back.

"All right, I'm going to release you now. Remember if you ever see me again it means you are about to meet God." Shine slowly pulled the gun back, stepped off the porch, and started whistling, *Somewhere Over the Rainbow*.

He backed down the walk and with a spring in his step, walked to the van.

Chapter 49

The President and Jimmy entered the Situation Room after the rest of the committee was seated. Each member emptied their briefcases and piled notebooks and printouts on the table before them. The friendly chatter that usually preceded meetings such as this was absent today. Each member had experienced reporting casualties of war, but this was a tragedy before the event.

The President stood behind his chair and spoke before he sat. "I don't need to remind you, that what we say here stays in this room. You must, and I can't say this strongly enough, act normally with your family. We can't have Jimmy's wife telling her friends at the PTA meeting that the Chief of Staff is depressed over something."

"No chance of that," Jimmy thought.

"You understand what I mean? Your behavior could endanger millions of lives."

"Okay, General," Jimmy said, "Let's hear what you have. And remember guys, we only need your input for what will happen when the news breaks, not after the collision."

"For our projections, we feel the most endangered components of the US military would be our overseas bases. There would be no fear of retaliation for any government that would launch an attack. The bases closest to the countries that are the least friendly to the

US would have a higher percentage of attack. These bases would also have a much lower AWOL rate.

The bases in this country may have as much as a seventy five percent AWOL rate during a non-war related incident. These percentages were calculated for planet killer asteroid hits and biological disasters.

"Finally," the General went on, "the chance of nuclear attack on the US from unfriendly countries is high. If they have the nukes they might as well use them. Also, Israel would probably unload everything they have on the Arabs. And vice versa."

"Thanks," Jimmy said, "how about you, Kenny?"

Ken Jenkins was the head of Homeland Security. He had the second biggest pile of notes before him. The tallest and most fit of the group, his quiet presence could be intimidating.

"We monitor dozens and dozens of groups constantly. There are hundreds of possible terrorists in the country that have not broken any laws, yet. This one was pretty simple. Every one of these people is going to do whatever they can to kill US citizens. They believe the path to Heaven is over the bodies of the infidels. If this is their last chance to prove themselves worthy, they are going to take it, no matter how incomplete the plan is. If they don't have a bomb, they can set buildings on fire, or just go on a shooting rampage. The harbor and government buildings would be targets. The studies also show that they may work in teams for something so last minute. It's hard for us to sniff out a plan if they don't really have one. Biological and chemical threats are low because they take too long to spread. But we do agree with the General, whatever they have, they will use."

He put his pad down and looked at the others. "The prudent thing to do is to jail any suspected subject as soon as the news breaks. It may not be Constitutional, but prosecution of violations may be a moot point, and everybody will be interested in the safety of their own family, not the rights of suspected terrorists."

"Thanks Kenny," Jimmy said. "You got any good news for us, Ron?"

"Nope," said Ronald King from the Energy Dept. "Our projections have determined that people aren't going to want to go to work. They will want to stay with their families or go to their churches. People with a very distinct set of skills are needed to man nuclear power plants. They can't be replaced and if the workers stop showing up, we are not going to have to worry about The Ghost, we will have meltdowns all over the world." He shuffled through his papers.

"On a smaller scale we will have the same problems with power plants; no employees and the plants will blow. Even with automation, the plants can't run themselves. We can't get a good feel for what would happen at Hoover Dam, it's well built, but dams need to be manned. Cities like New York will go dark when the grid goes down. Subways and security go down, hospitals and airports can only run on generators for so long. It's not good."

The room was quiet. They were each lost in their own thoughts, knowing this was not a practice drill they were talking about, but something that was actually going to happen. Jimmy felt it most of all. He had been splitting his time between the cloning situation and this. The joy of Emmanuel balanced this out, up until now. The gravity of this was beginning to wear him down.

"Anybody need anything?" Jimmy said. "Water, Coke, something to eat?" A few of them nodded. He picked up the phone and asked for some drinks, sandwiches and pizza. "I'm not going to get any Diet Coke." That got a couple of chuckles.

"Frank, do you have anything new?"

"Sorry, no. The timeline for impact is still the same. We don't really know what it is, what it will do, or where it came from."

"Thus the wonders of modern science," the President said smiling.

Brenda James, Secretary of State was seated next in line.

"Brenda, your turn." Jimmy said.

"Our thought is that the industrialized countries will have the same problems we do, mostly the breakdown of the infrastructure due to absenteeism. Most of them will look to us to see how to handle things. Continents such as Africa, Australia and South America will have problems in the larger population centers, but the rural areas will be unaffected. Same with China and Russia, the cities are hit the hardest.

"In Japan, Europe, and the US there will be wide spread panic due to better communications. Too much info means more fear. We will see no difference in the behavior, regardless of race, culture, or religion."

"Well, okay, Jude, what have you got. There has got to be a ray of light here somewhere. The human race isn't this fragile, is it?" the President asked.

"Well, sir," said Jude Johnson, CIA director. "Our studies show the same scenarios as Homeland Security and the Department of Defense. The top two threats are the splinter groups that are already here but dormant, and the lack of workers in certain jobs. The latter is by far the biggest threat."

"Judge, you got anything useful to say?" the President asked.

"No, no. Like you I'm just gathering information," he said. He picked up his pencil and scribbled something down. He had sweat rings under the arms of his light blue shirt.

The food came and was dispersed. The drinks were gone in no time, but only a couple of them were composed enough to eat.

"Mike, I didn't mean to leave you for last. I should have introduced each of you at the first meeting. Most of you have heard of Dr. DeRose and the wonderful studies he has done on religion."

Jude Johnson, the CIA director, nodded, "I think we have a whole file on him, don't we?" He looked at the Head of Homeland Security, who nodded back.

"No doubt," Jimmy said. "Dr. DeRose has great insight into religion in this and other countries. In one way or another, that is going to come into play."

Dr. DeRose was the only one at the table without notes.

"I agree," Dr. DeRose said. "When punishment is no longer enforced, a group think situation is the only glue that will hold a society together. Religion is our best group think vehicle."

Secret Blood

He stood, "Without our interference nearly all practicing Christians will find refuge in the church. Of the remaining population of the non-practicing population, forty percent will also look to the church for answers. This reflects our country and the rest of the world.

"The numbers for Buddhists and Hindus are nearly the same as the Christians. The nonracial Muslims and the Jewish religion will be even higher. This is good news; they will follow their religious leaders. If we factor out all the students and the unemployed people of the world, then exclude the religious, we are left with a relatively small group who could cause problems in absenteeism."

"So you are saying that one religious leader can talk everybody into going to work when they know the world is going to end?" the President asked.

"This is where there are complications. The world does not have one religious leader. If we did there would be no wars. The Christians do not even agree among themselves. A large percentage here in the United States does not see the Pope as their leader, although in Europe they do. Throughout the world it would be very difficult to find enough common ground to even start."

"Well, then, what do you suggest?" Frank asked.

"Nothing," Dr. DeRose said. "I can think of nothing that would bring the religions of the world together."

Judge Aston said, "Why are we even worrying about this? Who cares what the Jews and Arabs do if this thing is going to smash into us anyhow?"

Jimmy rubbed his forehead. "We're preparing for what we can," he said. "Somehow I think this is important."

The President said, "Let's take a long break. Go out, have some lunch, clear your heads. Let's meet back here about six."

Chapter 50

Jimmy sat in his office looking out the window. The raindrops ran in disjointed paths down the pane. The grounds were soaked and dark puddles formed in the pavement he could see from his window. The trees were bare and in the distance he could make out the highway, an endless line of shapes and colors. Drivers singing along with the radio or thinking about work, not knowing that in a few days all this could be gone.

The destruction of the Earth was unimaginable. He could not comprehend the totality of it. He was sure it was weighing heavily on the others also. Maybe that is why he was so concerned about the effect before the collision. It was his way of dealing with the loss of the planet. His way of dealing was to work through it.

What would Patricia do when she heard the news? Would she think of him? Would she pick up the kids and run back here to Washington? Nothing like a world crisis to bring the family back together. Enough's enough, he thought, I'm calling her right now. But his hand wouldn't move, it lay zombie-like on the desk. He couldn't do it. He wasn't calling because he wanted to apologize, he was calling because he was scared. And because he might never see her again once the trouble started. Calling would be like giving up and not finding a way to do his job. It was a crutch and he didn't want it.

I walked into the Chief of Staff's office feeling about as out of place as a priest at a biker rally. I wore a large name tag on a lanyard around my neck. No one I passed said anything, but they all squinted to see my name. I'm not sure they didn't break into smiles as they passed, laughing at the interloper in the wrong kind of clothing.

The secretary was startled at my sudden appearance at her desk. I suppose she was not used to walk up customers. I tried my best smile.

"Do you have an appointment?" she asked, looking at her desk blotter which was pristine in its emptiness.

"No," I said holding up my nametag. "But I got one of these."

She reached down and pushed a button on her phone without taking her eyes off of me. "Someone with a name tag to see you Mr. Reinhart."

The inner office door opened and Jimmy stuck his head out. He smiled and waved me in.

"I thought you were a member of the committee," he said and sat down.

"What committee?" I asked.

"Thank you, Kim," he said to her. "So are you just walking around, watching the wheels of bureaucracy in motion?"

"Wheels inside of wheels, I've heard. No, I've been sent to ask when we can leave. Simon and Shine are going stir crazy and Emmanuel wants to go back to Africa. And I have to admit, the walls are starting to close in on me also," I said. He motioned for me to sit on a black leather couch, then walked around his couch and sat.

He turned away and stared out the window to his left. He tapped a pencil on the desk. For the first time I saw him as a man, not the second most powerful man in the country. He was a little frail from this view, and it kind of unnerved me. He didn't look like the man I met in the church or the one that had eaten dinner with us. He was becoming a shell.

"I didn't know why I brought him here at first." He spoke slowly and carefully. "I did it without hesitation or regard for anyone's well-being. But now I'm starting to wonder."

The intercom buzzed and we both jumped.

"A Dr. DeRose to see you Mr. Rienhart. He does not have an appointment either." Jimmy smiled again.

"Of course it would be Dr. DeRose, Send him in."

Dr. DeRose was as dumbfounded as I, when he walked in.

"Well, Father, I thought your clandestine adventure with the administration was finished, but I must be mistaken," he said in his formal voice.

I asked him what had brought him here, to the White House. He looked at Jimmy. Jimmy had a shrewd smile that was not there before. He was the only person who knew the pieces to both puzzles.

Jimmy said, "Why not," and explained the whole Ghost mess to me. I was shocked to say the least. I began to tear up. I don't know why exactly, it wasn't for me. Maybe it was the sadness for those who would never know happiness or love. Or maybe it was for those who would lose it. Like those who became aware, I had feelings beyond my ability to explain.

DeRose, seeing my discomfort, asked me why I was with the Chief of Staff. I glanced at Jimmy and he nodded. He already knew part of the story. I told him everything he did not know and Jimmy filled in his part. Dr. DeRose didn't think his story could be trumped. He realized he was wrong.

At the end, the three of us sat motionless for a while.

Finally Jimmy said, "Am I the only one seeing something here?"

"Certainly not," Dr. DeRose said. Now he looked a little shaky.

I consider myself fairly sharp, but by no means in the same league with these two. They were both becoming excited and animated. I did not understand what they were talking about. But, whatever it was, I seemed to be a big part of it.

Jimmy picked up the phone. "Kim, get me Director Snider at the FBI. Yeah, I'll hold." He looked over to DeRose, "Wait till you meet him." He tapped his pencil rapidly. "Hey, I know I already owe you. Yeah, listen; you know the situation you helped me with before? I need everything you have on it; every scrap, DNA markers, pictures. And start digging again. Put everybody you got on it. It doesn't have to be quiet any more. E-mail it to my secretary. I don't think I can get outside e-mail on this computer. Okay send it right now." He hung up. "Now we're rolling."

DeRose looked at me and asked, "Father, do you believe in destiny?"

Chapter 51

"Destiny?" I asked.

"Maybe even more than destiny. A Divine plan. The events that are unraveling as we speak may have been set in motion thousands of years ago." DeRose stood. He was not a man to allow a dramatic moment to pass without making sure everyone was aware of it.

"We have been brought together for a reason. Think of all the twists and turns our lives have taken to bring us together at this moment. Then think of the unusual way we have handled circumstances lately.

Jimmy, I've been wondering, once you got the journals, why didn't you destroy them? Why bring Emmanuel here? It was not the prudent thing for this administration to do. I've seen you defend your brother like a mother tiger and yet you set him up for a possibly devastating blow. He would have been blamed even though he was by no means responsible. He would have been eaten alive for this and you didn't see it."

He paused for a second, and then looked at me. "Why didn't you turn the journals over to the diocese? What possessed you to go to the people you did? If you were a popular priest with a growing parish you wouldn't have risked it."

"Are you saying that God never wanted me to be a good priest? That he wanted me to fail?" I asked.

"What did all your instructors tell you? You had the spirit but not the gifts you needed in the pulpit. I think you are doing this because God knew you were the right person. This fills your gaps, you need to serve God but not in the usual way."

I thought of Emmanuel's story about Mother Teresa. She called it, the calling inside the calling. I handled being on the run better than my weekly homily. I carried Jesus' blood better than his message.

"And you, Mr. Rienhart," he said to Jimmy. "What burden have you had that has caused you to act differently?"

Jimmy was looking out the window again but was listening to us. He frowned. "My wife has left me. I didn't realize this until now, but I probably would not have brought Emmanuel here if things were right at home. I wouldn't have felt the need. I wouldn't have felt so lost or…"

"Hopeless," I interjected, knowing how I felt.

"Hopeless is the perfect word for my situation," Dr. DeRose said. "Prostate cancer. Fast growing, according to the doctor. I too, feel the need to be here."

"I'm sorry," I said.

"No need," he said. "That is of little consequence considering the planet's situation."

The intercom buzzed. "Mr. Reinhart, I'm receiving e-mail from the FBI. I'm not sure I'm supposed to see this."

"It's all right Kim, just forward it in here." He checked the printer to see if the paper tray was full.

"I'm going to print it all." A few keystrokes later the printer was humming and paper began to spew into a tray. Jimmy started to browse through it on the monitor. There were over seven hundred pages. Too much to view and understand now. It would have to be divvied out and analyzed by someone, but whom? Maybe DeRose had a staff that might know what was important and what wasn't.

He noticed an attachment for photos and clicked on it. There were a number of pictures of Emmanuel, some looked like photos taken for ID badges, and others were group shots of him with villagers. Older black and whites of him as a boy with groups of nuns. Another series were photos of documents, like immigration papers and passports and medical records.

The last section caught Jimmy's eye. A group of six photos that were tagged Smithsonian Institute. He clicked. The goose bumps were back.

There, as photographed for documentation, was an alabaster jar. Discolored, but in pristine condition, it sat on a purple cloth. It was shot from all four directions, plus one from straight down with the lid off, and from the bottom. A gloved hand held it over on its side exposing the bottom and a small hole that had been drilled there.

"My God," Jimmy said with such emotion that Dr. DeRose and I looked up. "Come here and look at this." He pushed the monitor back so when we came around his desk we could see.

"That's it, that's the way he got the Savior's blood," Dr. DeRose said. "There is a hole drilled in the bottom."

It hit the three of us at the same time, exactly what we were looking at. The blood of Christ dried in the desert and passed through history. I felt His presence. It was palpable. The monitor began to swim as my tears welled. With no preamble, each of us made the sign of the cross. I'm not exactly sure why.

It was obvious the jar had not been restored in any way. Tiny threads of cracks like spider webs covered the lid and bottom.

Age had made the scratches around the middle of the jar more visible. They had symmetry or a rhythm that looked both organic and manmade. Clicking around the pictures, the scratches made a pattern that repeated itself four times, so at every angle you could see the same markings.

"I don't understand what this is," Dr. DeRose said, referring to the markings. "There are not enough lines to be a language. They almost look like the scribbling of a child."

Jimmy was seated behind his desk. Dr. DeRose and I were on either side of him, leaning on the desk and studying the monitor. He looked up suddenly and rolled his chair back and looked to his left, out the window. He rolled back to the screen.

"It's a drawing," he said. "You're not going to believe this one." He slid the monitor forward and turned it so the window was behind it.

The view from the window was partly of the D.C. skyline with just the tip of the Washington Monument in the distance. The naked branches of the trees dominated the foreground. They looked like a child's scribbles. The skyline, if etched, looked like a series of vertical and horizontal lines. It made no sense unless you could see the real thing, which was on the screen.

It was an exact rendering, in lines, of the view from their window.

Chapter 52

Jimmy stood before the committee. Even though he was convinced, convincing the others could be a problem. Explaining it in words took the power out of it. He had considered using a Power Point to show the jar, but that cheapened it. Using the blood of Christ to solidify a point was something he could not bring himself to do.

"What are we doing about the thing itself?" the Judge asked. He, of all others, looked the most frightened. Jimmy guessed the Judge's blood pressure was up several points, and his eyes were puffy and red. Probably been drinking too.

"The President and his science adviser, Dr. White, have considered a few different alternatives, none of which seem very promising. Frank, would you like to elaborate on that?" Jimmy asked.

"The problem is, we have to know what it is before we start trying to destroy it. The panel we created to gather information was in disagreement on its composition. Many thought it was comprised of Dark Matter, but the jury is still out on its characteristics. It may be a concentrated mass of neutrinos. Shooting it with a laser, which is still a possibility, could be even worse than an impact. We could start a molecular chain reaction. That could give birth to a new sun closer than the moon. We're dealing with real science fiction stuff."

"What about HARP?" the Judge asked.

"No," said Frank. "Sound waves may be a solution, but HARP produces too small of an area and the waves bounce back off the ionosphere."

"Well, we got to do something. We can't just sit here on our hands, the American people are our responsibility," he said looking frenzied.

"We are doing what we can," the President said sharply.

"I think this committee needs to concentrate on the problem at hand, which is to keep the world safe after word gets out on a possible impact," Jimmy said. The President glared at the Vice President, but kept quiet.

"I'm going to propose something. I want you to hear me out because this may come out of left field, but I think this is exactly what we need to keep order."

He started with the call from Dr. DeRose, about getting the journals and tracking down the clone, and bringing him to the US. Then told them about the gunfight where no one was injured, and then about meeting this amazing man who only worked to help others. Finally he spoke of the jar photos and how the etchings mirrored the view from his window.

"I think he should be the face of reason. He could ask the people to go to their jobs and keep to their posts, to keep the country running as smoothly as possible."

Dr. DeRose was the only person looking back at him. Each of the other members looked at their notes, or their hands, or at the President who was also looking away. He had lost them. They didn't believe a word.

"No, I have to disagree. The President is the person the people will respond to. We have to have a known leader, not an unknown," Gen. Parker said.

"The General is right," said Ken Jenkins of Homeland Security. "In no way can the President relinquish power; the bad guys would not hesitate to strike. They will see it as a sign of weakness."

Dr. DeRose stood. "But you said they would attack as soon as they learned the Earth's fate anyway. So that is not an issue here. I do not see this as giving up any power; we have two unprecedented situations here. I know minds such as yours do not believe in coincidences. 'Acumens' Razor', ladies and gentlemen—all things being equal, the simplest solution is usually correct.

"I submit that since these are not random acts, there is reasoning behind it. And that God, in his infinite wisdom, is allowing us the decision to choose Jesus or not. This, my friends, may be the Second Coming."

No one else was convinced. They looked at DeRose as they had looked at Jimmy, like they had lost their minds. But their vote was not requested or needed. This was the President's decision to make, and his alone.

"What do you think, Mr. President?" DeRose asked.

He looked at his brother for a long time.

"What are you trying to do, Jimmy? We worked so hard to get here, and you want me to give it up? You've been different lately and I've gone along with most of your ideas, but I can't this time. Let's say the thing turns around and flies back into space. I'd never win a reelection cowering behind a clone, if that's what he really is."

Jimmy was stunned. And hurt.

"Let's do this," the President said. "When the news breaks I will address the matter rationally and we will see what happens."

"That's the plan?" Dr. DeRose asked. "We'll see what happens?"

The President said, "Stay in town, I will be calling all of you, when things begin to happen. We can discuss strategy then." He stood and walked out without another word to his brother.

Jimmy and DeRose veered to the side as the others left the room. Judge Aston stepped up to them.

"I don't know what you're playing at, but I know you're not this dumb. Listen, I'm next in line after the President and I will not allow you to slip some "peacenik" in ahead of me. Do you hear? I don't care if he can walk across the reflecting pool, I'm the Vice President!"

They watched him walk away. "Jimmy, my friend," Dr. DeRose said, "that's what I love about you, you make friends wherever you go."

Chapter 53

"They didn't go for it?" I said. "How could they not?" I was absolutely shocked. I waited in Jimmy's office with a growing feeling of comfort; a feeling that everything was going to be all right. Like the feeling of going to sleep as a child, knowing your parents were right across the hall.

"I think the idea lost some of its punch in the retelling," Jimmy said. They both walked in and sat heavily on the couch. Jimmy loosened his tie and kicked off his loafers. "And now my brother thinks I'm losing my mind and the Vice President believes I'm cutting him out of the batting order."

"All is not lost," DeRose said. "We've presented an idea. They didn't like it, but have not come up with a better one. Let it stew in their minds. If we are right and this is God's plan, I'm sure we will get some help from somewhere."

"You mean we should do nothing and wait for Divine inspiration?" I asked.

"No, no," he said. "We need to work hard on this. I'm saying we are not alone in our efforts." He put his fingers to his temples and rubbed in a circular motion. "We need to convince the President, but we can't be the ones doing the convincing. It can't be Emmanuel because he is the one the power is being transferred to, so he cannot seem too anxious. The President would think that was really fishy. So the only people left are the committee members. We need to work on them individually. Decide what we can do to change their minds."

"I'll go along with that, but the clock is ticking. It could be five days or five minutes," Jimmy said.

"I agree with all that," I said. "But none of this is going to happen if Emmanuel disappears, and I think he is almost to the point of trying to sneak out of here. If we tell him what is going on and that he can help, I think he'll stay."

"Okay, I'll cut Shine and the other guy loose," Jimmy said. "I'll look into some background of the committee members, DeRose, you do some lobbying, and Father, you talk to Emmanuel. All three of us should do some praying."

Chapter 54

From what I could gather, much of the White House staff was eager to see Simon go. Apparently he thought his ID badge allowed him access to all parts of the building. He walked in on meetings, gave suggestions to speechwriters and policy makers, and bothered all female employees to no end. He had a small stash of coffee cups, pens, windbreakers and towels in his room. Anything he could find with a White House logo, he lifted.

At one point he stopped a group of cattlemen who were invited to a lunch with the President and the Senators from Texas. The President was not able to attend, much to the dismay of the Senators. But Simon treated them to a shortened speech on how to water the dry areas of Texas.

Shine mostly stayed in his room, much to the relief of everyone involved with security. They were happy it was the goofy guy running around, not the scary one.

Without anything to pack, the good-byes took only a few minutes. We shook hands in the hall and told each other we would get together again and meant it. When the men came to escort them to the van, Simon stepped back into his room and returned with a bulging sheet slung over his shoulder like some kind of Santa Clause. Its weight caused him to stumble and bounce against the wall. Shine shook his head.

"I'm sorry sir, you will not be allowed to take anything from the building," the man with the ear piece said.

"What? You mean these things? Babe, these are mementos from the President, we had dinner the other night. Do you see this damn name tag?"

"Sir, it looks like you have a chair wrapped up in there."

It did. Four distinct bumps protruded from the bottom.

"No, man. Those are ink pens, they just in there at a funny angle."

Shine said, "Leave it."

Simon looked at him, then made a face like he had bitten into a lemon.

"Man, can't a brother make a dollar. It's the man holdin' me back again."

He let the sack drop to the carpet. There was a distinct sound of heavy porcelain butting together. They walked out, following the men in navy blazers, with Simon's voice trailing off; "Man, I thought you had my back, but nooo. Leave it here he says …"

Chapter 55

"So you and I are staying?" Emmanuel said. We sat on the couch in his room. I was uncomfortable sitting and turning sideways so I moved to a wingback chair opposite him. He wore the same white cotton shirt and jeans but for some reason it looked a little whiter. Perhaps it was a better grade of laundry soap here at the White House.

"There are some things I've only recently become aware of. I would be remiss not speaking of them. I think the country is going to need your help," I said. He nodded.

I waited for a reaction, or questions, but none came. He simply nodded. He folded his legs under himself and sat quietly in that celestial way he had.

He looked at me and saw what must have been a quizzical expression on my face. "I figured as much. I was brought here for a reason."

"No, I didn't know about this until just recently," I tried to explain.

He held his hand up and smiled. "This has happened to me my entire life, although now, it happens more and more often. People, good people, want me around for reasons they do not understand or cannot explain. Then, later there is a need for me to be there." He smiled self-consciously.

"I knew when Mr. Rienhart brought me here without his brother's approval. And you, without any regard for you own safety were instrumental in my being here. Neither of you knew why. God's plans are not easily outlined for us. If they were, we would probably want a say in them."

"Have you always known this? You have an aura about you. You have something special, a gift?"

"I'm not so sure it's special, different perhaps. You must remember that being reared in a convent and mothered by nuns gave me an altered perspective. In retrospect I think they knew more than I did about this gift as you call it. Looking back, there is a feeling that I was being prepared for something, that I had a goal only they knew. I didn't realize any of this until the President informed me of my ancestry. I didn't understand why I was made to learn so many languages, or made to read all the other religious books along with the Bible."

I thought about what Dr. DeRose said, about the events being set into motion thousands of years ago.

"There is something in space, the news channels are calling it 'The Ghost'," I said. "It's on a collision course with earth. Only a few people know that. No one knows what it is or what it will do."

Saying it again brought back the fear. It curdled in my stomach and rose up in my throat. I felt drops of sweat pop on my forehead. I saw my parishioners, alone with no one to console them. I felt the agony of pregnant women who may never live to bring a life. After a moment I realized that I had been staring at the deep blue carpet. I looked up and saw that Emmanuel was watching me. His eyes were what? Glittering? A feeling of total calm washed over me. My arms were covered with goose bumps. I was able to steady myself and continue.

"The powers that be; are worried about public reaction. Will the nation become hysterical? Will we become violent? How will the other nations react? They want to do everything to prevent panic from destroying the earth before The Ghost has a chance to."

Again he did not have much of a reaction. He readjusted himself and looked at me.

"And what is it I shall do?" he asked.

"I think you are here to save us," I blurted out. I wouldn't have said it a minute ago, but there it was—lying out there like a bad line from a Superman movie.

"We think you are here to save us," I didn't want to sound like I was crazy, alone.

"You see me as a clone of Christ," he said. "I'm a man, no matter how I was conceived or ill conceived. To put your faith in anything, other than God, is wrong."

It was the harshest I had heard him speak. We sat in silence still facing each other. The building was very still. The sky was darkening enough that you could see the grounds outside the window and see just the hint of a reflection of the two of us, sitting in the room.

"Who are 'we'?" he asked.

"Jimmy, Dr. DeRose, and myself. You have not met DeRose, but he believes as strongly as I do."

"And the President?" he asked.

"He has not yet given it his full attention," I lied.

"So he does not believe as you do?"

I hesitated, then said, "He has not seen the things we have seen nor felt the revelations that were shown to us. He'll come around and see the light. Dr. DeRose is working on that, we all are. I wanted you to know the truth, about us staying, about the thing in space, about what we are doing to present you to the people. I just hope I'm up to the task. Sometimes I do not feel I'm worthy to do the Lord's work."

"Oh, ye of little faith," he said. Then he smiled.

Chapter 56

"He wants you out, both of you," Jimmy said. "I'm very sorry, but I can't do anything." Then he winked at me. We stood in the doorway to my room. It was still dark outside and sleet was tapping against my window.

"He thinks you two are affecting my judgment. You can call someone to meet you and I'll have an agent drop you off. I'll escort Emmanuel to the plane myself. Let me know when you are packed and you can get your life back to normal. Make the drop off place somewhere public but not too public."

I couldn't believe it; we were getting thrown out of the White House after being invited here. Jimmy was referring to the President when he said 'he'. And once I gave it a moment's thought, I wasn't surprised at all. We had been a distraction at best, and now we were becoming dangerous by influencing his brother. If I were in his shoes I probably would do the same thing.

But the wink told me Jimmy had a plan. So I didn't object and immediately and called Father Craig since he was really the only friend I had left. I was sure he would be home on a sleeting Wednesday morning, although probably not up yet.

"I'll be seeing you around," he said and stuck out his hand. I felt something in it. I shook it and he smoothly transferred a piece of paper into mine. He smiled and nodded.

Secret Blood

Before I packed, I took the paper into the shower and opened it. Either I was becoming more aware of surveillance or more paranoid, I wasn't sure which. The only thing written on the paper was a phone number.

We decided the drop off point would be McDonalds on Glass Ave. At nine thirty in the morning it was the closest open restaurant to Father Craig. The weather was getting worse. Sleet and freezing rain were gathering on trees and power lines. The footing on the sidewalks was dicey and several accidents were already slowing traffic on the beltway. Headline News was reporting that delays of several hours were to be expected at the airports.

The black van pulled to the curb and we stepped out carrying our belongings in military style duffel bags. Inside Father Craig sat in a booth by himself sipping coffee. He froze when he saw Emmanuel. His typical smirky-smile dropped and he stared.

As we neared the booth he stood and didn't say anything, which was not the Craig I knew. I introduced them. There was an uncomfortable silence. Emmanuel sensed this and said, "Would it be all right if I ordered some food? I've always wondered what it would be like to do that."

"Sure," I said, and then realized I didn't have any money. I knew Emmanuel didn't either.

"Could we borrow a couple of bucks?" I asked Father Craig.

He reached into his back pocket and pulled out his wallet. Opening it, he counted out some ones. It must have broken his awe, because he said, using one of his lines he used on any of us that had ever borrowed money from him. "I always like to help the less fortunate." When he realized what he had said he was horrified.

"Thank you," Emmanuel said, and got in line. Father Craig and I sat.

"I can't do this, why didn't you warn me?" he said, not taking his eyes off of Emmanuel.

"What?" I asked.

"He looks just like Him, I mean, it's like it's Him."

"Maybe it is," I said.

Other people were looking at him now. The customers in line were inching nearer. A couple to his left were whispering to each other and looking him over. A little girl, probably three years old, left her family in a booth and stood beside him in line. She reached for his hand just as her mother got there. The mother muttered an apology and dragged the youngster back to the booth.

"It's like you take whatever you think Jesus is and dress him in our clothes, and he is standing right in front of us. It's more than just what he looks like. Watch how they react to him," Father Craig said.

Emmanuel was at the front of the line now and the McDonalds guy was smiling as he took the order. A short pudgy girl working the fry baskets looked around and stared. She said something to the employees working behind the warmers. Faces started popping through the openings between the stainless steel.

That's when I noticed it. His shirt, under the olive green coat, was whiter. So were his eyes and teeth. In contrast to his dark skin he was nearly glowing. There was an aura around him and it was affecting the people near him.

The guy that took the order shook his head several times. He was refusing to take the money. I saw Emmanuel take the money and stick it in a clear plastic barrel on the counter. It was a March of Dimes container. He lifted the tray and began walking our way. The crowd parted, smiling and nodding to him as he passed.

He sat the tray down and slid in beside Father Craig. He had ordered a small fry and water. He offered to share the fries with us.

He looked around at the other customers, who quickly looked somewhere else, realizing they were staring. We had the attention of the entire restaurant.

"They are using ketchup on their French fries. Is that a custom here?" he asked.

"Yeah, let me get you some," I said and slid out of the booth. I squirted some into the tiny paper cups provided at the condiment table and set them on his tray.

"I thought ketchup was used for hotdogs and hamburgers," he said. He took one, dipped the end, and tasted the fry. He didn't like it, although he tried not to show it.

"It's all right, I don't like them with ketchup either," I said.

"I do not like wasting the ketchup," he said looking around. "Would anyone like some extra ketchup?" he said loudly. Everyone looked in our direction. An elderly man in a navy parka and green work pants got up from his booth and hobbled over. Emanuel smiled and handed it to him. The man nodded and turned, and I could swear he stood a little straighter and walked more smoothly on the way back to his seat. Father Craig noticed it also.

"What now?" Father Craig asked.

"I think we go back to the church and wait," I said.

"Wait for what?" Father Craig asked.

"I don't know," I said. "I don't think we're driving this bus anymore."

"I don't think you ever have been," he said.

Chapter 57

Father Craig was as nervous as I had ever seen him. Emmanuel had taken the front seat and I sat in the back. I'm not sure if he was tense from driving with such a valuable passenger in the front seat or from Emmanuel's questions about the church and its policies. Regardless, Father Craig relaxed a bit when Emmanuel asked about the radio. It seemed, in Africa, talk and informational shows took most of the radio channels. Emmanuel was interested in what people listened to in America.

"If you were not a Priest, but a businessman or a teacher in the car right now, what would you be listening to?" he asked us.

"No problem with that," Father Craig said. He turned on the radio to a classic rock station, relaxed his wrist on the steering wheel, and settled back into his seat.

As if on cue the first strands of a Doobie Brothers song began. From the back seat I looked into the rear view mirror at Father Craig. Our eyes met and I heard him breathe, "Unbelievable."

The song was, *Jesus Is Just All Right*.

We parked in front and entered the church as a cold wind swept down the street. A hollow metallic clanging rang from a flagpole as the wind slapped the cord with metal fittings against the aluminum pole. It was a lonely sound you would expect to hear on a vacant playground.

The large front door opened against the wind and we shuffled into the golden warmth of the church. The lighting was subdued in the entry, but inside the sanctuary hundreds of prayer candles flickered near the walls. Blue on the right and red on the left, they induced the same feeling as sitting in front of a giant fireplace. The majesty of the room opened before us with the huge vaulted ceilings and the massive altar. The altar was not as grand as the one in the President's church, but that did not diminish its passion. In the center, illuminated by the most intense lighting in the room, was the crucifix.

We stood in the wide center aisle, three abreast, as Jesus, on the cross, gazed down upon us. The power of the moment was lost on no one. There was a tangible feeling of God, and love, and absolution in this place. The wind gusted outside and a low whistling escaped the windows. Instead of feeling the cold, I felt warmer and more connected to God than I ever had; a rush of love, as if God had just smiled.

Emmanuel turned to me. "I would like to receive communion."

I hesitated for only a second and looked at Father Craig. He nodded slowly. I could not think of a greater honor. A month ago I could not have done it.

As Father Craig and I prepared, I found my hands were trembling. He was unusually quiet also. I don't know what he was thinking but he had lost, at least temporarily, his sense of irony.

Emmanuel was kneeling in the front pew. During the time I had known him, I had not thought of him as Catholic, even though I knew nuns raised him. Since I had known him he had been much more "priestly" than I. But he had asked me. And I felt more than a small amount of pride in that. I knew that was wrong, but I would be lying to myself if I couldn't admit it.

We donned our vestments and took the wine and wafers to the table. I felt a part of history, and wondered if the three wise men knew they were a part of Christ's story two thousand years later.

By the time we changed and put things away it was midafternoon. I was hungry and I figured Father Craig was too. Emmanuel was never hungry. He could go all day without showing any sign he needed something to eat.

I was nearly ready to say that lunch had passed us by when Father Craig's cell rang. He answered and slowly walked away from us, talking quietly.

Emmanuel looked at me and smiled for some reason. He looked genuinely happy, not the "I'm just doing this until I can get a plane back to Africa" look. His grin became more sheepish.

"What?" I asked.

"What do you mean? What?" he asked.

"Why are you looking at me with that grin on your face?" I said.

"I think I am going to be able to help," he said.

"You agreed to do that before."

"Yes, but now I'm happy about it," he said.

I stared at him and resisted the urge to cock my head.

Father Craig walked briskly back toward us.

"We have a bit of a situation," he said. "I am going to have to leave you two for a while. You can make yourselves at home; there should be some food in the fridge." He started to walk by us.

Emmanuel touched him softly on the arm as he passed. "Where are you going?" he asked.

I'm not sure whether it was the touch or that the question was asked so directly, but I knew Father Craig was going to answer it truthfully. He glanced at me, and then turned to Emmanuel.

"That was Mr. Stubbs. Shine has been taken into custody. If it were Simon I wouldn't have been surprised, but not Shine. Shine is too much in control to allow himself to be arrested. The whole thing was strange."

"Shouldn't he handle this, it is more up his alley than yours?" I said.

"That's what he wanted to know. He could call the lawyers, but once push comes to shove, it's public knowledge. He wanted to do what would jeopardize our relationship the least and that turns out for me to go and try to smooth the waters before things get out of hand."

"What is he charged with?" I asked.

"Nobody really knows yet. He was caught hanging around a school."

"A school?" I said.

"Yep, like I said it's weird. He had been sitting in his car all morning watching the kids and someone called the police. I think there was probably a scene when they tried to take him in."

"Then we should go help our friend," Emmanuel said as he gathered his coat.

"No, no. I'll take care of this, you two go to the parsonage and relax for a while. Have some stew, watch a little TV," Father Craig said.

I knew right off, this was of no interest to Emmanuel. He was not the kind of person to just kick back. It was not the way he relaxed.

Father Craig realized this too and said, "The station house will be packed; it's not a nice place to be. It'll be full up with criminals."

Emmanuel's face lit up. Father Craig realized this was exactly the wrong thing to say to him.

"This place, this is where the troubled and the needy are taken?"

Father Craig looked to me for help. I had to shake my head.

"He's not going to stay behind now. The three of us might as well get going and not waste time arguing," I said.

Father Craig gave a resigned look. Emmanuel smiled knowingly. We got our coats and left, without eating a bite.

Chapter 58

What normally would have taken twenty minutes took an hour and a half. The road conditions had improved but downed power lines and stop lights that only blinked yellow brought the flow of traffic to a standstill. Parking for the station was in a lot to the left of the main building. It had been plowed and a wall of chunky mush rimmed the perimeter. A uniformed guard raised a mechanical gate without offering to slide his window open. He pointed to the multitude of empty spaces.

The plants around the building had been rounded and mutated into glassy lumps of ice with portions of yew frozen just below the surface. The sidewalk was sprinkled with salt which left it sporadically wet and slippery. Near the door was a 'No Smoking on the Premises' sign and under it a blue plastic trash can containing sand but was now covered with ice two inches thick.

As the doors slid open, Walmart style, we were hit by a blast of hot air. Another sign asked us to press a button and wait for assistance. Father Craig sidled his way to the front and said, "Let me do the talking here. I know some of these officers and I don't want to come off as meddling." Before he could press the button, the door behind them opened again, and the heater shot another blast of hot air.

"Well, what we got here looks like a large percentage of all my white friends!" Simon said, smiling and strolling in out of the cold.

"Probably about ninety nine percent of all your friends' are right here," Father Craig said. Simon shook hands with us then pressed the button before Father Craig could stop him.

"Bubba, you on duty tonight?" he said into the speaker. "Put those doughnuts away and let us in."

A metallic voice replied, "Get out of here, Simon."

Simon looked up at a camera in the corner or the room.

"What you mean get out of here? I got a right to city property. My tax dollars are payin' for those Krispy Kreme's you got hidden under your desk."

The laughter from the speaker made the tin around it buzz. "Your tax dollars? You ain't ever done anything legal enough to pay taxes. Go on home."

Simon turned sideways and leaned on the button with his shoulder. When the speaker came on again they could hear a buzzer whining away inside. He kept leaning. Bubba's voice came through so loud his words were unintelligible, the speaker blared. Simon smiled at us and kept leaning.

Finally the door swung open and a very large, red faced officer came out. His shirt was pulled taunt across his belly and the collar strained to hold back his neck. His movements were quick, and even though he was fat, there was hardness under it. He reached for Simon and grabbed him by the front of his shirt with one ham-sized hand. It looked as though his feet were barely brushing the floor. Simon kept smiling like this was the result he had expected.

"I expect you'd like to know that the gentleman in the collar is my spiritual guide and the other two are my legal representatives."

Bubba looked at Father Craig, who still wore his collar, then at Emmanuel and me.

"They don't look like no legal representatives," Bubba said.

"They from the ACLU, kind of nonconformist," Simon said. Bubba released his grip.

"Now we on the same page," Simon said straightening his shirt and coat. "We're here to see Shine, where you keeping him?"

Before Bubba could answer, Emmanuel walked through the open door into the booking area. Father Craig and I followed; I could hear Bubba yelling at us from the lobby.

The area was bathed in bright florescent lights. There were maybe a dozen desks with inexpensive office chairs around each. Officers occupying the desks were typing or reading reports. Another pair was talking to a suspect they were booking. Cameras were mounted on the walls and on the ceiling so every part of the room could be videotaped.

Two officers sat talking and drinking coffee at a desk in the corner of the room. They glanced at us as we entered but paid little attention until one focused in on Emmanuel. He put his cup down and stared.

Of course Emmanuel was in a place where people were scared and needed help—a place where he thought he could comfort someone. He marched to the nearest desk and knelt beside a girl with neon green hair and black lipstick. They talked softly while the police officer watched in amazement. He stopped typing and listened to Emmanuel. At one point both the officer and the girl nodded collectively.

The two officers in the corner were now in a serious conversation and kept glancing in our direction. I had a sinking feeling.

A set of metal double doors were framed in the back of the room, the kind that swung both ways. Probably for suspects that were unruly or so drunk they had to be carried to a cell. At the back desk one of officers stood and pushed his way through these doors. The other walked toward us and said something to Bubba, who had just reentered the room.

They spoke for a moment and looked at Emmanuel. Bubba rested his hand on his gun holster and walked over and tapped Emmanuel on the shoulder. Father Craig, Simon, and I followed.

"I'd like to see some I.D.," Bubba said to Emmanuel.

Emmanuel looked at me, not scared but a little uncertain. "I have no I.D., at least not here with me in this country," he said.

"What's wrong?" Simon said. "What you botherin' my man for?" He tried to step between him and Emmanuel. With a sweep of his arm Simon was sent flying across the room. Before I knew what was happening I was bent over a desk and felt steel clamp my wrists together. Officers swarmed in through the double doors and overwhelmed us. I could hear Simon yelling in the background and the crashes of office equipment breaking on the floor. Someone was applying pressure to my back, keeping my chest flat on the desktop. Emmanuel was in the same position on the desk next to me. A tiny smile crept across his face.

"Your authorities are certainly serious about identification in this country," he said.

The officers were having a much harder time corralling Simon. He was running down the aisles made by the rows of desks with a swarm of police in pursuit. Each time they had him cornered he would leap up onto a desk and jump to another then back on the floor. In the end they were smart enough to channel him into the corner of the room. Once he was tackled, plastic wrist restraints were used to secure his arms. He was fighting, spitting mad.

"You in real trouble now," he yelled. "Wait till my lawyer gets here! You got no right attacking us."

"I thought these were your lawyers," Bubba said. Simon fell silent for a moment.

"No, you moron, I said legal representatives."

"What is the problem, officer?" Father Craig asked. His voice was muffled as if he, too, were being bent over.

"At last one civil voice," Bubba said.

"Detective DeMoss recognized this man as the person on the video from the gang shoot out. He could be armed and dangerous. But we were only going to question him until Simon here started jumping around. So now you are all going to be held for questioning. Be glad you're not being held for resisting arrest."

That brought a chorus of shouts from everyone, including myself. But nevertheless we were marched through the double doors and out the back into cells. We were frisked then; our cell phones and personal effects were taken.

Just like in the movies, cells on both sides flanked the bright linoleum floor. Black iron bars ran from floor to ceiling and the walls were painted cinderblock. Our footsteps echoed. We each were placed in separate cells and the doors clanged closed behind us.

I heard Father Craig say, "How did that happen? We weren't doing anything and we end up here."

"Welcome to the black experience," Simon said.

Chapter 59

The place was quiet, so I thought we were the only ones incarcerated. There were four cells on the left and three on the right. Emmanuel was placed in the first on the right and I was placed in the second leaving the third empty. The first cell on the left was vacant, and then Simon, straight across from me, then Father Craig was in the third.

As we settled I saw movement in the last cell on the left. Someone moved to the bars at the front and tried to look down the row. I would not have seen him at all if I had not been across on the other side of the cells. The person's movements were silent, he was listening.

"Shine?" I said.

At first he said nothing, and then he moved out of sight and said, "Yeah."

After the trouble with Bubba, I had forgotten the reason we were here. We hadn't done such a great job of keeping things off the record and cordial. I could see no upside on any level.

"What you doin' Babe?" Simon shouted. There was only silence from the cell. We waited.

"You all right?" Simon said. He was directly across the aisle. He looked at me and raised his eyebrows. "This ain't like Shine.

He's not troubled by a little jail time. He too tuff to be all up tight over a small thing like this."

We waited. No one said anything for a while, each drifted into our own little world, wondering what it would be like to spend a longer amount in a place like this, and how long we would survive. I thought about The Ghost and if it did collide with the earth, how many prisoners would never feel freedom again, how many would die in a place like this?

I thought about each of the people that were here with me now and how I, since entering their lives, had led them right here to jail. I thought about Father Craig, who had the love and respect of an entire parish, sitting in his cell. I thought about Emmanuel, who was greeted by smiling and grateful people in each village, now incarcerated in our country of freedom. Had this also been in the grand plan set into motion two thousand years ago? Or had I bungled it into this dead end?

The double doors swung open and I heard footsteps. Before they got to us Simon began yelling.

"Hey, when do I get my phone call? You can't hold us here without reading us our rights! Who you think you dealing with, some juvenile delinquent?"

"Detective DeMoss will take your statements concerning the shootout. You will go one at a time," Bubba said as if he were reading off of a cue card. "Do not discuss anything with each other while you are waiting to be questioned. You are under surveillance and anything you say will be recorded and is admissible in court. Do you all understand?"

"I hope you understand," Simon yelled, "that you are going to be one sorry mother big time when I get my phone call. Cause I got big time friends now."

"Simon," Bubba said, "the only friends you got are locked up with you. Might call your Mama, but she's probably glad to be shed of you."

That brought a round of laughter from all the police in earshot.

"You leave my Mama out of this," Simon said in a distinctly docile voice.

"All right, you, Father, if you are a Priest. You're first." Bubba unlocked the cell door and slid it to the side. All the doors were heavy and needed oiled. He had to put his weight into it to get it to grudgingly roll open.

Father Craig stepped out and left with them without saying anything to us. Before they exited Bubba said, "We'll be back to get you Simon, probably around midnight." More laughter from the other officers.

We lapsed into silence again. I wondered how long we had been here. It seemed like hours but it may have only been a few minutes.

I heard Emmanuel stirring in his cell. He stepped up to the bars.

"Mr. Shine, are you all right?" he said.

There was nothing from Shine's cell. If I had not seen him earlier I would have thought the cell empty. My view allowed me only to see the front angle of his area. He must have been sitting on the aluminum bench at the rear of the cell.

"I sense you are very troubled by something. I would like to speak with you, if you would allow me."

"I'd like to talk, but in private, and I don't think that's going to happen in here."

Simon, across the aisle, had a view inside Emmanuel's cell that I did not. I could hear Emmanuel stir then I watched as Simon stood and gripped the bars and stared toward Emmanuel's cell.

Light pulsed from Emmanuel's cell and lighted even the back of Simon's cell. It reflected off the aluminum bench. I felt the tingling sensation on my neck and down my back. I looked at Simon and he was shivering too.

I heard Emmanuel say, "Ephphatha," and the cell door smoothly slid open. It softly clanged against the iron frame. The place was filled with his light. Not like a harsh florescent, but warm and golden, like a fond memory. As he moved out of his cell and into the hallway, the light filtered into the cells and created striped shadows on the floor. Moving between the cells soundlessly, he stepped to Shine's door.

He held his hand, fingers slightly apart, to the lock on Shine's door and repeated the word he had used before. "Ephphatha." It slid open and he entered.

Simon looked at me and said, "You better call the Pope. I believe Jesus is back."

I knelt there in my cell and crossed myself.

Chapter 60

Before long the door at the end of the hall clanged open and Detective DeMoss and Father Craig entered. The detective had Father Craig by the arm, but they both looked very relaxed, almost friendly. DeMoss quickly noticed the open cell door and reached for his gun, which was holstered on his belt. He pushed Father Craig to the wall, pulled the gun, and held it, barrel up, in his right hand. Then he spotted Shine's door ajar.

Simon jumped to the bars and looked down the hall toward the two men. DeMoss leveled the pistol at him, all the while pinning Father Craig to the wall. Simon smiled sweetly.

"Step back to the rear of the cell," DeMoss ordered.

I stood and looked out of my cell.

"You, too," DeMoss said, this time with a little more concern in his voice. He was slowly making his way down the hall, inching towards Shine's cell.

"I think you done tellin' us what to do. I was goin' to call the President. I know he could get us out of this jam. But I think we can even trump the President now," Simon smiled at me.

"How'd you get the door open?" DeMoss said, still trying to trick someone into giving away his position. He was not sure whom the empty cell belonged to.

"I wouldn't go down that aisle any farther if I was you," Simon said. "Lest you wanna get zapped by a blindin' light, you better be cool."

I was starting to see what Simon was trying to prevent. The closer DeMoss got, the more certain there would be some type of confrontation. I wasn't sure who needed to be more careful, the man with the gun, or Emmanuel. Either way the situation needed to be defused now before there was no way out.

Father Craig spoke for the first time. "Listen, I've called Dr. DeRose, and he is calling our other friend. We will be out of here in no time, so please everybody, calm down." He whispered to the detective, "Let me go down the hall and I will pull the door closed. You can stay here and keep the gun on me. They won't give me any trouble, I swear to you, I'll just close the door and walk right back into my cell."

"I don't want to have to shoot you, Father," said the detective, slowing to a stop and releasing his grip on Father Craig. The hum of the overhead lights grew louder and their light seemed a little brighter. DeMoss glanced side to side, then up to the lights. None of this was making any sense.

He kept the gun pointed at the Priest until he had done what he promised to do. Only when Father Craig wrestled his door shut did he lower the gun. He walked softly to Shine's door and peered around the edge of the frame. Emmanuel and Shine sat on the aluminum bench, praying.

"I'm going to ask you this one time. How did you get the door open?"

Emmanuel sat quietly until Shine finished his prayer. Then he stood and said, "Like this."

He repeated the word he has used before, Ephphatha, and the door slid open without being touched.

DeMoss didn't even react. He held his gun limply at his side and watched Emmanuel walk softly back into his cell. He didn't bother to close either door. He took a couple of steps and stopped, then looked back at the row of cells. There was a frightened look in his eyes as he turned and walked back out the double doors. His gun dangled at his side as he disappeared.

Father Craig was as taken aback as the detective, but being a man of God, he tried not to show it. He glanced at me, the best he could from the angle of our cells. I nodded, to let him know that it really happened, he wasn't seeing things. He closed his eyes and crossed himself.

After spending a few moments contemplating what had happened, and hearing no sound whatsoever I said, "Emmanuel, are you all right over there?"

"I'm not sure what is happening to me," he said in a small voice.

Chapter 61

The power of the White House is an amazing thing, within mortal terms of course. Within eight minutes of Father Craig making the call, the police station was awash with dark suits and headsets. The street hardened D.C. cops, were completely overwhelmed by the NSA. The perps, which consisted of two Priests, two gang members, and one illegal alien were released and taken back into custody for reasons of National security.

The station itself was ringed with dark colored SUV's with blacked out windows. Agents talked into their jacket sleeves and fanned out though the building. They cleared the room and confiscated all the arrest records for the group. The videotapes of the security cameras were removed and collected. They moved through the station calmly and efficiently.

The D.C. cops were outraged. But once phone calls were made and careers threatened, they begrudgingly relented. The agents, who were used to getting whatever they wanted, but always doing so politely, met the hard stares of the police with little notice and were allowed to remove the prisoners.

Father Craig was the only one of the group who had not been taken into custody before today and was reeling from the turn of

Secret Blood

events. The other four had been through capture and release and were beginning to believe it was part of the price paid for being near Emmanuel. That did not preclude Simon giving a little love back to Officer Bubba.

"Hey, Bubba, I told you I had friends in high places." He looked around at the other policemen in the room. "You need any help with anything, you know, in case a crime wave erupts or somethin', give me a call. I'll bring in my boys and we'll give a hand." He held his thumb and pinky to his ear and mouth and winked at Bubba as he passed.

We were led out and ushered into the back of one of the dark SUV's. Our days of trouble with the police were over, forever.

Chapter 62

John Thomas started out as most other part time astronomers. He loved looking into the sky. As a kid in West Virginia, summer was Little League, Johnny Quest, and his telescope. There was also an occasional trip to the Public Library for books on planets and stars.

The patio was the permanent stargazing platform. Ringed with citrine candles for his mother and plastic and aluminum lawn chairs for his father, the patio was his private center of the universe. Watermelon seeds spit out into the yard, and a transistor radio when the Pirates were playing, no music allowed, was what his dad called a little slice of heaven.

His dream was to work at the Green Bank Observatory, the world's largest telescope, which was conveniently located in West Virginia. But very inconveniently, the coal mines were there also. His dad was a miner, and very few miners of the era were left unscathed by black lung. His father was no different and died in his fifties leaving a wife and a son with no means to pursue his dream. A big university and at least a Master's degree was downgraded to the local liberal arts college and a teaching degree.

Downgraded was too negative of a term. He had a good life. The family was good, teaching high school science was rewarding, and summer vacation allowed for stargazing. Instead of the patio he had a deck, and the transistor radio was replaced with a laptop.

He felt a little disloyal to his father because he did listen to music instead of baseball. He listened to anyone from Yanni, to the Beatles, to Tesh, to the Stones, all the while clicking through star charts.

Tonight he was listening to the *Pirates of the Caribbean* sound track and plotting the course of the Ghost. It had been an obsession to him since the news channels had briefly reported it. His wife Lori said he was like Richard Dreyfuss in *Close Encounters*.

He was here on a cold evening, hoping the cloud cover would break and his laptop wouldn't freeze up. He wore his oversized down jacket and scarf and was, as his daughter told him, the definition of an astro-nerd.

The frightening images the President and his brother had seen had not been made public. So the semi-excitement over The Ghost had dwindled from the main stream news outlets. The scientific world was still very interested, but only in the way a paleontologist would be with a new bone. Most thought we had seen the last of it and worked on angles for grants to research the data that it behind.

John's wife, with a sweater wrapped around her shoulders, brought him out a cup of coffee after dinner. He took off his gloves and held it in both hands, the steam fogging up his glasses.

"So, Galileo, how's it going?" she said pulling the sweater a bit tighter.

"Well, so far, I can only find one little break in the clouds, and that isn't where I need to look," he said dimly. "The clouds are just hanging there, nothing's moving. The weather is just sitting here."

"Then why don't you point your telescope at the hole in the clouds, look there, then come inside. It's not like you can really see anything if the weather isn't cooperating."

"All right," he said, lying. "Let me change the coordinates and take a quick look, then I'll be in."

"Yeah, right," she moved toward the door. "I know you don't give up that easy."

He took a sip of the coffee. It was already starting to get cold. It didn't take him long to rearrange the telescope and find the opening. The scope was the best of a long line of scopes he had owned since childhood. It was only a few steps down from the weaker ones used at real observatories. Of course, what it was hooked to designated the real power. But this was almost perfect for his limited work.

It was wired to the laptop and although he could magnify using the arrow keys, he had to physically move the scope to adjust the area. He did this while viewing through the weaker side scope then switching to the main scope while watching the monitor.

Once he found the hole in the clouds it was only a matter of minutes until his findings reached the President of the United States.

Chapter 63

The SUV cruised along the beltway with the five fugitives in the back two rows. The driver was alone in the front and watching traffic, he acted like they were not there. When they asked where they were being taken, he explained the Chief of Staff had given instructions to take them to his private residence. The snow was drifting down and flattening against the windshield.

"So what's up with you? Hangin' out in front of a school, man, that ain't like you," Simon turned around in his seat and asked Shine, who was in the back row.

Shine looked out the window at the passing cars, their headlights now becoming necessary. He looked at Emmanuel. Emmanuel nodded.

"I have a daughter." He hesitated for a moment to steady himself. "She goes to that school, I wanted to see her, you know, I wanted to know how she's getting along, how she plays with the other kids."

"What are you talkin' about, I don't know nothin' 'bout you havin' a daughter?" Simon looked almost hurt.

"When her mother got pregnant I got these feelings that I never even knew I had. I was happy, I was even lookin' forward to getting married," he took a resigned breath and continued. "We didn't tell anybody because we were in the middle of a turf war. I was scared she might get involved, you know kidnapped or worse if the other gang knew it was my baby."

He looked down at the darkness between his shoes. "I got jammed up and had to leave town until things cooled down. I should have told Mr. Stubbs about them, but too many things were going on at the time. If I'd have told him he would have given us protection and I could'a stayed, but I didn't. Her mom died during childbirth. I wasn't around when it happened and didn't know until a couple of days after."

Simon looked stunned. The SUV turned off onto a smaller street and rolled to a stop at a traffic light. The only sound in the car was the pinging of the turn signal.

"I guess I could have proved she was mine, but what was I going to do with a baby? Court probably wouldn't deem me a safe father anyway with my record and all. She went into foster care, put into the system before she could even walk. I finally talked to Mr. Stubbs. With his police contacts, we've kept track of her. She been bouncing around with different foster parents for eleven years."

This was the most I'd ever heard Shine say at one time.

"Mr. Stubbs knows and you didn't tell me?" Simon asked indignantly.

"Mr. Stubbs was there when I found out her mother died. That's one of the reasons he wants to go legit soon. He has been working on this a long time. He thinks we go legitimate, I got a good chance of getting her back."

The chirp of a cell phone came from the front. The driver reached into the breast pocket of his blazer. He listened for a moment then replaced the phone and said, "Change of plans."

He pulled into a gas station and pulled right back out, now going in the other direction.

Father Craig's cell rang. He pulled it out and peered at the caller ID. It was Dr. DeRose. Father Craig's concern showed in the light of the oncoming traffic. Finally, he put the phone away.

"Apparently Dr. DeRose's condition is much worse than he let on. He saw his doctor today and was taken straight to the hospital. He's in critical condition and non-responsive."

"We must go," Emmanuel said.

"Hey, Kato," Simon said to the driver. "We got to get to the hospital. Turn this boat around."

"No, sir," he said politely, "we are to return to the White House." He faced straight ahead and paid little attention, the way a parent might do to a child who asks for something outrageous.

"We been there and done that," Simon said. "Listen here, I'm telling you we got to get to ….. Hey we know what hospital he in?"

"He's in Bethesda," Emmanuel said.

"How did you know that?" Father Craig asked.

"I don't know how I knew it, but I can see him lying there. The lights are dim and there is a painting of sunflowers on the wall. His eyes are closed."

"See what you dealing with?" Simon said to the driver. "Who you think you got back here, The Amazing Kreskin? You best do what he want you to do." The driver kept his eyes on the road.

Emmanuel, with his eyes closed said, "I can hear a soft beeping, there are many tubes attached to him. The number on the door is 1217."

"May I see your phone?" I asked Father Craig. He handed it over and I dialed the number Jimmy had slipped me. It rang several times before he answered. It sounded as if he was in a train station. There were all sorts of background noises. Several different voices and shuffling sounds sounded like he was walking through the White House as he talked. I hung up and waited for the call as the others looked at me expectantly.

The driver's phone rang seconds later. Without any emotion he said, "Change of plans again, we are heading to Bethesda."

We changed course again and I prepared myself mentally to see my friend. His condition had barely registered in relation to the looming concerns we were facing at the time. But now I could picture him lying as Emmanuel described him, and I wondered if I could hold it together. I had never approached a hospital with such trepidation. What kind of a Priest could I be if I could give comfort to strangers but not to a friend?

The driver let us out, gave me his number, and said he would be waiting in the parking lot. We went to room 1217 without asking anyone if that was the correct room, we all knew it would be. And he was there, just as Emmanuel described, except that he looked very ill. He did not stir as we entered. I could not understand how he had gotten so bad so quickly.

Father Craig and I stepped to the bed and began to pray. Simon, Shine, and Emmanuel stood silently and waited. A young nurse walked by the open door and glanced in. She hesitated for a moment and kept going. Then she came back the other way and looked again, trying to keep her head straight ahead. Simon was the only one who noticed, he had been tossed out of too many places to not know the look.

Moments later a surly gray haired nurse marched into the room with the young nurse trailing behind. She chose Shine, who was certainly the most threatening of the group, and addressed him.

"Who are you gentlemen, and how did you get in here?" It really wasn't a question; it was more of a 'get outta here'. Shine looked down at her and she stared right back at him. No one said anything.

I broke off my prayer, crossed myself, and found my voice. Father Craig continued praying.

"My friends and I are associates of Dr. DeRose. We just found out he was admitted. To answer your question we just walked in."

She turned to me, "He was only admitted an hour ago and his paper work has not even gone through yet. How did you know what room he was in?"

"We got friends in high places," Simon said from behind her.

"Please, could we speak to his doctor?" Emmanuel asked.

When he spoke the nurse's demeanor changed, I'm not sure how, but she softened somehow. She looked at him quizzically.

"I can check and see if he is in the building." She turned and left the room. The young nurse followed.

"Man, I still say you some sort of Jedi," Simon said.

She came back a few minutes later and said, "No, the doctor was not in the Hospital, but he was on his way." We waited and prayed.

Chapter 64

"All right Frank, what have you got?" Jimmy spoke into the speakerphone. He was in the residence with the President. They were in their shirtsleeves sitting at a shiny ebony table. George Washington stared down at them from a portrait on the wall.

"An amateur astronomer spotted it," the voice came from a speaker on the table. The President clasped his hands on the table. They left smudges on the shiny surface.

"He started e-mailing it to all the news outlets; Fox, CNN, MSNBC. He got about four minutes of live feed, then the clouds rolled in, but unfortunately for us he was able to record it."

"I thought you were watching this for us, Frank," the President said, more harshly than he intended.

"We were trying. It hit our satellite at the same time the clouds opened for this guy in West Virginia. It's like it waited for the right moment to show itself again." He hesitated then started again.

"Another bad thing. Remember how awful the thing looked the last time we saw it? Well, it looks even worse now. The swirls inside it are more violent and defined. The colors are more, I don't know, vivid?"

"We're getting flooded with requests for comment," Jimmy told his brother. "It'll be the top story on the 11:00 p.m. news, we're going to have to give them something, even if it is just a 'We're monitoring the situation'."

"Ah, Mr. President, it's positioned itself just outside the Van Allen radiation belt," Frank said.

"What does that mean?"

"On a clear night you could see it with a Sears and Roebuck telescope. All the observatories around the world are going to be locking onto it. It's not going to be our secret anymore."

"Okay, Frank, thanks. I didn't mean to jump down your throat there. But please, keep us informed with anything, and I mean ANYTHING that happens."

"Yes, Mr. President," he said then hung up. The dial tone came on and Jimmy hit the button to silence it.

Before either could say anything the phone rang again.

Jimmy answered with a simple, "Yes," then listened.

"Thanks," he said and laid the phone back in its cradle.

"Come on," he said to the President. "It's time to check the regular programming."

They walked three doors down to a viewing room. The lights were dim and the room quiet. One entire wall was covered with flat screen televisions. The sound was muted on all of them. One by one the channels began stopping their shows and flashing the BREAKING NEWS, or SPECIAL REPORT banners across the bottom of their screens. Nearly all showed a reporter beneath the rolling image of The Ghost. To Jimmy, the silent mouths of the newsmen seemed to be moving faster than usual. They sat down on a leather couch without taking their eyes off the screens.

Above each TV was a plastic number running from one through twenty-six. On a large coffee table were twenty-six remotes each with a corresponding number to a TV. Jimmy hit the mute button for TV1.

"..as for now there is no comment from the White House or NASA. The object was nicknamed The Ghost because of its history of disappearing then reappearing in a different area of space. No other object in the known universe has had the ability to do that. Or the ability to cross the vast distances it has before showing itself again." The reporter checked his notes.

"Later in the show, our guest will be Dr. John Williams, whose latest book *Why Would E.T. Phone home? He's Already Here*, hits the shelves this month. Dr. Williams will explain why he thinks The Ghost is in our neighborhood for a reason…."

Jimmy put the remote down and picked up another. By now every screen was reporting the sighting. Somewhere in these United States a guy was downloading the image to a machine that would turn it into a tee shirt. By morning it would be available for sale on the Internet. John Thomas, the man in West Virginia, would already have been contacted for spots on the morning talk shows.

Jimmy hit the mute button of another TV. This channel had already brought on an expert guest who must have been in the studio for some other reason.

"What about intelligence?" the anchor asked.

"Well," the expert said with just the slightest trace of an English accent, "It seems very unlikely, that an object that has traveled a staggering distance to get here, making adjustments in its course right to our doorstep, has done so by accident. It calculated what it needed to do to get here."

Jimmy clicked the mute button. "That right there is going to be enough to spook half the country."

The President sat staring at the bank of silent TV screens. Jimmy knew what he was doing; he was tracing little ovals on the roof of his mouth with his tongue. It was something he had done since childhood.

"The next few hours will probably define my presidency," he said.

"And affect how the world is going react to this news," Jimmy said. "This could be 'End of Days' stuff. Look at them, he nodded to the faces on the screens, "the news guys are scared, you can see it in their faces. Look how fast they are talking."

Chapter 65

They waited in silence; the only sound was the soft steady beep of the monitor that was attached to Dr. DeRose

"Man, somethin' goin' on," Simon said to the others. He was leaning against the door jamb watching out into the hall. Waiting around was difficult especially since the hospital room felt just as confining as the jail cell. In the minutes he had stood there, the pace of the staff had increased, and many were going to the floor's visitor area and not returning. He was watching for the young nurse who had been in earlier.

"What do you mean, something's going on. It's a hospital something always going on," Shine said from his chair against the wall.

"I know where we are. I'm tellin' ya, something's happenin'," Simon said and slid off the wall and began to sander down the hallway.

Father Craig, sitting in a chair closest to the bed said, "Emmanuel, is there anything you can do?"

"Do?" Emmanuel asked.

"Can you save him?"

"Only God can do that." He smiled, "And God listens to you as closely as he does me."

"I've been praying. I know what we are about to go through, and that I should be praying about the fate of mankind and not, I hate to say this, worrying about one man."

"Tell me a memory of your friend," Emmanuel said.

Father Craig took a breath and looked at the floor. Then he smiled a little.

"In my last semester at the seminary I took a class on writing the homily. Dr. DeRose was the instructor. Each of us was to go through the entire mass at least once during the class. All of us played a part. We were altar servers, deacons, lectors, you know everyone needed for the Mass." Father Craig was smiling fully now.

"Well, one day Father Brian was doing Mass and I was supposed to do the readings."

The monitor beeped loudly. The graph that provided some type of data spiked. The beeping became more rapid. I stood to get the nurse.

"Sit, Father," Emmanuel said. "Father Craig, continue with your story."

He began again, with all of us watching the equipment.

"The second reading was from the Book of Numbers."

The beeping got faster again; lights in the back of the monitor began to flicker on. A nurse stepped into the room. I had no idea if this was good or bad.

"See, Father, you have as much pull with the Almighty as I," Emmanuel said. "Please continue, we are all enjoying this."

"I stepped up the podium and said, without knowing why I said it, 'A reading from the Book of Numbers. 7, 21, 42, 9.' Then I went and sat down. Father Brian didn't know what to say, everyone else was ready to bust out laughing, but were afraid they'd get in trouble."

The machine went berserk, with a single high pitched whine and lights flashing red and yellow. The nurse stepped to the monitor and others entered the room. A young doctor pushed his way to the front and placed the stethoscope into his ears. Emmanuel cupped the listening end before the intern could place it on Dr. DeRose's chest. As Emmanuel touched the metal, the monitor went silent. DeRose opened his eyes.

Without a word he looked into Emmanuel's eyes and slowly crossed himself.

He reached for Father Craig's hand and pulled it to his cheek. He blinked back the tears while Father Craig did the same.

His voice was a whisper. "You were the one who could always make me laugh."

He looked around the room until his eyes landed on me. He held the other hand out in my direction. I took it and he pulled me closer.

"And you were the one that was the most worthy," he took a long rattling breath. "Maybe not to lead the flock, but to save it."

He saw I did not understand what he was saying but then his focus became distant. He was leaving us and looking toward what was to come next. With his gaze far away, he said, "Convince them with their names."

"What?" I said. "I don't understand." But it was too late. His eyes closed and the machines hummed back to life, the monitor showing a weak but steady heartbeat.

"Everybody out," the nurse said sternly.

Chapter 66

By seven o'clock the next morning the Internet had crashed. The morning news shows were ninety nine percent stories on The Ghost. Experts were flown in from all over the world to be interviewed on any related topic the news directors thought the other networks had missed. Newspapers ran headlines ranging from; SOMEONE'S OUT THERE to IS THIS THE END?

The White House was in full disaster mode. Wanting to be kept in the loop, members of the Senate and the House had started calling the President at daybreak. They did not want their constituents thinking them uninformed. Leaders of foreign nations were also insisting the United States keep them abreast of the situation.

In parts of the world, America was being blamed for The Ghost's appearance. The most radical religions believed we were about to be punished for our sinful ways. Others thought we had polluted the Earth and a *Day the Earth Stood Still* ultimatum would be forthcoming.

One group, which contained a few very intelligent members, believed SETI was responsible. We had been sending signals out for so long, that something finally heard them and didn't like the tunes we were playing.

No matter which group was accusing, the responsibility fell into the President's lap. He was the king spider that had cast the web of evil over our planet.

Jimmy had spent the night at the White House and arranged meetings for the next morning. There was to be a speech around noon to calm the nation and assure them the government was still in place and that it was working on the situation. The first business was to calm the government officials who would have a microphone stuck in front of their faces every time they left their homes. The reporters could smell fear and would begin to circle if a Senator came off as scared or shaken.

Jimmy sat in the Oval Office with a paper and pencil waiting for the President. He began making checklists. He soon found there were too many variables to make a list that would be anything but a starting point.

There was nothing to do until the reactions of last night's news could be measured. If the public were to panic, it would become evident pretty quickly.

The school systems would be a place to start. There, absenteeism is hardwired into the system. Before noon each state could get the number of teachers, cooks, and custodians who did not show up for work. They could also get a good read on how many parents were keeping their children home from school.

Local, state, and government employees, would be the next to monitor. Retail and service personnel would be more difficult to monitor.

They would have to watch the stock markets here and overseas. The market would be a place where a few scared individuals could cause a definite panic. What would the ultra-rich do if there were only a few days left? What would they do when their money became worthless? What would the average citizen do?

The NSA had been notified to identify key words for an immediate attack on web sites or e-mails. The CIA and FBI were also on high alert. If the agents of these groups started calling in sick to stay with their families, our ability to protect against the terror threats would become nil.

The news services were an excellent tool for measuring public response. Interviewing people on the street, even though the opinions that actually showed up on the screen or in print could be one-sided, usually provided good insight into the mood of the public. It wouldn't be long before some of these reports would be taped, edited, and aired.

Then there was the coverage of riots, heaven forbid. There was also the National Guard. If there was a chance of seeing your family for the last time, who in their right mind would leave to stop the looting of iPods and designer purses, the smashing of windows?

The President strode into the room with a speechwriter and his secretary trailing behind. He was wearing a navy suit, light blue shirt, and a darker blue tie.

"You look very presidential today."

"Thanks, Jimmy." The President hesitated for a moment. "Are you saying there are times when I don't look Presidential?"

Jimmy brushed off the question and went straight to the incomplete list of potential problems. They went over it together and the President passed it along to his secretary that would disseminate it to the proper agencies. They drafted the statement he was going to make sometime within the next hour.

Jimmy opened the door and a group of advisers entered to prep the President on questions the press may ask after the statement. Jimmy leaned back on the sofa and closed his eyes for the first time since the news broke. He began to plan how to bring Emmanuel back into the scenario.

Chapter 67

Father Craig asked to be taken back to the rectory as they climbed into the back of the SUV. The driver must have been advised of the situation because he seemed a little more human than on the trip in. Father Craig prayed at the foot of the bed until the nurses began lining up at the door to perform their duties.

Clearly upset, he sat, with his head down, in the darkness of the last seat with Emmanuel beside him.

"Your friend, he seems like a good man," Emmanuel said.

"He is. A very kind and spiritual man," Father Craig replied.

"Good," Emmanuel said. "It is much better for a good man to be called before God than a bad man who has not asked for forgiveness."

We were taken to a house in a residential neighborhood. It was a large white home, that while not overdone, whispered of affluence. The driver had the code to the front door and checked the house as we waited. It was quiet and empty. In the corner of the entryway stood an antique grandfather clock, silent for lack of winding.

The agent came back and told us there were four guest bedrooms on the second floor and to make ourselves comfortable and we would receive a phone call later in the morning.

"Hey, man, whose house is this anyway?" Simon asked.

"Chief of Staff Rienhart's," he said. "Don't break anything." He closed the door.

We stood in the entry and looked at each other.

Finally, Emmanuel spoke up. "In this country, is it the custom to spend so many nights in homes other than your own?"

"Only when you on the lam, baby," Simon said. "And since I met the Father and you, we been constantly buggin' out. Now, where's the fridge and the TV?"

That night, as the clouds cleared, a speck of light shone dimly just to the left of the moon. The Ghost was on its way.

Chapter 68

West Wood Home for Children

Zonnie Walker marched down the hushed hallway carrying a small bowl of vanilla ice cream. It was not a proud, arrogant march but a march of a linebacker or a power forward. She moved as people of great strength and weight do. Zonnie was a woman that tipped the scales at nearly 300 pounds and could move as effortlessly in her white shoes as a ballerina. Her uniform gleamed in contrast to her ebony skin.

New orderlies kept their distance. Stories circulated that she had grabbed an abusive father by the throat and pinned him against a wall. There was another popular one, where she had taken a junkie mother into a room, and emerged hours later with the mother visibly shaken and a signed form putting the children in the custody of the state.

But now, as she had been doing for the last several months, she was taking a little treat to her favorite patient, an eleven year old she called Tadpole. The doctors at the West Wood Center did not look favorably on special treatment for residents. Zonnie thought differently.

She passed the muted colors and subdued lighting and stopped at room 21. Putting her ear to the door she listened, a habit she had picked up her first year working with special needs children. She heard nothing so she opened the door slowly.

The lights were out and the room was still.

"Tadpole, you in here smokin' those big cigars?"

Silence, then a giggle. "Zonnie, I fooled you!" The 'you' came out 'Yoo'l. He spoke as a deaf person sometimes does, elongating the vowels.

"You did fool me, Tadpole. I thought you had skedaddled," she said flipping the light switch. "I got a little something for you."

He sat up on his knees in the middle of the bed. He had a funny way of holding his hands. The fingertips of the first and second fingers rubbed against his thumbs like a gambler who couldn't wait for the next hand to be dealt. If he became really excited he drummed his fingertips against his thumb. He was excited a lot.

Zonnie produced the bowl from behind her back to delighted giggles, thumbs drumming. She handed him the ice cream and pulled up a chair and said, "All right Tadpole you want a story, or do you just want to talk?"

The idea was to get him to make as many decisions himself as possible, which was part of his program. Steven Cooper was found at the age of four at a Greyhound station in Cleveland. A note pinned to his dirty tee shirt gave his name. Scrawled in big letters was the message HELP ME. He was diagnosed with RETT syndrome and an accomplice, Pervasive Developmental Disorder. Simply put, he was going to have trouble with life in general, being socially accepted, specifically. Even now, Zonnie was the only person who had heard his voice. He would speak to no one else and all of her interactions with him were recorded, except these little covert visits after hours.

When he was mainstreamed with other children he would stand alone in a corner of the room or stand and spin. He could spin for long periods of time without becoming dizzy. Often his encounters with other children became violent. The normal provocations did not bother him; calling him a freak would only arouse a giggle. But another child building a castle with his blocks may enrage him. He would often tear up instructions for games. His drawings, although having an artistic quality to them, were grotesque and not proportioned. There was always one sad looking character with a misshapen, elongated head. The doctors had a field day with those.

He held the bowl against his chin to avoid dripping any ice cream onto his Sponge Bob pajamas. "You read a story to me while I eat the ice cream, and after we can talk," he said with a mouthful. Talk came out "Taullk."

"I know what you're doing. You're trying to get old Zonnie to stay in here longer. You tryin' to get me fired?"

Giggling again. "No you're gonna' get me fired, Zonnie. You keep bringing me cigars." He pretended to smoke the spoon. The ice cream was now wide around his lips.

Zonnie opened a drawer in the nightstand and pulled out *The Big Book of Bible Stories*. She settled herself in the chair and Steven, AKA Tadpole, stood beside her slurping his ice cream and looking at the colorful pictures of Noah and the Ark.

No one could possibly know, that in a few days' time, he would become the most famous boy on the planet.

* * *

At exactly ten o'clock the President stepped to the podium to deliver the most important speech of his career. He had to look in control but be honest, to seem concerned but confident, and to be great but humble.

"As all of you are aware, we are witness to a scientific phenomenon that has not been observed in recorded history. As of now it is beyond our comprehension and our ability to predict its origin or its design. I will be honest with you and tell you that we just don't know much about it. That leaves us to our imaginations, and for the people of the world at this time, imagination is a very dangerous thing."

The President looked down and traced the edges of the podium top with his fingertips. When he looked up again he wore his most sincere face. "Speculation will be thick in the next few days or weeks, or whenever this event comes to its conclusion. I ask that you are calm and sensible, to ignore all those who would create discourse for their own personal gain. I would ask you to go about your life as you always have, love your families and go to work. Plan for the future. Help all those you can. We, as a nation, need to show the world that we will not flinch in a time of uncertainty, not break in the face of the unknown, and face each day with a resolve that is the human spirit."

The staff that flanked the sides of the stage, some in front of the royal blue curtains and some behind, applauded. This President was known for his dry intellectual wit, not this type of motivational outburst. Some of the staffers nodded to each other as they clapped.

"Now, if there are questions, I'll start with Mr. Urse." There was a clamor, then everyone settled down to hear the question.

"Mr. President, how much of a threat is The Ghost to our planet and what steps are being taken to protect us?"

"Jeff, our scientists have been monitoring the situation and at no time has this object caused any type of destruction or shown any hostile behavior. I believe our biggest problem is that we have never seen anything like it and we don't know how to feel. It goes against our intellectual grain to see something new without making predictions or reacting to it in some way. As to the rest of the question, we have taken no military actions. We are not a nation that fires without provocation. And if we were," the President smiled for the first time, "it would be very dangerous to attack something we do not understand. It could be like putting out a fire with gasoline."

The President pointed to a familiar face in the crowd, "Mrs. Stephens?"

"Mr. President, have we received any type of communication from the object?"

"No, Ridgely, E.T. has not phoned home." The reporters laughed and the President smiled for the second time.

"I'm sorry, I do not mean to be flip. I know there is a lot of talk that The Ghost is an alien, how should I put it, a galactic census taker. Or that it is a scout from a distant civilization. But, no, we have had nothing in the way of a message."

The longer the press conference went, the sillier the questions became. After thirty minutes the President abruptly turned and left the room, and told the press that if anything new developed they would be informed promptly.

As he walked past, Jimmy filed in with the staff that swarmed after the President. Looking back, the President said, "What did you think?"

"Calmed MY nerves," Jimmy said.

"Yeah, I guess we'll see."

Chapter 69

I awoke to the smell of bacon frying. The room where I slept was much nicer in the daylight than I had noticed last night. It was more like a very nice hotel room than an extra guestroom in a home. I wondered if the bed had ever been slept in.

I gathered my clothes, which were in a heap at the foot of the bed where I had left them last night, and pulled them on. I followed the aroma downstairs and into the kitchen. I was the last one there.

Shine was at the oven and had his back to me. Emmanuel was sitting at a granite topped island that was situated in the center of the kitchen, and Simon was standing in front of a glass panel that comprised the back wall of the kitchen.

"Well, look here, if it ain't Rip Van Reverent," Simon said. "You almost missed breakfast babe. Can you believe it, this guy, the President's brother, doesn't even get cable?"

Emmanuel motioned for me to sit at the island with him. I wanted to talk about the jail and the light that opened the door. Something was telling me that he hadn't even realized it had happened. I noticed his plate had two strips of bacon and a small pile of scrambled eggs with peppers and onions. He was chewing and put down his fork. "Our friend here is a wonderful cook," he said. He took a sip of water from a glass and picked up the fork again.

Secret Blood

"I got to tell you, Father, since we started runnin' with you, we be stayin' in some five star places. I could learn to live like this," Simon said looking out the glass wall. "But we got to get cable; this is like a fourth world nation."

The snow began again in earnest, huge flakes in a swirling wind. The glass panel overlooked a large backyard that sloped down to expose about 500 yards of golf course. On the other side were dark skeletons of leafless trees, their black trunks and branches silhouetted against the steel gray of a river. Even though the wind blew the flakes in their infinite patterns, it was silent in the kitchen. Unlike the windows of my former church, these windows were well sealed.

"In a place like this, I could sit and have deep thoughts," Simon said breaking the silence.

"What deep thoughts have you ever had? You know, besides the giant Space Straw," Shine asked without turning around.

"All right," Simon said rubbing his chin like he had a goatee, "what if all these snowflakes were the souls of everybody who had ever died. You ever think about that? And they got to float all the time, each one havin' its own journey. Kinda' of like they did in life. Maybe that's what Heaven is, floatin' around like angels. Then when you hit the ground you join all the others. Then you melt and join all the others in the ocean."

"What are you saying, heaven is just one big water cycle?"

Emmanuel coughed and took another sip of water.

"I am just sayin', What if?" Simon said, "That's what science is, thinkin' about a bunch of what ifs."

"What if you get away from those deep thoughts and do the dishes," Shine said as he slid a plate of eggs in front of me.

"Man, you are always marshing my mellow." Simon said. "Emmanuel, you been eating that for about an hour, how come it's taking you so long?"

"We were taught to take a bite, put the fork down, take a sip of water, and then do it again. It teaches one to slow down and enjoy the food, to savor it."

"Tell you what, Babe, at my school you would have never got to go to recess. We used to spit on everything we wanted so nobody would steal it. We…"

The telephone rang and interrupted Simon.

Chapter 70

Simon was the closest so he picked up the receiver. He looked at the caller ID. He grinned. "Pearly Gates, Saint Peter speaking."

"Anything still left in my house or did you already pawn it all?" Jimmy asked.

"I don't know, but that kinda sound like a racist remark to me." Simon started to hand the phone to me, and then took it back. "Hey, why don't you get cable, you some kind of intellectual or something, don't believe in it. Don't your wife watch the soaps?"

Jimmy hesitated. "I guess I didn't pay the bill. I haven't turned a set on at home for a few months. My wife is living up state for a while," he lied.

Simon handed the phone over to me. "He a racist and got domestic problems. And not payin' his bills. Life as a thug lookin' more respectable all the time."

"Hello," I said.

"Gypsies in the castle," he said. I wasn't quite sure what that meant so I ignored it.

"Any word on Dr. De Rose?" I asked.

"Yes," he said, his voice cheering a bit. "His condition is improving. All the vital signs are strengthening. They don't really know why, in their words they are cautiously optimistic." I repeated what he said to the others who were acting like they weren't listening, but were.

"I guess you guys haven't been watching the news," he said.

He knew it was a rhetorical question so he went on. "The President just addressed the nation and things are going to start happening, so try to keep Emmanuel ready."

"Ready for what?" I asked.

"An onslaught," he said. "You saw what the press did when that woman had eight babies. No amount of security will be enough."

"I will try to prepare him the best I can, but for some reason I think he could handle just about anything. There are some things that have happened that I need to tell you about."

"Maybe later, I'll see if I can get the cable back on for you and I'll send some more clothes. Margaret has the sizes. I'll keep in touch." He paused, then said, "We are doing the right thing aren't we? You feel the same about this being one big plan?"

"After what occurred during our unfortunate incarceration, I'd say we're on the right track."

Chapter 71

"Man that ain't a cable company van, and that don't look like no cable guy," Simon said peeking through the drapes. The man wore a navy work suit that looked brand new. He had opened the access panel in the yard and was pulling tools out of a carry-all.

Shine, ever serious about security, pulled the curtains open a fraction of an inch. He watched quietly. "You still got the Chief of Staff's number?" he asked me.

"Back home somebody just shimmy up the telephone pole and fix the cable," Simon said. "But out here you got to go down a hole, people sure live different."

I dialed the number from the house phone wondering who else was listening. All the utilities came through the access where the guy was working.

"What's wrong," Jimmy said instead of hello. I had only talked to him a couple of hours earlier.

"Nothing," I said. "Maybe nothing. There is a man in your yard messing with the access to your utilities. Something we should be worried about?"

Simon yelled in the background, "We don't want to be cruisin' through the channels and see ourselves watchin' TV like Will Smith did in that spy movie."

"No, no, he's one of ours. They're connecting the house with the same hookup we have at the White House. This way Emmanuel can see what is happening around the world. I thought it might be helpful."

"How come you didn't have it before?" I asked

"I was rarely at home and I wasn't so sure it would be good for the kids."

"What about the kids now?" I asked. "When will they come back home?"

He ignored that. "We are getting the data back from the school systems and some of the state departments. Things are still looking pretty good for now."

Simon turned on the TV. It was a large flat screen that was hidden behind an oak panel which slid across a shelving unit. The screen flashed shows as Simon used the remote to speed through the channels. He had zipped through the three hundred and was coming back around the horn when he gave up and threw the remote on the couch.

"Aw man, it's all news shows, we don't even get ESPN!"

Chapter 72

Dinner at the West Wood Center was usually a barometer of how the day had gone. Children who had problems during the day would have problems at night. Many had nightmares about the lives they led before becoming residents. For others, the responsibility of preparing for the next day was stressful. Even on the best of days, there were a large number of children, with very difficult problems, forced into one area. The doctors and staff were diligent and ever present. This was a private and expensive clinic, which did award scholarships and in turn was rewarded by state and federal tax breaks.

Zonnie's Tadpole was a recipient of one of these scholarships; he fit the criteria by being a ward of the state and having multiple disorders. He was a candidate for various studies by the psychologists on staff and several articles were being prepared on his treatments. The fact that he would talk to none of them only added interest to their studies.

Tadpole carried his lunch tray past several rowdy groups of children and planted himself in the back corner of the farthest table. This was the most troubled part of his day, the part with the least supervision. He was learning to like the structure and the routine of the school, but dinnertime allowed more freedom and with that, more opportunity for uncomfortable encounters.

A trio of boys spotted him and made their way over. Two sat across the table and one scooted in beside him. They surrounded him, like lions spotting a weak animal. He had watched them before, with other students, and was sure of what was coming. Pressure built behind his eyes and under the table his fingers furiously rubbed against his thumbs. He looked around for Zonnie, but the night shift had not shown up yet.

He remembered the three boys as FUD. One had freckles, one was ugly and the other was dumb. Freckles was the mean one, the leader, the one who decided who would be harassed. The students were not supposed to know the reasons for being enrolled at the West Wood Center, but Tadpole was sure Freckles was here because he was a sociopath. Although he didn't know what the word meant, he knew Freckles could hurt people without feeling bad about it.

"So what's the freak having to eat today?" Freckles said to the group. Tadpole didn't look up, he wanted to flatten his hands on his thighs, something he was practicing to keep his fingers still, but his arms weren't cooperating.

"What you asking him that for?" Dumb said, "This is the kid that don't talk."

"I know that, you moron. It was, you know a conversation starter," Freckles said, keeping his eyes on Tadpole.

"How can you have a conversation with somebody who don't talk?" Dumb asked. Freckles kicked him under the table.

"Ouch," Dumb mumbled.

Ugly, who was sitting right beside Tadpole glanced down. "Man what are you doing with your hands?"

Tadpole sat sit staring at his food. His chest moved in and out with rapid breathing. His jaw set firm. Ugly grabbed a forearm and pulled it to the top of the table. The other arm came up automatically. His fingers were hammering against his thumbs.

"That's weird," Dumb said.

"I'm sorry," Freckles said. "I thought you were just a freak, but you're not, you are Lobster Boy." The three laughed.

Secret Blood

"I'll tell you what, Lobster Boy, we're going to make this a special treat for you tonight. We're going to allow you to eat dinner like a real lobster would. You see, I think they search through the sand at the bottom of the ocean to find their food. We don't got any sand but we got mashed potatoes."

Freckles leaned back, crossed his arms, and said, "I'll watch the teachers, you boys load up." With that the other two took spoonfuls of the mashed potatoes and started plopping them down on tadpole's plate. With each spoonful the pressure behind his eyes became greater and greater. Soon his ham was covered and they started giggling. They started covering his green beans.

"See," Freckles said, "It will be like a little treasure hunt." He smiled with satisfaction. Another soul tortured, another job fulfilled. It was the last natural smile he would ever have.

At that moment the pressure became too great. For the first time, Tadpole looked up and smiled back at Freckles. In one motion he grabbed a fork and punched it across the table into Dumb's eye. There was a soft pop and the fork stuck, quivering slightly. The other two watched with horrified disbelief. As the thought that they just might be next began to form in their minds, Tadpole stood.

Grabbing his tray with both hands he swung with an almighty force, sending the edge of it into Freckles mouth. The blow knocked him backwards off the bench splintering both top and bottom teeth, nearly ripping off the upper lip, and sending mashed potatoes in a spraying arc across the cafeteria.

Ugly was next. He was beginning to stand and was looking down at the bloody mess that was Freckles mouth when Tadpole began his second swing. The bottom of the tray connected with the top of Ugly's head with tremendous force as Tadpole brought it down with both hands. He collapsed and landed beside Freckles, both on their backs with their feet still on the bench. The remaining potatoes had popped off the tray on impact and rained down on the table.

It all had happened in two seconds and for a few seconds after that there was complete silence. The table was scrambled and

Tadpole was standing above it with half a tray in his hands. Then Dumb began to scream and Freckles began to blubber through his wrecked mouth. Noise filled the dining hall.

The students nearby were yelling for help, others farther away were climbing over each other to see what was happening, and Dumb was sitting rigid, screaming. With every scream the fork bounced up and down, like a vacated diving board. The noise and chaos in the hall was starting to affect Tadpole.

He sat back down, laid his head on the table, and put his arms over his head, and began rocking. Zonnie had just walked into the dining hall. She was the first to get to the table. She came out of nowhere, pushing aside tables and knocking over students. She didn't know whom to attend to first. Her heart was with her Tadpole.

"Lord, Lord, what have you done?" she said putting an arm around Tadpole and looking at the other boys. The words stung him more deeply than anything the boys had done or could ever do. The pressure behind his eyes built immediately. He thrashed from side to side as if he had become possessed. He flew off of the bench and lay convulsing on the floor. More orderlies came, shouting directions. There was a heated discussion as to whether to leave the fork in or pull it out. The din continued to get louder as more staff poured into the room.

Zonnie pulled Tadpole up and held him against her chest, facing out. She gripped his arms so they were crossed over his chest like a straight jacket and carried him out of the dining hall away from the noise and gore that had started only minutes ago.

She carried back to his room still churning in her arms. It felt like he would dislocate his own shoulders. Hoisting him up a little higher she managed to grab the knob to his door and backed in. She used her elbow to hit the light switch and kicked the door closed behind her.

On the dresser was a cheap CD player. She wanted to turn it on, but Tadpole was not making it easy for her. He reeled back trying to bang the back of his head into her face. She let him slide down a little further and loosened her grip on one arm. She had just managed to tap the play button as he got his head around far enough to bite down on her forearm. She didn't let go, even through the searing pain. The first few notes of *All My Loving* blared through the speakers and Tadpole stopped jerking. By the end of the first verse he was slack in her arms.

An administrator was standing at the door when she looked up.

"The Beatles?" he asked.

"Yep," she said. "The Beatles."

He wrote the time and the song in a black leather notebook.

Chapter 73

They soon figured out the TV. The channels were divided into sections. There were foreign news channels, domestic news channels, local channels, and network TV.

Simon flitted through the channels and got bored with the programming quickly. Emmanuel took the remote next, much to everyone's frustration. He had no pattern or logic when he charged through the channels. He did not stop at the things most of us would. He would spend a minute on C-Span then to a commercial selling something he would never need, then to a public information announcement.

"Man, what are you doin'. Trying to find the absolute worst thing on TV?" Simon said. "Who watches C-Span? Gimme that remote back."

"What you talking about?" Shine said. "I seen you watching the Antique Road Show."

"Yeah, well I caught you watching Lawrence Welk. He was trying to dance a polka, too." Simon was serious. That made us laugh harder.

By chance we landed on a news channel and saw The Ghost. It was unnerving. The laughter stopped abruptly. I had the goose bumps again. All of the stories were related to The Ghost, but it

Secret Blood

became evident fairly quickly there was little to report. Basically, it boiled down to the fact, there was something out there, we didn't know what it was, or what to do about it. And, yes, it was heading straight for us.

With a lack of real information, the discussions turned philosophic and religious. This is where the first seed of fear started. People were forced to think deeply about things they had taken for granted. Some began to question the things they had always thought of as truths.

But in the depths of everyone's mind was the fear that this just may be the end of everything we hold dear. The closer the fear came to the surface, the more we looked around at each other and wondered if we were all thinking the same thing, and the closer we were to worldwide panic.

It was time to tell Simon and Shine everything. They knew bits and pieces, they had witnessed some of the events Emmanuel had created, and they had become our friends. I think they were as much a part of the chain of events as Dr. DeRose and me. I think Shine already had a grasp of what was happening, but probably not the two thousand-year script that led us here. And I think maybe I needed to hear the story again, from beginning to present.

It took about an hour and I was right about rejuvenating myself with the story. In context, it didn't seem so outlandish. If fact my convictions were stronger than ever. It was the feeling of being part of something that was greater than myself. I think Simon and Shine felt the same. It clicked that they had been chosen, not by Mr. Stubbs, or me, but by a higher power.

We were quiet, allowing the thoughts to sink in when Simon said, "What's wrong with you man, look at your hands?"

I looked at my hands and they looked fine, then I glanced at Emmanuel's.

He turned them over. His palms were bleeding. There was a large puncture in each palm. He stood, dripping blood from each hand, and headed for the sink in the kitchen. He left stains of red across the carpet where his feet had started to bleed also.

Chapter 74

Tadpole slept. He slept more deeply than he ever slept before. He slept through Zonnie changing him into his pajamas. And he slept through the next two times she checked on him. And he was asleep when she turned off his boom box. The Beatles were the only thing that had ever calmed him down. The album or era was irrelevant, it worked every time.

But while he was sleeping his clouded mind became clear. A seed had been planted there, a crystalline vision of what he was supposed to do. Its clarity allowed him to see four or five moves in advance. He had never been so happy or so complete in his life. He awoke giggling, but then he thought of Zonnie and his heart ached. He would have to leave her, and she might be fired because of him. What he was going to do?

But, he thought, he would make it right in the end. He would come back and they would be happy again. That is, if he did things right. The way he was feeling now, he knew he would do things right, it would be impossible to do anything wrong.

So, he went to his closet and put on a pair of jeans over his PJs. He pulled his coat off a hanger and chose a pair of heavy socks. Giggling and fingers drumming he arranged his pillows so it would look as if someone were in the bed. He found his shoes and went to the window, which he knew from his dream, would be unlocked. He heaved up the sash and hesitated, but only for a moment. Something flashed across his mind that wasn't in his dream. In the drawer of the nightstand was a red marker. Giggling, he retrieved it and pulled off the cap with his teeth.

On the back of his door he wrote, 'I (heart you) Zonnie' in a sprawling hand.

He climbed out the second story window and sprinted across the roof, only inches from the edge. He was sure he wouldn't fall, that did not even enter his mind as he reached the end of the building and leaped. His fingertips just snagged an oak branch 30 feet off the ground. He swung to and fro giggling because he had known the branch would be waiting for him. After all, his leap was the reason it had grown in that direction anyhow. It was the reason the landscaper had planted the tree there 50 years ago, although he didn't know it at the time. He shinnied down the tree and disappeared into the darkness. He needed no streetlights; he knew exactly where he was going.

Chapter 75

Jimmy sat in his office waiting for the other shoe to drop. The numbers from the danger zones, the places where absenteeism was dangerous, were still holding, but the public was starting to get anxious. He could feel it the way he could feel the momentum of a campaign tipping in a different direction.

The committee and the President would change their minds about Emmanuel when the nation started to panic, of that he had no doubt. He just didn't want Emmanuel to be their last choice. Somehow that seemed very wrong, almost to the point of being sacrilegious. He hoped his determination would not waver. Without Emmanuel or the Priest nearby, the story did seem a bit preposterous. Now he could see why the committee thought he was nuts. He had been so sure, but now, in the daylight of reality, he was starting to doubt. He had asked for reassurance from the Priest and he was still steadfast.

That helped but he wanted a sign. Anything out of the normal that would show him he was on the right track. He hated his own lack of faith in his reasoning, but the stakes were too big to have doubts.

There was a knock on the door and Kim stuck her head in.

"You have a phone call and you will take it," she said.

Secret Blood

"Who is it?"

"Your wife." And without waiting for an answer, she said before closing the door, "Line two."

Was this it? Was she going to ask for the divorce he knew was coming? How had it come to this? All the confusion in his life had convinced him of two things. Emmanuel was here for a reason and he wanted to save his marriage. He lifted the receiver carefully; his heart was pounding in his chest. He figured 'Hello' was the best way to start.

"Is this a bad time?" she asked. She sounded small, hurt.

"No, not at all. Are you okay, anything wrong with the kids?"

"No, everybody is fine. Listen I don't want this to feel strained." Now she sounded tense, nervous.

"Please come home," he blurted out. "I can't tell you how many times I've picked up the phone to call you."

"Why didn't you then?"

"I don't know, I wish I could tell you, but I don't know why. There were times when something came up just as I was starting to, but there were plenty of times when I had the chance but I couldn't do it. Maybe I was afraid I'd ask you to come back and you'd say no."

There was a silence. Then, "I wouldn't have said no," she said softly.

"I know I've been wrong, I promise things will get better. We'll work this out. We can make it happen," he said. He felt himself starting to tear up, which was a surprise to him. What was going on?

"I've missed you and I've missed the kids," he suddenly realized she had not positively said she was returning. "Now that I'm hearing your voice I feel more like myself, I didn't know how far I'd drifted away. It's been like the best part of my life has been erased."

That sounded pretty good, he thought to himself. He'd meant it but he wasn't used to expressing his feelings so well. In the past when he'd try to say something romantic it would sound more like a press release.

He thought the conversation was going pretty well, she still hadn't committed but she had not put up any arguments against coming back.

"The reason I called was...."

Uh ho, he thought, these next few words will determine where I'm going to be when The Ghost hits; alone or with the ones I love.

"....to ask how you'd feel about giving this another try."

The tears started. There were no tissues around.

"I just," she was crying also, "I want us to be together when whatever is going to happen, happens. I want to come home."

He wiped his eyes on his shirt sleeve. "Just pack and come back, now, as soon as you can. I'll leave work and meet you guys at home."

She sniffled and laughed, "You, leave work? You must have missed us."

"Just call when you start home, I can arrange to get you a police escort if you want."

"No, they drive too fast. I'll wait until morning—that will be better for the kids and give me time to pack up."

"Whatever you want. I really can't wait to see you guys. Give the kids my love. Be careful driving home."

"Jimmy, I love you."

"I love you too, always have, and always will." He hung up the phone.

That was the sign he had asked for. The feeling of euphoria surged. He was rejuvenating in his loyalty to the plan. There was only one snag. He had forgotten that a Priest, two street thugs, and the Messiah were now living in his house. How was he going to explain that?

Chapter 76

We were back in the family room gathered like a family on a rainy Saturday afternoon. We were waiting for something, although we didn't know what. The impending gloom of The Ghost began to gain weight and started to wear us down emotionally.

Simon's idea of a bandage was a paper towel wrapped with masking tape. Emanuel sat sideways on the couch with his legs elevated, a bandage on each appendage. The bleeding had stopped as quickly as it had started. I cleaned up the tiles and Shine worked on the carpet with a spot cleaner we found under the kitchen sink.

"I saw that in a movie," he was telling Emmanuel. "That's called stigmata, when you bleed like Jesus on the cross. Did you make that happen?"

"I'm all right now," he said. He unwrapped his hands and feet. There were only shallow marks left, none that looked deep enough to break the skin.

"Well, that kinda freaked me out. I hope that don't happen' anymore," Simon said. He looked around and resigned himself to the fact that there was nothing to do but wait. Shine was standing by the window, keeping an eye on anything that looked peculiar to the neighborhood.

"What we gonna' do now, another day of just sittin' around."

"You spent your whole life sittin' around, why you complain' about it now?" Shine said.

"Yeah, but then I was sittin' around where I wanted, not some place I know nothin' about." He looked at Emmanuel. "That nothin' on you, I mean, I don't mean no disrespect."

Emmanuel smiled but said nothing.

Simon started flipping through the channels, trying to find something that would hold his attention. He stopped on the giant smiling face of Rev. Grace, the television evangelist they had seen some time before. He had taken his show on the road.

"God is knocking on our door, friends, and this time it's not a tap. He's pounding with both hands calling for you to get out of your homes and do something Christian in these times of tribulation." Behind the face was a montage of catastrophes. Mt. St. Helen's exploding, the body armor shootout in L.A., starving children in Africa. Every four seconds a different heart-wrenching scene.

"We are taking Christ's love to the streets of America. Come on down to a Revival like the world has never seen. We want to start off the quest with you."

Next, was film footage of the Reverend on a multi-leveled stage, in ecstasy, filled with the spirit. His sky blue suit was soaked with sweat and a chunk of his comb over hair was pasted to his ample forehead. A gospel choir, filled with the same joyful spirit as the Reverend, belted out a spiritual in the background.

"God wants to see you there, so don't disappoint him!"

An announcer's voice repeated the invitation and gave the times and dates. The first of five revivals in the city were to start tonight at the Capital Center.

"Let's go see this man, Reverend Grace," Emmanuel said.

"What?" Simon said. "That man is a Charlatan. He just in it for the money."

"Yes, to help people like those I helped in Africa."

"No, man. Look at that guy's hair. That's how you can tell. If they on religious TV and they got whacked out hair, they crooked. They want you to pay to pray."

Emmanuel stood. "I would like to visit him now."

"No, you don't. Emmanuel you kinda naive about the way things work in this country. You gonna' be disappointed in people if you believe everything they say. Anyway, how we gonna' get there?"

"Cadillac in the garage," Shine said. "Keys on a hook by the kitchen door."

I watched the two talk, wondering where this was going to take us. But deep down I wanted to see Emmanuel meet Rev. Grace.

"I'm in," I said.

"What is wrong with you people? Why give this guy the time of day? We don't even know where he is," Simon said.

"But I do," Emmanuel said. He closed his eyes. "He is in a hotel and preparing to leave for the arena. There are others with him wearing suits but he is not. He wears something that is blue and soft."

Simon smiled, "I am partial to Cadillac's."

"What are we waiting for?" I said.

Chapter 77

"Go to the service entrance," Simon said.

Shine pulled the Cadillac through the area's parking lot. It was empty except for a few cars near the entrances, probably owned by arena workers who had nothing to do with the Revival. Five big rigs sat idling at the far end of the lot, each bearing a photo of the good Reverend plastered across the sides of the trailers.

Shine started to slow at the entrance.

"No, keep going," Simon said. There's a ramp that goes to underground parking." About 100 yards ahead was a ramp, disappearing into a lower level. The door, which was open, was large enough to drive a tour bus through. The place was unattended.

When I was young, we would try to sneak into better seats at ball games. Even if we weren't thrown out immediately, I didn't enjoy the game for fear we would get caught. That's how I felt every time I did something with Simon. Everything he did had a feeling of guiltiness about it.

"Got The Commodores autographs' down here one time," he said. "Got clear through and on stage with War another time. Got tossed out during Cisco Kid. Don't blame them though, can't have that kinda' thing going on."

We rolled down the ramp and into a cavernous parking area. Everything was cement-gray and industrial looking. Huge pipes bisected walls on the ceiling. Everything echoed.

Shine stopped the car in what appeared to be a parking place for a limo. We got out and closed the car doors, which seemed loud enough to send every security guard in the pace running toward us. There were a series of doors along the wall, all of which had numbers and letters above them in battleship font.

"Okay, Nostradamus, which door?" Simon asked. To his credit or doom, whichever way you looked at it, Simon treated Emmanuel the same way he had, before learning of his heritage.

"This one," Emmanuel said. He walked towards the door marked D-4.

The door opened into a long hallway, which veered to the left and out of sight. The farther we walked the deeper into the bowels of the area we went. The hall ended with metal double doors, the kind that has an aluminum bar to push open. We exited onto the arena floor, stage left and looked out onto a sea of chairs. There were hundreds, evenly spaced in neat rows with a large center aisle running ruler straight down the center.

The stage was about six feet above the seats, located at one end of the oval arena. The house lights were on, which usually diminishes the impact on the stage, but not in this case. The stage itself ran from one side of the arena to the other. There was a massive lighting rack overhead and a shining steel cross hanging at the back of the stage above a drum kit. A pair of spotlights set it alight and the edges of the metal reflected in every direction. To the back and sides of the stage were green grassy meadows that looked fake and inexpensive.

A man, wearing jeans and a tee shirt, with large headphones, walked across the stage tapping on microphones as he went. He hesitated at one stand and made a thumbs up gesture to another man adjusting a control board at the other end of the arena.

I became aware of more people working around the stage. There were men in chairs with spotlights hanging incredibly high in the rafters. I noticed a boom with a camera swinging across center stage. Cameras were also positioned to capture the Reverend from both stage right and stage left.

The grassy meadows must have had hidden speakers; *Rock the Casbah* by the Clash started blasting out of nowhere. Emmanuel jumped as if he had been stung. It was so loud we could not talk to each other, so I motioned for the others to sit down in about row ten.

We watched the roadies through *I Wanna Be Sedated* and *Twenty One Guns*. I began to think this guy's religious views may not be exactly the same as Rev. Grace's. On the tour didn't mean on the team.

The music cut off in the middle of *Less Than Zero* and someone made the announcement that the Reverend was arriving. The music had been a physical presence and its absence left the place empty. I felt like I needed to whisper.

The Reverend and his entourage burst through another set of doors stage left and began mounting the stage by means of a hidden staircase. Emmanuel was right; the man himself was wearing a blue velour jogging suit. The four men with him had on dark suits, white shirts, and pastel ties. Television did not do Reverend Grace justice. He was a big man, a head taller than the men around him. He walked with strong purposeful strides. He looked like a general walking through a battlefield with bombs exploding all around him, knowing, that by force alone, he wouldn't be hurt. I could tell as soon as I saw the jogging suit that the ill-fitting suits he wore on his show were part of the illusion.

At this distance, I could only make out a few words, but I understood they were discussing camera angles and blocking. One of the men said something about a video. The union guys were keeping their distance; they kept their heads down, and finished what they were doing.

"Duane," yelled one of the men, "Reverend Grace would like to see the ark."

Secret Blood

The man who had been tapping the microphones looked over, and then said something into his walkie-talkie. The Reverend held up his hand as a signal to stop, and then slowly walked toward Duane who was standing fairly close to us, and put an arm around his shoulder.

He started talking to him in a low voice and by the time he was finished, he was shouting. "It's not you, it's not your moron brother-in-law, it's me, standing on stage looking like an idiot if this thing doesn't work. I don't want to turn around and see only half of it on the stage!"

Duane broke away and spoke into the walkie-talkie again. He rubbed his sleeve across his forehead. Almost instantly the house lights went down and Aaron Copland's *Fanfare for the Common Man* blasted through the arena. The steel cross rose out of sight and an image of a huge wave was projected on a screen at the back of the stage. The wave looked like it was about to crash on us when the screen split and a truly majestic version of Noah's Ark appeared and began rolling toward the front of the stage. It kept rolling on and on, until it filled the entire stage. Then, when it was completely out, it started turning sideways, so the audience could get a complete view of the port side. For the first time, I could see animals on the deck and some looking out the windows. They were plastic, and not quite as good as the Ark, but still pretty realistic. The fanfare rose to a crescendo. It would have made Walt Disney envious.

A door opened on the Ark like a drawbridge door in a castle. As soon as the door hit the ground the music stopped, and the arena was quiet again. The ark sat majestically while the plastic animals watched out the windows.

"Now that's what I'm talking about," the Reverend yelled. The men with him applauded. Duane looked relived.

The Reverend turned and pointed towards the door or the Ark. "This is where the smoke starts…" He stopped as he noticed us sitting there.

"Who are they?" he asked the men with him. They looked at each other.

Emmanuel stood. "We've come to help."

"To help with what?" one of the men asked.

"To help raise money for the people on the television ads," Emmanuel said.

"Then buy a ticket," Reverend Grace said. The men laughed. Reverend Grace didn't smile.

Emmanuel didn't give up. "I've seen your show; you ask for money to help the needy, to clothe the poor, that is why you are having this show, is it not?"

I could see it coming, the Reverend thought he was being backed into a corner and he was not going to let it happen. He was doing well, flying under the radar, until we showed up.

"Who sent you?" he said. "The newspaper? Men of God have always been targets of abuse. There are those who are always willing to try and taint the righteous. None of you look smart enough to try something on your own."

I knew we were doomed when Simon stood up.

"Who you callin' dumb? Don't you call this man here dumb. He believed that you were honest, he willin' to come down here and help. I knew you were a charlatan, but he believed. Same way you got millions of people believin' in you. And look what you're doin', raking them out of all their money."

"I don't know how you got in here, but go out the same way," the Reverend growled. His voice was low and that somehow made it scarier.

Shine was sitting there, staring at the stage like he was watching a boring movie. One finger was tapping out a slow rhythm. I don't think he had moved since we sat down; absolutely still like a submerged alligator at the edge of a river.

"Don't worry about that, I can't wait to get out of this place, but don't think some 'velvet suit wearing gypsy preacher' is gonna' make me leave if I don't have a mind to."

The Reverend spoke to one of the men without taking his eyes off of us.

"Get security down here. I want to see if any of these heathens are miked or have cameras."

"Let's go," I said to Emmanuel. "Simon was right; he's not what we thought he was."

"I would like to speak with him," Emmanuel told me. "Maybe I could explain the true nature of the need in Africa. Surely he would understand what even a little could do to lessen the suffering."

"He ain't that kind of man," Simon said. "He just a crook usin' the Lord's name." He looked at the stage with disgust.

"But God has given him such a gift, he has the power to move people, to gain their trust and to drive them to act," Emmanuel said. "Surely he could use this ability for good."

Doors slammed open behind us at the far end of the arena. Simon and I turned to look, Emmanuel continued to watch the Reverend and Shine stared straight ahead, drumming his fingers on the chair in the row in front.

Six men, ranging from stocky to fat, were walking down the center aisle. Their black shirts had Event Security silk screened across the fronts. All had their hair high and tight, so they were either ex-military or ex-military wannabes.

The one leading the pack was shorter and stockier than the rest. He reminded me of a grown up Spanky from the "Our Gang" show. He actually had some sort of military belt that none of the others wore. They stopped beside Shine, who was seated at the end of the row. I was in the next seat, then Emmanuel and Simon.

"Check for listening devices or any kind of cameras," Reverend Grace said.

Duane, who had been watching the confrontation develop from the side of the stage, said into his walkie-talkie, "Are you getting this?"

"Yeah," a voice came back, "all seven cameras are rolling. And I heard him call me a moron."

"Get up big boy," Spanky said.

Shine sat motionless, I couldn't even tell for sure that he was breathing.

"We can do this the easy way or the hard way," Spanky said.

Simon said from the other end of the row, "You ain't got enough guys to do it the easy way, and Shine here, he a hard case, he ain't gonna' do nothin' the easy way."

Spanky smiled and looked down at Shine sitting motionless.

"Up big boy," he grabbed the shoulder of Shine's leather jacket and pulled him up.

Shine came up easily and swung around with a left jab to Spanky's nose, breaking it easily. He shook off Spanky's grip and landed a right hook on the side of his chin. His head snapped to the left and he staggered two steps knocking over folding chairs and obliterating the neat rows of seats.

The next security guy reached for Shine's lapels and tried to head butt him, but was too slow. Shine unleashed four sharp upper cuts into the solar plexus and the man dropped to the floor, gasping.

Shine stepped over him into the aisle and squared off against two more guards. "Nice shirts," he said.

I stood, turning away from Emmanuel and Simon without realizing it. The guards that were still standing stopped and turned their attention behind me. A moment later Shine did the same. I felt warmth coming from behind, then watched a shadow form at my feet and extend into the aisle. I turned to see Emmanuel standing. He had allowed his army jacket to slide off and drop into his seat. He was standing with his head tilted back and his arms out, like he did the day of the shootout. But, today he was glowing.

Simon took a step back. He shielded his eyes and blinked. It was almost as if he took a step back into darkness because Emmanuel's white shirt was becoming so bright it was difficult to see. Along with the light was an energy that was invisible, but I could feel it crackle on my skin.

Everybody stopped and became quiet; we stood watching without a sound.

Spanky regained his senses rolled over and raised up on one elbow, but said nothing. His nose dripped blood onto the cement floor.

In the silence there came a loud snort, then another. Then a grunt and a squawk. Everyone, including the Reverend and his men on stage turned to look at the Ark.

A toucan flew from one of the windows. It flew over our heads, circled the floor seats twice, and landed on an exit sign in the rear of the arena.

We heard the grunts again and turned to see a pair of pigs barreling out of the Ark. They rocketed down the gang plank and slid to the edge of the stage. Their pinkish hooves pumping for all they were worth. Duane stepped back and watched as they disappeared behind the Ark squealing all the way.

I glanced at Emmanuel, he had returned to normal. He watched the stage with just the tiniest smile on his lips. It was the first time I had seen him amused. He had lowered his hands and now rested them on his hips.

Rev. Grace and his friends were anything but amused. In fact they looked absolutely terrified. One of the men had clamped himself to the Reverend's arm and was holding on for dear life. They stood frozen and watched as several species of monkeys pulled themselves out of the windows and climbed topside on the Ark. A couple leaped off and landed on a support structure that contained lights. They were up it and into the rafters of the arena in no time. The others jumped up and down and hooted at the Reverend

A rectangular section of the hull was being splintered from something on the inside of the ship. With each blow, the carbon fiber logs separated a little further, and soon the metal supports from the interior were visible. With one final blow, the panel crashed down and hit the stage with a bang. The massive horn of a rhinoceros emerged from the opening, followed by an equally massive head and body. It turned its head to see the Reverend and his party standing only a few feet away. With one loud snort it charged and would have impaled someone in the group if Reverend Grace had not stepped back and inadvertently pulled the man attached to his arm with him.

The beast didn't see the end of the stage, or didn't care. It plunged off the edge into the chairs below. The front legs buckled and it fell flattening the seats in section A5. Quickly, it righted itself and began a jog across the arena, swiveling its massive horn and tossing chairs through the air. It left a swath of mangled and overturned chairs in its wake.

Next was a pair of ostriches, which in its own odd way was more unsettling than anything else that had happened. They made a beeline for the Reverend and hovered around the men, their heads bobbing, while their bodies were stationary. They pecked at their suits, their heads, and their ears, claws scraping on the stage floor.

A deep throaty roar came from deep in the Ark, followed by a mass exodus of creatures, some I recognized and some I didn't. They were spilling over the gangplank and across the stage.

I'm sure there are people that can tell the difference between the roar of a lion and the roar of a tiger. Not being one of those people, I was positive it was one or the other that was going to step out of the Ark next. The Reverend and his party felt the same way I'm sure, because each of them were "roared" out of their stupor and either climbed or jumped down from the stage.

The fight or flight response comes into play when a human hears a roar like the one we heard. The first response will always be flight. Simon was already at the double doors waving us to him in large wild circles. The monkeys were hooting in the rafters, the toucan was back circling the arena, and the rhino was still destroying the seating.

We were to the door and out in the hall in seconds. When the door slammed behind us, the jungle sounds of the animals ceased. The four of us were again surrounded by the silence of cement and metal pipes. We looked at each other, knowing that, even though we had left them surrounded by dangerous animals, no one was going to be hurt. I don't know how we knew it, but we did. We started to the car, knowing it would be waiting for us.

I realized also that we had just seen a miracle. We had seen a couple of very odd things from Emmanuel, but this could not be classified as anything else. I had actually witnessed a miracle. For the first time in my life I knew I would never feel fear again. After witnessing this, of what should I be afraid?

We reached the car and climbed in. Shine turned the key and we roared up the ramp and out of the parking lot, and under security cameras that could easily view the license plates of the Chief of Staff, of the President of the United States.

Chapter 78

The phone was ringing when Shine pulled the Cadillac back into Jimmy's garage. Strangely enough there was a phone there on the wall between the two stalls. I thought, *wow, it does pay to have money and influence.* Simon must have been thinking along those same lines.

"White people never fail to amaze me," he said as he walked by.

"How are things?" Jimmy asked.

"Good, good," I said. I wondered if he could have found out about the Ark already. We should not have left the building with the animals running around the arena, but I knew Emmanuel would not have put them in any real danger. When he was around, I was not the voice of spiritual reason, he was. I realized I had become a follower, not the leader I had wanted to become. I was better at this, at least when I was following him.

"Got a couple of things for you, if you've got a minute. First of all Dr. DeRose is doing really well. Father Craig has been with him and it looks like he will pull through this with flying colors. And you can take this any way you want; he is showing no signs of the cancer. They are still running some tests, but it looks like he'll be leaving the hospital soon."

I was amazed but not shocked. How could I be shocked at anything anymore?

"Secondly, you are going to be getting some visitors tomorrow. My family is coming back." I could almost hear him smiling over the phone.

"That's good news, right? I mean nothing has happened. They're all okay?"

"Yep, it's great news. I wanted to give you guys a heads up so your posse doesn't attack them when they walk in. I should be there when they arrive, but sometimes my wife strays away from the plans I make. She's a little independent sometimes."

"That," I said, "sounds like a good thing."

"It is," he said. "Everything about her is a good thing."

We were both quiet for an instant then I asked, "Should we leave? I'm sure Mr. Stubbs could find us a place again."

"No. I'm still not so sure about Mr. Stubbs. I've never heard of a crime boss that wanted to change his ways at the height of his power."

"Bet you never met a Priest who was running from the FBI either," I said

"You got me there. Besides, I want the family to meet you, Shine, and Emmanuel. The other one, I could live without."

I looked at Simon and Shine. Shine was at the window watching to see if we were followed. He stood motionless blending into the shadows of the drapes, ever vigilant. I had no doubt that he would take a bullet for any of us, only because that was what he was supposed to do. I couldn't tell if he thought about what he was doing here with us or if he thought about it at all. I just knew he would do what he was supposed to do. Not what he wanted to do or what he thought was right. Just do what he was supposed to do. It kept his world orderly.

Simon was drinking milk out of the carton at the refrigerator. He saw me looking at him and smiled.

"Sorry," I said. "The four of us come as a set."

"The other thing is, she doesn't know anyone is living at the house other than me. I plan to be there, but just in case something happens, I wanted you to know that she doesn't know about any of this."

I smiled and said, "I'll wear my collar, that usually settles people down." I wanted to tell him about the Ark, but I thought that might go better in person. I didn't want him in the dark and thinking I was holding back things he should know. Maybe I should have Emmanuel tell him. In the end, he sounded so happy about the family coming back that I didn't want to do anything to dampen his mood.

So the four of us settled in for an evening at home. Not our home of course, I guess I haven't had a home that felt permanent since I left the Seminary. But we felt like a real family.

Shine made pasta and garlic bread which gave the house an aroma of a celebration. I never felt stronger in my faith and I was happy. I thought back to a slogan I read once. It said, 'Imagine what you could do if you knew you could not fail'. That's how I felt.

While most of the world's population was becoming more and more anxious about The Ghost, I was looking forward to seeing how it all played out. But the world had not had the good fortune of seeing Emmanuel in action.

* * *

"Now what? Man I can't take this waitin' around." Simon had been pacing around for the last forty minutes. "What we waitin' for, the end of the world?"

The news channels had been reporting on The Ghost non-stop. As usual, when the flow of information dwindles, each network finds angles to quench the thirst of the viewers. The ramifications of The Ghost ran from religious to unreal. Most of the mainstream scientists had made their rounds through the guest lists and now the producers were gravitating towards the fringe of science types. Many times, with space science and astronomy, spiritual beliefs were questioned and discussed and sides taken.

Secret Blood

This is what led to 'the end of the world' comment by Simon. The light in the sky, combined with the nonstop coverage of the news outlets, began to wear on the country. People were divided into two camps, those addicted to the news and those who tried to ignore it.

"All right," I said, turning the TV off. "Let's do something different. What can we do together, here at home, without turning on the TV?"

"Does that include video games?" Simon asked.

"No video games. Something where we can also talk while we're doing it."

"In Africa we sit around the village fire at night and the older ones tell the children stories of long ago," Emmanuel said.

"Shine and I know all each other's stories. Father, you a Priest and you shouldn't have any stories. Emmanuel, brother, all your stories are so sad I get depressed every time you tell me something about Africa," Simon said.

"How about cards?" Shine said.

"That's perfect," I said. "If we can find a deck."

"Bottom left drawer, black cabinet in the hall way," Simon said. We all looked at him.

"I didn't lift anything, relax. Man, you can't blame a brother for looking," Simon said.

Emmanuel had never played poker before, so Shine gave a quick explanation as we cleaned off the kitchen table. Simon cut the cards expertly and dealt.

As we looked at our hands, I began to get the feeling that this might not go so well. Emmanuel had a quick look and laid the cards flat on the table.

"What you need?" Simon asked me.

"Two," I said laying down two of my cards.

"Three," Shine said when it was his turn.

"Emmanuel, how many you want?"

"None, thank you," he said.

"What you mean none, you gotta' need something?"

"No, thank you," Emmanuel repeated.

When it was time to show our hand, Emmanuel was correct. He didn't need anything else. He had a Royal Flush.

"Aw, dang man. How we gonna' play with him?" Simon stood and tossed his cards on the table. "He don't even need to 'remote view' our hand if he gets deals like that."

Emmanuel smiled happily at him.

"You know you aren't gonna' ever lose," Simon said.

Out of nowhere Shine said, "Are you Jesus?"

Emmanuel dropped his smile, but only a little.

"No, I'm the same person I was on the day we first met. It's just that I have been filled with the Spirit."

"Spirit of who?" Simon asked. "Jesus?"

"No, it's not like that. I just feel so happy, and I'd like everyone to be happy with me. I want to help everyone feel the same joy as I do."

"I always thought that when Jesus comes back, we would be bowin' down and washin' feet, biblical things like that," Simon said.

"Maybe because back then, people needed that kind of thing, today we don't," I said. "Instead of bowing down we should be asking how we can help."

"I don't know 'bout that, I just know I ain't gonna' be playin' cards with someone who has a direct affiliation with the hereafter," Simon said.

Chapter 79

Tadpole had walked for nearly ten hours. He had a brief stop around 1:00 a.m. at a warehouse. A loading dock door had been left open and he slipped in unnoticed. Factory sized heaters on the ceiling warmed the place to a very comfortable temperature. Whoever was working the night shift was nowhere to be seen. He found a tarp and pulled it behind some palettes and fell asleep.

He dreamed the wonderful dreams again, about holding hands with a man that was pure white light. They stood in front of a cheering crowd and everyone was very, very happy. Then he floated away, he wasn't sure if the man was with him or not. It felt like he was but he couldn't see him, he could only see the ground getting farther and farther away.

He awoke to a loud beeping. A semi backing into the building. He watched for a while and decided to escape like a mouse, so he kept low, close to the walls, and behind things.

The night was cold when he got outside again but he felt good, rejuvenated. He walked without hesitation or fear. Before long he would have to find a Walmart. For that he didn't need a map, this was America after all. You couldn't walk for an hour and not see a Walmart.

Sure enough, one loomed ahead after only thirty minutes of walking. Still thinking like a mouse, he kept to the sides and away from the main aisles. The store felt very empty at this time of night. The self-checkout registers were vacant and the one human at the front of the store had been sent to straighten up the candy aisle.

Hood up and head down he went directly to the paint department and found the spray paint. He giggled as he pretended to browse for a color. He knelt down on one knee to examine the cans on the bottom shelf, but instead, quickly shoved a can up each of his jacket sleeves. He stood and walked out of the store as unnoticed as at the warehouse.

He was still hours ahead of the early morning commuters. The cold air wafted in front of his mouth leaving it chapped. He fought the urge to lick his lips and the skin around them. The cans felt good against his arms. He pretended to be a cowboy with six shooters concealed up his sleeves. In a way, they were the guns he needed to wage his war.

He came upon a four lane street. It was deserted but would probably be very busy during the day, especially since the Walmart was only a few blocks back. He wondered if the street was busy because the Walmart was there or if the Walmart was there because the street was busy. He giggled.

That thought was automatically lost when he spotted a blank billboard three blocks away. It even had three spotlights above it to light the missing message. There were actually two signs but the bottom one was plastered with an ad for the circus which had passed through months ago.

Tadpole had not seen a car or truck since he had left Walmart. A bus passed through an intersection a hundred yards away but he would not even have noticed if it had not downshifted between buildings.

Nope, he was alone with the spray paint and a giant canvas to start spreading the news.

* * *

The radio car pulled off the road under the once blank billboard.

Officer Lowers put the car in park and notified dispatch that they were 10-96, No Backup. She got out and met her partner Officer Hayden, who stood with his hands on his hips looking up.

"Should I get some pictures?" she asked.

"Yeah, I guess. It sure doesn't look like any graffiti we've had before, though. It's kinda good, in a simple sort of way."

The figure was simple and elegant and as tall as the billboard. A stick man with his back arched looking toward Heaven. The arms were bent but outstretched, palms up. Three straight lines made the eyes and mouth but even then the figure looked like he was smiling. He had long hair and a beard. The caption read: He Is Risen. And it was signed, Walrus.

Lowers brought the camera back from the cruiser and snapped several shots for the Gang Unit. They stared, as did the hundreds of early commuters driving by.

"Kinda spooky," Lowers said. "Maybe ominous is a better word."

They returned to the car and left the scene, the image branded into their minds. Before their shift was finished they took photos of the same drawing again in seventeen different places.

Chapter 80

Jimmy woke at the White House a little confused. He had spent many nights here, probably more here than at his own home since his brother had taken office. He had slept later than usual for a working day and he was a little out of it. Someone knocked on the door.

"Yes?" was all he could muster.

Kim stuck her head in the door. "Are you all right? I've knocked several times. I was about ready to get security."

"No security, I'm okay. What's going on?"

"I don't want to explain it. You need to see it for yourself and I think you better see it before the President does." She walked into the room in a business length blue dress, opened the armoire, and turned on the TV set.

"Let me know what you'd like me to do," she said as she tossed the remote to him and left the room.

Jimmy bunched up the pillows behind him and scooted himself into a sitting position. CNN was on a commercial so he flipped to Headline News. It didn't take long to find what Kim was talking about.

The video, which looked to be done professionally, showed a glowing Emmanuel standing below a life-sized ark. As he lifted his arms the animals began spewing out causing chaos and generally wrecking the arena. It was evident to anyone watching, that he was the catalyst of the entire melee.

Jimmy, the political animal that he had grown to be, was already working out a way to spin this to the committee and the President. The announcer on the screen was talking to another reporter who was covering the story.

"Well, Robin, arena management reports that extensive damage was done to the stage and audience areas, as well as equipment of the Grace Production Co. This company is owned by Rev. Grace, the popular evangelical minister, who has carved out a lucrative chunk of the Television Ministries market."

"Bob, what is his take on what happened?" she asked.

"We've tried to contact Grace Productions but have not had any response. Interestingly, if you watch the video closely enough it looks like the Reverend himself scampering across the stage just after the appearance of the rhinos." Bob said. "Though I am hearing this video was leaked to us by someone working for Grace Productions."

"What are the chances this is fake?" she asked.

"We're looking into that," he said. "But arena security has confirmed the wild animals were contained and captured in the arena and that the Grace Revival has been canceled. We have also confirmed that a company called Animal Replicas sold composite animals, like the real ones in the video, to Grace Productions."

"Are you saying they started off as plastic and became real?" she asked.

Bob smiled nervously, "I'm just confirming facts. You can come to your own conclusions. But here are two more facts that are very interesting. First off, we have security film of the men who were on the floor of the arena."

"Could we see that footage now?"

Several security cameras shot the grainy film as they passed from one area to another. It was filmed at different angles and distances but showed quite clearly their escape and their departure in a Cadillac. Jimmy watched as his family car, one he hadn't driven since moving to D.C., pulled away from the arena.

"Here's the thing," Bob said. "We got a visual on the license plates, and guess what. They are registered to none other than the Chief of Staff at the White House, the President's brother." He waited for the dramatic effect, "James Rienhart."

"The second thing is this, Robin, remember the 'Miracle Shoot Out' a while back? Look at the man in both videos." They had a side by side blow up of Emmanuel from each video.

"Oh, my gosh," Robin said. "It's the same man."

Jimmy turned off the television. It was 7:02 a.m. He would have to intercept the President before he saw this.

Chapter 81

Tadpole was exhausted. With the exception of a couple of hours here and there, he had been up for almost a day; and he had been walking for most of it.

At 7:02 a.m. he was passing through a section of town the locals call the Knob. It never had been a place law enforcement patrolled regularly. Its beginnings started with prohibition and the bootlegging trade and grew with each illegal fad the country had endured. Through the fifties, one particular Mafia family used the area as a headquarters and distribution center. They operated in full view of the police and population because they owned both, and rumor was that the place was so heavily fortified the army would have a tough time digging them out.

During the sixties, the Knob was the place to try all the psychedelic drugs. LSD, mushrooms, and experimental drugs were commonly passed out on the streets.

Many of the locals thought it was a covert government testing ground studying the effects of drugs on the human brain. Although there were no men walking around with lab coats and clipboards, people could be found passed out on street corners and in alleys.

The eighties gave way to cocaine and later, crack. The nineties turned even harder with heroin and crystal meth and the crime that accompanied them.

The new decade saw the insurgence of the homeless. Cuts in mental health institutions and the downsizing of American business ushered in wave after wave of transients. It became a haven because the police left them alone. This was an area ignored by the rest of the city. Crimes were not reported, streets were not patrolled, and each person was left to survive on their own.

This was the neighborhood Tadpole walked into. He walked down Key Street and took a right at Green Avenue, passed by the vacant bank building and the old G.C. Murphy store. He stopped and squinted into the rising sun and saw a burned out Methodist church. There, under what was left of an awning, was an old black man. He was sitting in a wooden shelter made from pallets like the ones Tadpole had hidden behind at the warehouse. He was playing a harmonica. When he saw Tadpole, he stopped and waited.

His hair and beard were white. His suit, he wore a jacket and tie, had once been black, but now was a sooty gray, only a few shades darker than his once white shirt. The whites of his eyes had a yellow tint, probably due to a failing kidney.

Tadpole shaded his eyes and focused on the black man, then smiled.

The man shifted the blankets and with effort stood and stiffly beckoned Tadpole to him. Tadpole ran to him giggling.

Chapter 82

At 7:02 a.m. I heard the first car door slam. I rolled over and pulled the covers a little tighter. By 7:05 a.m. I had heard six car doors slam and the doorbell had begun to ring. Shine stuck his head into my room.

"Don't turn any lights on or go near the windows. Come down to the basement as soon as you dress."

By the time I reached the basement Emmanuel and Simon had joined Shine. They were on the black leather sectional, Simon looking a bit dazed, Emmanuel, as peaceful and calm as ever, and Shine wound a little tighter than usual.

"What's going on? Who keeps ringing the doorbell?" I asked.

"There's what's going on," Simon said. It was the same footage Jimmy had seen, complete with the announcement of the license plate owner.

"We busted. We busted good on this one," Simon said. "I told you all from the beginning, that man was not worth our time and see what it got us, nothin'. Nothin' but busted."

"Shut up," Shine said.

They listened to the report and watched the film. As the reporter, Bob, told Robin the revival had been canceled, Simon looked at Emmanuel.

"That why we went… you played us." Simon looked at me. "He knew this was gonna' happen. That's why he wanted to go, to shut Rev. 'Gimme Yo Money' down."

We all looked at Emmanuel, who sat silently while the corners of his eyes crinkled a bit.

The phone rang and made us all jump. It was Jimmy.

"So, when I asked how things were yesterday, you forgot Emmanuel had brought plastic animals to life. I would have thought you might have been mentioned that in the conversation some place."

"Well," I mumbled, "I didn't think it was the right time to bring it up. I was going to tell you." Shine looked at me and pointed up the stairs. He was going up to make sure they were still outside and not crawling in the windows.

"What, so you just put it on the back burner?" He was mad and not doing too well controlling it. "A little thing like that."

"You're right, I'm sorry I didn't let you know, we didn't know it was filmed, if we knew I would have let you know."

"Are there any other things that weren't filmed that you haven't told me?"

"No, this is it," I said. Trying to change the tone, I said, "Is your family still coming this morning?"

There was silence. "Oh, Jeeze, I forgot."

"Listen," I said, "the place is crawling with reporters. They have been ringing the doorbell every five minutes. How'd they know to come here?"

"That house is provided by the government because I'm the Chief of Staff, it's all on public record. Once they had my license number, they could easily find out where I live."

"What are we going to do?" I asked.

"I can't come home; they'd be all over me."

"Can't you call your wife and warn her away?"

"She won't answer her phone while she's driving."

"What about calling the state police and have them warn her?"

"That's no good. The news people all have scanners; they'd probably find her before we did."

"I'm out of ideas," I said.

"I asked her to call before she left this morning, so maybe she actually will and I can make some other arrangements."

Shine came halfway down the stairs and said, "The garage door is going up."

"Too late," I said, "I think she's already here."

Chapter 83

Tadpole giggled. He hugged the man tightly even though the man didn't smell too good. He supposed he didn't smell too good either. The hug was good, not as warm and fleshy as Zonnie's embrace, but hard and strong.

"I walked a long way to get here," Tadpole said. He looked up at the man and for the first time noticed the curly white hairs blossoming from his ears.

"I know you did son, and it was a pretty brave thing for you to do all alone," the man said, and led him back into the shelter. They sat and the man pulled a couple more blankets from a stack near the back of the shelter.

A man in a long olive colored coat rolled a shopping cart up the sidewalk. One of the front wheels fluttered as if from an unseen wind. He stopped in front of the shelter. Long dirty hair hung in curtains beneath his toboggan. His face was greasy and his teeth were rotting out.

"Hey, Eggman, got anything to recycle, I'm goin', I'll give you half."

"No, I don't and if I did, I wouldn't give it to you. You stiffed me last time. I know you took the money and bought Scope. Keep walkin'," Cleo shouted.

Secret Blood

The man dismissed them with a wave of his arm and rolled his empty cart down the sidewalk. He was muttering to himself as he stopped at a trash can and began to dig.

Tadpole said, "He took your money and bought Scope? His teeth didn't look like he gargled in his whole life."

"He doesn't gargle it son, he drinks it." They watched him to the end of the block where he rounded the corner and disappeared.

"So, your name is Eggman?" Tadpole asked. "That's a funny name."

"Nope, Eggman is my nickname."

"How come they call you Eggman?"

"Because I can do this." He reached behind Tadpole's ear and pulled out a plastic Easter egg. They both laughed.

"My real name is Cleo, Cleo Johnson, how about you? What's your name?"

"Zonnie calls me Tadpole; she's the only person I talk to."

Cleo smiled at the boy, "You're talking to me now."

Tadpole furrowed his brow and thought hard about that. He drummed his fingers on his thumbs.

"Listen," Cleo said, "seems to me that a boy that's brave enough to do what you did should have stronger name than Tadpole. What's your real name?"

"Steven Cooper."

"I like that," Cleo said. He pursed his lips and scratched his chin. "I like that a lot, name like that got a ring to it. Sounds good to roll it around in your mouth. Steven Cooper."

Tadpole must have liked it also. "From now on call me Steven Cooper." He giggled. "So, what do we do now?"

That stunned Cleo. He looked down at the boy who was starting to nestle up against him. "Don't rightly know, I thought you were going to tell me what to do."

They were quiet and watched a blue plastic bag blow down the street.

"I'd like to know, Steven, how'd you find me? How did you know I'd be here at this particular time?"

"The voice told me," Steven said, starting to doze off. "The man that showed me what was going to happen."

"Steven, what did he sound like?"

Steven's eyes were closed and his speech was even more garbled than usual. Just as he was drifting off he said, "His voice was deep and friendly, it made me happy… and want to laugh."

"Yep," Cleo said. "That would be him."

Chapter 84

The car pulled into the garage without anyone noticing Shine standing in the shadows. The reporters were such a shock to Mrs. Rienhart that an intruder being inside was the last thing on her mind. Shine moved to the entrance of the garage as the first reporter started to step in. The cameraman was just to his left and filming when Shine moved in front and blocked the lens.

Veterans of many such encounters, they were moving and shouting questions at the same time, gaining access to the garage and trying to cut off any escape route other than directly by them.

Shine put the flat of his hand on each of their chests and pushed.

"Out of the garage," he said. The force knocked both of them back onto the driveway. To their credit they continued to film and shout questions. They tried to ignore Shine, which is like trying to ignore a shark.

He hit the garage door button and the door began to slowly roll down between them. Not to be dismissed so easily, the reporter stuck his foot under the closing door breaking the laser safety guard. The door stopped and began to rise again.

As the door began to rise, Shine reached under and swept his massive forearm across the legs on the other side. The reporter's legs were knocked out from under him and he landed on his backside on the concrete. Shine hit the button again and the door went down for good.

Mrs. Rienhart was frozen in the front seat. Shine tried to open the car door for her, but she quickly locked it. She pushed the garage door opener inside the car. Shine was way ahead of her. He stretched up over the car and pulled the release. The chain on the door opener slid harmlessly down its channel.

Simon appeared at the kitchen door, smiling widely, "Hey, Mr. President's sister-in-law, we the welcoming committee."

Mrs. Reinhart was an attractive woman with blondish hair, make up flawlessly applied, and completely terrified. The barrage of unexpected news vans and reporters had surprised her completely, and now she was undoubtedly being taken hostage in her own home. Her growing fear of The Ghost was now forgotten. So much for surprising Jimmy by coming early.

The daughters, Cooper and Elise, looked just as rattled. They sat motionless and round-eyed in the back seat, dressed in cute outfits to surprise Daddy. Shine looked at the frightened girls in the back.

By the time I reached the kitchen door and moved past Simon, Shine was already stepping away realizing that he was causing the panic.

I held the phone to the window and said, "It's your husband."

She looked at the phone, then back at me. I smiled assuredly. Either it was the smile or she realized she had no other options. She rolled the window halfway down and gently took the phone from my hand. She did roll the window back up but smiled while she did it.

I watched her talk into the phone with a controlled panic. She looked at me, then her eyes shifted to Shine, then Simon. She spoke into the phone for several more minutes. Then she ended the call and spoke to her children.

When she stepped out of the car she had regained her poise and smiled brightly. It was not a fake smile. She was even more attractive standing, than sitting in the car. The rear door opened and the two girls slid out.

"I'm sorry I acted, well, afraid," she said. "I was not expecting anyone but my husband to be here."

"That's all right," Simon said, "Shine frighten everybody. He don't try, he just born that way."

"Your husband had planned to be here," I said, "but things have been hectic for him this morning, and most of it is because of us."

"He really is in the doghouse now," she said smiling. "He told me he has a lot of explaining to do. I'm sure some of that concerns all of you."

"And the sleeping arrangements," Simon said under his breath.

"Well, let's not stand here in the garage, girls get your things from the trunk, and take them up to your rooms."

"We can help with those," Simon said and went to the rear of the car. "How would you like Uncle Shine to cook you some breakfast?" He nodded toward Shine.

"You know what he could make for you? Some scrambled eggs with green peppers, onions, and spinach. How does that sound?"

"Yuck," the oldest said.

Shine looked at me and said, "Yuck?"

Chapter 85

Steven stirred. It was nearly two in the afternoon. He opened his eyes and found he was alone in the shelter. It was warm under the mound of army blankets and he decided to stay there.

He was hungry. Food was something that was missing from his dreams. Suddenly he felt very sad. He wondered if Zonnie had brought his ice cream last night and he wasn't there to eat it. He never once thought of the boys he had injured.

He heard Cleo before he saw him. Harmonica music came drifting up the street, and a few seconds behind it, came Cleo. He held a bulging bag in one hand and the harmonica in the other. He was playing *Love Me Do*. Giggling and clapping Steven stood and bounced from foot to foot.

"Young Master Steven," he said formally as he reached the shelter, "would you care for some breakfast on this fresh, fine morning?"

"Yeah boy, I would. I'm super hungry," he said. "Where'd you get this food?" He reached into the bag Cleo had set down.

"There's a Homeless Shelter down the road a piece. They're not supposed to let anyone take food out of the building, but for you, they made an exception."

"You told them about me?"

"Yes, I did Steven. I told them, the person I had been waiting for, finally made it. I also told them, I might be leaving these parts soon."

Steven reached into the bag and was eating a strawberry pop tart. He stopped chewing when he heard the last part.

"Where are you going?"

"Not me Steven, us." He pulled a cup of coffee out of the bag and took off the lid. Steam rose from the cup. "I think we need to be ready to depart quickly for whatever our mission is."

"Okay," Steven said, chewing again. They sat in silence, Steven eating and Cleo sipping his coffee. When he was finished, Cleo took out his harmonica and played *The Long and Winding Road*.

"Cleo," Steven said, "you told those people at the shelter I was the person you have been waiting on. How long have you been waiting?"

"Now that, Steven, is a good question. And the answer depends how you look at things. If you want to go back when it really started, then we gotta go back almost fifty years, to the Vietnam War. You ever heard of that, Steven?"

"No," he said still chewing.

"It was a terrible time. I was in the Marines."

"Is that a good thing, to be in the Marines?" Steven asked.

"A very good thing Steven, that's probably the thing in my life that I'm the proudest of." He smiled and Steven felt the reassurance of the harmonica in his hand. "But one particular night I became separated from my friends. It was dark, so very dark, there was no moon that night and I found myself lost in the middle of a big rice paddy. Do you know what that is?"

"No."

"It's a big watery area where they grow rice. And I was there all alone sloshing through the water when I heard voices speaking Vietnamese. I heard them and they heard me but we couldn't see each other. So I laid down in the water and tried to hide myself. The water was only a couple of feet deep, so I laid there with only the top of my helmet, my eyes, and nose out of the water. Even my mouth was under the water." He closed his eyes and was quiet. "I can still taste that foul water, even now."

Steven started on another pop tart.

"So all night I was there with the enemy soldiers searching for me. I could hear them walking through the water, sometimes I would have to lean a little to the left or to the right so they wouldn't step right on me." Cleo readjusted himself and tried to shake a bit more coffee out of the cup.

"And every time one of them came near I silently prayed 'Dear God, get me out of this and I'll be yours forever.'" I must have prayed that a hundred times that night. First light of the morning when I could see, I was alone in the paddy. They must have given up and left right before sun up. I got up, soggy and waterlogged, and walked back to my unit like nothing had ever happened. But something had happened. I had given my life to the Lord."

"But how long have you been waiting for me?" Steven asked

"Well, my young friend, that's just the first part, the rest don't make any sense unless you hear the first part. Kinda like seeing the end of the movie and not knowing what's going on." Steven nodded his agreement.

"So when I come back to the states, I don't know what to do with my life, and I hear that voice one night. You know the deep happy one that just fills you with joy. And IT says, 'Don't you worry, Cleo Johnson, I got a plan for you. All you got to do is be ready.' That very next day I packed my suitcase and set it in the closet; a black suit, shoes, socks, shirt and tie. I was ready.

"I became an ordained Minister and had a wonderful church in St Louis. We did wonderful things in the community; we helped the old and the lonely. And I met a girl. Her name was Jean and I fell head over heels for her. I could go on for hours telling you about her, but I know you want to know how long I've been waiting for you."

Steven nodded, in many ways he had changed, but he still had tunnel vision for his mission, no matter how interesting his story was.

"We were as happy as two people could be, but at night I would still hear the voice. 'Cleo Johnson, I have a plan for you, so be ready.'

"And I thought, if this isn't the plan what is?

"The only dark spot was, we were not blessed with children. My wife prayed constantly but it just wasn't to be. So we clung to the church and each other. Then one day she came down sick, doctors said it was cancer. Within two months she was gone. Twenty-some years of happiness, then I'm all alone with my suitcase still packed and in the closet.

"My faith got me through those terrible days. At first I wasn't much good for anything, but I started coming around. My church family gave me jobs, made me feel needed. Just about decided I was happy for the time I had with her instead of being angry, missing her, when I got some bad news myself. Liver disease, can you believe that? Never had a drink in my life.

"I can hear the voice again saying, 'Cleo Johnson, you don't have much time left there on Earth, so you better be ready. It won't be long now'."

He stood up, stretched, and rubbed his worn hands over his scalp.

"So, Steven Cooper, I resigned from the Church I loved, got my harmonica and suitcase that I had packed all those years ago and started walking. People thought I had gone crazy, wanted me to stay right there and they'd take care of me, watch me die. I told them the Lord had other plans for me; I'd been living on borrowed time since that rice paddy back in Vietnam. That was three years ago this spring. Came across this corner in November of last year. That sweet old voice came back to me and said, 'You stay right on that corner and wait.' That's how long I've been waiting."

"Okay," Steven said. His question had been answered, it was a long answer but now he could go on. He liked this man, but boy did he talk a lot. "I have to get some paint."

"Paint?" Cleo said. "Why do you need paint?"

"That's how I spread the word until it's time."

"Time for what?"

"You'll see." he said, then giggled. "You'll see."

Chapter 86

Shine cooked and watched. If I had not been around him for the past few weeks, I would have thought he was concentrating only on the food he was preparing. I was sure he was aware of everyone in the house, where they were and what they were doing. His back was to us but he could have spun around and thrown a carving knife into any of our chests.

Our hosts, the Rienhart family, disappeared upstairs and apparently had a sort of conference; perhaps the proper etiquette for the approved home invasion. On their arrival, Patricia was cordial but a little aloof. The kids, by some weird quirk, gravitated to Shine. The oldest, Cooper, was about the age of Shine's estranged daughter. The other one, Elise, was about three years younger. They drifted over to the cook top and stood on either side of him as he expertly managed three pans and chopped the vegetables on a cutting board to the side.

He mostly ignored them, but every once in a while he would raise an eyebrow and flash a look at them. He showed no signs that they were annoying him; in fact I think he was starting to enjoy himself.

"Why do you have to put in that green stuff? It looks gross."

I'm sure they would have sensed it if he really didn't want them around. The less he spoke, the friendlier they became. They talked to each other from either side of Shine as though he wasn't there.

Secret Blood

I wasn't sure where Emmanuel was, he had not made an appearance since Mrs. Rienhart arrived. Simon was watching TV from the couch. He had no guilt about watching someone else's TV in their home without their consent.

"Here we go," he said as he switched the channel to a show airing the clip of the Ark again. Apparently Mrs. Reinhart had packed the children up and been on the road too early to catch the news. She drifted over to Simon and watched. It didn't take long for her to realize that we were the men in the video. Her face went from fear to shock to complete confusion.

"My husband knows about this?" she said.

"Oh, yeah," Simon said. "That's why he so tied up this morning. I got to say we been leavin' that man some big messes to clean up, ain't that right, Father?"

I nodded to her but she wasn't seeing me. "Is he here, 'The Man in White'?"

The press, not really knowing how to refer to the main character in the clips, had started calling Emmanuel, 'The Man in White.'

Before I could say anything Shine said, "We got more company."

From the glass wall in the kitchen I could see the golf course. Three golf carts were winding their way up the path toward the house. From behind the house they were unseen by the mob of reporters camped out in front. As they approached I could make out the sunglasses on the men in the first and third carts; standard Secret Service issue. All the men in the carts wore overcoats, but only the two men in the second cart had scarves to accessorize them.

The carts left the path, drove through an opening in the landscaping, across the Rienhart property, and converged at the house. I saw Jimmy slide out of the middle cart and disappear across the flagstone patio. Seconds later he was in the kitchen embracing his wife so tightly that I wondered if she could inhale.

The children left Shine as soon as they saw their father and joined the hug. Each grabbed a leg and snuggled their heads between their parents. Jimmy released his wife and embraced each daughter individually and only then did he remove his overcoat and use a sleeve of his jacket to wipe his eyes.

Simon stealthily removed himself from the couch and tapped my arm and nodded toward the door. I saw Shine had set the pans off to one side and turned off the stove and was following us to the door. I was constantly amazed at how they acted in unison without a single spoken word, and most of the time without even looking at each other.

When we were back in the basement I said to Shine, "How did you know we were leaving the room? Your back was to us."

He shrugged, "Just doing the right thing."

Simon spoke up, "Me and Shine, we like, twin brothers from different mothers."

Emmanuel was sitting motionless on the couch with his eyes closed. The TV was off and the room was silent with the exception of a clock ticking somewhere. He was so still that for a moment I thought there was something wrong. Fear hit me like a cold shower, paralyzing and stifling. We had been increasingly dependent on him for the last few weeks without understanding that other options were rapidly evaporating. I realized then what I should have known, he was going to be our only way out of this. Only Him. The Savior.

His eyes opened and I allowed myself to breathe again. "I need to speak with Jimmy. Things need to be arranged."

* * *

The White House has had occasion to host many improbable dinners in its history. Many we've known about and no doubt many more we have not. The business of government is not as transparent as many would like, but that is nothing new.

This night was notably an exception because the Chief Executive was not invited or notified that any type of gathering was taking place. It was a small affair with a guest list known only by Jimmy and Emmanuel.

They had discussed something quietly and Jimmy spent the next several minutes working the phone. They both seemed pleased with themselves when we gathered back together and Jimmy introduced his family to Emmanuel.

Patricia broke into tears as they shook hands. She didn't know why, and neither did we. But I think we all felt a subtle change in our relationships with Emmanuel. It was much more emotional, more powerful now.

We left the Rienhart house by golf cart, to avoid the press, just as Jimmy had made his entrance. The weather had warmed up considerably and the residual snow was melting. The sky was clear and the moon was out as we snaked our way quietly through the golf course. Again the strangeness of the situation hit me. Where we were, who I was with, what we were doing. But it felt so right, like all the gears of a clock spinning correctly to keep precise time. Maybe I was only a cog in this whole thing but each cog was invaluable.

Jimmy made arrangements with the chef to leave the kitchen open. Patricia, her daughters, and Shine headed there and started the pizzas. Jimmy, Emmanuel, Simon, and I went to one of the smaller reception rooms and arranged some tables and moved some of the furniture. It seemed like a lot of moving for our little group but what did I know? Jimmy was the happiest I had ever seen him. He was downright chipper. He even scooted a couch across the room with Simon still lying on it.

Once things were arranged, Emmanuel sat on one of the leather couches and said, "I believe we should bring your wife and children up to date. They know about the two video clips, perhaps they should know about the rest." He smiled with the blinding white teeth. "The truth may be a bit of a shock if they find out some other way than through us. And I don't want to give the impression that we are only running amuck to get ourselves on television."

"Yeah," Simon said. "Our running amuck is for real."

"I think," Emmanuel said, "that I should speak privately with your family." He looked at Simon and me.

I stood and pulled Simon to his feet.

"Aw man, I wanna see this part. It's like that punked guy, Ashton Kutcher, you know when he jumps out at the end to see the reaction. Come on, man. I wanna watch," Simon said.

"I hope you're going to see a lot of that later, but not now." I nodded toward the door. Jimmy led us through the back halls to the kitchen. We could hear the excited chatter of the children before we actually entered the stainless steel kitchen. Shine had a gigantic oven door open and was sliding in the fifth mammoth pizza. The girls were leaning in, watching. All three wore chefs' aprons, the girls had theirs folded up somehow so they hung to their knees instead of dragging the floor.

Jimmy walked in and said, "Smells good, guys."

"Daddy!" the girls ran and clung to his waist happy and oblivious to where they were and what was happening.

"We'll let Shine watch the pizzas and we'll go back to the party. I want you and Mom to talk a friend of mine."

"Do you mean the one that looks like Jesus?" Cooper said.

"Well, yeah, honey. His name is Emmanuel."

"Looks like Jesus to me," Elise said. "He's nice; I saw a painting of him with kids crawling all over him. He was laughing."

All of us, no matter what we believed, were reluctant to call him Jesus. I wondered why.

"That was a man who lived a long time ago."

"Believe what you want, Dad," Elise said. "I know who he is."

Jimmy took them by the hand and they left, Shine smiled.

Chapter 87

Cleo and Steven went to Kmart and bought the paint. Cleo, the ex-pastor, had become a skilled panhandler. They walked to the city, a trip that had taken them all morning and found the perfect corner to hit the office lunch crowd. Cleo played the harmonica and Steven clapped and giggled and the pocket money fluttered into Cleo's fedora. Experience told Cleo to move after right after lunch. So they moved to the subway to catch the five o'clock commuters. The two made over a hundred dollars for the day while avoiding the authorities. To celebrate, they hit a deli and bought sandwiches.

The rising temperature took the winter chill off the benches and tables in the downtown area. Steven was focused and happy and devouring a pepperoni roll. Cleo, who now was known only as the Eggman to Steven, was feeling the pain of the day's walk. This was the end game for him, and he had accepted that, but the pain was a constant reminder. His hot pastrami sub lay half-eaten in its greasy paper.

"What's next Steven?" Cleo said.

"We're really going to paint things up tonight," he said and licked the sauce off his fingers. "He is risen."

"But what does that mean, He is risen. Doesn't that just mean Jesus has gone to heaven?"

"I don't know what it means, why don't you ask Him?" Steven said, and then giggled. His fingers began frantically drumming against each other.

"Ask who?"

"Jesus, you silly." He was laughing so hard now that they were drawing stares.

Cleo sat stunned. He always knew the voice he was hearing was the voice of God but…

"You mean in prayer, right? I should pray and ask Jesus?"

"You can pray and ask him if you want, or you can ask him tomorrow night. Whatever you want."

Cleo's back hurt. Now his head hurt. "Are you saying that he is here with us? Now?"

"Yep, he's among us like a fungus." Steven laughed again. The food had energized him. He was nearly bouncing and he was getting louder. The last thing Cleo needed was a beat cop asking how he had come about an underage white traveling companion.

"And that is what I've been waiting for all these years, so we can announce to the world that the Second Coming is at hand?"

"Nope," Steven said. He was running circles around the table now; Cleo had to swing his head around to watch him.

Steven stopped and became serious. He looked into Cleo's eyes.

"You have to get me in, and I have to convince the people."

"Get you in where?"

"To see the President."

"Oh, Lord," Cleo said. "The President of the United States?"

"Yep."

"Oh, Lord," Cleo said.

"I don't know if he will be there, but he'll probably be listening in," Steven cackled and started running around the table again.

Chapter 88

I couldn't contain Simon. He wanted to watch Mrs. Rienhart meet Emmanuel so bad that he gravitated toward the door without even moving his feet. It was as if an invisible force was pulling him. I have to admit, I felt the same way, not the meeting part but being away from his presence. We have spent a great deal of time together and I physically felt his absence when he wasn't near. He was like an emotional magnet.

I looked at the pizzas through the oven door then glanced back to see why Simon wasn't complaining. Then I realized he wasn't complaining because he was gone.

I followed him back to the door to the party room. He had slid the pocket door open a crack and was looking through the slit. I pushed him over just a little so I had a view also.

Jimmy was standing beside his wife; the two daughters were on the other side of her. He had opted for a blue broadcloth shirt, open at the collar and khaki pants. It was the most informal I had seen him. The misses and the daughters were all wearing jeans and pretty sweaters. Emmanuel, wearing his faithful faded jeans and white baggy shirt, was standing casually and smiling that brilliant smile. They were across the room and partially behind the couch but standing in such a way that we could see everyone. One of the daughters was looking up at her mother and the other was looking absently at her shoes. Mrs. Rienhart looked at her husband, then Emmanuel and back again.

As Jimmy continued to explain things, Mrs. Rienhart became disjointed. They both reached to steady her and I could tell the moment she felt Emmanuel's touch. She started to cry. Jimmy produced a tissue from somewhere and she wiped her eyes and was able to gain some composure. She straightened herself; pulled back her shoulders, crossed herself, and knelt down on a knee in front of Emmanuel.

He gently pulled her up and embraced her. The kids looked like they wanted to crawl up his back.

"I'm just now startin' to believe all this," Simon said. "My Mama made me go to Sunday school and all that, so I know the story. But up to now, it was too freaky to be real." His voice dropped a note. "It's like God is really watchin' us. I mean really watchin." Man, I thought it was like Santa Claus or somethin', you know, he's watching all the time to see if you're good or bad."

He closed the door and leaned back against the wall. "If I would have known....man, I wouldn't have done half the stuff I did."

I smiled. "Remember, I'm still a Priest, and that sounds like a confession."

Now it was his turn to smile. "Father, we comin' from two different places. In your line of work, a confession is a good thing, in my line of work, it means jail time."

We heard voices from the other side of the door, happy, unexpected voices. Simon opened the door and we looked in. There, in a wheel chair, was Dr. DeRose. Father Craig was rolling him into the room. The last time I saw Dr. DeRose he was near death. The turnaround was miraculous. He was thinner and paler, but his eyes sparkled.

Emmanuel walked to him and knelt beside the wheel chair. He took Dr. DeRose's hand in both of his. DeRose looked into his eyes and began to weep.

"That's starting to be a trend," Simon said.

Secret Blood

Jimmy and his wife greeted Father Craig with handshakes and introductions. Emmanuel continued to talk with DeRose. Simon and I joined the group and added to the hand shaking. I felt the tears start to come myself as I leaned down to hug my old mentor. He was so thin he felt hollow.

"He did it you know. He saved me. I don't know why and I don't know for how long, but Emmanuel brought me back."

After a couple of minutes Emmanuel turned his attention back to Jimmy and his wife, and Father Craig slid over to us. Simon stood near the fireplace, resting his elbow on the mantle and sipping a tumbler of coke.

"He's changed. He's stronger," Father Craig said. "Before he looked like Him, but now it feels like Him."

"I know, but I'm around him so much I haven't noticed. But I've seen the reactions of other people. You're right, something is happening." I hated whispering and I was sure he knew we were talking about him.

The door Dr. DeRose and Father Craig had entered swung slowly open. The President's social secretary, Terri Barker, scanned the room. She wore an olive green business suit that brought out the blue in her eyes. She found Jimmy and motioned for him to join her in the hallway.

He excused himself and closed the door behind him. Almost instantly we could hear muffled voices. Not shouts but close, agitated maybe, and all coming from one voice.

I looked around for Emmanuel. I was relieved to see him still with Mrs. Rienhart with a sort of bemused look.

There was a shatter of glass. Simon had dropped his tumbler on the granite hearth and it had broken into a hundred pieces. He stood motionless staring at the hallway door.

Terri and Jimmy entered the room followed by a large black woman in a wild flowered dress. She had a necklace consisting of black spheres about the size of golf balls. Her make-up was overdone and her hair was straight, shoulder length, and flipped up on the ends. There was a strong possibility that it was a wig.

She marched in and sized up the room. For the first time I noticed a large print purse. It dangled from her arm like a tire swing from a mighty oak.

Simon had not moved from the fireplace, but he had lost the noble stance he had struck earlier. He had shrunk. "Mama?" he said weakly.

She was to him in about five steps. He disappeared from view as she embraced him into her ample bosom. Finally his arms snaked free and slid them across her back in a hug.

"I have no idea why they brought me here, damn Secret Service," she pulled away and looked at him, then squeezed him again. Everyone in the room was smiling now. She let go and gave Jimmy and Terri an evil looking glance, then turned her attention back to her son. She held him by his shoulders and looked him over. "What has been goin' on with you? Did they bring you here too?"

Simon looked around at the rest of us with a 'help me' expression.

"Please tell me this has nothin' to do with your gang bangin'."

"No, Mama," he said. "I'm all done with that."

"That's wonderful Simon." She grabbed him again and squeezed. "You're welcome back in my house then. As long as you're still not knockin' around with that hard case friend of yours. My children at school see you actin' all gangbusters and I lose all my credibility."

I could understand where Simon got his conversational genes. She barely let him get a word in. She changed the direction of the conversation so many times, I could barely keep up. But there was something honest about her. She had the feel of a teacher that could love you to death, then land on you with both feet if you stepped out of line.

She turned and looked at Jimmy and Terri. Terri turned on her heel and was out the door.

"I would like to know," she said in a voice that could wake the President, "why no one will tell me why we're here!"

I was the closest, so I felt I had to step up to the plate.

Secret Blood

"Your son has been protecting me," I said. I offered her my hand. She took it and held it and looked at me sort of sideways.

"Who are you?" she asked. She looked to Jimmy. "I thought he was in charge." Thankfully, there was a muffled noise at the door that led to the kitchen.

The aroma arrived before the pizza actually got there. Shine, who had lost the apron, was wearing a shiny, tight, black tee shirt and black dress pants, opened the door without looking in. He pulled a stainless steel serving cart behind him. The pizzas were beautifully prepared, red sauce, colorful toppings, and golden crust like an ad in a fine dining magazine.

I felt the pressure of her hand increase to the point that my knuckles popped. I sagged.

"So, he's here with you?" she said still crushing my hand.

Simon stood still, having about as much to say as a patch of moss.

"I thought you said you weren't running with that crowd anymore?"

Shine stopped moving as soon as he saw her there clamping down on my hand. Pizzas forgotten, he crossed his arms and stood impassible. His face rarely showed any expression but now his eyes were steely and his mouth only a thin line. The absence of any emotion from him usually caused fear in the observer, although this time, I sensed sadness.

At that point, Emmanuel stepped in and touched Mama on the shoulder. The sensation of his touch passed through her, down her arm, and into my hand. We both felt a jolt. It was a relaxing, joyful feeling. I looked at Emmanuel and for the first time I could see an aura around him. It glowed in waves, a white light emanated from him like in old paintings.

He lifted his hand and the light melted away, but the feeling remained. Now I understood why the others had been moved to tears. I understood how he was untouched by the coming of The Ghost and how those of us around him were less affected by it than the rest of the world. His power, unbeknownst to us, was a shield protecting our group for whatever we were about to undertake. I had never felt so ready and able, so capable.

Mama had seen the light also. She knew instantly. She didn't understand any of it, but she knew. Big tears began to roll. She was the hugging type and I could tell she wanted to squeeze the life out of Emmanuel, but after the feeling and the light show, she was torn.

"Perhaps we should revisit the story of the prodigal son," Emmanuel said, smiling a winning smile. She released my hand, and turned with him. Simon joined them and they walked toward Jimmy and Mrs. Rienhart who had watched the entire thing without moving.

I turned back to Shine who was still standing motionless, except now his eyes didn't seem focused, he was in deep thought.

"I don't mind jail," he said. "As long as it's for something I did. Don't much like being accused of something I had nothin' to do with."

"She thinks you brought Simon into the gang?" I asked.

He nodded slowly.

"Did you?" I asked

"Nope." He lightened slightly. "If you think he kinda foolish now, you should have seen him back then. He the Duke of Windsor now, compared to how he was." He uncrossed his arms and pulled the pizzas into the center of the room.

"I protected him."

The Rinehart's, including their daughters, began to drift toward the pizzas. Father Craig and Dr. DeRose followed. Shine began cutting the pies into slices.

"He could have gotten himself whacked so many times that I had to set up a sort of mentorship. To keep him alive I had to harden him up. Then one day I realized I was turning him into another me. That made me reevaluate my life. I had the rep so there were things I didn't have to do anymore 'cause everybody already know I did them once. Kinda' like being around a snake that already bit you once, he don't have to bite you again to prove himself. So we became a kind of gentler, more sophisticated kind of thugs. People still back away, just cause of who we are."

Secret Blood

"Like corporate lawyers," I said, trying to be funny.

Shine looked at me sideways while still slicing pizza. "But with a hard reputation."

It took me a moment to notice Terri was standing by the open door again and she was looking in our direction. She had her hand up to her mouth like someone about to cry. Then I saw her.

A beautiful little girl with smooth ebony skin walked between the two Rienhart girls. Elise was holding her left hand and Cooper was on her right. She wore a pink party dress with matching pink shoes. She had a saintly look on her face, the kind of happy look only a child can have. They stopped right behind us and the room went completely quiet.

Shine stopped slicing and looked around with the pizza cutter still in his hand. Their eyes met.

The girl offered her hand. "Hi, I'm Raye," she said. "I think you might be my dad."

Shine shifted the pizza cutter to his left hand and clumsily shook hands.

"I think I am," he said.

They stood there awkwardly shaking and looking at each other. Everyone watched, not sure exactly how this was going to go. Her smile faded when she could find no warmth in his face. Both of their lives were balancing on the next couple of moments. Then she let go of his hand and lunged, burying her face in his stomach and throwing her hands around his back.

Shine looked down at the top of her head and slowly brought his massive hands across the pink back of the dress. Emmanuel was smiling that self-amusing smile of his. Mama's hatred had melted and she was fishing for a tissue in her huge purse. The two Rienhart daughters were smiling nonchalantly, as if this was an everyday occurrence. The rest of us were pretty fatigued from the emotions of the day.

Without looking up, Raye said, "You're strong."

Shine looked at me, then at the floor. A single tear formed in the corner of his eye, "Yeah, I'm strong."

Chapter 89

Even though the temperatures had become spring-like, the evenings were still short. Darkness set in early and allowed the two more freedom to paint their messages undetected. It also increased the danger of being struck by a car since most of the messages were near the roadways. Steven and Cleo made the most of the darkness and had sprayed a dozen or so messages by the time Shine had met Raye.

They had one close call when a patrol car pulled off the highway under a blank billboard Steven had just begun to paint. The billboard was about twenty yards away from the road, mounted on the side of an embankment. It was lit from scaffolding that ran along the bottom of the billboard, a place for workers to stand when they hung a new sign.

Steven dropped flat and lay on the scaffolding as soon as he heard the patrol car crunching the gravel in the breakdown lane. Cleo had hidden in the bushes that were dormant on the embankment. Thank the Lord, he thought, it was winter and there were no varmints around to sneak out and bite him on the behind, as his mother used to say.

He could hear Steven giggling above him, louder than the road noise. He tried to shush him several times but to Steven this was like

Secret Blood

a big game of hide and seek. One he thought he couldn't lose. At one point Steven made shadow animals on the billboard like it was his own private theater.

Finally, after an hour of crouching, the patrol car pulled away and joined the wash of taillights heading east. The incident left Cleo drained and for the first time, wondering if he would be alive to see this through.

When Steven climbed down and met Cleo back on the berm of the road he noticed his friend was pale. Cleo was sitting on the pavement with his arms wrapped around his stomach looking defeated.

"Don't know how much farther I can go, Steven," Cleo said.

Seven smiled at him, "Don't have to walk much farther, we're going to ride. Yep, me and the Eggman. We are going to ride." He began to drum his fingers against his thumbs. "Come on," he reached down to pull Cleo up. It took an effort but Cleo finally got to his feet.

One step after another Cleo trudged down the edge of the highway while Steven hopped along beside him. They disappeared into the darkness as the taillights joined into long thin lines of scarlet.

* * *

Within the hour, the pair was on a Greyhound bus. Steven bought the tickets for his step-grandfather who was, as he told the ticket agent, feeling poorly. He paid for the tickets and still had about a hundred dollars left.

Cleo dozed off in the seat, warm, comfortable, and confident they were on their way to Washington D.C. Steven watched the darkness pass by, confident in his decision to buy tickets to New York City. The road to the White House would not be a straight one.

Chapter 90

It was a very joyous occasion, the pizza was cold but excellent, the conversations were loud and punctuated with laughter, and thoughts of an unknown presence in space, with the earth in its sight, were nonexistent. A brotherhood was developing, one that was bound by some strange force. Maybe we all knew that it was truly He and we were honored to be a part of it. Maybe it was because we knew that it was going to come down to us in some way to save mankind. Or maybe it was because we had all changed enough that we loved each other.

Simon's mother had taken to the children, especially Raye. She sat talking with them and every once in a while gave a voodoo eye to Shine. But, there was no real menace behind it like before. The Rinehart's held hands or touched constantly and Father Craig laughed and conferred with Dr. DeRose.

Then, I was struck with a slightly selfish thought. I was alone. Emmanuel had seen to it that everyone was with loved ones. Everyone except me. It became very noticeable from my point of view. I wasn't normally one to have jealous feelings, but I had to admit, I felt a little abandoned. I was basically the one that brought all these people together, and yet I was the one who had been left out.

Terri slipped back into the room and went directly to Jimmy. They spoke softly and the cheerful look slipped from Jimmy's face. Without saying anything to anyone he went to the bar and found a long black remote control. He pointed it at the wall across the room and an oak panel opened soundlessly revealing a large flat screen. It clicked on, with the same remote, showing a jerky picture somewhere in the Middle East. There were thousands of people in the streets, fists pumping and stomping burning American flags. From somewhere off camera a machine gun let loose a barrage of shots, followed by several other guns being shot into the air.

An interpreter was translating the message that had been dubbed over the footage. She said, in her own heavy accent, that the Americans were responsible for the object in the sky and the only way to save the world was to crush the infidels and appease Allah. Jihad was coming.

Emmanuel gently took the remote from Jimmy and hit the power button. He smiled at us and said, "And so it begins."

"So that's it? It's just a battle between us and the rag heads?" Simon asked.

Emmanuel's smile did not waver, "No, we are not the Knights Templar. We will not fight anyone. We have been chosen to do God's work, fighting may be someone else's work, but not ours."

"Then, what is the plan?" Jimmy asked. "I get the feeling that things are really going to start happening now."

"There is no plan," Emmanuel said.

I'll have to admit, that was one of the most frightening statements I had heard in a while. The others had the same look on their faces.

"I think I can speak for the others here," Simon said, "We were hopin' that someone could, you know, hook us up with a plan." He nodded his head toward the ceiling.

Emmanuel smiled again, the smile that strengthened the heart. "God may have a plan, but he does not always share it with us. Have faith."

"We got plenty of that," Jimmy said. "It is a great burden for us, for just the people in this room to carry."

"Is it any more of a burden than Mary had to carry? There are only two messages. Love God and love each other. Stay with those two and you can do no wrong." He paused for a moment then added. "You are wrong about one thing. It is not just those of us in this room. We have the easiest tasks ahead. There are two others who have not joined us yet. They are the ones that will show us and the world the sign."

That took the air out of the room. I felt very close to the people here. I could not imagine anyone outside the group that I could trust as much. I thought the others were thinking the same thing. It was almost snobbish, but I didn't think anyone else deserved to be invited in. Instantly, I thought, that is twice tonight I've put my feelings before the good of the group, what's wrong with me?

"Everyone," Father Craig said, "Dr. DeRose has found some interesting things on the Internet." Dr. DeRose had wheeled himself up to a computer and was typing. We gathered behind him to see the screen.

"The night we first saw the jar," he began, "I thought there was something familiar about the shape and the design. The design haunted me for days. The only thing I could recollect was that it was not the focus of my memory, but a secondary object in the memory. Sort of like not being able to remember a name but being able to remember the first letter of the name." He hit a button on the keyboard and a painting of Mary Magdalene appeared. There, in the background was an alabaster jar. It was not exactly like our jar, but close enough to make one wonder.

He hit another button and another painting emerged. It was apparent that it was another artist's impression of Mary Magdalene, but there again was another jar.

"Mary is pictured with a jar of some kind on at least half of the masterpieces I have found. The Masters like Fontana, Di Buoninsegna, Campi, Lorenzetti, and van der Weydeu. The list is long."

I think Father Craig and I were the only ones in the room that were not astounded by this revelation. I thought Dr. DeRose should not have been surprised either, but he seemed very excited by the fact. I spoke up before Father Craig.

"But isn't that what Mary was known for? The salves and lotions and washing feet were her trademark; until Dan Brown, that's how most people thought of Mary."

"True, true," said DeRose. "But I find it interesting. Given the information the FBI has provided, along with the legend that the Holy Grail was once held in the same area where Mary Magdalene was thought to have died, one can draw a line, from the time of the Crucifixion, to the break-ins at Fort Knox."

"If that's so, why didn't the Vatican keep better track of it? How could they let the Blood of Jesus just disappear?" Jimmy asked.

"Maybe no one knew. The first person to have all the facts must have been Rundell," DeRose said. "I don't know how he added it all together, maybe we'll never know."

"So what's this all mean?" Simon said.

"Maybe nothing," DeRose said. "But maybe it means that down through the ages, someone has left a trail to follow. A way to backtrack the trek of the Blood. They might not have even known they were doing it. The artists might have put the jars in the pictures without knowing why they were doing it."

He typed in one final name. Jan van Scorel. A rather unflattering likeness of Mary came up. She looked a little plump and had a kind of milkmaid look to her.

"Look at this one. It seems a bit of a controversy has brewed over her clothing." He arrowed down until he found an insert that focused on the wide collar of her dress. There were letters sewn in around the edge.

"What does it say," I asked.

"That's the thing," he said. "No one can identify the language for certain. Researchers can't agree if it's Hebrew or a language even older. According to the experts the closest interpretation would be 'mother'."

"Why would Mary Magdalene be mother?" Father Craig asked.

"Looking at it from our perspective," DeRose said, "perhaps it is she who brings life to Jesus, or brings life back."

We stared at the screen, each contemplating our own place. History was unraveling faster than we could comprehend it.

"It's like that Ian Hunter dude said," Simon mumbled, "We ain't the chain, we're just a link."

Chapter 91

Phillips and Farrah, the two over enthusiastic FBI agents that had so vigorously pursued the suicide of Anna Rundell had been busted down to the lowest grade possible without being completely tossed out of the agency. They were transferred to a different section, under a different chief, who had no loyalty or affection for them. To him they were just a couple of screw-ups who were dumped on him.

They were assigned to a special task force, the special team only having two members; them. This task force was to evaluate the possibility of gangs being infiltrated by terrorist groups and the implications thereof. There was absolutely no chance of this happening, but it was the perfect way to keep the overachievers out of the chief's hair. Because of the nature of this job, most of their waking hours were spent looking out the windows of large, plain sedans. They spent so many nights on stakeouts that no one in their section could identify them as working there. They filed reports no one ever read, made no new friends or allies, and were destined to be cemented to the bottom rung of any career ladder.

But even though they were smug, cocky, and a bit on the Buzz Lightyear side, they were not dumb. The fruitless hours of gang observance did produce one small interesting tidbit. They started to observe the graffiti around the area. The first thing that caught Phillip's attention was a very simplistic stick figure. Its head was raised to the sky and its arms spread wide. The whole body was bent as if to gather in the heavens in one large embrace.

He remembered the figure from somewhere. It didn't click until he read the message with religious overtones beneath it. It couldn't possibly be the work of the Rundell woman, these paintings were new. They took it upon themselves to contact the local police and set up a database of any other religious vandalism in the vicinity. They needed to find some hard facts to prove the cases were related, and then take it to their old boss. Maybe there was another chance for two "can do" kind of agents. And there was the big question. Why was the graffiti signed, "The Walrus"?

Chapter 92

There is nothing like an overnight bus ride for thinking long and deep thoughts. The cushion suspension, the low background noise of the tires on the pavement, and the gentle sway of the interstate turns, induce a relaxation that leads to contemplation.

Cleo glanced at the fragile boy sleeping in the seat beside him. Here in the dim light, he looked small and innocent. He had a general idea he had come from some kind of special home and that his departure had been hasty and probably illegal. No doubt, he himself was breaking several laws, including crossing state lines with a juvenile whom he had no business with anyway.

The seats he and Steven occupied were called theater seats, which meant they were slightly raised so the driver's head was about the same height as their knees. Cleo watched out the window, then out the windshield.

Cleo saw that the driver was watching him from the mirror above the windshield. He would watch the road for a few moments then glance up. He was a black man with salt and pepper hair that curled around the band of his driver's cap. His shirt and tie were pressed nicely and his chrome name badge said J.B.

"You feeling better?" J.B. asked, his eyes still surveying the road then returning to him.

"Yes, I do," Cleo said. "Just a little tried. My grandson has been running me ragged."

"That your grandson?"

"Yes, he is," Cleo said.

"Uh huh," J.B. said.

They rode in silence for a few miles. Cleo, after reconsidering his situation, realized that maybe giving false information was more suspicious than pretending to fall back asleep. The seats were made for comfortable riding, but not for comfortable sleeping. He snuggled in but for only a second.

"Ever been to New York before?" J.B. asked.

"Not for a long time," Cleo said. "Why do you ask?"

"I was just wondering if you were bringing your grandson here for the first time or bringing him back home."

"New York? Isn't this the bus to Washington D.C.?"

"New York," J.B. said still holding onto the wheel and studying Cleo more closely. "Your grandson seemed to know where you were going."

Cleo didn't say anything. He was furious at Steven. Mistakes like this could put him in prison and send Steven back to wherever he came from. J.B. was still watching him.

"I've been driving for a good while and seen all kinds come and go. I can tell you ain't right, don't know how yet, but I know something about you just ain't right."

Cleo inhaled and let it out slowly. His back was starting to hurt again.

"We're about the same age, aren't we?"

"Maybe," J.B. said.

"You in the service?"

"Yep."

"Vietnam?"

"Sort of," J.B. said. "The war, not the country."

"Come again?"

"Stayed here in the states the whole time. Had three brothers deployed over there. They didn't want to send the whole family; I was the youngest, so I stayed. Stationed at Fort Bragg the entire time."

"That must have been tough."

J.B. watched the road. "Yeah. Spent half my time thanking God for my good luck, spent the other half feeling guilty for not being there."

"So," Cleo said, "you know what it's like to promise things to God?"

"I think every solider does."

"Well J.B., that's what I'm doing now, fulfilling my promise. This young man here is leading me somewhere, and I'm going take his hand and follow as long as I am able."

J.B. slowly nodded and kept his eyes on the road. "So this boy, he ain't your grandson?"

"No, he isn't. I could tell you the story, but you'd probably throw me off the bus and call the police. You would think I was a nut job." Cleo shook his head. "Maybe I am."

"No, the real nuts never think they are wrong, they think they're the sane ones."

Steven began to stir. He opened his eyes and looked at Cleo and smiled.

"You found out, didn't you? You found out where we are going."

"If it wasn't for Mr. J.B. here, I'd be looking for the Washington Monument."

Steven giggled. He sat up and looked around. His new jeans were stiff and the plain blue shirt had come untucked. His hair had always been a mess but now it was flattened on one side. He noticed J.B. looking at him in the mirror. He waved. J.B. just gave a little nod.

"Okay, Steven, what's the plan. What are we going to do in New York?" Cleo asked.

"You got to go see Matt," Steven said, looking at J.B.

"Matt. Who is Matt?" Cleo asked.

"Matt Lauer, silly." Steven said. At the name, J.B.'s head jerked up. He stared at Steven. Cleo noticed and looked back and forth between them.

"Why do we have to see Matt Lauer?" Cleo asked.

"You have to tell him about me so we can go make the committee believe."

The bus rolled on seemingly more quiet than before. J.B. shifted in his seat and took his cap off. He upped the air conditioner. He looked at the road less and at Steven more. Steven looked pleased with himself and Cleo was watching what was going on between them.

"This is the news guy on the Today Show, right?" Cleo asked.

"Yep."

"And how are we going to introduce ourselves to Matt?" Cleo asked.

"Not me, at least not at first. You are going to talk to him before I do." Steven said and smiled at J.B. "Mr. J.B. is going to help you get in to see him."

Cleo looked at J.B. He appeared very uncomfortable now, almost to the point of being ill.

J.B. looked at the road and said, "I'm going to stop at the first gas station we come to, then I'll be dropping you two off."

"Why? What did he say? I promise you I have no idea what is going on." Cleo said. "Why do you care who we go to see?"

"This kid is spooking me."

Cleo looked at Steven and tried to remain calm. He didn't want to be stuck at some gas station in the middle of the night. "Tell me what is making J.B. look at us as though we were from Mars."

"Because he has a connection to Matt Lauer, don't you Mr. J.B.?"

J.B. was not saying a word and it looked like he wasn't going to acknowledge the question. He kept both hands on the wheel and drove a little faster.

"I got to go to the bathroom," Steven said. He got up stiffly and scooted down the aisle toward the restroom in the rear of the bus.

"I know he is…..different," Cleo said. "And maybe a little spooky. But we are doing something here that is very important. Don't ask me what it is because I don't know. I don't know if you want to believe this or not but I have had visions of him for a long time. By the looks of your reaction you have had something happen too."

J.B. shook his head like he was arguing with himself.

"You know I haven't thought about this for a long time." He shook his head again and his eyes reddened. "I told you I was the only one of my brothers not sent overseas. Maybe I didn't tell you the real reason I stayed here. Not that it made any sense at the time. Not until now." He looked back and forth between the mirror and the road.

"When I was in basic, the base commander sent for me. I thought I was in trouble because a base commander just doesn't invite a new recruit in for lunch."

Cleo leaned forward, J.B.'s voice was getting lower and it was getting harder to hear him.

"So they take me to his office and I'm standing at attention there in front of him. And you know what he does?" Cleo was right behind his left ear. He shook his head no.

"He shakes my hand. He says, 'at ease,' and shakes my hand." J.B. isn't telling the story to Cleo anymore, he's telling it to himself remembering something forgotten with time.

"He says that it's an honor to meet me. I was sure he had me confused with a football player or a singer or something. He was a stiff old white guy, gray flattop, everything strictly by the book. Kept looking into my eyes. Told me nothing was going to happen to me on his watch. Then finally he said it was an honor to meet me and told me to be ready. And I left. Never saw him again."

Cleo leaned back. "That's a strange story, but what does that have to do with us?"

J.B. wasn't an emotional kind of guy, but it was easy to tell he was fighting back tears. "I have one brother who made it back alive. So, it was just he and I, the others were all killed." He hesitated then looked into the mirror. "My brother is the limo driver for Matt Lauer."

* * *

The horizon began to lighten and the traffic started to grow thicker. From the back, passengers started to move around and make morning noises. Steven sat up quickly and looked around, then realized where he was. He giggled and drummed his fingers, plans in place.

J.B. and Cleo had both come to the conclusion that Steven was the one driving the bus. Not the physical one they were riding on, but the decision-maker who was really controlling the journey. Steven had explained the plan in a clear concise manner, like a general laying out an intricate battle plan. The constant giggling and drumming gave credence to the fact that he was receiving direction from above, something both J.B. and Cleo decided silently.

It actually was a very simple plan given the fact that the most difficult components were laid right in their collective laps. Steven needed to be invited into the White House. The messages in spray paint laid the foundation for that. The stick figure he had seen in his dreams and painted could not be dismissed as a bunch of 'the end is near' messages.

Now he had to be seen, in public, in a rational way, as a prophet. He had to be credible and believable without being found out and taken back to the Center. He could not walk up to the White House and announce himself. Once he had accomplished all of this he had no idea what was to come next. The only thing he knew was, to convince them with their names, whatever that meant.

The on air talent for the Today Show arrive very early at Rockefeller Plaza. Not as early as the support staff, but earlier than most of America wants to think about. The drivers, who bring them to the studio, do so knowing they have a few hours break until the show is over and they can whisk them off, back to their homes or to other business they might have. During this break they congregate at a coffee shop in the plaza that opens early for them.

The drivers are employed by the same company and wear the same dark suit, white shirt, and dark tie. J.B. had given them the name of his brother and a note to hand to him. Steven had written a note of his own.

The air breaks shot off a blast of air as the bus rolled to a stop. Cleo took the note and shook hands with J.B. Cleo told him they would be within a couple of blocks of the coffee shop if he needed to contact them. J.B. had a two-day lay over, a rarity that surprised no one. Then they would finish the deal.

Chapter 93

About the same time Cleo and Steven began the short walk to the coffee shop, Jimmy was awakened by a ringing telephone. He reached for the phone, which he always left on his nightstand, when he realized his nightstand wasn't there. He was not in his bed at home; he was in the one he slept in when he stayed at the White House. And the warm bundle of covers beside him was his lovely wife, whom he had not woken up with for weeks. These things passed through his mind instantly, along with the realization that the phone was on the nightstand on Patricia's side of the bed.

"Well, that's one thing I didn't miss," she said distantly.

Jimmy got up and walked stiffly around the end of the bed.

He had stopped saying, "this had better be good." It was never good when someone called this early. He was afraid that good in this situation meant horrific or catastrophic.

"Yeah," was what he could manage.

"The Ghost is gone. It disappeared like before."

"It's gone just like that?" Jimmy felt a sense of happiness began to surge, he began to pace with the phone. "This is great. Unbelievable."

There was silence from the other end of the line. "Is this Frank?"

"Maybe, it's great. Just remember, every time it's disappeared before, it has reappeared closer."

Jimmy let that sink in.

"I've got some significant numbers you should see. The Random Number Generators around the world are spiking some amazing strings."

"Random what?" Jimmy asked.

"There are generators all over the world and…"

Jimmy cut him off. "I don't know what you're talking about, but if it's important, get over to the White House within the hour. And you'd better be able to explain it to the President."

He sat back down on the side of the bed and looked at his wife. Someday his life would calm back down. Maybe he could just finish this term with his brother then step down. Washington was not great for relationships. Funny, he was considering long range goals when the reappearance of The Ghost loomed ahead. The doom of a few days ago had lightened considerably.

The first time he had a good look at it, he was frightened. A thought hit him. The more powerful Emmanuel became, the less intimidating The Ghost became. That was a good sign, he guessed.

Chapter 94

One by one, the heads turned to look at Cleo as he walked into the coffee shop. Their conversations dissipated as he wove his way around the maze of tables regarding each face he passed. The place wasn't really open to the public, but it wasn't closed either. This was the first non-chauffeur patron they had ever seen at this time of the morning. The shop smelled like breakfast food.

The tabletops were orange Formica with chrome legs, the chairs were plastic. There were four or five drivers to a table, some with bagels, some with doughnuts, and all with coffee. They look friendly enough, Cleo thought, but he felt like an outsider. Someone at a family reunion that nobody knew. They looked at him expectantly.

He wore his black suit that he had kept ready for years. It appeared worn compared to the chauffeurs' suits and it hung on his frail body like it was borrowed. He trudged in slowly and slightly stooped, hoping someone would ask if they might be able to help him. No one did.

"I'm looking for Dwight Gill," he said.

"That's me," said a man a couple of tables over.

"I wonder if I could have a word," Cleo asked smoothly.

The man didn't move, clearly hesitating. He felt the pressure from the faces in the room.

"I have a message from your brother," Cleo said.

Dwight stood and motioned toward an empty table near the back of the room. Cleo followed and gradually the conversations started again. Cleo had a bit of trouble sitting, the back pain was advancing. Flashes of biting agony circled forward across his stomach and ribs.

He took the note from his left pants pocket and slid it across the slick table. It was a folded up piece of paper torn from a spiral notebook. It looked like a note slipped to someone during study hall.

Cleo had no idea what the note said. He had no idea what Steven's note said either, but it was still safe in his right pants pocket. Dwight unfolded the note, still staring at Cleo. Cleo stared back, smiling his warmest smile and tracing little figure eight's on the table.

He read the note, then looked at Cleo again.

"Is this a joke?" he asked. "I could lose my job over something like this."

"No Joke," Cleo said. Dwight sat, thinking. "Let me see the other note."

Cleo pulled out the other note, Steven's note. It was written on the same type of paper as the first, only this one was stapled shut.

"I don't know what this says. But whatever it is, it's important, more than you can comprehend at this time," Cleo said.

"You want me to pass a note to a network anchor man without reading it?"

'You can do what you want as long as I have your word that you will pass it to him. You brother said that you keep your word."

Dwight looked doubtful but started peeling the paper back from the staples.

Cleo could see Steven's labored handwriting through the paper.

"If your boss finds this interesting, call your brother and we will set up a meeting about this time tomorrow," Cleo said. "If he doesn't, we won't bother you again."

Dwight finished reading and laid the note down on the table. "You aren't a terrorist are you?"

That shook Cleo a little. Steven had gone vacant when he wrote the note.

"How do you know my brother, he doesn't explain that in the letter here." He held the first note his hand.

Cleo explained, Dwight listened. He was still hesitant about passing the note. Some of the other drivers were starting to get to their feet, probably some of their fares were the earlier guests and their interviews were finishing up. Time to move the limos into position.

Dwight laid Steven's note on the table. It was open but upside down to Cleo.

"Sorry, I got to know what it says. I'm as curious as you were." Cleo said as he spun the note around so he could read it.

> Dear Mr. Lauer
> Today, at 1:00 p.m., United States time, there will be a big explosion at the Datang power plant near Beijing. I am sorry to tell you that a bunch people will die. They are switching from a coal fire to a gas fire or the other way around I'm not sure. I can predict stuff. I can tell you much, much more if you want.
> The Walrus

Cleo leaned back in his chair and blew out a breath. Steven was scary, no doubt about that. He looked at Dwight. He still looked doubtful. He reread his brother's note.

"Sounds crazy, doesn't it? I thought the same thing. No reason we should be doing any of this." Cleo was drawing the figure eight's again and looking at the table as he spoke.

Then he stopped and looked into Dwight's eyes. "But we are. It feels like we should. I don't even know why you are here listening to me. But you are. This just feels like something I have to do. I can feel it clear to my bones, and my guess is, you can, too."

Secret Blood

Dwight slowly began to nod. It wasn't much, but it was enough to see he agreed. He stood, picked up the note and put it in his breast pocket.

"I hope this is legit," he said and started to walk back to his table. He stopped and turned back to Cleo. "You're not the Walrus, are you?"

"No," Cleo said, "He is only a boy."

"Great," said Dwight. "Just great."

* * *

Cleo walked back to the McDonalds where he had left Steven. He had told him to eat slow and order something else when the management started looking at him. The breakfast crowd was just starting so he wasn't that noticeable. He looked a little like a vagrant but he was spending money and he didn't smell. No odor is always a plus.

When Cleo sat, Steven smiled and pushed a cup towards him.

"I got you coffee. What did Mr. J.B.'s brother say? Is he going to do it?"

"I think so," Cleo said, smiling. The walk had helped his back. "Why didn't you tell me about the explosion, that's a horrible thing."

"I didn't make it happen. I am just reporting it, like a reporter."

"Before it happens?"

"Yeah, what's the big deal reporting it after it happens? Anyone can do that."

Cleo sipped the coffee and watched his young friend. He had a pile of NYC brochures laid out on the table. Some were maps and others more informational. Each had been opened and clumsily refolded. Steven organized them in an order that only he could understand and shoved them into his coat pocket.

"Do you want to go and try to make a little money? I thought maybe we could get a hotel room tonight."

"You mean, you play and I sing?" Steven asked. "Beatle songs?"

"Yep, Beatle songs."

Chapter 95

The President and his brother waited for Frank to arrive in the same room he had first reported to them concerning The Ghost. All three men would agree, that seemed like years ago. Frank had been offered something to eat but declined, per orders of Margaret. They did not offer twice and got down to business.

"All right Frank, explain to the President what you were explaining to me," Jimmy said.

"Okay," he said as though he had rehearsed it several times. "There are generators in different places in the world. All these generators do is spit out numbers. Some do zeros and ones, other do integers up to ten, I think there are even some that do larger numbers. Anyway, they generate random numbers, supposedly. There is still a lot of debate over this whole branch of science."

"Frank," Jimmy said, "just tell us what we need to know."

"Sorry," he said going back to his rehearsed speech. "The numbers the researchers are getting now are abnormal. There are long strings of numbers that are apparently not random."

"How can that be?" asked the President.

"That is where this kind of science gets even a little mystical. Many of the people that believe this kind of thing think there is a collective consciousness for humanity."

"Like the Force in Star Wars?" Jimmy asked.

Frank chuckled. "Sort of, but I haven't got to the strangest part yet. Several of the labs are generating the same number. 5646316. Either in groups of ten or separated by a group of zeros."

"So that's a big deal?" the President asked.

"Yeah, these guys get excited when there are three like numbers in a row. Now we have hundreds, maybe thousands."

"Anyone know what that number is?" Jimmy asked.

"Not yet, not enough time to examine it."

"Maybe," Jimmy said, "we should hold back on the solving part. At least officially. We don't want someone translating it into some kind of message of doom."

"Does it look like some kind of message?" the President asked.

Frank thought about it for a second. "In nature and society, patterns always mean something, so yeah, if there is anything at all to these generators, these are some pretty specific patterns."

"When did this all start?" Jimmy asked.

"Last night at the exact moment The Ghost disappeared."

"Let's call the committee together this afternoon and get a handle on the reaction this will have," the President said.

"Which committee?" Frank asked.

"There's more than one?" Jimmy asked.

The President gave Jimmy a look that could wilt a cactus. "I've put some people together to look at a different aspect of The Ghost situation."

"Without telling me about it?" Jimmy said, with his voice rising.

The President said, "At the time you were not yourself. You were having weird ideas about the cloning thing. I decided we needed to look into the military aspect."

"Without my advice. When were you going to tell me about it?"

"Calm down, let me remind you that you are not only talking to your brother but also to the President of the United States."

Jimmy stiffened.

"Anyway, we came up with no viable solution. The military option is out," the President said. "Jimmy is right, we need to get the first committee back together and see what we have."

Jimmy stood and left without saying a word.

Chapter 96

Later that morning, Dwight passed the note to Matt Lauer. He had opened the rear passenger door and handed him the note as he sat. He read it, then stuck in his pants pocket and forgot about it. He was surprised his driver would take advantage of his position and pass crazy notes to him. He liked the guy. They discussed events and people in the car. He reported craziness almost every morning; he didn't want his drive to feel the same way.

Later that afternoon as he was checking his e-mail, Yahoo was reporting an explosion at a power plant in China. He pulled the note out of his pocket. He looked at the clock. It read one thirty. He pulled out a cell phone and dialed his producer. The ball was rolling.

* * *

By two o'clock Dwight had talked to J.B. and the two of them were cruising the area near the coffee shop looking for Cleo and Steven. J.B. was kicking himself mentally, wishing he had made better plans for reconnecting. Driving around looking for someone in Rockefeller Center can be almost impossible. The warm temperatures were setting records, which added strangeness to the afternoon.

Initially, Dwight had not been happy with his brother's decision to involve him in this escapade. But once the producer had called

Secret Blood

the agency to find him and he realized his job was not being terminated, his reluctance dropped. They talked about the odd pair, that for some reason, they were willing to help. Talking and searching they decided they too were going to follow this to the end, much like Cleo said he would do.

J.B. finally spotted Steven carrying a cup of coffee down the busy sidewalk. He was dodging people left and right, spilling coffee, and giggling.

Dwight pulled over and J.B. yelled out the window.

"Hey, Walrus, how you doing?"

Steven spun around and looked in the window. He smiled.

"They called, didn't they? They want The Eggman and me to get interviewed by Matt Lauer."

"Yep, you called it. Where is Cleo?" J.B. asked.

"He's right down the street."

A cab started honking its horn behind them. Dwight waved him around, which drew more honking.

"We'll follow you," J.B. said.

Within an hour Steven was getting make up and a stylist was trying to figure out what to do with his hair.

* * *

The big four, Jimmy's nickname for Emmanuel, Shine, Simon and I, were confined to our rooms and the dining room of the previous evening.

Shine was in constant motion around the room. Meeting his daughter had made him anxious. He was eager to make her a permanent part of his life and he was not the type to waste any time getting what he wanted. He could wait for hours in surveillance for Mr. Stubbs, but to get his daughter back, he did not want to wait another minute.

Emmanuel spent most of his time now in prayer. He would pray for long periods of time oblivious to the things around him. I liked to watch him, although I felt a little like I was invading more than just his privacy. He was so serene, so calm that it affected my emotions. Each moment he prayed I gained strength.

Simon sat on the couch and watched TV. He seemed affected the least by the surprises of the previous evening. He was happy, but it was not a life-altering event for him. He hadn't changed. He was interested in the same things yesterday as he was today. And none of the things he was interested in were on TV. He switched channels even more fiendishly than he usually did.

"Oprah, I can understand. At least she tryin' to help folks. But Judge Judy? Man, you know how much she worth?" He started flipping again. "Like my Mama used to say, what's this world comin' to?"

He stopped, reversed and came back to a channel that had a close up of a young boy with his hair plastered down. He was talking to Matt Lauer.

"What's Matt Lauer doing on in the afternoon?" he said.

Matt was sitting at his usual interview spot, the left side of the screen, in an uncomfortable looking chair, holding a legal pad. The interviewee was to the right, separated from Matt by a small round coffee table. The usually personable Lauer seemed a bit unhinged by the fidgeting and laughing guest.

"I don't know your name. What should I call you?" Matt asked.

"I'm the Walrus, that's the Eggman over there," Steven pointed off screen.

"Coo coo kachoo," he sang. Then he giggled and stood, drumming his fingers. He wore jeans and a Pirates baseball jersey, complete with yellow wristbands.

"Okay, Walrus, I wanted to talk to you today about the note you sent me this morning. Do you remember the note?"

"I wrote it, do you think I'd forget it?" He giggled again. He sat back down quickly and pulled a banana from the bowl on the table. He held it to his mouth like a microphone.

"All right," Matt said. He began to look as if this was a horrible idea.

"Just to let the listeners know," he explained, "a note was given to me this morning, informing me about an explosion that had not even happened yet."

Steven remained silent and held the banana.

"So tell me, how did you know that power plant was going to explode?"

"I don't know, I guess God just showed me."

"But why you, why not me or Inky, the camera man, over there?"

"Because I am the Walrus, coo coo kachoo," Steven said into the banana. He jumped up again and dragged the mike, pinned to his shirt, across the bowl on the table.

Lauer jumped at the sudden movement. The camera tried to follow Steven but it was not designed to follow quick movement. The scene was chaos momentarily, while a sound girl clipped the mike back on and a stagehand retrieved the rolling fruit.

Then the vacant side of Steven appeared. He sat slowly and put the banana on the table. His eyes softened and he spoke in a different voice.

"There is something happening now, only it's in another country. France, yeah it's France." The drumming of his fingers was barely noticeable now, the voice lowered to a whisper.

Simon yelled to the others, "Hey, you gotta come in here and see this kid."

I sat on the couch with Simon; Shine stood behind the couch watching the screen over our heads. Simon was watching for the entertainment value, I was captivated by the kid, and Shine was, well, he was watching to get his mind off of his daughter. Simon turned up the volume when Steven started whispering.

"The water level in reactor A is getting too low, the core is getting too hot and no one is doing anything about it." Steven stared straight ahead without blinking.

"Where is this power plant? Is it nuclear? What city?"

It was impossible for me to tell whether Lauer believed him or if he was trying to save the interview. He motioned for someone off camera to check it out.

"Saint Alben, that's the name of the town. Somebody needs to tell them. Reactor A is still overheating."

Steven switched back into his bubbly self. He popped back up and giggled. Lauer jumped again. Steven grabbed the banana.

"But that's not what I came to tell you. That's nothing compared to what I need to tell you," Steven said.

"What did you come to tell us and why did you choose me?"

"I picked you cause I knew you would talk to me, cause your ratings are down."

That took Lauer back considerably.

"I came to tell you that He is back and He is going to save the world."

That took me back considerably.

"Man, he knows," Simon said. "That crazy kid knows."

We watched as Steven took the legal pad and Sharpie that Lauer was holding and began to draw. He used short jerky motions and drew quickly. The cap of the Sharpie flew off the back but he kept on drawing. When he finished he dropped the marker and held the pad in front of his chest. He walked toward the camera, moving out of focus.

"Are you getting this?" he yelled.

"I'll show it," Lauer said, "Just bring it back here."

Steven was stretching the cord to its limits when he turned to take the drawing back to Lauer. He held it still and the cameraman focused in on a stick drawing with the arms extended and palms up.

"What's that remind you of?" Shine asked.

I knew what he was thinking. It resembled the pose Emmanuel struck during the shootout. Resembled was an understatement. It looked exactly like him. I wondered how many people were making the same connection.

"Maybe you should call Jimmy," said a voice from behind us. It was Emmanuel, standing in the doorway. A smile creased his face.

"He may find this boy very interesting." I started dialing and the others focused back on the TV.

"And something else," the boy shouted, loud enough to make the speaker blare.

"The Ghost is coming back and this time it's going to hit us." It felt like everyone in the studio froze. You could feel it over the airways. Lauer didn't say anything; the usual cutting from one face to the other stopped and left us only looking at Matt. There was an uncomfortable silence before the one camera panned back to Steven.

Steven looked into the camera and said only one word. "Kabam!" Then he ran off the set and straight to Cleo. They embraced.

"I did it!" Steven said. "I told the world, I told the word. The truth is out there!"

Cleo had to laugh.

Back on stage Matt was composing himself.

"That was the self-proclaimed 'Walrus' making several predictions. We are going to play this interview again in its entirety after this commercial break."

He stood, unclipped his mike and dropped it in his chair. He didn't know or maybe didn't care that the director hadn't cut away yet. But we watched as he left the stage slightly perplexed and visibly shaken. An Insurance commercial started.

Jimmy finally answered his phone. "Did you see the kid on with Matt Lauer just now?" I asked.

"Just now? What's Matt Lauer doing on in the afternoon?"

"I don't know. Listen, just turn on MSNBC and watch for a few minutes," I said and hung up.

Matt was back, looking a little ashen. He explained how he had received the note and the circumstances with which it came.

"Understanding that," he said, "along with the odd interview we are going to replay now, I would be remiss if I did not report this. Only moments ago a nuclear reactor near the city of Saint Alben entered a dangerous cycle that would have led to a meltdown. Our staff alerted the engineers at the power plant, possibly saving millions of lives. To say it more clearly, the boy's predictions were right."

As we began to watch the interview from the beginning, the telephone rang.

Jimmy said, "I got a car on the way."

* * *

Hundreds of miles away, at the West Wood Center for Children, Zonnie sat motionless. She was staring at the television, a spoon dangling halfway between her mouth and a bowl of vanilla ice cream. There was her little Tadpole, the boy who spoke only to her, talking to Matt Lauer.

Chapter 97

The committee convened in a newer and more comfortable room than the last time. They were seated around the outer rim of a semi-circular table, nameplates in front of each, as if they didn't know each other. At the open end was a thin podium and behind that was a marker board, like the ones coaches use in the locker room.

Most of those in attendance had taken their things out of their briefcases, placed them on the table, and then parked the briefcases on the floor. They waited grimly, in silence, for the President. The Judge was his usual abrasive self and slapped his walking stick on the table beside his folder.

Jimmy was waiting in an outer office for the President. He had watched the replay of the boy several times and was certain this was one of the people Emmanuel had meant when he said there were two left to join us.

His cell phone buzzed. "Yeah," he said.

"This is your old buddy at the FBI," Snider said. "You know—the one you already owe a favor to?"

"Yes, I remember, how'd you get this number?"

"I just said I work at the FBI. Hey listen, remember the two geniuses that broke into the church? On that thing you wanted me to look into?"

"Yeah, I remember," Jimmy said.

"Well, they came up with something. There was a drawing of a stick figure at the Rundell woman's house. A little weird, seemed insignificant at the time. But dozens of these drawings have been showing up all over Ohio." He waited on some kind of response. Jimmy said nothing.

"Are you still interested in this case?" Snider asked.

"Somewhat, keep me posted." He hung up leaving Snider confused and a little disappointed.

He was thinking about this and replaying the interview over in his mind and did not hear the President walk in behind him. He jumped when the President spoke to him.

"Jeeze, I didn't mean to startle you." The President looked sheepish. "Listen we need to talk before we go in."

"It's all right," Jimmy said. "It was my fault; you clearly have the right to call for any meeting you like. I was just kind of stunned I didn't know about it. Maybe I'm getting a little too big for my britches."

"I should have told you what I was doing," the President said. "You're only going to be the Chief of Staff for a few more years, but you're always going to be my brother." He extended his hand and Jimmy took it.

"By the way, Patricia is back. With the kids."

The President smiled and grabbed his brother again. "That's great! You'd better not mess it up again."

Jimmy grinned and opened the door for the President. As they stepped into the room everyone around the table stood. Judge Ashton was the last to rise. Jimmy took a seat at the end of the semicircle. The President switched from happy brother to the leader of the free world.

"First off, has anyone got anything new?" he asked them.

Ken Jenkins was first to speak up. "We have a very negative rating in the e-mail chatter; it's the worst we've had since the weeks following 9/11."

"What's that mean, a negative rating?" the President asked.

"We monitor the nation's e-mail to get a sense of the nation's morale. The more negative the vocabulary, the lower the population feels. We can tie announcements to the mood of the county. Let's say we want to increase troop strength in a certain country. We don't want to release that news when the population is in a negative cycle."

"So what does that mean for us?" Jimmy asked.

"It means people are worried about The Ghost, even more so now that it has disappeared. We were counting on the opposite."

There was a knock on the door. The room became silent, meeting of these types were never interrupted. The President looked at me as if to say 'what now'?

Kim poked her head in and motioned for Jimmy to step out of the room. He said to the President, "I'll be right back." He stepped out and closed the door.

"They are here," she said. "In your office."

It took about five minutes to walk back. When Jimmy opened the door, Cleo was sitting on the couch looking very apprehensive and Steven was sitting at Jimmy's desk throwing pencils toward the ceiling trying to make them stick into the ceiling tile.

"Are you going to take me?" Steven asked.

"Take you where?" Jimmy said.

"To see the committee."

"How do you know about a committee?"

"Just do that's all."

Cleo stood and approached Jimmy with his hand extended. "I'm with the boy. He's awful anxious to see this committee." A stab of pain etched its way across his back. He grimaced enough for Jimmy to notice.

"Are you all right?" Jimmy said, taking his hand and guiding him back toward the couch.

"Yes, fine. Like I was saying Steven here, is in a powerful hurry to talk to this committee. After that, I expect we'll go."

"He wants to talk to the committee about The Ghost?"

Cleo hesitated. "I don't know exactly what you're talking about, but he hasn't said anything about a ghost. He wants to change their minds about someone. He says he knows how."

"I gotta' do it 'cause you couldn't," Steven said. "Come on, let's go!"

Jimmy excused himself, stepped out of his office, and spoke to his secretary. "Kim, could you round up the others and take them to the meeting. Have them wait in the outer office." He thought for a second. "Tell Emmanuel that I think we've found the final two pieces of the puzzle."

Chapter 98

We were waiting in the outer office when Jimmy walked in with the boy we had seen with Matt Lauer and an older gentleman. The older guy had a distinguished look about him but he also looked intimidated by his surroundings, just as I'm sure I did the first time I was here. He stood erect, even though it seemed a little difficult for him. His threadbare clothing made him almost noble as they hung on his slight frame. He was someone that had given everything to get here, and it showed.

Jimmy introduced everyone and we shook hands. The boy's name was Steven but he insisted on being called Walrus and had no interest in any of us. He wanted to get into the committee and I think would have busted into the meeting if he had known they were on the other side of the door.

The old man's introduction to Emmanuel was a different story.

Emmanuel told him he was glad they had finally joined and the old eyes teared up instantly.

"It's you," Cleo said softly. "It's been you all along. I recognize your voice."

He dropped his hand and embraced Emmanuel. As he did his back became straighter and the rigidity left his body. He pulled back, tears now streaming down his cheeks, and knelt in front of Emmanuel. We all watched, realizing that Emmanuel had touched many more lives than we had realized.

Then, for the first time since the jailhouse, Emmanuel began to glow, not as brightly as before, just a velvety incandescence that pulsed, then faded away. Emmanuel smiled and helped Cleo up.

I wanted to laugh, there was such joy rising in me. The others looked the same. Big smiles were breaking out on their faces.

Jimmy, not wanting to let this moment pass said, "Let me go in first and prepare them. Don't expect this to go easily. This may be our last chance at them."

"How can you possibly base anything on Random Number Generators? It's voodoo science Frank." General Parker said, color on his cheeks. He scooted back in his chair and slapped his folder shut.

Jimmy slid in the door and closed it behind him. The President stared at him and raised his eyebrows, giving him a 'where have you been' look. Apparently the conversation had become somewhat heated. The President's strengths were more along the lines of impassioned speeches and the day to day workings of the government. Keeping the lid on the power players like these people was more up Jimmy's alley.

"I'll handle this," he whispered. "But you have to trust me."

The President nodded his approval, but looked a little wary.

Frank was still trying to make his point. "General, your inability to comprehend anything newer than Sputnik should not enter into it. You have to admit that number strands like these are relevant in some way."

Jimmy stood in front of the podium but they ignored him. He waited a couple of beats before interrupting. "Guys, listen." The arguing continued as if he wasn't there.

"General, shut up," he said. The General turned his attention from Frank to Jimmy, his face reddening even more.

"Did you just tell me to shut up?" the General said, standing.

"Shut up AND sit down," the President said from behind Jimmy.

Secret Blood

He sat, slowly.

Jimmy smiled. "I have someone here you need to listen to. I have no idea why he needs your approval, but he thinks he does."

We waited in the outer office still warmed by the glow. Simon sat on a desk and dangled his feet. "Hurry up and wait, man that's all we do."

Steven looked at him and said, "Who do?"

"What?" Simon said.

"Who do voodoo? Kobe had forty-six last night. What do you think of that?" Steven said and laughed hysterically.

Simon looked at Shine who was standing perfectly still. "You tell him I think Kobe overrated?" Shine shook his head slightly.

Steven bounced over to the door and put his right eye up to the crack. "Hurry up!" he yelled.

"He some kind of Rain Man?" Simon asked Cleo.

"He's some kind of something," Cleo said.

Steven stepped back and the door swung open.

Jimmy ushered us in.

* * *

We huddled in toward the back of the room, all of us except Emmanuel and Steven. Emmanuel stood beside Jimmy, noble, even in his jeans and cotton shirt.

Steven launched himself into the center of the semicircle, the committee wrapped around the table only a few feet away. He giggled and drummed his fingers.

The President was as shocked as everyone else. Jimmy looked back at him and said, "I have to do this, you'll understand."

"Let me make a few introductions before we start. This is Emmanuel."

The Judge said, "Are we back to this? Jesus Christ!"

"Yeah, something like that." Jimmy said.

Emmanuel smiled brightly.

Steven was prancing in front of the group, jumping from one foot to the other.

"The excited young man in front of you is Steven. He predicted two disasters, one that prevented a nuclear meltdown. Both predictions were documented prior to the event."

"I'm the Walrus and over there is my friend 'The Eggman'. Koo Koo kachoo." Steven made a gun out of his thumb and index finger and shot the Judge. The two men to my left are Simon and his associate Mr. Shine."

"Associate? They're criminals," the Judge said.

"Alleged," Simon said.

"And on my right is Father Kenzee."

Steven stopped hopping and turned toward me. "What's your first name?" he asked.

I was taken back a little, "Matthew," I said.

Steven laughed and became even more animated.

"Father Matt Kenzee!" he shouted. "Where were you last night? Darning your socks in the night when there's nobody there?"

The President stood. I thought he was going to throw us out and that was going to be it. But either the brotherly love had sprung where it had not before, or the aura of Emmanuel had infected the President in a way that it had not previously. "Steven, what did you come to tell us?" he asked.

Steven stopped. A calm came over him. The fidgeting and laughing stopped. He spoke in a calm measured voice.

"Think for a moment, the events that brought us all here today. How many career moves you've made, how many personal decisions you made early on to be in this room today." He paused allowing this to sink in.

"Mr. Vice President, didn't you win your first election on the county commission because your opponent won the state lottery?" The Judge's eyes narrowed.

"Dr. White, what about the scholarships you received? The ones you thought you had no chance to win? And Ms. James, didn't you decide to pursue Political Science only after having a dream about saving the world?"

Each person Steven spoke to remained silent, reflective. The rest seemed to draw within themselves, asking their own private questions. Even Simon, Shine, Cleo, the President, Jimmy and I were silent. I remembered standing alone in front of that huge, handcrafted altar. That was my fork in the road. I think the others could pinpoint theirs, also.

"Now picture all of our paths like little streams; all the twists and turns leading to one point where we converge as one. This is it; this is the room where it has led us, as an entity."

"This is insane!" the Judge burst out. "I will not listen to this drivel." He stood to leave, knocking over his chair and pushing past Ken Bartholomew, the Homeland Security director.

Emmanuel held his hand up, like a crossing guard signaling a car to stop. The sound in the room was extinguished. It just ended. The Judge stopped. I stopped. Steven stopped. It was like being in a movie theater and the sound going out. Only in a theater you can still hear yourself breathing, you can slap your leg, or tap the seat in front of you. Now, you could do none of those things. I saw the General pound on the table. Jude Johnson clapped his hands. Nothing.

We all looked at Emmanuel. He smiled then let his hand drop. I heard myself breathe. Everyone let out a sigh of relief, including the four of us, who had seen these miracles before. To my left I heard Simon say, "I saw Darth Vader do somethin' like that once."

Steven had the committee's attention now, though they were looking at Emmanuel. "We want you to know you are a part of this now. We cannot go on without the approval of this committee. If one of you casts any doubt, the cause will be lost."

"I'm convinced," the President said.

"I don't want to convince you, I don't want to talk you into something. I want your soul to rejoice in the Truth. The Truth that comes from Knowing," Steven said.

He lost me on the last part. I think he lost the committee also. What did he mean by Knowing?

He spun around, went to the marker board, and picked up a black marker. "You," he pointed at Frank. "What is your full name?"

As Frank said, "Franklin Thomas White," Steven wrote the name on the board neatly and very quickly. Almost as fast as a printer. He pointed to the next person.

"Brenda Ann James." He wrote it.

"Next,"

"Jude Thaddeus Johnson."

"General Levi Phillip Parker" Steven wrote the name omitting 'General'.

"Kenneth Bartholomew Jenkins."

Then I remembered. The thing Dr. DeRose had whispered when we thought he was dying. It was what Steven had said he was going to do when he was interviewed, "Convince them with their names." This group was assembled, like everything else, years and years ago. And we didn't even know it. It was here all along.

Steven pointed at the Judge, but he sat brooding.

"Keep it up and you're going to get a time out," Steven said.

"My God," Jimmy said looking at the names. He sat down in a chair next to the President. "Can't you see it?" He grabbed his brother's wrist. "Dad's name was Jeb, we lived on a farm!"

Jimmy began to weep; it was the first time since they were boys that his brother had seen him cry.

"Look at the names, Mr. President," I said.

Then he saw it, too. He looked at his brother, then at Emmanuel, and back to the board.

Steven slipped into a trace. He kept writing names on the board with his eyes closed and without asking for names.

John William Rienhart

James William Rienhart

Ronald Simon King

Steven used the marker to underline the parts of the names he wanted them to look at. He stopped writing and started giggling. He

Secret Blood

ran over and leapt into Cleo's arms. "I did it!" he yelled. "Now they know!"

Frank was the first to say it out loud. "The Last Supper. We each have one of their names."

"It's happening again," Jimmy said.

I felt the surge of goose bumps run along my spine and down my arms. There were only eight names on the board. I felt tears rolling down my face as I took the marker and wrote my name on the board.

Matthew Allen Kenzee

I turned, "Shine what's your real name?"

"Andrew," he said. That was good enough.

I looked at Simon, confused. We had a Simon already. This wasn't the way it was supposed to go. We were a team, how could he not be one of us.

Simon grinned, embarrassed. "My uncle used to call me Simple Simon. The name kinda stuck. Actual name is Peter."

I felt a surge of relief. That only left one.

Judge Aston stood with fear and anger in his eyes. He started backing away.

"I'm a big fan of the saying, 'If we don't learn from the past, we are bound to repeat it,'" the President said.

Shine was around the table and to the Judge before anyone else had time to react. The Judge took a weak swing with his walking stick, but Shine easily grabbed it out of the air and snapped it like a twig. The Judge lunged at him. With a right, that could not have traveled more than five inches, Shine knocked the Judge back across the table, breaking it and dumping everything on the floor. This included the Judge's nameplate, which snapped into four pieces. The 'g' and the 'e' broke from Judge and the last three letters broke off of Aston. Those sections rolled away, leaving two pieces that read Jud As.

Jimmy's cell phone buzzed. Two seconds later, Frank's did the same. Within the space of ten seconds every cell belonging to a committee member was ringing and someone was knocking on the door. Jimmy opened the door while still on the phone. Margaret was in the outer office beckoning the President to follow her.

Two Secret Service agents rushed past her toward the President. Each took hold of an arm and began to escort him out of the room.

"Sir, we have to get you to a secure location in the building," one said as they had the President nearly off his feet. Shine stiffened. I could see his muscles go taunt across his shoulders and neck. He had already decided which agent to pick off first.

"Go," Jimmy said. "We'll work it out from here to see if it's real." He gathered himself. "Everybody sit down, calm down."

The Judge started to moan. "Margaret can you get someone to get him out of here and lock him up somewhere? And take his cell phone."

"What's going on?" I asked.

"Possibly a cyber-attack. Protocol dictates that the President get to a secure location just in case a literal attack may follow."

Frank was still on his phone. "It's the number. The one from the Random Number Generators," he said, continuing to listen and talk at the same time. "It's popping up everywhere."

"Is there a TV around here?" he asked.

"Two offices that way," she pointed. "Flat panel on the wall," Margaret said. We filed out like a fire drill.

Jimmy had it on by the time we squeezed in. It showed Times Square. The number 5646316 was running around the message board over and over. It was flashing on the jumbo screen. Jimmy switched channels. A film crew was at an airport for some reason. The camera man focused on the arrival and departure screens. The numbers were systematically switching to 5646316.

"Look at your phones," Ken Jenkins said. "Are yours doing what mine is?"

Everybody looked, even Frank who was still talking to someone. The number was flashing on each of their phones.

Frank said, "We're getting word from all over, all over the world that is. It's happening everywhere. Just about all forms of communication have been affected."

"Who has the ability to do it all over the world?" Jimmy asked.

"God," said a voice from the hallway. Steven was sitting on the carpet, Cleo was standing behind him.

All of us turned to look. "What does it mean?" Jimmy asked.

"Jeeze, you people are supposed to be smart, didn't any of you go to Sunday school?" Steven said. His fingers began to drum. "Read the numbers and letters on your phones. Part of it is a word."

I looked. 5646 spelled out John. John 3:16.

"For God so loved the world he gave his only begotten son," Jimmy recited.

"Something like that," I said. No one moved, no one said anything.

"Is there anyone here, not in agreement, that we publicly acknowledge Emmanuel?" Jimmy asked. No one made a sound. "Mr. President, am I correct in assuming that the full power of this committee will be used to identify Emmanuel as a clone of Jesus?"

"Yes," the President said. The rest of the committee nodded in agreement.

"Good," Steven said. "Cause in about an hour we're not gonna' be able to see much of the sky."

*　*　*

The President was 'made up' for a short message he would deliver at nine o'clock eastern time. Everyone involved, agreed it would be best to get out in front of the story, and prepare the world for the return of The Ghost. Just the fact the President knew it was showing up again, provided a small amount of assurance that he had a handle on the situation, which was not the case. The 'make up' people went to work applying a layer that removed the haggard look that was beginning to appear around his eyes.

The message was to be short and on point, The Ghost was going to be back soon, please do not panic. Another statement would follow the next morning. That one was going to be much more difficult to spin in the correct way. Most of the night, after the President's message, was going to be devoted to making the unbelievable, believable.

Chapter 99

That night The Ghost reappeared in all of its alien majesty. And true to Steven's prediction, it took up most of the sky. Some parts of the globe were in darkness much longer than usual because of the shadow cast from The Ghost. The moon was dwarfed and drifted in the background like a small child watching a bully cross a playground. It was horrifying in its sheer size. The hysteria was immediate. The Internet crashed again only moments after it reappeared. The news networks brought the full attention of their assets to the story, but TV failed miserably in comparison to the view from the back yard. The incandescent colors swirling below the surface would have made a smaller object seem wondrous. But with something this big, it just looked macabre. At the time of its appearance, the United States was on the opposite side of the world, allowing its citizens a reprieve from an actual sighting for a few hours.

It was a giant heart that pumped fear across the Earth. Those on the other side of the world could only watch the news broadcasts and wait for the planet to rotate under The Ghost to get their own sky full of horror. In some areas civilization began to break down. Supermarkets were ransacked without reason, as if The Ghost was going to zap all of our food and allow us to starve. The highways brimmed as everyone tried to get back to their loved ones before the end came. Many of the foundations of our lives became irrelevant.

Working toward and saving for retirement seemed silly now. The vacation home that had been the center of a dream was now sheer folly. The protestant work ethic was laughable.

Tribal leaders across Africa tried in vain to calm the fears of their fellow tribesmen. Most had never heard of The Ghost or its trek across the galaxy. In the parts of the world where the Internet and television had no reach, this was the first glimpse. Panic spread across each horizon as it rose across nation after nation.

The news outlets were grateful the President was going to address the nation. The stories they were broadcasting were no different than what they had been broadcasting since The Ghost reappeared. They had a lot of people watching and a lot of time to fill. Many networks started a countdown to when the President would speak.

First came the Seal of the President of the United States. Then the screen faded to a podium standing precisely in the center of a royal blue carpet runner. The President stepped out of an office and strode purposefully to the podium. He wore a navy suit and a blue oxford button down open at the collar. It was the least formal anyone had ever seen him in public.

"I usually start my speeches with 'My fellow Americans', but today my message transcends nations and politics. Today I speak to the entire human race. Our planet sits in the cross hairs of something so alien to us, something so inconceivable, that we virtually have no response except to stare and expect the worst." He stopped, straightened, and looked around the room. "I'm sorry to say that our government has no viable response. It is difficult to prepare for something so unknown, so for that, I make no apologies.

"There is something else to report. Something I think has more importance than The Ghost and its unknown agenda." He told the story of the Holy Blood at Fort Knox and about the clandestine operation to clone. Even the jaded reporters were genuinely shocked; he could see it on their faces. He knew the public response was tenfold that.

Secret Blood

He described his surprise when they found the clone was alive and working in Africa. "As many of you know, I am a religious man." He paused for effect and to control his racing heart. "At first I was horrified at what we as a nation had done. It was unthinkable. But I have since changed my mind. I believe now, that this has all been part of God's plan. And we are witness to it.

"His name is Emmanuel Shepherd and I'm sure you have seen him without realizing who you were watching. It was he, in the middle of what was called the 'Miracle Shootout' where hundreds of shots were fired and no one was injured. He was also involved in the events that surrounded the ark footage where very real animals emerged from a plastic ark. I would like to introduce you to the man involved in both of these miracles."

In a state of panic, Jimmy burst into the area behind the camera, stepping over power cables and pushing people out of his way. He tensely slashed his hand across his throat in a 'cut' sign. The President was thrown off completely and stopped before starting his next sentence. For one extremely long moment he was baffled. He looked down at the podium, took in a long breath and exhaled slowly.

"I am now going into an area where I can do that." The picture went back to the Seal of the President.

The President controlled his anger long enough to make sure the camera and sound were off. He stormed back down the hall and into the office. Jimmy followed.

"What was that all about?" the President yelled.

"They're gone," Jimmy said.

* * *

It was my idea. It seemed to me, so horribly wrong, to have Emmanuel introduced like a guest on a talk show. It was demeaning and seemed like a ruse. I also thought it would anger other countries to have our President seem responsible for the 'Second Coming'. He spread the word and that was good enough. Now, this was a story nearly equal to the giant sphere hovering overhead.

After a conference call with the Vatican it was decided I was not to wear my collar if I was to accompany Emmanuel. At this point they would not take a stand one way or the other concerning Emmanuel. Procedures were to be followed, which could possibly take years before they would confirm or deny Emmanuel's relationship with the scriptures.

Jimmy realized early on that we could not dress in the fashion that we had been dressing. He also knew it would be hopeless to convince Emmanuel to wear something other than his white shirt and faded jeans. So in an effort to create a semblance of uniformity, Simon, Shine and I were issued nicely tailored black suits. Black crew neck shirts completed the ensemble. I didn't look much different than usual except that the white patch was missing from my collar.

Cleo argued and won, and was still sporting his old black suit. He said that was the one Jesus told him to pack and that was the highest power he was listening to. Steven wanted a white suit, so he and Cleo could look like Lennon and McCartney on the cover of Abbey Road.

We left our designated green room and went to the Front Lawn of the White House. Since Emmanuel had 'Become' getting places was easy. He simply smiled and people would do whatever. The guards and Secret Service stepped aside and granted us passage where we liked.

The Front Lawn, home to Easter egg hunts and other children's' events, was calm in contrast to the events taking place inside the building. The lawn was perfectly manicured and the sky was a brilliant blue above. High altitude cirrus clouds appeared stationary, their ice crystals creating a wispy feathery illusion.

My cell rang as I expected. It was Jimmy. He began with, "You better have a good explanation for this!"

"I do, and I'll tell you later, but for now, call a couple of reporters you can trust. Tell them we're on the Front Lawn. I think things will start to happen quickly after that." There was silence on the other end.

Secret Blood

"Okay, I see where you are going with this," Jimmy finally said. "But you have to keep me informed, you can't disappear like that."

"Sorry" I said. "It was a last minute thought. But you do understand that for now, at least. The President and anyone associated with him has to stay away."

"I don't like it, but I understand. I'll make some calls." He hung up.

Emmanuel sat on a bench, legs folded under, and prayed. Somewhere in the distance a bird filled the openness of the lawn with song.

"This is weird," Simon said. "Feels like, *The Day the Earth Stood Still*. Not the last one, the first one, you know, the black and white one."

He looked at Shine and smiled. "Black and white movies, black and white TV. We were getting first billing back in those days and people didn't even know it. Bet George Wallace didn't know that."

A lady in a blue business dress and heels sprinted out of a doorway and aimed herself at us. A cameraman followed, trying to keep up. As she neared, two more reporters, a man and another woman, burst out of the door and raced their way. Emmanuel raised his head and opened his eyes.

The reporter in blue stopped in front of him, out of breath, and asked, "Are you Emmanuel Shepherd?"

He smiled and nodded once.

The other reporters caught up and started blurting out questions.

"Are you the Son of God?"

"Yes, as are we all."

"Are you here to save us from The Ghost?"

"No, only God can do that."

"What proof do you have that you are who you say you are?" asked a reporter in a wrinkled tan suit.

"None. What proof do you have to say that I'm not?"

By now there was a trickle of people coming from the door, all running and looking for Emmanuel. I saw Steven bolt out the door with Cleo following slowly. Both were laughing. Within a few minutes the crowd was three deep around Emmanuel with reporters and cameramen jostling for position and lines of cable running toward the White House.

Out on Pennsylvania Ave. a satellite truck screeched to a stop in the No Parking zone. Two more followed and the images of Emmanuel began their trek around the world. The security force around the White House was ordered to stand down and to help the news people with anything they needed. The actual security nerve center monitored the Front Lawn with dozens of cameras. This was all very unsettling for the officers and guards used to protecting the White House. People were flooding onto the grounds from different directions.

As the breaking news began to hit the airways, the roads around the White House became impassable. Drivers pulled off any place they could and began walking. Traffic came to a standstill. Cell phones in hand, they wandered onto the Front Lawn. For some, the horror of The Ghost took a backseat.

A security guard, monitoring the Front Lawn cameras, got the attention of his supervisor. "Sir, someone has opened the front gate on Pennsylvania Ave., people are pouring in."

The supervisor was stunned and stared at the monitor himself. "There is no gate on Pennsylvania Ave."

"There is now sir," he said.

Emmanuel rose from the bench, and began to move through the mass of gathering people. The reporters trailed quietly behind, waiting for him to speak. He is like a shepherd now, I thought. I remembered the scriptures that described Jesus walking from town to town, attended by his followers. A white seagull drifted across the sky.

"Many of you ask for proof as to who I am," Emmanuel said. "It does not matter who I am, the real question is, who are you? Are you a lost soul, a dry leaf that drops and falls into a steam only to be carried away by the current?"

The sky began to fill with gulls. They soared in from all directions using only a weak updraft to keep them aloft. There was no sound, no squawking, they floated silently, majestically.

The pedestrians now outnumbered the reporters. Emmanuel walked to the highest point on the lawn. Without instruction the crowd settled in below him. There was no commotion, no one rushed forward to try to touch, and questioning had ceased. His physical presence touched those in the distance as well as the people near him. Many were crying, many more were smiling. Steven found his way to the mound and stood beside Emmanuel. He rested his hand on the boy's shoulder. Ten thousand seagulls dropped from the sky, lighting on anything available. Many found the trees; others landed on the buildings, and still more found the vans and other vehicles. No matter where they landed, they each faced Emmanuel.

My cell rang again. "This is not a good situation," Jimmy said. "We have no good way to stem the flow of people. The Front Lawn is not an infinite space."

"I know," I said. "I'm getting the same feeling down here. In ten minutes we will be so packed that someone is going to get hurt."

Emmanuel answered the flow of questions. The man in the wrinkled tan suit was becoming increasingly abrasive. "People want to believe in you, so that makes anything you say more believable. We've been sucked in by the David Koresh's and Jim Jones's of the world, what makes you any different?"

"I am only conveying God's message," Emmanuel said. "I am asking no one to follow me."

"That's what they said."

Emmanuel stood. He held his hands out, palms up and looked skyward. "In these trying hours ahead, you must remember two things, love God, and love each other."

Steven glanced at Emmanuel and said, "The love you take is equal to the love you make." Emmanuel looked down at the boy and nodded.

Each time I looked closely at Emmanuel he grew stronger, kinder, and wiser. I could feel the presence of God in him. He knew the secrets to everything we wanted to know. The mysteries, beyond this life and the next, were clear to him. He could explain the universe if he desired—the how and why of everything.

"Go in Peace," Emmanuel said and began to glow. He turned from a golden yellow to a radiant white as bright as the sun. People shielded their eyes, unable to see but unable to look away.

He stood that way for several seconds. A breeze began to blow, as if something powerful was happening very far away. High above, the cirrus clouds began to bend, and then rotate.

The sky was changing before our eyes. The clouds that had once been fairly straight were now curving. They swirled high in the atmosphere creating a vortex and pulling in more clouds from the far reaches of the horizon. Looking up, everyone was frozen in place, quiet, transfixed. There was no sound and only a slight breeze blew.

The warmer air drawn in from the lower levels of the atmosphere generated huge amounts of static. Lighting flashed, as the clouds became denser. The bolts branched through the wind and entangled themselves throughout the cloud wall looking, for the entire world, like a thorny crown. They gained speed and changed from their wispy form into a more ragged dark gray.

"What is that?" Simon said.

"Glory," I said.

Then with a flash, it stopped. The clouds stopped swirling and began to float slowly back into a natural position. Emmanuel was smiling contentedly. The gathering of people, now several thousand strong, froze in silence. A slight breeze fluttered hair and gave the watchers a stone-like appearance. The man in the tan suit was kneeling and crossing himself.

I saw, through the crowd of stunned people, Secret Service dispersing from the White House and making their way toward us. They were moving quickly, and they were moving with a purpose. Something was happening.

Chapter 100

My phone rang. "The Ghost is rising; it will be visible in Nova Scotia. It's moving at 12,000 miles an hour," Jimmy said. "The President wants you all to evacuate."

"Why evacuate?"

"The public knows you're here. It's not safe. The White House wasn't designed to house thousands."

"Where do you want us to go? Where is the President going?"

"Listen, when in doubt, we follow protocol. At this point he will be taken to the most secure part of the residence, against his wishes I might add."

Overhead I heard the thudding of powerful rotor blades. The seagulls rose as one white wave of wings and feathers, scarcely missing the three green helicopters descending behind The White House. People in the crowd stood, some embracing the person beside them, others running in panic.

A firm hand seized my arm. "This way sir," an agent said, and began to guide me toward the building. Emmanuel, Simon, Steven, and Cleo were each being escorted in the same fashion. Only Shine had resisted the agent and broken the grasp. He was walking, dignified, with the agent following him.

Inside, the staffers were in an orderly panic, the building was being locked down and readied as if for attack. Protocol booklets were disseminated and studied. This was happening throughout Washington and cities around the globe. They took us through the building and out the other side. Jimmy was impatiently waiting for us.

"Gotta' go," he said.

"Where?" I asked.

"The Greenbrier," he said. Then to the agents, "Get them in number two."

The Greenbrier is an elegant resort tucked into the mountains of West Virginia. Regal enough for European heads of State, Kings and Queens from the world over, and movie stars since the inception of moving pictures. The place was a massive jewel tucked into the wilderness. And like a set from a James bond movie, the Greenbrier had a secret bunker built beneath it large enough to house congress for the duration of a nuclear attack. It was the prime location for evacuation since the sixties, complete with fortified walls and massive blast doors that became invisible when closed.

Even the locals and the staff were unaware, until the project was declassified some thirty years later.

"But it's not a bunker anymore," I said.

"Not the part under the West Virginia wing," he said and winked.

"Ain't going nowhere." I heard Shine's voice from behind me. "Not without my daughter." He was telling Jimmy and anyone else who was near.

"I'm not leaving Mama either," Simon chirped in, "Get her on the phone, we can pick her up somewhere."

"No time," Jimmy said. "We follow protocol. If we stop to get your mother, she'll want to get her sister, or her friend, and she'll want to get someone else."

"I bet your wife and kids are going to be safe with the President," Simon said indignantly.

"No, I'm going home to be with them," Jimmy said. Our group grew quiet.

"Sorry," Simon mumbled. "I was just worried about my Mama and I thought….."

"She will be safe," Emmanuel said.

"Safe, yeah, but Raye will be scared. I don't want her to be afraid," Shine said with a slight waver in his voice.

"Go get her and her foster family," Jimmy said. "Bring them to my house; we can ride this out together." Something passed between the two fathers without anything more being said. The slight nod Shine gave him spoke volumes. He shook hands with me and did a shoulder bump with Simon.

Shine held his hand out to Emmanuel. They shook for a moment then Emmanuel pulled Shine close for an embrace. They released and Shine walked past us and disappeared into the chaos. It would be the last time the two men would see each other.

In the courtyard outside of the window, TV crews were being led to the other two helicopters. The shouting through the building was getting louder. The rotors on the helicopter thumped as everyone boarded.

Jimmy shook hands with each of us, smiling and controlling his emotions. As with Shine, Emmanuel could not make due with a simple handshake. He embraced Jimmy as he had Shine, a little longer perhaps. Emmanuel whispered to him, "Have faith." Then there was a Marine yelling at the door and we were hurried outside where the wash and the roar of the rotors knocked us back.

Cleo collapsed. He and Steven were behind me and I wasn't aware until Steven grabbed my arm. The engines were deafening and no one heard my shouts for help. The Marine who was at the hatch saw what had happened and sprinted to help me pull Cleo up. With an arm over each of our shoulders we drug him into the helicopter.

The medic assigned to our vehicle helped Cleo into a seat and buckled him in, then advised us to do the same. He continued to examine Cleo as we ascended and gained speed. Looking out the window I watched the grass flatten in waves. Jimmy stepped out of the building and looked up. I watched him until the pilot banked left and he was out of sight.

"Do you know anything about this man's medical history?" the medic asked.

"No, not really, I know he didn't look very healthy," I said. "Steven, was Cleo sick?"

"The Eggman? Yep, he's dying," Steven said, his face mashed against the window. "It's okay, the dying though. He wants to; he wants to be with his wife."

The medic put a stethoscope against Cleo's chest and listened. He pulled Cleo's lower eyelid down with his thumb and examined the white of the eye. "He's in pretty bad shape. I'll radio ahead and we will unload him first."

Emmanuel unbuckled himself and moved up the aisle. He knelt at Cleo's seat, facing him, and took Cleo's hand in both of his.

Cleo's eyes sprang open and he smiled. He looked at Emmanuel dreamily. "I was ready wasn't I? I heard your voice and I've been ready all these years, just like you asked."

"You did fine Cleo, just fine." He looked at Cleo with such loving eyes, such strength, such knowing. "Are you ready?"

"Yes sir, I am."

The medic was half sitting in a seat a few feet away, not knowing what to think. Apparently he had not seen the President's briefing this morning and had no idea of who any of us were. He watched Emmanuel, sensing who he was, but trying not to allow himself to believe. Simon and I were watching with our hearts in our throats and Steven was still looking out the window.

Cleo said to the rest of us in a waning voice, "I wish you all the luck in the world, but my place isn't here anymore. My place is with my wife." He was wearing his black suit, the one he had kept ready.

Steven finally sensed what was happening and broke from the window. He came over and stood beside Emmanuel. With his free hand Cleo reached up and touched Steven's cheek. "I'll be seeing you around, Walrus."

"You're a good man, Cleo Johnson," Steven said.

Cleo smiled and said, "That's all I ever wanted to be."

"Close your eyes and rest," Emmanuel told him, "You have a reunion to attend." Cleo looked at each of us; Emmanuel last, closed his eyes, and was gone.

Chapter 101

The medic covered him with an army blanket. He looked like an olive colored cocoon transforming into a realm where only souls tread.

I lost track of time. I watched the trees and hills flow beneath us and thought of Dr. DeRose and Father Craig. I wondered about my parishioners and how many had inquired about my sudden departure. I pondered how many had lived and given their lives, as Cleo had done, for the sake of the alabaster jar. Two thousand years of devotion and faith would culminate in the next few hours.

My phone jolted me back into the moment. "I've got everything set up at the Greenbrier" Jimmy said.

"Set for what?" I asked.

"A message from Emmanuel," he said. "The assets are in place. We have the capability to broadcast worldwide from there. The plan was for the President to appear before allies and enemies in a safe zone, other than D.C. Right now all of our satellites, and even some that don't belong to us, are being aligned to transmit from West Virginia."

Chapter 102

The helicopters skimmed over the crest of a craggy mountain, and descended into a long rolling valley. From the corner of my eye I saw Emmanuel stand, then walk up the aisle of the swaying helicopter. He sat beside me.

"We are heading toward a resort of some type?"

"Yes."

"I have a better idea." He said, "Let's call Jimmy."

Five minutes later the pilot banked sharply and we headed back to the north. The other two helicopters following us did the same, changing direction in perfect unison. A new flight plan had been filed and the airspace cleared. Emmanuel returned to his seat and folding his legs under himself, began his prayers.

Simon had not been himself since Shine had left. He was quiet and subdued, almost reflective. As I considered this, two air force jets blasted past us, one on either side of our formation. Steven let out a yell.

"You must be a hot ticket," the medic said. "They're plowing the road for us." We climbed to a higher altitude and increased speed.

An immense marine stepped from a door near the cockpit holding an alien looking phone. "Are you Mr. Simon?" he asked me.

I pointed to Simon who had snapped around at the sound of his name.

"Sir, you have a phone call," the marine said. "This is a line we must keep open, so please be brief."

He handed the phone to Simon who did not take his eyes off the massive solider.

"Hello," he said then paused. "Mama... no, I'm in a helicopter... Yeah, he's here with me. No, no it's not the end of the world. I just know, all right? No, he never actually said so but,....I can't, I'm in a helicopter."

"Sir?" the marine said.

Simon covered the mouthpiece and said to the marine. "Hold on."

"Mama, there is a stern looking dude wantin' his phone back…..Listen, I get the feelin' we're going to be on TV in the next few minutes, if things are going to be okay I'll give you a signal, all right?"

The marine cleared his voice and held out a huge hand.

"Hold on Shaqzilla..no, no, not you, Mama." He turned toward the window.

"I promise, everything is gonna' be all right… I love you, too, Mama."

I expected him to say something smart to the marine as he handed the phone back, but he did so quietly.

I decided it was time that I should have a word with God and found the idea tremendously comforting. I closed my eyes and began to pray. I'm not sure how long, but before I was finished we had begun our descent into New York City.

* * *

From the sky it looked like an emerald with razor straight edges enclosed in gray concrete. We dropped lower and more detail materialized. The trees were still leafless and provided a brownish cast to the grass and evergreens beneath the branches. The engines whined to a different pitch and the airspeed receded as we circled the rim of the park.

Secret Blood

We passed over ponds and an obelisk, then the Vanderbilt Gate, all the while descending in a spiral. I could see no one in the park. The ball fields were empty, as well as the paddle boats, and the running paths.

At this height I could see the horizon by looking over some buildings and between others. A vague glow emanated from the east. In that faint line, where the land meets the sky, I could just mark a curved ribbon of scarlet. The Ghost was about to make its appearance in New York City.

Our helicopter touched down so lightly that I wasn't sure we were on the ground until I heard the engine begin to throttle down. Through the small window I could see the other two helicopters do the same. Dust kicked up from the softball field as their tires touched and the helicopters settled down into their shocks.

The large marine stepped out from wherever he had been and began the procedure for opening the fuselage door. Steven was already bouncing down the aisle, excited. He ran back and forth in front of Cleo's body without a thought of who was under the blanket. Emmanuel watched and smiled.

The marine stood at the door and made sure we didn't stumble as we exited. As Simon passed, he said, "My mother is scared, too."

The air smelled almost like spring as we walked away from the diesel engines. The grass felt springy, not dead as it usually does in the last weeks of winter. I wondered if the comfortable temperatures were a part of the divine plan also.

The TV guys were already assembling their equipment, which looked like something a research exposition would have in the Rain Forest. A shed was being constructed with satellite dishes of varying sizes tethered to it. I could hear a generator burp to life, which activated banks of lights and switches inside the metal building.

"Bye for now," Steven said as he ran past Simon and I. He giggled and ran, clomping his feet and squeezing one of the maps he had picked up earlier at McDonalds.

"Wait," I yelled. "Where are you going?"

"Where do you think silly," he yelled back. "Strawberry Fields."

"Wait!" I yelled and started after him.

"Let him go," Emmanuel said softly touching my arm.

"A kid in Central Park? By himself?"

"He has proven himself quite capable."

I watched him go, running in a nonathletic stride, up a path and disappearing into a grove of trees. Now there were only three of us left; Emmanuel, Simon and me. A sparse number compared to the collection of people we were at one time.

The sky to the east was turning ugly. I couldn't see the horizon but the area of the sky in that direction had turned dark, the colors of a day old bruise. Like splayed fingers, streaks of burgundy tinged with violet spread wide as if reaching for the blue sky, only to devour it. I could imagine standing in a cornfield in Kansas watching a violent storm bear down on me.

"We're ready when you are," said one of the TV guys.

Emmanuel did not hesitate. "Could you take the picture so the sky is visible behind me?"

"You got it," said one of the cameramen.

There were two men with shoulder mounted cameras. A guide person was assigned to each to keep track of the cable that spewed from each camera. They decided on cable instead of wireless in the chance that The Ghost could cause some type of atmospheric interference. That same interference might disrupt the satellites, but that was beyond their control. A director in the shed could cut from one camera to the other and give directions through earpieces each cameraman wore. Techs in Washington, West Virginia, and the NSC in Atlanta, were readying the satellites, which would beam Emmanuel around the globe.

"So what do we do? Walk around like two stooges?" Simon asked.

"We are stooges," I said.

"I know that, but we don't gotta' look like stooges," he said. He stared up at the eastern sky. "You know, I'm not even worried about that anymore. Not worried about dying either."

Secret Blood

"Why not?" I asked.

"Don't know."

"Are you worried about anything?"

"Yeah. Yeah, I guess I am. I'm worried about my Mama being all by herself, her being scared and all. I guess I feel bad about all the people out there who are alone."

I smiled. "I think you have evolved."

"Evolved? Is that some kind of racist comment?"

"No, I didn't mean...."

He grinned, "Man, you white people are so gullible."

* * *

"Thirty seconds," the guy behind the cameraman said.

"Are you ready?" I asked.

"Yes. My entire life seems to have been in preparation for this moment. Are you at peace?"

"Yes, Emmanuel, I am, thanks to you."

"Counting down in ten," the man said.

"Would you give me a blessing Father?" Emmanuel asked.

I was taken back. I nearly refused. Who was I to bless him?

He was aware that I was hesitant. "Perhaps your whole life has been in preparation for this moment also."

I put my hand on his shoulder and asked for God's strength, for the both of us.

"You're on," the man said and pointed at us.

Emmanuel's image instantly appeared on every television screen in the world. In Kanpur, India, Prakash Patel and his family gathered around their TV. They had been awake for nearly forty-eight hours, watching the worldwide coverage of The Ghost and praying for answers.

In Mexico City, the Hernandez and Gomez families gathered in the common room of their apartment complex. As Emmanuel's broadcast commenced, they shouted for their neighbors to come and see the Savior.

At the Vatican, St. Peters Square filled with worshipers. For the first time, the Pope did not attend the people from the balcony. He and the Cardinals in attendance appeared on the floor of the Square, holding hands and singing.

In Christian and non-Christian countries alike they watched and waited to see what he had to say. The cell phones began to ring. Around the globe, every cell with a screen proceeded to play the broadcast, even if it was not fitted with the correct technology to do so.

Aide workers in Haiti and Africa, scientists in Gambia and the South Pole, were able to watch and listen to Emmanuel.

"This day humanity is frightened," he began. "Many are frightened for their lives, but I suspect most have an even deeper fear. A fear, not of what will happen to them, but of what will happen to all of mankind. Masked by our hostilities and bravado, we fundamentally care about each other. And perhaps that is the greatest, the most noble of all our attributes."

The nearest camera was catching the close-ups and the other camera framed us, strolling in the grass, with The Ghost ever present in the background. It appeared as a gigantic boulder rolling down a trough, moments away from impact.

"For all of our rituals and beliefs, our arguments and wars, for the millions of lives lost, God gives two rules to live by; Love Him and love each other."

A man came from somewhere to our left was looking at his phone. He was dressed in jeans and a golf shirt. When he saw us he closed his cell phone and put it in his pocket. His eyes filled with tears.

A family of four, a mom, dad, and two girls walked across the softball field toward us. Emmanuel continued to speak while he welcomed them.

"We are our own greatest treasure, God's greatest treasure also. Yet, we have strayed away from each other and isolated ourselves with those who have the same beliefs, the same hatreds."

Secret Blood

Like on the Front Lawn of the White House, people began to flood into the Park. They came, not knowing exactly why they needed to be near him. They came, not knowing why they needed to be near each other. They came to us, humbly and reverent, without fear or anxiety.

"Close you eyes now, and think of someone near you, someone who is alone or needs help. Someone who is afraid, that you might be able to comfort."

At the White House, Jimmy manned the phones while his family kept a vigil at the television. Shine and Raye were there also. Raye snuggled against his bulk as he put his arm around her shoulder. They sat like that on the couch and listened to Emmanuel.

Jimmy got off the phone and motioned for Shine to follow him. They stepped into the room with the satellite feeds from the other countries. Emmanuel was on each screen. The pictures should have been exactly the same, but they weren't. "The mouths are different," Shine said.

"Yeah, watch this," Jimmy said. He picked up the remote for a German channel. Emmanuel was speaking in German, his lips moving with each of the syllables he was enunciating. Jimmy pushed the button on the next TV for a French channel. There, Emmanuel was speaking perfect French. And again, it was clearly him, no voice-overs or interpreters.

"We're not doing this," Jimmy told Shine. "He is speaking in every language. All at the same time."

"Now, go find that person and take them outdoors, join hands with your neighbors. God has given this beautiful day; let us show Him we do care about each other, that we are a people worth saving. This does not have to be the Apocalypse." The Ghost loomed overhead, its fiery center churning faster than its surface.

The number of people at the Park was increasing; radically. Times Square began to fill. The crowd faced the giant Sony screen where Emmanuel appeared. Many people, who sought refuge in their places of worship, joined hands and left their buildings and merged into their neighborhoods. At the White House, the Mall, and the Capitol, crowds grew.

In Darfur, villagers joined together and began a trek out of the Marrah Mountains to join others in El Geneina. The villagers carried their belongings on their backs down from the mesas, led by missionaries who watched Emmanuel on their cells.

"I know many of you have been praying, many for the first time. You have been making deals, striking accords, to save us from total annihilation. This, my friends is entirely acceptable. You may promise God whatever you like. Only remember, you must carry through with what you promise. If you swear to attend church more, or show more kindness to those who are unkind to you, then you must do exactly that. Someday you will be held accountable for your honesty."

The Ghost rose upon them now. The entire sky was blotted out as it positioned itself directly above us. Its rounded edge began to bulge through the Earth's atmosphere. We were at the epicenter of the collision. The cloud formations were forced away in oval patterns. The fabric that comprised The Ghost engulfed the satellites in orbit overhead. The audio transmission of Emmanuel continued through some divine technology beyond our comprehension. The video went dark, leaving the world with only his voice.

The sky darkened and grew odd. Faces in this light became misshapen and grotesque. We looked like visions from Dante's Inferno. The light became denser and the sounds around me were thick and dulled. Everything appeared far away and I felt myself drifting, drifting, and slowly falling. I was being drained of all hope, all happiness.

I felt the warmth and saw the light at the same moment. Emmanuel was to my left. He was glowing. He stood in the same stance that we had seen in all the drawings, gazing at the heavens. Pure white light emanated from his body like a lighthouse. It repelled the darkness, casting light and illuminating us.

Then it stopped, the darkness drained away and left a toxic orange cast on everything. It seemed to penetrate every pore, every atom in sight. I stood still, erect. I saw Simon doing the same, while Emmanuel continued to glow.

"Now is the moment," Emmanuel said, "For us to gather as one. For once in our existence, as the human race, to stand together as one, to Praise God and to love each other."

They laid their phones down or kept them open in their pockets and joined hands, people all over the world flooded into the orange mist. They left their churches, synagogues, and mosques. In the cities, cabbies stepped out of their cars, leaving the doors open and radio blaring. It had enveloped the entire globe. It was neither day nor night in any one place on the planet; the orange of The Ghost replaced the dark and light. Emmanuel's glow was the only light on the planet.

We were at a stalemate.

I found Simon on the other side of Emmanuel. Walking to him was odd, like the disjointed movement in a dream.

"Feels like we balancin' man," he said.

I knew exactly what he meant. Emmanuel could only take us so far. He had fought The Ghost to a standstill. He had brought all of humanity together. It was up to us now. We needed something to unite us completely.

I heard something from the wooded area behind us; like a song coming through a snowstorm. Quiet and muffled at first, then I understood. An unseen chorus was marching our way, its song so familiar it seemed organic.

I glanced at Emmanuel, he was smiling and his glow was strengthening. Simon understood also.

Steven led them through the path and into the open; like a shepherd followed by an endless multitude of sheep. Hundreds of homeless people followed him singing,

Na na na na na na na

Na na na na, Hey Jude

Steven, still in his white suit, brought them through the park like a psychedelic drum major. The melody was so intoxicating it was nearly impossible not to sing along. I joined in, so did the masses in the Park, along with the millions listening on radio, television, and cell phone.

In a line that ran block after block Mr. Stubbs and his associates, joined hands with Father Craig and his parishioners. Dr. DeRose sang along with them. The line ran from the church to Sampson's, with hundreds of people who once had been frightened of the gang, joining in.

Shine and Jimmy took their families outside into the street and merged with Jimmy's neighbors, most of whom they had never met. They emerged from their homes and gravitated toward the singing. Many embraced, still singing, ignoring the orange mist that surrounded them.

In Afghanistan tribal chiefs brought their charges together to sing the same words that were being sung in China, Mexico, and Canada.

Na na na na na na na
Na na na na, Hey Jude

Overhead the sky filled with rivers of energy. Beams of purple and magenta undulated across the sky, whipping back and forth from one orange horizon to the other. They produced a burnt electrical odor and caused a static build up on the planet's surface like a gigantic electric motor. These were the electrical events that gave The Ghost its violent appearance; the horizontal lightening bands, the orange mist, the features that could be seen from a distance.

The static on my hands and face intensified.

I examined my hands more closely. There was a dust there, an outer layer that began to crumble. Like ash, it flaked off and floated. It was coming off everyone except Emmanuel. Underneath the skin looked new, healthy.

"Somethin' happenin," Simon said.

The orange glow grew fainter. I could see some of the buildings in the distance but the sensations on my skin grew more profound. I looked down to see the sparse hair on the back of my hand and wrist waving in the nonexistent breeze. By the time I gazed back up, the buildings that had seemed clear became fuzzy around the edges.

My exposed skin felt like it had been rubbed with sandpaper. My eyes burned. But all around me the voices singing *Hey Jude* did not waver. I could hear Steven's voice through all the others.

The buildings now were only smudges looming above the trees, which were losing their definition also. It was a vibration. I could feel it now, so strong and fast that everything it contacted blurred. The world vibrated like a tuning fork. It washed across the park like a wave striking on a sub-atomic level. The woven texture of my blazer transformed into smooth material. Sound ceased. It was like being under water. The vibration trapped the sound waves and snuffed them out, leaving in its place only a piercing hum. The ash was floating up in massive waves, cast off by the vibrations.

I glanced at Simon, he was becoming blurry too. I turned to Emmanuel. He was still solid. Whatever was happening was not affecting him in the least. I felt disembodied, unable to move, hardly able to think.

The people in the park smeared into odd shapes, barely recognizable as human. The vibrations enveloped each individual, creating a mist cocoon around each of us. Steven moved toward us still singing, I couldn't see his mouth clearly, but I knew. He was not allowing the vibration to affect him. He continued to move when those around him, including myself, were frozen in place.

He came to me, gesturing for me to continue singing. I fought to break free from my stupor, but the vibration was stronger than my will. I closed my eyes, wondering if my brain matter was liquefying. As Steven passed by, his vibration brushed against mine and jolted me enough to reopen my eyes.

I watched him walk into Emmanuel's aura of white light. Instantly he was less blurry. He was smiling and drumming his fingers as he entered the light, I could hear his sweet child voice. So could everyone else.

Na na na na na na na
Na na na na, Hey Jude

The light that surrounded them overpowered the vibration. I watched it simply melt away. Warmth blanketed me as the glow engulfed us. It radiated across the park and warmed the air, like the sun coming out from behind a cloud. The glow grew and I found my voice, as did all the others. The piercing hum receded as our voices strengthened. Again we were a thundering chorus, this time even stronger than before.

The faces I could see, and there were thousands, smiled with pure joy. Tears traced down their faces. Children danced around their parents, broken from the vibration that bound them only moments before.

From the east, at the edge of the horizon, appeared a miniscule slice of lustrous blue. It quickly widened, rolling back like a giant canopy, unveiling a sky both familiar and reassuring. The television guys were giving us the thumbs up, the signal was back and we were broadcasting again.

The cheering started then, as the people in the Park realized The Ghost was pulling away from the planet. What we thought was going to be a collision turned into more of an entrapment. Through faith and prayer we had shown ourselves as members of a race that could join together and work peacefully. Simon leaped into my arms and clung to me like we were wearing Velcro.

Emmanuel's voice thundered above the cheering. "We have asked for God's blessing and received it. Now we must thank Him for the results He has bestowed on us."

Each man, women, and child bowed their heads and offered their own thanks. Many knelt, others held hands, and others still wrapped their arms around their neighbor's waists, forming large circles, and recited the Lord's Prayer.

Emmanuel waited and watched the many races and classes of New Yorkers in the Park, a true brotherhood of man. Simon and I were doing the same. "You know," I said "They have the exact same life they had a couple of months ago and no one was happy. Nothing's really changed, yet look at them."

"They changed, we changed, everything's gonna' be different now," Simon said. Then something in the sky caught our attention. I saw the cameramen were angling the cameras straight up.

The sky was now completely blue, except for a darkish circle in the sky about the size of the moon. The vacuum left by The Ghost was producing an odd silvery white cloud. It generated out of thin air and grew with alarming speed. Billowing and spreading, it grew majestically, a divine object like nothing seen before.

The masses looked to the sky and quieted. They stood in disbelief, thinking the spectral display was over and they could go back to their lives, loved ones and homes.

Tendrils of dazzling white oozed from the cloud in dozens of places. They curved snake-like through the sky, independent of each other. New tendrils burst from the widening cloud, as if the contents within, were too much to contain.

As they reached lower they became more visible, more comprehensible. The tendrils were comprised of thousands of particles, still too small to discern, but visible. Shimmering in the light, they moved in unison like a compact school of minnows in the surf. One in particular appeared to be flowing toward us.

The tip had just a trace of reddish orange. It continued to flow out of the cloud, surging forward like a shining tentacle of smoke. The sky was a mass of twisting, swooping lines of moving particles.

"We have visitors," Emmanuel said to me in calm, reassuring voice.

Now I could see them, not clearly, but well enough to see they were angels. Millions of angels. Their wings shown like mirrors, catching the wind, outstretched, only the very tips moving. The angel leading his tendril toward us was larger than the others. He grasped a fiery sword in his right hand. Their beauty and majesty was unparalleled by anything on Earth.

The angel, grasping the sword, touched down softly near Emmanuel. He took several steps toward Emmanuel, his wings folded perfectly behind him. Then he did something that no one watching expected. He knelt before Emmanuel and bowed his head. The others soared overhead, watching, uninvited.

Emmanuel moved to the angel and laid a hand on his shoulder. The angel looked up into Emmanuel's face.

"It is time," the angel said. His voice was deep and resonant.

Emmanuel slowly exhaled, "There is much more I can do, the suffering is great."

"You have fulfilled your destiny; you have a place in paradise."

"And if that is not my choice?" Emmanuel asked.

"Then you are free to follow your own path."

"Then that is what I choose."

The angel smiled and stood, holding the flaming sword at his side. He towered over Emmanuel. "That decision surprises no one. Peace be with you until the day we meet again."

"And with you," Emmanuel said.

The angel turned and looked at the rest of us. In comparison I'm sure we appeared a motley crew, disheveled and even dirty, staring back in awe.

His eyes swept across us, touching the thousands there, each of us feeling he had looked directly at us. And each of us knowing what he was thinking, 'He's doing this for you.'

The angel bowed his ahead once again, and then unfolded his massive wings. With one powerful thrust he pushed off the ground and ascended toward the soaring masses above. His sword thrust before him and wings outstretched, the others joined him forming a line to the west. Without warning every group in the sky disbanded with individuals flying off on their own. Like a million fireworks exploding at once, sending sparkling particles off in every direction.

"I hope you got that," one of the cameramen said to their director.

"Wow," was all Simon could say.

Steven ran by us, jumping and pointing at a glistening pair of angels that were dipping toward us. He stopped and began waving, hopping on one leg, then the other.

Secret Blood

The pair shimmered as they came to a soft hover above us. Cleo and his wife each held a hand up toward Steven. Cleo looked healthier and thirty years younger. She was beautiful, but in a plain way. Her smile was infectious. Cleo grinned widely and his wife took his hand. They hovered there radiating white light. Steven continued to wave. Other angels zoomed off in all directions.

"Thank you, Steven, for helping my husband."

"That's okay," he said.

"Live a good life, Walrus," he said. And with one last wave they flew away, joining the other sparkling points spreading across the sky. They disseminated and jetted out of sight, spreading around the world on orders from beyond.

The crowd in Central Park was not ready to disperse; there was no fatigue, even with the emotion of the past hour. Happy and forever changed, they were ready to start the lives they had pledged to live. In many parts of the world the celebrations were about to begin, in others, they were beginning to be planned. A new holiday was in the making, a new way of life for everyone.

The homeless people Steven had rallied, were mobbing Emmanuel. Each wanted a hug and to give him some kind of offering. A lady with very few teeth removed her dirty nylon jacket and placed it on Emmanuel's shoulders. It was her most prized possession.

Another man placed his Yankee baseball cap on Emmanuel's head. The mass of people grew.

"Simon," I yelled. "Cause a distraction over there."

He gave me a "thumbs up" and moved to a spot about thirty yards away. We were beginning to communicate like he and Shine.

"Hey, everybody! Line starts here to get a blessing!" As soon as everyone's head turned, Emmanuel tucked his hair up under the cap and pulled the collar of the jacket up. He turned and slowly walked away, head down.

Luckily, few in the crowd had seen the jacket or the hat and they were searching for a long haired man in a white shirt and jeans. By the time they looked back we were twenty yards away. We walked for a while and found an arch where we could talk and not be seen.

"What now?" I asked. "Do you want me to call Jimmy and set up our next move?"

Emmanuel smiled. It was a tired smile, a forced smile. And it scared me. His eyes appeared a little weary, strained. I had never noticed that before.

"Yes, you should call Jimmy to retrieve Steven, Simon and yourself."

"But, what about…"

"Me?" he finished my sentence. "Not me. It is time for me to go."

"Go where? You are the angel; you are going to continue to work for those suffering. I want to go with you."

"You cannot," he said. I felt the world come crashing down around me. It must have shown on my face. A clock was ticking in my mind.

"I have been a guest in your country long enough to know what will happen."

"We can change the world. People love you, they will listen to you."

Emmanuel nodded. "Yes, at first. But soon there will be photos of me on the news and in the papers. The people will be interested in not what I say, but what type of shoes I have, what kind of jeans, where do I get my hair cut, whom would I like as the next President. They will want answers that I do not know."

"But maybe we can use that type of exposure to help people," I said noticing his eyes and teeth were not as bright.

"No, I am myself now; my time of Holiness has past. The way I was when we first met. People will want to see miracles that I can't produce. Some will think I was a fraud. Then this will all be for naught."

He was right, of course. The first thing we want to do when we have a hero is to tear them down. A group of people ran across the bridge over us. They were laughing and singing.

Secret Blood

"Do you see what has happened?" He stood straight and placed his hands on my shoulders. "Its name was not accidental. It was not a Ghost, but The Ghost, The Holy Ghost. When it was discovered, I was discovered. The closer it came, the more powers I had at my command."

Simon and Steven were following the path to where we were standing. They were alone but casually were looking back over their shoulders. They hesitated.

"Now, the Holy Ghost has passed from me to the people of the Earth."

It took a moment to comprehend. Now it was very clear, but still not what I wanted.

"Will they know what to do without you leading them?" I asked.

"Some will and some won't, but it is a fresh start for all. A revelation."

He could see how dejected I was. I did not want to show my depression, but I had already lost that battle.

"Do you remember, Matthew, the party at the White House? The night where Simon and his mother were reunited and Shine met his daughter for the first time? I know you thought everyone had been given something but you. You should have known that your gift had already been given."

I looked at him, knowing already that this was the last time we would be together.

"When we met, you were failing at a job you didn't like. Being a servant of God does not mean you have to be a priest. Now you will go on to do the work we have begun. That, Matthew, is your destiny and your gift."

"There are too many things I don't know. We all have questions only you can answer. What about things like the death penalty, abortion, gay rights?"

Simon and Steven were nearing as I spotted a large group of people following them on the path. They were still searching for Emmanuel.

"There are only two things, Matthew; love God and love each other."

"What about the Arabs and the Jews. What about the Holy Lands?"

"Two things, Matthew, just the two things." He touched my cheek, then turned and walked past Simon and Steven into the mass of bodies. For some reason, they focused on me and didn't give Emmanuel a second glance. He melted away in the swirling humanity, a Yankee cap flowing against the current of colors and faces. In my mind I could hear his voice. "Two things, Matthew, just the two things."

"Where's Emmanuel?" Simon asked.

"He just walked by you," I said.

"No way, I didn't see him."

"Let's go find him," Simon said, a little panicked.

"You can't," Steven said. "He won't look the same to us. He's gone."

We stood silent as the rejoicing group of celebrators surged by, still intoxicated by the egress of The Ghost.

"You mean, it's over? He left us just like that?"

"How'd you think it was going to end?" Steven said.

"Not like this," I said.

"Ended better than last time, I guess," Simon said.

A single seagull floated above, swiveling its head from side to side, watching everything below. It caught a draft and effortlessly drifted away.

My phone rang. I let the seagull slip out of view.

"You guys did it!" Jimmy yelled. He was clearly in the celebratory mood. "I just spoke to the President, The Ghost is heading out into space. It turned tail and took off." There was a muffled sound and Jimmy said, "Hold on a second." I could hear him talking to someone, he said 'and peace be with you'. There was the rustling sound again.

"Okay, I'm back," he said.

"What was that?"

Secret Blood

"Some guy wanted a hug. He hugged Shine, too. You should have seen Shine's face." He hesitated a moment and switched gears. "People are going nuts here, how is it in the Park?"

"Yeah," I said. "Everyone seems relieved and happy."

"How's Emmanuel? Let me talk to him."

"Can't do that at the moment. What did the hugger look like?"

"I don't know, just regular looking. Had on a Yankee cap."

"And a dirty looking windbreaker?" I asked.

"How'd you know?"

I ignored the question. "Can you have someone bring us back?"

"Choppers are already on the way."

"We'll need to talk about the future," I said.

"The future's wide open," he said and hung up. I could hear him smiling.

We made our way through the Park, the three of us unusually quiet. I was experiencing a mixture of emotions.

"I feel good, I mean really good," Simon said. "I feel like I'll never be cold again, no matter what. You know what I mean?"

"I do," said Steven. "I feel like there's always going to be an answer."

I could hear the thump of rotor blades in the distance. The air felt light, clean like after a thunderstorm. The buildings in the distance had sharp clear edges. It wouldn't be long until the trees started to bloom.

"I know what you mean," I said to Simon. "The future is wide open."

* * *

Anguish has taken wing, dispelled is darkness;
For there is no gloom where but now there was distress.
The people who walked in darkness
Have seen a great light;
Upon those who have dwelt in the land of gloom
A light has shown.
　　　　　　　　From the book of the Prophet Isaiah

Award winning author, **Don Stansberry,** is a native West Virginian and an elementary school teacher. He is the author of two middle school books, *Inky & the Missing Gold* and *Inky, Oglebee, & the Witches*, and his children's book, *Crusty*, was named a Finalist in the USA News Best Book Awards.

He is part of Headline Books School Show Program and visits many schools throughout the year. Don is also a popular speaker and presenter at conferences, book clubs, and corporate events.

He has been a public school teacher since 1984 and always had an interest in writing. He was the head coach for the Parkersburg High Girls' Basketball team for 16 years and retired from this position with four state championships.